Praise for
M. M. KAYE

"With its satisfying plot, deft characterization and emphasis on setting and atmosphere, [*Death in the Andamans*] . . . is both fresh and credible."
—*Publishers Weekly*

"M. M. Kaye outdoes Agatha Christie in palming the ace!"   —*San Diego Union*

". . . *Death in the Andamans* is a frothy cocktail . . . equal parts of manners, money, flirtations and nostalgia, spiced by a dash of literary allusion, served up just as the sun sets on the last days of the British Raj."   —*Los Angeles Times*

". . . an excellent, very suspenseful mystery story, with a double dose of romance thrown in for good measure."   —*The Pittsburgh Press*

"M. M. Kaye is a master at providing suspense!"   —*UPI*

"*Death in the Andamans* is one of her best."
—*Richmond Times Dispatch*

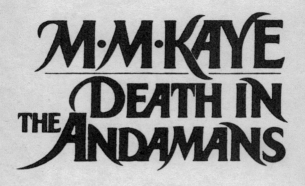

M·M·KAYE
DEATH IN THE ANDAMANS

ST. MARTIN'S PRESS/NEW YORK

DEATH IN THE ANDAMANS

Copyright © 1960, 1985 by M. M. Kaye

Library of Congress Catalog Card Number: 86-1825

ISBN: 0-312-90619-6

Printed in the United States of America

First St. Martin's Press mass market edition/March 1987

10 9 8 7 6 5 4 3 2 1

In fond memory
of
'Fudge'
(Rosemary Cosgrave)
and the Islands

'The isle is full of noises . . .'
THE TEMPEST

AUTHOR'S NOTE

This story was roughed out during a wild and stormy afternoon towards the end of the long-ago thirties, on a tiny island in the southern waters of the Bay of Bengal.

I happened to be there because a great friend and fellow art student, to whom this book is dedicated, had accompanied her parents to this far-flung bit of Empire when her father was appointed Chief Commissioner of the Andaman Islands. Shortly after her arrival in Port Blair she had written inviting me to come out and spend the winter with them: an irresistible invitation that would have had to be resisted had it arrived any earlier, since my art had not been paying very well and I could not possibly have afforded the fare. But as luck would have it I had recently put away my paint-brushes and tried my hand at writing instead, and to my stunned surprise a children's book and my first novel, a crime story, had both been accepted for publication. What was more, an advance had been paid for them!

The sum involved was, by today's standards, incredibly meagre. But it seemed vast at a time when a return tourist-class passage by sea, from England to India and back again, cost only £40 (which is less than $50 at the present rate of exchange), and suddenly I was rich! I hastily bought a one-way ticket to Calcutta, where I eventually boarded a little steamer, the S.S. *Maharaja*, that called once a month at the Andamans, and four days later landed at Port Blair and was taken by launch to Ross—an island about the size of a postage stamp that guarded the entrance to the harbour and was topped by Government House, the residence of the Chief Commissioner.

The largest building in Port Blair was a pink, Moorish-style jail; for the main island had been used for almost a century as a convict settlement, and more than two thirds of the local population, many of them Burmese, were either convicted murderers serving life sentences, or the descendants of murderers—this last because 'lifers' were allowed out after serving a year or two in the jail, permitted, if they wished, to send for their wives and families, given a hut and a plot of land and encouraged to settle. Even the majority of house-servants and gardeners on Ross, including those in Government House, were 'lifers': and a nicer lot of people I have seldom met! But the house itself was another matter . . .

It was a disturbingly creepy place. What my Scottish grandfather would have termed 'unchancy.' And if ever there was a haunted house it was this one. The incident at the beginning of this book happened to me exactly as I have described it, except that the figure I saw was not a European but a malevolent little Burman armed with a *kriss*—the wicked Burmese knife that has a wavy-edged blade. Other and equally peculiar things happened in that house: but that, as they say, is another story. The settings, however, and many of the incidents in this book, are real.

There actually was a picnic party at Mount Harriet on Christmas Eve, and there was also a British Navy cruiser visiting Port Blair. We saw the storm coming up, and ran for it, and a few of us managed to get back to Ross on the ferry: though I still don't know how we made it! Once back, we were cut off from the rest of Port Blair, and from everywhere else for that matter, for the best part of a week. The various Christmas festivities that we had planned were literally washed out, and by mid-afternoon on Boxing Day there was still a horrific sea running and every jetty in Port Blair had been smashed flat. But since the worst of the hurricane appeared to have passed, Fudge and I fought our way around Ross, ending up at the deserted Club, where we sat sipping gimlets* and staring glumly at the damp patches on the ballroom floor and the wilting decorations that we had put up so gaily only three days before.

Perhaps because I had just written a crime novel I remarked idly that the present situation would be a gift to a would-be murderer. No doctor on the island, no police, only a handful of the detachment of British troops, no telephone lines operating and no link at all with the main island, and despite the gale, the temperature and humidity so high that any corpse would have to be buried in double-quick time—and probably without a coffin at that! To which Fudge replied cheerfully: 'You know, that's quite an idea! Who shall we kill?'

We spent the next half hour or so happily plotting a murder, limiting our characters to the number of British marooned on Ross, minus Fudge's mother, Lady Cosgrave, because we decided that our fictional Chief Commissioner had better be a widower with a stepdaughter, and plus two naval officers who had, in fact, been members of the picnic party on Mount Harriet, but had managed to make it back to their ship by the skin of their teeth. And since

---

*A popular short drink in the days of the Raj, consisting of gin, ice and a dollop of Rose's lime juice, plus a dash of bitters (optional). These, too, would appear to have vanished along with the Empire.

our real-life cast seemed much too average and humdrum, we derived considerable amusement from endowing them all with looks, characters, colouring and quirks that the originals did not possess.

All in all it proved a very entertaining way of passing a long, wet afternoon. But it did not occur to me to make any use of it, because I had gone back to painting again. I never gave it another thought until a year later, by which time my mother and I were in Persia—or Iran, if you insist, though I prefer the old name. (A 'Persian' carpet or a 'Persian' poem sounds far more attractive than an 'Iranian' one any day.)

The Second World War had broken out that autumn, so sightseeing and sketching were not encouraged—particularly sketching!—and time was hanging a bit heavy on my hands. It was the period known as the 'phoney war,' and there being little else to do I decided to try my hand at writing another crime novel, using the plot that Fudge and I had concocted in the Andamans. Which I did: though by the time I finished it I was unable to get the manuscript home to my British publishers, owing to the fact that by then the war was no longer in the least 'phoney.' And it was not until a long time later that it appeared in print in England under the title of *Night on the Island*.

This is how a tale that was invented during an idle afternoon on a tiny, storm-bound island in the Bay of Bengal came to be written in Persia, in a small town on the banks of the Shatt-al-Arab, called Khurramshah, which not so long ago was reduced to rubble in the fighting between Iran and Iraq. Sadly, Ross had long since predeceased it; falling a victim to Japanese bombing that demolished Government House and its ghosts, together with every other building on the island—including the little club-house where this story began.

I am told that the jungle has taken over Ross and that no one goes there any more. But that nowadays there is a modern hotel for tourists at Corbyn's Cove. Time and the Tourist march on!

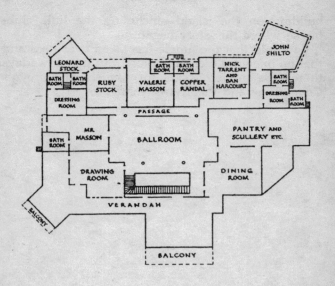

LEONARD STOCK

BATH ROOM | BATH ROOM

RUBY STOCK

DRESSING ROOM

BATH ROOM | BATH ROOM

VALERIE MASSON

COPPER RANDAL

NICK TARRENT AND DAN HARCOURT

JOHN SHILTO

BATH ROOM

DRESSING ROOM

BATH ROOM

PASSAGE

BATH ROOM

MR. MASSON

BALLROOM

PANTRY AND SCULLERY ETC.

DRAWING ROOM

DINING ROOM

BALCONY

VERANDAH

BALCONY

E
E — W
N

PLAN OF FIRST FLOOR,
**GOVERNMENT HOUSE,
ROSS**

=== 1 ===

Something bumped lightly against the side of her bed and Copper Randal, awakening with a start, was astonished to find that her heart was racing.

For a moment or two she lay staring into the darkness and listening. Trying to identify what it was that had woken her so abruptly. And why she should be afraid? But apart from the monotonous swish of the electric fan blades overhead there was no sound in the silent house, and the hot, windless night was so still that she could hear the frightened pounding of her heart. Then somewhere in the room a floorboard creaked . . .

Every nerve in her body seemed to jerk in response to that small, stealthy sound and suddenly her heart was no longer in her breast but had jumped into her throat and was constricting it so that she could barely breathe. She had to force herself to sit up and ease one hand out from under the close-tucked mosquito netting, moving very cautiously, and grope for the switch of her bedside light. She heard it click as she pressed it, but no comforting light sprang up to banish the darkness.

This, thought Copper, swerving abruptly from panic to impatience, is absurd! She rubbed her eyes with the back of her other hand and pressed the

switch a second time. But with no better result.
Yet there had been nothing wrong with the lamp
when she turned it off, so either the bulb had given
out during the night, which seemed unlikely, or
else . . . Or else I'm dreaming this, she thought uneasily.

The idea was a preposterous one, but nevertheless
she pinched herself to make sure that she was
awake, and reassured on that point, pressed the
switch a third time. Nothing. Then the bulb must
have . . . It was at this point that irritation changed
swiftly back into panic as she remembered the yards
of flex that lay across the uncarpeted floor and connected the lamp on her bedside table to a plug on
the far side of the room. Supposing someone—
something—had passed by her bed and tripped
over the flex, jerking the plug from its socket? She
had done that herself more than once, so there was
no reason to suppose—

'Stop it!' Copper scolded herself in a furious whisper: 'You're behaving like a lunatic! And what's
more, if you sit here in the dark for just one more
minute, you'll end up screaming the house down.
So get going!' Thus adjured she took a deep breath
and summoning up all her courage, pushed up the
mosquito netting and slid out of bed.

The smooth, polished floorboards felt pleasantly
cool to her bare feet as she groped her way across to
the switch by the bathroom door, and finding it,
pressed down the little metal knob with a feeling of
profound relief.

Once again a switch clicked beneath her unsteady
fingers, and this time a light came on. But it was not
the bright, warm comforting one she had expected.
Instead, a queer, greenish, phosphorescent glow
filled the room, and aware of a movement beside
her, she turned sharply and saw, standing so close
to her that without moving she could have touched

him, the figure of a little wizened man in a suit of soiled white drill.

Copper shrank back, both hands at her throat and her mouth dry with terror. But the intruder did not move. In that dim light his blanched face glimmered like that of a drowned man coming up out of deep water, and she could see that his wrinkled features were set in an expression of malignant fury: a blind, unseeing rage that did not appear to be directed at her, for the unfocused eyes stared past her at someone or something else. But there was no one else, and the whole house was still. So still that the silence and the queer greenish light seemed part of one another, and Time had stopped and was standing behind her, waiting . . .

I ought to scream, thought Copper numbly; Val's only in the next room. I've only got to scream——— She opened her mouth but no sound came from her dry throat, and the green light began to flicker and grow dim. It was going out and she would be left alone in the dark with . . . with . . .

And then at last she screamed. And, astonishingly, woke to find herself in her bed, shivering among the pillows, with the last echoes of her own strangled shriek in her ears.

A light snapped on in the next room and seconds later a dark-haired girl in pink cotton pyjamas, newly aroused from sleep, burst through the curtained archway that separated the two bedrooms, calling out encouragingly that she was coming and what on *earth* was the matter?

'N-nothing,' quavered Copper through chattering teeth. 'Only a nightmare. But a perfectly beastly one! I still can't believe . . .' She reached out a trembling hand and switched on her own light, apologizing confusedly for making such an appalling din: 'I didn't mean . . . I was going . . . I *am* sorry I woke you, but I thought he—it———And then the light started to go and——Oh Val, am I glad to see you! D'you mind staying around and talking to me for a bit until I've simmered down and unscrambled myself? Bless you——!'

She lifted her mosquito net and Valerie crept in underneath it and having annexed a pillow and made herself comfortable at the foot of the bed, observed crisply that any talking to be done had better be done, pronto, by Copper. 'Have you any *idea* what a ghastly noise you were making? It sounded like an entire glee club of love-lorn tom cats yowling on a rooftop. What in heaven's name were you dreaming about?'

'I'm not too sure that I was dreaming,' confessed Copper with a shudder. 'In fact I actually pinched myself just to make sure I wasn't: and it hurt, too.'

'Tell!' ordered Valerie, and composed herself to listen while Copper embarked hesitantly on an account of the peculiar happenings of the last fifteen minutes or so, ending defensively: 'It was *real*, Val! Right up to the time that I switched on the light by the bathroom door, I could have sworn I was awake and that it was all really happening. It was far more of a shock to find myself waking up in bed than it would have been to find myself being murdered!'

'*Hmm*. I'd say that the trouble with you,' diagnosed Valerie sapiently, 'was either too many of those curried prawns at the Club last night, or else you've been letting the fact that you are living on a sort of Devil's Island—anyway, a penal settlement—get on your nerves.'

'The latter, probably.' Copper relaxed and lay back on her pillow, watching the whirling, white-painted blades of the electric fan flicking swift shadows across the high ceiling, and presently she said slowly: 'It's a bit difficult to explain, but don't you think there must be something a little out of kilter . . . something unchancy . . . about the Andamans?

Just think of it, Val. In this particular bit of the Islands almost three quarters of the population, including most of your father's house-servants, are convicted murderers serving a life sentence. They've all killed someone. Surely that must have *some* effect on a place—any place? Murderers being sent here year after year? All those dead people whose lives they took . . . the atmosphere must get choked up with them like—like static . Or wireless waves, or—or something——' She hesitated and then laughed a little shamefacedly. 'I'm sorry. I don't seem able to explain it very well.'

'Try not to think about it,' advised Valerie practically. 'Otherwise you'll be waking me up nightly dreaming that you're being murdered by convicts or haunted by the ghosts of their victims, and I'm not sure that I could take any more of that scarifying "woman wailing for her demon lover" stuff. It scared me rigid.'

'Don't worry, I'm not likely to have a dream like that twice, touch wood!' said Copper, reaching up to rap the nearest mosquito pole with her knuckles. 'And anyway, it wasn't a convict I was dreaming about. Unless there are any European convicts here. Are there?'

'No, of course not. What did he look like?'

'Rather like a rat. If you can imagine a rat with wrinkles and a lot of grey, wispy hair. A mean, vindictive sort of face. He wasn't much taller than I am, and he was wearing a grubby white suit and a big ring with a red stone set in it. You've no idea how terribly solid and detailed it all was. I saw him so clearly that I could draw a picture of him; and it wasn't like a dream at all. It was *real*. Horridly real! I was here, in this room. And I not only felt that switch click, I heard it. The only unreal thing was the light being green.' She shivered again, and turning her head, sat up in sudden astonishment and said: 'Why, it's morning!'

The clear pale light of dawn had seeped unnoticed into the room as they talked, dimming the electric bulbs to a wan yellow glow. Copper slid out from under the mosquito net, and crossing to the windows drew back the curtains: 'It must be getting on for six. I don't know why, but I thought it was the middle of the night.' She leant out over the window-sill, sniffing the faint dawn breeze that whispered through the mango trees on the far side of the lawn, and said: 'It's going to be a marvellous day, Val. Come and look.'

Valerie snapped off the bedside lamp and joined her, and the two girls knelt on the low window-seat to watch the growing light deepen over the sea and stretch along the ruled edge of the far horizon.

Below them lay a wide strip of lawn bordered on the far side by mango, pyinma and casuarina trees that overlooked the grass tennis-courts, a tangled rose garden and two tall, feathery clusters of bamboo. Beyond this the ground sloped down to the beach so steeply that the clear, glassy water that shivered to a lace of foam about the dark shelves of rock appeared to lie almost directly below the house, and only the tops of the tall coconut palms that fringed the shores of the little island could be seen from the upper windows. Sky, sea and the level stretch of lawn seemed to be fashioned from Lalique glass, so still and smooth and serene they were: the still, smooth serenity that presages a perfect Indian Ocean day.

The fronds of the coconut palms swayed gently to a breath of scented air that wandered across the garden and ruffled Valerie's dark hair, and she stretched a pair of sunburnt arms above her head and sighed gratefully. 'So cool! And yet in another hour it will be hot and sticky again. A curse upon this climate.'

'That's because you've been here too long. You're blasé,' said Copper, her eyes on the glowing horizon: 'After that endless London fog and rain and drizzle, I don't believe I could ever have too much sun, however hot and sticky.'

'You wait!' retorted Valerie. 'I may have been in the Islands too long, but you haven't been here long enough. Two more months of the Andamans and you'll be thinking longingly of expeditions to the North Pole!'

Valerie Masson, born Valerie Ann Knight, was the stepdaughter of Sir Lionel Masson, Chief Commissioner of the Andamans. A childless man, Sir Lionel had been a widower for close upon seventeen years; during which time he had paid school bills and written cheques at frequent intervals but, since his visits to England had been infrequent, had seen little or nothing of this stepdaughter who had taken his name. He knew that the child was well looked after in the home of a couple of devoted aunts, and his only anxiety on her behalf (in the rare intervals in which he thought of her at all) was the fear that in all probability she was being badly spoiled.

His appointment as Chief Commissioner to the Andamans had coincided with Valerie's nineteenth birthday, and it had suddenly occurred to him that he not only possessed a grown-up stepdaughter, but that it might be both pleasant and convenient to install a hostess in the big, sprawling house on Ross. The idea was well received. Valerie had welcomed it with enthusiasm and for the past two years had kept house for her stepfather, played hostess at Government House, and enjoyed herself considerably. Which last was not to be wondered at, for although

she could lay no particular claim to beauty, her dark
hair grew in a deep widow's peak above an endear-
ingly freckled face in which a pair of disturbing
green eyes were set charmingly atilt, and these as-
sets, combined with an inexhaustible supply of good
humour, had worked havoc with the susceptibilities
of the male population of Port Blair.

Her present house-guest, Miss Randal—Caroline
Olivia Phoebe Elizabeth by baptism but invariably
known, from an obvious combination of initials,
'Copper'—had been her best friend since their early
schooldays, and at about the time that Valerie was
setting sail for the Andamans, Copper had been reluctantly embarking upon the infinitely more prosaic
venture of earning her living as a shorthand typist in
the city of London.

For two drab years she had drawn a weekly pay
cheque from Messrs Hudnut and Addison Limited,
Glass and China Merchants, whose gaunt and grimy
premises were situated in that unlovely section of
London known as the Elephant and Castle. The
weekly pay cheque had been incredibly meagre, and
at times it had needed all Copper's ingenuity, coupled with incorrigible optimism, to make both ends
meet and life seem at all worth supporting. 'But
someday,' said Copper, reassuring herself, 'something exciting is *bound* to happen!'

Pending that day she continued to hammer out an
endless succession of letters beginning 'Dear Sir—In
reply to yours of the 15th ult.', to eat her meals off
clammy, marble-topped tables in A.B.C. teashops,
and to keep a weather-eye fixed on the horizon in
ever-hopeful anticipation of the sails of Adventure.
And then, three months previously, that sail had
lifted over the skyline in the form of a small and
totally unexpected legacy left her by a black-sheep
uncle long lost sight of in the wilds of the Belgian
Congo.

A slightly dazed Copper had handed in her resignation to Messrs Hudnut and Addison Limited, cabled her acceptance of a long-standing invitation of Valerie's to visit the Islands, and having indulged in an orgy of shopping, booked a passage to Calcutta, where she had boarded the S.S. *Maharaja*— the little steamer which is virtually the only link between the Andamans and the outside world. Four days later she had leaned over the deck rail, awed and enchanted, as the ship sailed past emerald hills and palm-fringed beaches, to drop anchor in the green, island-strewn harbour of Port Blair.

That had been nearly three weeks ago. Three weeks of glitteringly blue days and incredibly lovely star-splashed nights. She had bathed in the clear jade breakers of Forster Bay and Corbyn's Cove, fished in translucent waters above branching sprays of coral from the decks of the little steam launch *Jarawa*, and picnicked under palm trees that rustled to the song of the Trade Winds.

It was all so different from that other world of fog and rain, strap-hanging, shorthand and crowded rush-hour buses, that she sometimes felt that she must have dreamed it all. Or that this was the dream, and presently she would awake to find herself back once more in the cheerless, gas-lit lodgings off the Fulham Road. But no: this was real. This wonderful, colourful world. Copper drew a deep breath of utter contentment and leant her head against the window-frame.

Beside her, Valerie who had also fallen silent, was leaning out of the window, her head cocked a little on one side as though she were listening to something. There was a curious intentness about her that communicated itself to Copper, so that presently she too found herself listening: straining her ears to catch some untoward sound from the quiet garden below. But she could hear nothing but the hush of the glassy sea against the rocks, and after a minute or two she said uneasily: 'What is it, Val?'

'The birds. I've only just noticed it. Listen——'

'What birds? I can't hear any.'

'That's just it. They always make a terrific racket at this hour of the morning. I wonder what's come over them today?'

Copper leant out beside her, frowning. Every morning since her arrival in the Islands she had been awakened by a clamorous chorus of birds: unfamiliar tropical birds. Parrots, parakeets, mynas, sunbirds, orioles, paradise fly-catchers, shouting together in a joyous greeting to the dawn. But today, for the first time, no birds were singing. 'I expect they've migrated, or something,' said Copper lightly. 'Look at that sky, Val! Isn't it gorgeous?'

The cool, pearly sheen of dawn had warmed in the East to a blaze of vivid rose that deepened along the horizon's edge to a bar of living, glowing scarlet, and bathed the still sea and the dreaming islands in an uncanny, sunset radiance.

'"*Red sky at morning*",' said Valerie uneasily. 'I do hope to goodness this doesn't mean a storm. It would be too sickening, right at the beginning of Christmas week.'

'Good heavens,' exclaimed Copper blankly, 'I'd quite forgotten. Of course—this is Christmas Eve. Somehow it doesn't seem possible. I feel as if I'd left Christmas behind at the other side of the world. Well, one thing's certain: there won't be any snow here! And of *course* there isn't going to be a storm. There isn't a cloud in the sky.'

'I know—but I still don't like the look of it.'

'Nonsense! It's wonderful. It's like a transformation scene in a pantomime.'

As they watched, the fiery glow faded from the quiet sky and the sun leapt above the horizon and flashed dazzling swords of light through the dia-

mond air. Hard shadows streaked the lawns, and
the house awoke to a subdued bustle of early morning activity.

The new day was full of sounds: the low, hush-
ing, interminable murmur of the sea; the sigh of a
wandering breeze among the grey-green casuarina
boughs; a distant hum and clatter from the servants'
quarters; and the dry click and rustle of the bam-
boos.

*'Be not afeard; the isle is full of noises, Sounds and
sweet airs, that give delight, and hurt not,'* quoted Copper, who had once played Miranda to Valerie's Fer-
dinand in a sixth-form production of *The Tempest.*

She had been thinking of the contrast between the
darkness and terror of the past night and the shining glory of the morning when Caliban's charmed,
immortal lines slipped into her mind, and she had
repeated them almost without knowing it: speaking
them as though they were an assurance of safety
and a spell against evil, and so softly that the words
were barely audible. But Valerie's ear had caught
them, for she said with an unexpected trace of
sharpness: 'That's all very well, but speaking for
myself I'm distinctly afeard, and at the moment I'd
say Keats was more on the ball than Caliban!'

'*Keats?* Why Keats?'

' "La Belle Dame sans Merci". That place by a lake,
where "no birds sing". Well, there are still none
singing here this morning and I don't like it—or that
red sky either! I don't like it one *bit!*'

Copper stared at her: and puzzled by her un-
characteristic vehemence, turned to lean out of the
window again and listen intently. But Valerie was
right. The isle was still full of noises. But in its gardens no bird sang.

2

The Andaman Islands, green, fairy-like, enchanted, lie some hundred miles off the Burmese coast in the blue waters of the Bay of Bengal. Legend, with some support by science, tells that their hills and valleys were once part of a great range of mountains that extended from Burma to Sumatra, but that the wickedness of the inhabitants angered Mavia Tomala, the great chief, who caused a cataclysm which separated the land into over two hundred islands, and marooned them for ever in the Bay of Bengal.

For close on a hundred years a small part of the Andamans had been used by the Government of India as a penal settlement. The only important harbour, Port Blair, lies on the south-east coast of South Andaman, with its harbour guarded from the sea by the tiny triangular islet of Ross, the administrative headquarters of the Islands.

Ross covers less than a mile in area, and into its narrow confines are packed over forty buildings that include a clubhouse, barracks, two churches, a hospital and a native bazaar. Topping this heterogeneous collection of dwellings, and set among green gardens, stands the residence of the Chief Commissioner: a long, rambling two-storeyed building that for some forgotten reason is known in the Islands as 'Government House', and whose windows look down on roofs and tree-tops and out to sea where the lovely, lost islands stray away on either hand to the far horizon like a flight of exotic butterflies.

On this particular Christmas Eve morning the Massons and Miss Randal were breakfasting as usual in the dining-room of Government House. It was not yet nine o'clock but the day was unusually hot and close for the time of year, and the electric fans were whirring at full speed as Valerie filled in the details of the day's programme—an all-day picnic to the top of Mount Harriet followed by a large dinner party at Government House—to an inattentive audience.

The Chief Commissioner, normally an amiable though somewhat absentminded man, was frowning over a letter that had arrived half an hour earlier with a batch of official correspondence, and which he had already read at least twice, while Copper's gaze had strayed to the open windows that looked out across the harbour mouth to the pink, Moorish-looking walls of the cellular jail and the little town that some homesick Scot had named Aberdeen, which lies facing Ross on the mainland of Port Blair. A 'mainland' that is in fact only the largest of the Islands, though always referred to by the inhabitants by the more imposing title.

To the right of the town the land curves in a green arc between Aberdeen and North Point, embracing Phoenix Bay with its boats and steam-launches and lighters rocking gently in the blue swell; tiny Chatham Island with its sawmills and piled timber; Hopetown jetty where, in 1872, a Viceroy of India was murdered; and rising up behind it, on the far side of the bay, the green, gracious slope of Mount Harriet.

For once, however, Copper was not alive to the exotic beauty of the view, her attention at that moment being centred upon the slim, gleaming lines of a cruiser that lay at anchor far up the reaches of the harbour.

His Majesty's Ship *Sapphire* was paying a fortnight's visit to the Andamans; to the delight of the British denizens of Port Blair, for the problems of an enclosed society are many. It becomes difficult to infuse much enthusiasm into entertaining when every dinner, dance, bridge party or picnic must of necessity be made up of combinations and permutations of fifteen or twenty people, all of whom have lived cheek by jowl for months past—often for years—and whose individual interests and topics of conversation have become so well known that any form of social gathering is apt to become a routine performance. Which explains why the arrival of H.M.S *Sapphire* had been welcomed with relief as well as pleasure.

Copper's thoughts, however, were not concerned with the *Sapphire* either as a social saviour or a decorative addition to the scattered collection of seagoing craft reflecting themselves in the pellucid waters of the bay. To her the cruiser existed solely as the ship which numbered among its company of officers and men, one Nicholas Tarrent R.N.

There was a certain electric quality about Nick Tarrent that had nothing whatever to do with his undoubted good looks, for possessing it a plain man or an ugly one would have been equally attractive, and Copper had been in love with him for precisely eight days, seven hours and forty-two minutes. In other words from the moment she had first set eyes on him, two hours after the arrival of H.M.S. *Sapphire* in Port Blair.

'—and some of them,' continued Valerie, 'want to sail from here to Hopetown jetty, where a lorry will meet them and take them up to the top of Mount Harriet. Charles had the boats brought across from Chatham last night so that they can start from the Club pier. The rest of us will take the ferry to Aberdeen and then go on by car. Harriet is only just across the other side of the bay, and I don't suppose it's more than two or three miles from here as the crow flies. But to get to it by road it's over thirty miles and—Copper! you're not listening.'

'I'm sorry,' apologized Copper in some confusion. 'I was looking at the view. It's fascinating.'

'Yes, I know: but if I'd realized you'd be able to see him at this range I'd have had the blinds drawn. Really, Coppy, you might *pretend* to take some interest. Here have I been going over all the arrangements for your benefit, and you haven't bothered to listen to a word. If you could just stop thinking about Nick Tarrent for five minutes, I'd be deeply grateful!'

Copper had the grace to blush, and Valerie laughed and said contritely: 'I'm sorry, Coppy. That was abominably rude and scratchy of me. I can't think why I should be feeling so jumpy and cross this morning. I suppose it's the heat. I shall be glad when we reach Mount Harriet: it's always much cooler up there.'

'It does seem to be a lot hotter today, doesn't it?' said Copper, relieved at the change of subject. 'Or perhaps it's just because it's so still? There doesn't seem to be a breath of air. Who's coming on this picnic?'

'Almost everyone. They're all finding their way there under their own steam. Rendezvous about twelve to twelve-thirty, at the top. You and I are going with Charles.'

'Who's Nick going with?'

'He's sailing over. He and Dan Harcourt and Ted Norton are taking one of the boats, and Hamish is going in another with Ronnie and Rosamund Purvis, and I think George Beamish is supposed to be taking that gloomy girlfriend of his, Amabel, in the third. Mr Hurridge is having a lorry sent to meet them at Crown Point jetty, so they ought to fetch up at Mount Harriet a good bit ahead of us. Except that there's no breeze today.'

'And what about *dear* Mrs Stock? I suppose she'll be there—worse luck!'

'Don't be catty, Coppy!'

'Why not? I enjoy being catty about Ruby. I heard her telling Nick in a honey-sweet voice at the Withers's barbecue that it was "*such* a pity that dear Copper gave the impression of being just a *tiny* bit insipid, because *actually* the girl was really terribly, *terribly* efficient—a complete blue-stocking in fact— she used to hold a *dreadfully* responsible executive post in London"!'

Valerie laughed. 'Dear Ruby! She probably still believes that old story that men are terrified of intelligent women.'

'And in nine cases out of ten, how right she is,' commented Copper gloomily.

'Perhaps. But at a guess I'd say that Nick is the tenth; if that's any comfort to you. As for Ruby, she hasn't a brain in her head.'

'She doesn't appear to need them! You have to admit that she has what it takes. And I suppose she *is* rather attractive in an overblown "Queen of Calcutta" way; what with that black hair and those enormous eyes—not to mention her vital statistics. What really defeats me is how she ever came to marry someone as depressingly ineffectual as poor Leonard. Whenever I see them together I catch myself wondering why on earth she did it? I suppose he must have had *something* that she wanted: though I can't imagine what! Leonard always reminds me of one of those agitated little sand-crabs that pop up out of holes at low tide, and nip back again when they see you looking. An apologetic sand-crab. He ought by rights to have married someone like Rosamund Purvis; they'd have made a marvellous pair—not an ounce of guts or sex-appeal between them. Then Ruby could have married Ronnie, which would have been far more suitable all round.'

'I expect,' said Valerie thoughtfully, 'that Ruby considered one person with sex-appeal in a family to be quite enough. She seems to be allergic to competition.'

'Unless she is promoting it,' observed Copper tartly. 'Anyway, I still don't see why she has to go after Nick when she already seems to have every other available male in the Islands lashed to her chariot wheels—with the solitary exception of your Charles.'

'She collects them,' explained Valerie, helping herself to more coffee, '—the way some people collect stamps or matchboxes or Old Masters.'

'So it would appear,' said Copper crossly. 'And I can't think why her husband stands for it.'

'Oh, *Leonard*—! He doesn't count. And anyway, I don't suppose he notices it by this time. Or minds any more.'

'Perhaps not. But I should have thought Rosamund Purvis would. It can't be pleasant to see your husband dancing attendance on someone else's wife. Though if it comes to that, I suppose she's used to it, too. In fact her dear Ronnie and Leonard's Ruby are two of a kind; except that with Ronnie it's Old Mistresses! Oh dear—why am I being so bitchy and bad-tempered? What's the *matter* with us today, Val? We must have got out of the wrong sides of our beds this morning. I'm feeling all edgy and irritable. Not at all the right spirit for Christmas Eve. Or any other eve, for that matter! *"Peace on Earth, Goodwill toward Men"*—and Women, I suppose: which presumably includes Ruby Stock. When are we due to start off on this expedition?'

'Just as soon as you finish that mango. I told Charles we'd meet him at the Club not later than a quarter to ten, so we'd better get a move on.'

The Chief Commissioner, who had heard nothing of this conversation, folded up the single sheet of paper that had been engrossing his attention, returned it to its envelope and rose from the table: 'If you will excuse me,' he said, 'I have some work to do. By the way, Valerie, do you want the launch this evening?'

'No thank you, Dad. We'll catch the six-thirty ferry. We shall have to get back early if Copper and I are to change and then decorate the table and see that everything is set for the party.'

The Chief Commissioner groaned. 'Good lord, I'd forgotten that we had a dinner party here tonight. I take it this means that I shall not get to bed until after midnight? Oh well, I suppose one cannot avoid one's social obligations at Christmas time.'

He turned away from the table, and then paused and turned back: 'By the way, I forgot to mention that I have had a cable from the Captain to say that the *Maharaja* has been delayed and will not be in until late on Boxing Day.'

'Oh, *Dad*! Oh, no!—that means no Christmas mail.'

'I'm afraid so,' murmured the Chief Commissioner mildly. 'Well, it can't be helped.' He removed himself from the dining-room, Kioh, the Siamese cat, stalking sedately at his heels. And fifteen minutes later his stepdaughter and her guest left the house and walked down the short, steep, sunlit road to the Club, where Valerie's fiancé, Charles Corbet-Carr, senior subaltern of the detachment at present occupying the military barracks on Ross, was waiting for them.

Charles, a tall, fair young man of a type frequently described by female novelists as 'clean-limbed', possessed a pair of startlingly blue eyes and a sense of humour that was at present prompting him to model his conversation upon the only reading provided by the Calvert Library: an institution that would appear to have been last stocked during the frivolous twenties by a fervent admirer of such characters as Bertie Wooster, Berry and Co., and 'Bones of the River'.

Apart from this temporary aberration, Copper had no fault to find with him, and she grinned at him affectionately as he came quickly down the Club steps, kissed his betrothed, and spoke in an urgent undertone: 'There is a slug in our salad, honey. John Shilto, no less. He came over on the lumber boat this morning. I gather he's staying with old Hurridge for Christmas and wasn't expected until this evening, but as his host and everyone else is off on this picnic I more or less had to ask the old basket to come along too. You don't mind, do you? I couldn't very well leave him here *"alone and palely loitering"* for the entire day—Christmas Eve and all.'

'No, of course not, darling. I can bear it. But he'll have to sit in the back among all the bottles and—— Hello, Mr Shilto.' She went into the Club ahead of them to greet a heavily built hulk of a man who rose out of a wicker chair at her approach, and Copper, recognizing what she termed 'Val's Social-Poise Voice', realized that Valerie did not like Mr Shilto. Well, she needn't worry, thought Copper bleakly,

I'm the one who will have to sit in the back of the car and make polite conversation with him . . .

Valerie was saying: 'It's been a long time since you were last over here. We never seem to see you at the Club these days. You won't have met Miss Randal . . . Copper, this is Mr Shilto. He owns one of the largest coconut plantations in the Islands. You must get him to take you over it one day.'

'I shall be delighted,' said Mr Shilto extending a damp, fleshy hand. 'I hope you mean to make a long stay, Miss Randal? What do you think of our Islands?'

Why *must* people always ask that question? thought Copper with a touch of exasperation: like reporters! Aloud she said: 'I think they are beautiful.'

Charles ordered lemon squashes which arrived in tall, frosted glasses, clinking with ice and borne by a slant-eyed Burmese 'boy' who wore a wide length of vivid cerise cloth wound closely about his body, a short white jacket and a headscarf of salmon pink into the folds of which he had tucked a white frangipani flower. But while the others talked, Copper sat silent; sipping her drink and gazing out of the Club windows at the sunlight sparkling and splintering against the glassy surface of the bay, and thinking that she had never before understood the true meaning of colour. Where the water was deepest it was ultramarine, shading to a pure, vivid emerald in the shallows, with bars of lilac and lavender betraying the hidden reefs. And across the bay Mount Harriet rose up from the ranks of coconut palms in a riot of green, every shade of it— rich, tangled, tropical—against a sky like a sapphire shield . . .

A ship's hooter sounded twice from the Ross jetty, and Charles said: 'There goes the five-minutes signal,' and reached for his sun-helmet. Copper gulped down the icy contents of her glass and stood up, and they went out into the hot, blinding sunlight across the baked lawns under the gold mohur trees and past the little summer-house that is built out from the sea wall of the Club, and whose floor covers half the deep, dim tank where the turtles intended (though seldom used) for Government House dinner parties swim languidly in the gloom, to the small wooden jetty where the little steam-ferry jerked at her moorings as though impatient to be off. But with her foot on the gangplank, Copper checked and turned to stare across the harbour, puzzled and uneasy.

Far out in the bay and moving towards the foot of Mount Harriet, three small white triangles showed bright against the shimmering blue. But it was not the sight of the distant boats that had arrested her attention and brought a sharp return of the strange disquiet that had possessed her earlier that morning.

'A lousy day for sailing,' commented Charles, following the direction of her gaze. 'They must be rowing—there isn't a breath of wind. Well, rather them than me! What's up, Coppy? Anything the matter? Got a tummy-ache or something?'

'The birds . . .' said Copper confusedly. 'Why have the birds all gone? There were none in the garden this morning. And—and look——! There are no gulls in the harbour. There have always been gulls before . . . and birds . . . Do you suppose—?'

She shivered suddenly, aware of a curious feeling of tension and foreboding in the hot stillness of the morning and the fact that there were no gulls in the harbour. Though why their absence should worry her she could not have explained. Did birds know things that humans did not? Had the airless, breathless day sent them some warning that grosser senses were unable to comprehend, and had they obeyed it and—

Valerie said from behind her: 'What are you dithering about, Coppy? Do get a move on, you're holding everybody up.'

Copper started as though she had been awakened from a dream, and uttering a hasty apology, ran up the gangplank and on to the ferry.

3

'Caterpillars as big as that? How interesting,' said Copper; managing with considerable difficulty to turn a yawn into a bright social smile and wishing that Mr Shilto would not talk so much. She wanted to give all her attention to the queer, wild, fascinating country that was flicking past them as the big car whirled along the winding thirty-mile road to Mount Harriet, but there had been no stopping Mr Shilto . . .

Valerie was sitting beside Charles, who was driving, and Copper and Mr Shilto had been packed into the back of the car among a large assortment of bottles containing gin, beer, cider, gingerbeer, orange squash, soda water, and yet more beer.

The bottles clicked and clinked against each other as the car swung to the sharp bends in the road and John Shilto tried to find a more comfortable position for his feet.

He was a fat man who, had it not been for his height, would have appeared gross, and in spite of the burning suns of many years in the Islands his face had the unpleasantly pasty appearance of some plant that has grown in the dark. His narrow eyes, set between puffs of pale flesh, were too close together and markedly shrewd and calculating, while his conversation (which for the past ten miles had been concerned with the destructive activities of the coconut caterpillars) was as unprepossessing as his person.

Copper, who cared little for caterpillars, coconut or otherwise, once again allowed her attention to wander as the car swung into a green tunnel of shade. Giant trees arched overhead, their large, queerly shaped, exotic leaves blocking out every vestige of sunlight, while on either side of the road the dense tropical forest leant forward as though it were only waiting until the breeze of their passing had died away, before slipping forward to close over the road once more.

'Annihilating all that's made To a green thought in a green shade,' thought Copper: and wondered how Andrew Marvell could have known about tropical forests? Ferns and long-tangled creepers clung to the branches overhead or swung down in looping festoons, the tree trunks were garlanded with sprays of small white orchids, and here and there an occasional Red Bombway tree, its leaves flaming in an autumnal glory of scarlet, patched the shadowed forest with a festive fire and reminded her that this was Christmas Eve . . .

The car slid suddenly out of cool greenness into the bright sunlight of a small clearing that contained a tiny huddle of palm-thatched native huts, lime trees and banana palms. Here the forest had been forced to retreat a few reluctant paces and stood back—a towering wall of impenetrable shadow that seemed to stare down with hostility at that small, courageous attempt at civilization within its borders. A thin, flashing, emerald flight of parakeets flew screaming across the clearing, and from the edge of the forest a great slate-grey iguana—direct descendant of the dragon of fairy-tale—turned its scaly head as the car swung into a long, straight strip of roadway that ran through the star-patterned shadows of a coconut plantation.

It was at this point that Copper was abruptly awakened to a renewed sense of social shortcoming by the fact that Mr Shilto had at last fallen silent. She had the uncomfortable impression that he had stopped rather suddenly and in the middle of a sentence, and she turned hurriedly towards him with a bright smile which she hoped might be taken for intelligent interest. But Mr Shilto was no longer aware of her . . .

He was staring at the road ahead with an expression that was as plainly readable as it was startling. Rage, fury and fear were written large across his pallid features, and Copper had barely assimilated this surprising fact when he shrank into the extreme corner of the seat, pressing himself back until his head touched the hood, as though he were trying to keep out of sight.

I wonder who he thinks might see him and why it should matter if they did? thought Copper, intrigued by this peculiar manoeuvre. She said without thinking: 'Is this your plantation, Mr Shilto?'— and almost immediately remembered that Valerie had once pointed out the vast acres of palms beyond East Point as the Shilto plantation.

Mr Shilto did not reply and it was obvious that he did not even know that she had spoken. His eyes were warily intent on the white road and the straggling ranks of palm trees, and Copper saw him pass the tip of his tongue over his thick lips as though they were dry. She was about to repeat her question when her attention was suddenly diverted by a favourite and forcible oath from Charles: '*God-frey-and-Daniels-blast-iron-furnaces-from-Hull!*' howled Charles passionately; and jerked the car to a sudden stop.

'Anything the matter? Or are you just tired of driving?' inquired Copper.

'Engine's red hot,' replied Charles briefly, climbing out into the road and stretching his long legs. He threw up the sides of the bonnet and gingerly unscrewed the radiator cap, and pushing back his sun-helmet drew the back of his hand across his damp forehead and swore fervently.

'What's up, darling?' asked Valerie, joining him in the road.

'Believe it or not,' said Charles bitterly, 'those sinkminded saboteurs at the garage have apparently omitted the trifling precaution of filling her up with water. *Mea culpa!*—I should have checked up. She's bone-dry, and we shall have to push the brute. Thank God we're on a bit of a slope here and Ferrers's bungalow is only about a quarter of a mile further on. We'll be able to get water there.'

Mr Shilto, who had not yet spoken, shot out of his seat at speed of light, and stumbling into the road stood in the harsh sunlight, his pasty face no longer pale but patched with a rich shade of puce, and spoke shrilly and with inexplicable violence: 'Oh no you don't! I'm damned if I'll—'

He checked abruptly and appeared to recollect himself. The angry flush faded from his cheeks and he licked his dry lips again and spoke as though speech had become an effort: 'I mean—what I mean is—well, surely it would be simpler to walk back and fetch water from that spring we passed a few moments ago?'

'Using what for a bucket?' demanded Charles reasonably. 'And anyway that was over a mile back, and it shouldn't take us more than five minutes to roll this wretched vehicle down to Ferrers's bungalow. There's no need for you to go in.'

Valerie laid a hand on John Shilto's arm and said in a placatory voice: 'Charles is right, you know. It's the only thing to do. We're late as it is, and everyone else has probably arrived at Harriet by now. They'll be madly thirsty in this heat, and we've got all the drinks!'

The big man's flickering gaze shifted from Valerie to Charles and back again, and he forced a smile: 'Yes—yes, of course. I had only thought that it might be easier if—I mean . . .' He appeared to be unable to finish the sentence and Charles turned away and released the brake.

After the first few yards the car rolled along with comparatively little propulsion, gathering momentum until it was hardly necessary to do more than guide it, and presently they reached a wooden bridge over a muddy tidal stream fringed with mangrove, where Charles brought it to a stop.

A small side road, barely more than a rough track, branched off to the left among the columns of the palm trunks and led to a long, low, island-built bungalow which presented a forlorn and dilapidated appearance, as though it were slowly rotting from neglect, and a slovenly Burmese servant came down the pathway from the house and spoke in the vernacular to Charles, who said: 'Here, Val—you understand a bit of this language, don't you? What's he saying?'

'He says that Ferrers isn't here,' translated Valerie.

'What's that?' Mr Shilto, who had been keeping to the far side of the car, came out of hiding and addressed the servant in his own tongue, and after a moment turned to his companions with an expression of sullen ill-temper and said brusquely: 'Yes, that's right. This is one of the house-boys. He says that the Stocks stopped off here half an hour ago and that they've taken Ferrers on with them to Mount Harriet. Well if that's the case, you can count me out of this damned picnic, and that's flat.' He sat down abruptly on the dusty running-board, and pushing back his hat, leaned against the car door with the air of one who does not intend to move for some considerable time.

Copper, a bewildered spectator of the scene, saw Charles's mouth tighten and realized that he was keeping his temper with difficulty. His voice, however, remained calm and unruffled: 'Please yourself, of course. But I don't know how you propose to get back. I doubt if there'll be anyone passing here in the right direction to give you a lift. And Val and Copper and I have to get on; and that right speedily.'

'Of course,' put in Valerie sweetly, 'you can always walk. It can't be more than ten or twelve miles back to Rungal, and you could probably get a lift in a lorry from there.'

Mr Shilto appeared to digest the truth of these statements with considerable distaste, and after a moment or two he rose reluctantly from the running-board and said he would go up to the house and write a chit that one of the servants could take to the nearest telephone, asking for a call to be put through for a taxi: observing in conclusion that if Ferrers had gone to Mount Harriet for the day, he could wait here until it arrived.

'Good idea,' approved Valerie. '*Do* hurry and get that water, Charles darling.'

The two men turned and went up the path to the bungalow, followed by the house-boy, and Copper said explosively: 'Well I'm——! What on earth was all that about, Val? Construe, please.'

'Guilty conscience, I imagine,' said Valerie with a short laugh. 'I don't suppose he ever uses this road himself, so he'd probably forgotten that our shortest way to Mount Harriet is through Ferrers's plantation. If he *had* thought of it, he'd never have agreed to come.'

'But *why*, for heaven's sake? Come on, Val—tell!'

'Possibly for fear that Ferrers might take a pot-shot at him as he passed?—he's quite capable of it! In fact he's publicly announced his intention of murdering John Shilto on more than one occasion.'

Valerie sat down on the low rail of the bridge and Copper perched alongside her. A sour smell of mangrove mud hung on the humid air and below them huge, gaudily coloured butterflies dipped and drifted lazily over the slimy banks and the ugly, crawling, tentacle-like roots of the mangrove trees that the receding tide from the mile-distant sea had left uncovered.

'It's a longish story,' began Valerie, tilting her hat over her freckled nose to shade her eyes from the glare, 'and no one really knows the true ins and outs of it. The local gossips have collected the odd fact here and there and averaged the rest, so I don't swear by all of it. Anyway, Ferrers Shilto—the owner of that decrepit shack over there—is John Shilto's first cousin and only living relative, and a good many years ago, John, who was doing fairly well with a coconut plantation out here, apparently needed some ready-money badly and couldn't lay his hands on it.

'He eventually hit on the brilliant scheme of persuading Ferrers, who was living in some peaceful spot like Ponder's End on the interest of a smallish capital, to come out to the Andamans and make a fortune. He wrote home to say that there was a super plantation going dirt cheap in the Islands, its owner having made his pile and wishing to retire, and that he would have bought it himself except for the fact that he was already making such a packet on his own that he had decided to be magnanimous and let dear cousin Ferrers in on the ground floor.'

Valerie paused to flick a fallen leaf at a big scarlet dragon-fly that was sunning itself on a mangrove root, and said thoughtfully: 'I suppose Ferrers must always have had a yearning for romance in spite of—or because of?—Ponder's End. And perhaps John Shilto knew it, and so knew that he'd fall for the plantation scheme. Anyway, to cut a long story short, Ferrers swallowed it hook, line and sinker and could hardly wait to hand over his little capital to cousin John and come rushing out East to become a millionaire planter and live on a coral island. That was about fifteen years ago and old history by now. But I gather that it didn't take Ferrers more than fifteen days—or possibly fifteen hours—to find out that he'd been badly swindled, or that the rich planter off whom he had bought the plantation was in reality dear cousin John himself.'

'But what's the matter with it?' demanded Copper. 'It looks all right to me.'

'Well, for a start, over half of it is water. The plantation was supposed to cover about five hundred acres, but when Ferrers got out here he discovered that at least half of that was taken up by a tidal lagoon. You can't see it from here. It's right over there, about half a mile from the house, and a thin strip of the plantation cuts it off from the sea except for a narrow channel; which makes it technically part of the property. As for the palms, they may look all right but they hardly ever bear, because of the creeks which run through the plantation. Coconuts won't thrive properly near mangrove mud, you see.'

'What a filthy trick!' exploded Copper, straightening up with an indignant jerk that almost precipitated her into the muddy waters flowing sluggishly eight feet below. 'Why, it's no better than stealing! I can't understand why any of you even *speak* to that man!'

'It's difficult not to, in a community as small as this one,' said Valerie with a wry smile. 'Yes, it was a pretty rotten bit of dirty dealing. But then some people seem to be born into the world to be swindled, and poor Ferrers is obviously a Grade-A example. No one but an utter mug would have paid over their entire capital without having a searching look at the goods first.'

'He obviously trusted his cousin not to let him down!' said Copper indignantly.

'I suppose he did,' agreed Valerie. 'Anyway, he wouldn't have known if it was a good proposition or not even if he had come out and looked at it. You don't stand much chance of becoming an expert on coconuts in Ponder's End, and I expect John wrote merrily of copra and oil and "raw nuts" and so on, and it all sounded most impressive. Anyway, Ferrers came. And he's been here ever since. You see, he didn't have the money to get back, and of course no one out here would ever buy the place off him. It's the original White Elephant.'

'And that was more than fifteen years ago,' said Copper slowly. 'Oh, poor Ferrers!'

'He makes just enough to live on,' said Valerie, 'and I dare say he would be as happy here as in some dull little semi-detached villa, if it wasn't for his rage at being done down. He never forgets it for half a second. He and John haven't spoken for years, and I imagine they don't catch sight of each other more than they can help.'

'A bit difficult in Port Blair, surely?' commented Copper: 'I should have thought that it was next to impossible to avoid anyone in a community consisting of a handful of people all living practically in each other's backyards. How do they manage it? Wear blinkers?'

'Well, it is a bit tricky,' confessed Valerie, 'but of course we all help. They don't go about much, and no one ever asks them to the same parties. When John is present you steer the conversation off coconuts, mangrove and Ferrers, and when Ferrers is around you do the same of coconuts, mangrove and John. Quite simple, really.'

'Haven't they ever met by mistake?'

'Only once, I believe. Some muddle over the Government House garden party, about two Chief Commissioners back. Everyone is asked to those sort of crushes of course, but usually neither Shilto, or only one, turns up. On this occasion they evidently both thought the other had refused, so unfortunately they both turned up. I believe there was a most impressive scene. Insults fairly ricocheted around, and in the end Ferrers had to be forcibly removed by half the guests while the other half sat on John's head. It gave Port Blair a topic of conversation for months afterwards, and is still occasionally resurrected by the "old guard" at deadly parties when everything else has given out.'

'It sounds very exhilarating,' observed Copper, 'I wish I'd seen it. But I still can't understand why, when they know what a swindler he is, anyone ever invites John Shilto to anything!'

'My poor dear! In these islands if you once started cutting people off your visiting-list because you disapprove of things they've done or said in what is humorously termed their "private lives", you'd have an extremely sticky time with your entertaining. Now I'm being cynical and catty, so I'd better stop.'

'Ferrers Shilto,' said Copper thoughtfully, 'was on the *Maharaja* with me when I came down from Calcutta. What was he doing in Calcutta if he never leaves the Islands?'

'Oh, you've met the little man, have you? I think he goes up about once a year to see to the business end of what few nuts he does manage to sell.'

'I didn't actually meet him,' said Copper. 'All I saw of him was the top of his pith hat when he came on board. But I saw his luggage. Very aged

Gladstone bags. The Captain said he was seasick, but as the sea was like a mill-pond most of the way I was vaguely curious.'

'Probably the after-effects of a terrific yearly jag?' suggested Valerie. 'For all we know, Ferrers may have hidden depths. What *do* you suppose has happened to Charles? He's had time to fetch enough water to fill a swimming-pool by now. Let's go and—— Oh, here he is. What *have* you been doing, darling?'

'Drinking Ferrers's beer,' said Charles, sloshing water out of a battered bucket into the radiator. 'And now that both I and this hellish vehicle have received adequate liquid treatment, I propose that we set forth on our travels again. Get in you two.'

'What about Mr Shilto?' inquired Valerie, complying. 'Has he sent for a taxi, or is he going to try the alternative solution, and hike?'

'God knows!' said Charles cheerfully. 'I did not pause to ask. Ferrers's back premises stink like a sewer, so I was not disposed to linger. I've no idea what the little man is using to manure his plantation—decayed octopi and sea-slug, at a guess. The pong is fearsome. John Shilto went out to investigate, and I left him to it. It will do him no harm to be asphyxiated. Let's go——'

He pressed the self-starter and released the brake; and as he did so John Shilto came rapidly down the path between the palm trees, and breaking into a run, reached the car just as it began to move. His face was curiously flushed and he seemed to be labouring under the stress of some powerful emotion, for his pale eyes glittered with ill-suppressed excitement and his breathing was hurried and uneven.

He jerked open the rear door of the car and tumbled in beside Copper, and having settled himself back and slammed the door, said breathlessly: 'I've changed my mind. I think after all that I ought to come with you.'

He wiped the sweat off his face, and becoming aware that his three companions were staring at him with unconcealed astonishment, forced a rattle of singularly mirthless laughter.

'I—I have been thinking,' he said. 'About Ferrers, you know. It is really high time that we buried the hatchet—high time! The—ah, misunderstanding between us may have been partly my fault, and if so it is only right that I should try and make amends. We must shake hands and let bygones be bygones. He is my only relative—first cousins and all that. Blood is thicker than water and it is not right that—— Yes, yes, we must certainly see if we cannot make a fresh start . . . shake hands . . . After all, we must not forget that today is Christmas Eve, and *"The Better the Day, the Better the Deed"*—eh?'

Mr Shilto paused expectantly as though for comment.

'Oh—er—quite,' said Charles inadequately.

He released the clutch with unintentional abruptness, and the car shot forward down the sun-dappled road that leads to Mount Harriet.

=== 4 ===

Mount Harriet, the highest point in the Islands, was the hot-weather resort of the officials from Aberdeen and Ross, and the Christmas Eve picnic was an annual affair that took place in the grounds of the deserted summer-time Government House that crowned the flat-topped peak.

Charles brought the car to a standstill on the weed-grown drive, and Ronnie Purvis, the Forest Officer, a slimly built man in a spotless white yachting-suit, pulled open the door and greeted Copper with practised charm: 'At last, my lovely one! I'd begun to think you weren't coming and that my day was going to be ruined. But you're certainly worth waiting for. You look good enough to eat, and I don't know how you do it! Come and hold my hand . . .'

Copper descended from the car and said firmly: 'I don't feel like holding anyone's hand in this heat thank you, Ronnie. All that I'm interested in at the moment is a cold drink. And the colder, the better! Hullo, Amabel—did you have a good trip over?'

'No,' replied the damsel addressed: 'There wasn't any wind, so George had to row and he got blisters. They'll probably go septic. It just goes to show, doesn't it?'

Miss Amabel Withers, daughter of the Port Officer, was a plump, stolid maiden with a quite remarkable bent for pessimism, and her concluding remark, which might have been taken to mean anything from a comment on the weather to a reflection on the uncertainty of human existence, was a favourite observation that did not require an answer.

Copper turned to grin at the blistered George, a freckle-faced subaltern who was unaccountably enamoured of young Miss Withers, and said: 'Bad luck, George. Still, it may not actually come to gangrene, and if it should, we can always amputate. I can't think why any of you were mad enough to take out a boat on a day when there isn't . . .'

She broke off, leaving the sentence unfinished, for at that moment a tall man who had been lying in a patch of shade at the far side of the lawn stood up and lifted a hand in greeting and, as always at the sight of Nick Tarrent, Copper's heart gave a little lurch. Abandoning her sentence, together with George Beamish and the importunate Mr Purvis, she went straight across the lawn to him. And it was not until she was within a yard of him that she realized that he was not alone, or that a long, green wicker chair stood in the same patch of shadow, and in it, stretched at full length and wearing a scarlet linen dress that exactly matched her lipstick and the varnish on her long, pointed nails, languorous and seductive as a harem favourite, lay Ruby Stock . . .

Mrs Leonard Stock was a striking-looking woman of what is usually termed 'uncertain age', who might well have been accounted a beauty had her face not been spoiled for that accolade by an expression of discontent that had been worn for so long that it had eventually become an integral part of her features. But few critics would have found fault with her admirable figure and shining, blue-black hair, her great pansy-brown eyes and the smooth golden texture of her sun-browned skin. As the beautiful daughter of a subordinate in India's Post and Telegraphs Department, Ruby had been born and brought up in that country, and after completing her education at a convent school in the south of India, become the reigning belle among her set in Midnapore. But from the first, she had been both ambitious and consumed by envy of all those of a higher social status than herself, and that envy drove her like a spur until it became the mainspring of her being. Some day, she vowed, she would be the equal of any of the supercilious wives of high officials to whose dinner parties and lunches she was not invited. And with this end in view she had married Leonard Stock, son of an English country parson, who occupied a minor post in the Indian Civil Service.

Leonard was not earning anything approaching the pay that several other suitors of the dashing Ruby De Castres could offer, but for all that he was considered among her set to be a good match. First and foremost because he was what Anglo-India refers to, snobbishly, as a 'Sahib', and secondly, because rumour had it that although his present position in the Civil Service was a modest one, he would go far.

Rumour, however, as is frequently the case, had been misinformed. Leonard Stock was a pleasant enough little man, amiable, friendly, and unassuming, but totally incapable of firmness or decision—as Ruby De Castres, now Ruby Stock, was to discover within a few brief months of her marriage. Facing the fact that her husband would never rise to any heights if he remained in Midnapore, she had urged him to accept a position in the administration of the Andamans when that opportunity had offered. And so the Stocks had come to the Islands, and at first all had been more than well with them.

Here no echo of her past life had penetrated, and Ruby manufactured, with that facility of invention and superfluous falsehood that is so frequently the hallmark of her type, a father who was a retired Lieutenant-Colonel, an ancestral estate in Ireland, and a Spanish great-grandmother. She entertained lavishly, and to her Leonard's anxious remonstrances over their steadily mounting bills, merely retorted that it was necessary for them to keep up their position if he was ever to get on in the world. And when the four years' tenure of his post in the Islands was up, she persuaded him to apply for an extension.

The move was a fatal one, and he knew it. But he was too weak to resist, for Ruby answered his half-hearted protests with tears and temper, and eventually he gave in. With the result that his post in India, to which he could have returned, was filled. Other men moved up to close the gap, and now he must either continue to ask for and obtain extensions, or find himself out of a job. That had been sixteen years ago; and the Stocks were still in the Islands . . .

Beautiful, ambitious Ruby, the erstwhile belle of Midnapore, was now a soured and embittered woman who clung to her fading charms with despairing tenacity as being her only defence against the dragging monotony of her existence. And since women were few in the Islands, there had always been some man, often several, tied to her apron-strings. The pursuance of 'affairs' had become the sole interest of her shallow, childless life, and as a result of this she looked upon every other woman in the light of a possible rival.

Until the arrival of Valerie, Mrs Stock had possessed no serious competitor in Port Blair, and she had resented the girl's youth and distinction with an acid inward bitterness and an outward display of gushing friendliness. But Valerie had not proved the rival she had feared, for her instant annexation by Charles Corbet-Carr had made her impervious to the attentions of all other men. Copper Randal, however, posed a definite threat.

Ruby had decided on sight to add Nick to the 'chain-gang', as Port Blair was wont to refer, ribaldly, to Mrs Stock's admirers. But from the first it was painfully apparent that the option, if any, on Nick Tarrent's affections was held by that newly arrived tow-headed chit from Government House. Wherefore Mrs Stock's greeting of the aforementioned chit was characteristic——

'What on earth kept you, darling?' (Ruby had read somewhere that people in fashionable social circles constantly referred to each other as 'darling'.) 'No— don't tell me, I can guess. You had a puncture! Such a romantic road, isn't it? I expect John Shilto is completely *épris* by now! Quite a catch my dear, I assure you. Dear me, how useful punctures are! I wonder how people did without them before there were cars?'

The tinkling laugh that accompanied this pleasantry was not untinged with malice, and Copper's smoke-blue eyes widened into an expression of child-like innocence: 'Well, of course you'd know, Mrs Stock,' she countered sweetly.

'*Game, set and match*, I think!' murmured Nick to his immortal soul. Aloud he said briskly: 'Hullo, Copper. You're abominably late. I gather you brought the drinks with you—and about time too! I could do with one. And I'm sure Ruby could too. Let's go and collect them.' He took Copper firmly by the arm and walked her rapidly away across the lawn before Mrs Stock had time to reply.

'Oh dear, that was *beastly* of me,' said Copper remorsefully. 'But she did ask for it! All the same, we shouldn't have just walked off and left her.'

'Thanks,' said Nick grimly, 'but I had no desire to act as referee at a cat-fight. You are too quick on the uptake for one so young. It shocks me. It also appeared to shock poor Ruby considerably. Shall I mix you a gin sling, or would you rather have shandy?'

'Shandy, please. The box with all the gingerbeer and the rest of the soft drinks is still in the car, I think.'

'Here it is,' said Leonard Stock, appearing beside them with a bottle-filled packing-case. 'Where shall I put it? Good-morning, Miss Randal.'

'Dump it somewhere in the shade,' advised Nick. 'Here, let me help you.'

'Don't bother, I can manage.' Mr Stock deposited his burden in the shadow of a group of flame trees and hunted through the bottles for one containing gingerbeer: 'Shandy, I think you said. We might make a large jug of it. I could do with some myself. It really has been a very trying morning. Quite exceptionally airless. I had hoped that there would be a breeze up here; one can usually count on it. But there does not seem to be a breath of wind anywhere today.' He fumbled in his pockets for a handkerchief, and having wiped the palms of his hands, dabbed ineffectually at the sweat that trickled down his face and neck.

'Hullo, Leonard,' said Valerie, joining them. 'You're looking very hot and bothered. And so you should be!—what's all this we hear about you bringing Ferrers Shilto along to join the glad throng?'

Mr Stock threw a hunted look over his shoulder and said in an agitated undertone: 'Yes, I—I'm afraid we did. But how *were* we to know? You see, the padre and Mrs Dobbie brought us in their car, and as they wanted to ask Ferrers about bringing some bedding—he's staying with them for Christmas you know—we stopped at his bungalow, and . . . Well, it seemed only neighbourly to ask him to come on with us to the picnic, for of course we had no notion that John would be here. *None!* It really is *most* awkward.'

'You're telling us!' said Charles, accepting a glass of Mr Stock's shandy. 'In fact, here we go now. Stand by for fireworks! The cousins Shilto, Copper. Grand reunion scene in three sharp explosions. That's Ferrers in the beachcomber get-up: the skinny little shrimp with his back to us and seething fury in every line of it.'

The phrase was descriptive, for there was a tense and quivering animosity about the wizened figure in the stained and crumpled suit of drill who faced John Shilto's confident advance, and a sudden silence descended upon the company as the older man came to a stop before his cousin and held out a large, fleshy hand. Perhaps because of it, his voice when he spoke sounded unnaturally loud and forced: 'Well, well! This is a surprise!' said Mr Shilto with spurious heartiness. 'I must admit that I didn't bargain on running into you here, old man. But as we have met, what about taking this opportunity to call bygones bygones? Eh?'

His laugh rang as loud and forced as his voice, but it appeared that Ferrers Shilto was either short-sighted or else that he did not intend to take his cousin's proffered hand, for he did not move. The silence deepened and drew out until it seemed to acquire a solid entity of its own, and once again John Shilto's heavy features became mottled by a dark, ugly tide of colour. He dropped his hand but managed, with a palpable effort, to retain the semblance of a smile: 'Oh, come on, old man, be a sport! After all, it's Christmas, you know. *"Peace and Good-will".*'

Ferrers Shilto laughed—a shrill, cackling, almost hysterical sound—and said, astonishingly: 'So you've found out, have you? I wonder how you managed it? Well a hell of a lot of good may it do you!'

The words, meaningless as they appeared to the openly listening bystanders, evidently possessed a meaning for John Shilto. And afterwards Copper was to remember the way in which both colour and smile had been wiped off his face as though with a sponge, leaving it pasty white and raw with rage. To remember, too, the hot, bright sunlight and the dappled shadows, the silent group of people, and the strange, fleeting look that she had surprised on one other face . . .

John Shilto put up a fumbling and uncertain hand and tugged at his collar as though it were too tight for him, then turning abruptly, he walked away across the lawn with a curious stumbling tread.

Hurried and somewhat guilty conversation broke out again as the spectators of the recent drama awoke to a belated sense of social shortcomings. But as Ferrers Shilto turned on his heel, Valerie heard Copper draw in her breath in a short hard gasp and saw her stiffen as though the sight of the little man's face had given her a violent shock. 'What's the matter, Coppy?' she asked sharply: 'You look as if you'd seen a ghost.'

'I believe I have,' said Copper huskily.

She forced an uncertain laugh and said in a voice that was not entirely under control: 'Don't look so alarmed, Val. I'm not mental. At least I don't think I am. But—that nightmare I had. I know it sounds fantastic, but the man I saw in it was Ferrers Shilto!'

A period of deep, warm, post-luncheon peace had descended upon Mount Harriet.

Those members of the picnic party who had failed to secure one of the coveted beds in the house had disposed themselves for slumber on rugs and cushions in various shady corners of the garden, and Valerie, Copper, Charles and Nick, beaten by a short head in the race for the comforting though restricted shade of the fig trees on the eastern edge of the lawn, had retired with all the rugs they could muster to the lorry.

This capacious and utilitarian vehicle, the property of the Public Works Department, was ordinarily employed in carrying loads of gravel or stone for road repairs, but had on this occasion been borrowed to transport half the party from Hopetown jetty to Mount Harriet. Traces of its workaday occupation still lingered between the boards and littered the corners, but failed to discommode the four who, climbing in over the tail-board, spread rugs and cushions upon the dusty floor and settled down to a peaceful afternoon's siesta.

'This is bliss,' said Charles drowsily. 'Wake me up in time for a late-ish tea, someone. And let us pray that no hearty friends get bitten with the idea of going down to bathe and drive off with us, like last time!' He settled himself comfortably on his back on the floorboards and closed his eyes: only to open them a moment later as footsteps crunched the gravel outside and some unseen person approached the lorry and, pausing beside it, laid a hand on the edge of the tail-board.

Copper opened her mouth to speak, but stopped at a grimace from Charles. '*Ronnie!*' mouthed Charles silently; and indicated by dumb show that if Mr Purvis discovered their occupation of the vehicle he would undoubtedly add himself to their party. Whereupon the four lay quiet and made a creditable attempt to cease breathing, and after a moment or two the hand was withdrawn and the footsteps moved away in the direction of the house.

'Saved!' sighed Charles. 'That tedious Romeo would have pressed in and talked the entire afternoon.'

'It wasn't Ronnie,' announced Copper, peering through a crack in the side of the lorry. 'It was the Shilto cousin—Ferrers.'

'That's odd,' said Valerie. 'I thought it was Ronnie, too. I wonder why? What do you suppose Ferrers is doing wandering around loose? I'd rather hoped that after the Big Scene the padre would put a leash on him. Charles, do you suppose——?'

'No, I don't!' said Charles firmly. 'I see no evil, I hear no evil and I speak no evil. Not at the moment, anyway. I am suffering from post-prandial torpor and I intend to slumber. So pipe down, light-of-my-life, and let us have not only peace but quiet.'

The lorry had been parked in the shade of the house, and presently a faint, unexpectedly cold breeze stole across the garden, cooling the clogging warmth of the afternoon to a more pleasant temperature. A drowsy silence fell, in which Charles snored gently and a wandering bluebottle investigated Nick's unconscious chin . . .

Afterwards not one of them could be quite certain at what point they had awakened. But awakened they were, all four of them. And by the time they had arrived at full consciousness they had overheard sufficient to make them realize that this was no time to rise and disclose themselves. Therefore they lay still, concealed by the high wooden sides of the lorry, while a scant yard away the cousins Shilto exchanged words of an uncousinly nature.

Piecing together, in the light of after-events, what they could remember of that conversation, it appeared that John Shilto had offered to buy back his cousin's plantation at more than twice the price he had originally received for it; giving, as a reason for this astounding gesture, his desire to put an end to the old quarrel between them. This offer Ferrers was in the process of rejecting with every indication of scorn and loathing when the occupants of the lorry awoke to the fact that they were involuntarily eavesdropping on a private conversation.

'—and if,' announced Ferrers Shilto, concluding a speech generously interlarded with expressions of a distressingly personal and opprobrious character, 'you imagine for one minute that I am going to be had for a mug twice over by a crook like you, you can think again! You could offer me *forty* times the sum you swindled out of me for that stinking, rat-ridden, pestilential plantation, and I wouldn't take it! And what's more I shall make my will tomorrow—just to be sure that you never get your hands on it! No, my beloved cousin, this is where I get my own back at last. That plantation is mine. Every single, slimy acre of it, wet or dry. And if you so much as set foot on it, I'll have my servants thrash you off it!'

His voice rose until it cracked hysterically, and the elder Shilto, with one parting vitriolic epithet, turned on his heel and retired from the field of battle.

Presently Ferrers too departed, and Charles, having made a cautious survey, announced that the coast was clear. 'An exhilarating interlude, wasn't it? Teeming with drama, passion, human interest and mystery. The works! I enjoyed it immensely. What sort of dirty work do you suppose our John is up to now? Or have we witnessed a miracle and is he a genuine victim of remorse and the Christmas spirit? A sort of latter-day Scrooge? Somehow, I doubt it.'

'What about "*speaking no evil*" now?' inquired Valerie.

'Ah, but that was when I was feeling somnolent and well fed. As I am now no longer either, I am only too willing to believe the worst of everyone. So let us dismiss the case of Shilto versus Shilto and concentrate instead on getting some tea before my disposition deteriorates still further. Hand me down those rugs, my love.'

They walked round the side of the house, and passing under the creeper-clad porch, crossed to the far end of the lawn to where the remainder of the party were grouped about a well-covered tablecloth spread in the shade of the frangipani trees.

'Come and talk to me for a change, Copper,' invited Ronnie Purvis. 'There's room for a small one this end. Move over, Hurridge, and let us grab this damsel off the Navy. Have some sandwiches: the damp ones are cucumber and the mangled and messy ones are jam.'

'Cucumber, please,' decided Copper, inserting her slim person between the nattily yachting-suited figure of Ronnie Purvis and the large, khaki-clad bulk of Mr Albert Hurridge, the Deputy Commissioner. She was guiltily aware that her preoccupation with Nick Tarrent had had the effect of making her completely uninterested in every other person on the Islands with the exception of Valerie and Charles, and seized now with a temporary fit of remorse, she listened patiently to the Deputy Commissioner's incredibly dull and anecdotal conversation, bore equally patiently with the stereotyped flirtatiousness of that self-satisfied lady-killer Mr Ronald Purvis, and did her best, though without much success, to include his silent, faded wife in the conversation.

Ronnie Purvis was a member of that well-known genus, the compulsive philanderer, who imagines that his job in life is to brighten it for every woman he meets. Inordinately vain, he was possessed of a vain man's cheap attraction, and no one had ever quite understood how he had come to marry poor, dull, faded Rosamund Purvis. For if Mrs Purvis had ever had any claims to prettiness, the heat and fevers of the tropics had shrivelled them away long ago, and at thirty she succeeded in looking a good ten years older than her husband's bronzed and athletic thirty-six.

People were apt to refer to Mr Purvis as 'poor, dear Ronnie', and to add that it was a tragedy that he should be tied to that limp, uninteresting woman. Few would have believed the truth: that Rosamund Purvis had been a Bachelor of Arts at twenty-two, and one of the most brilliant students of her year at Oxford. A dazzling future was prophesied for her; and then, a year later, she had met Ronald Purvis, home on leave from India, fallen helplessly in love with him, and married him. That had been seven years ago, and the loneliness of forest camps, the damp, sticky, cloying heat of the Andamans, the birth and death of two successive children, and her husband's eternal philandering, had combined to turn the once-pretty and intelligent woman into the colourless nonentity that Port Blair knew as 'Poor, dear Ronnie's dreary wife'.

Meanwhile poor, dear Ronnie continued to flirt desperately with any and every girl he met, and to explain to them in turn, in sad, brave tones, how little his wife understood him—a phrase only too often in use, and which can generally be taken to mean that, on the contrary, she understands him only too well. He also continued, at thirty-six, to look as young as he had at twenty-five, and to conduct those of his flirtations which progressed into 'affairs', with unblushing openness in his wife's house.

'I can't think why on earth she stands it,' Charles had once said to Valerie: 'If I was in that woman's shoes, I'd clear out and leave him to his messy little affairs. She's got no guts.'

'Perhaps she's in love with him?' suggested Valerie.

'Rats!' retorted Charles inelegantly.

But as it happened, Valerie had been right. Rosamund Purvis despised her husband and bitterly resented his infidelities. But she still loved him, and so she stayed with him: tired, disillusioned, middle-aged at thirty, knowing herself an object of pity and contempt to the settlement . . .

Ronnie, however, was not having his customary success at the present moment. Valerie he had failed to impress from the first, and her subsequent engagement to Charles Corbet-Carr had effectually put a stop to any romantic adventures he may have anticipated in that direction. In the position of Public Boyfriend Number One, Mr Purvis had worked systematically through the present scanty female population of Ross and Aberdeen, and was suffering from the pangs of acute boredom at the time the *Maharaja* had docked at Chatham, bearing on board Miss Caroline Randal.

One look at the new importation and Ronnie decided that the gods had indeed been kind to him, and calling up all his well-worn stock-in-trade of charm, boyishness, impudence and romantic technique had confidently advanced to conquer.

But alas for high hopes! H.M.S. *Sapphire* and Lieutenant Nicholas Tarrent had between them effectively ruined the merry season of Christmas as far as Mr Purvis was concerned. And since he was not accustomed to competition, the spectacle of Nick Tarrent cheerfully monopolizing the new importation had done much toward souring his otherwise cheerful disposition: though little towards lowering his self-esteem, and Copper found herself parrying his ardent advances throughout the meal, while one half of her mind was engaged in actively disliking Ruby Stock and wondering what she could be saying to Nick that necessitated her draping herself across one of his shoulders?

5

. . . Jarawas,' said Mr Hurridge.

'I beg your pardon?' said Copper, suddenly realizing that the Deputy Commissioner was once again in full spate.

'Jarawas,' repeated Mr Hurridge impressively. 'I do not think you fully realize the fact that we are all actually sitting in Jarawa country at this very moment.'

He observed Copper's look of blank incomprehension and said in a slightly injured tone: 'I do not believe you have been listening to one word that I have said, Miss Randal.'

'I'm sorry,' apologized Copper. 'I'm afraid I was thinking of something else. What were you saying?'

'I was speaking of the Jarawas,' said Mr Hurridge with dignity. 'They are a tribe of aborigines that inhabit parts of these islands.'

'I thought they were called Andamanese,' said Copper brightly.

'No, no. The Jarawas are entirely distinct from the Andamanese: they are quite untameable little people who live in the forests, and no one has ever managed to learn their language or become friendly with them. They use bows and arrows and shoot on sight, and they are as wild today as they were when Marco Polo first wrote of the Islands.'

Mr Hurridge, now well away, launched into a long and pompous account of raids made on outlying settlements and lonely forest outposts by the savage little men, and of the impossibility of successful expeditions against them owing to the denseness of the wild jungle in which they lived. Mount Harriet itself, said Mr Hurridge, was well inside Jarawa country, and a dozen paces beyond the far edge of that smooth lawn would take one into the Jarawa jungles——

'We could all be murdered at any minute,' said Amabel Withers with automatic pessimism: 'It just goes to show, doesn't it?'

'Don't let 'em scare you, Copper,' cut in Ronnie Purvis. 'The Jarawas have hardly ever been known to come near this end of the island. And anyway they only kill for food or iron, or water in dry years; never for fun.'

'If that's supposed to cheer me up,' said Copper with a shiver, 'it doesn't. I thought this place was supposed to be nice and peaceful; no wild animals, not many snakes, and nice friendly Andamanese. Now I shall have heart failure whenever I hear a twig snap. Come and hold my hand, Mr Norton: I'm going to peer over the hedge at this Jarawa country, and I feel I should like some police protection.'

The tea party broke up and wandered across the lawn, and presently Valerie had taken Copper into the house and shown her a sight that was to remain clear in her memory for the rest of her life. They had mounted the staircase side by side and turned into a wide, glassed-in verandah that ran round three sides of the top storey of the house, where Valerie had pushed open a window and said, *'There—!'* And Copper had found herself gazing down at what must surely be one of the loveliest views in the world.

Far below her the Islands lay scattered over a

glassy sea that was so still and smooth and shining that the wandering currents showed like paper streamers straggling across a ballroom floor after a carnival night when the dancing is over and the dancers have gone. The air had cooled with the approach of evening and the Islands were no longer veiled by a shimmering heat-haze, but clear-cut and colourful: lilac and lavender, blue and green and gold in the tropic evening—

'Keats must have dreamed of this view,' said Copper. 'These are his *"magic casements, opening on the foam—Of perilous seas, in faery lands forlorn".*'

'Y-es,' agreed Valerie hesitantly. 'But there are times when I wonder if the magic is white or black?'

'Why do you say that?' asked Copper curiously.

'I don't know. Only—well, sometimes there is a queer sort of feeling about the Islands. Oh, not in the way you meant last night. But—but they seem so out of this world. As though civilization and the twentieth century had only made a little scratch on the surface, and underneath they were still strange and . . . And *"forlorn"* and *"perilous"*, I suppose! I believe that if one lived here for too long they might do odd things to one. To one's character, I mean. Change it, and make it different and—— Oh, I can't explain. I'm probably talking nonsense. You know, it's odd, but all day I've had a queer feeling; rather as though I were an overwound watch-spring wondering what happens when the breaking-point is reached? A loud, twanging noise perhaps, and all my nice, orderly, civilized little ideas flying in every direction in a gloriously crude and uninhibited manner. Now I *am* talking nonsense!'

'No,' said Copper slowly. 'I think I know what you mean. Everyone seems to be feeling a bit edgy today. I know I am! I was even driven to exchanging a catty scratch with La Stock. And then there were the Shiltos snarling at each other, and even Mrs Purvis got quite crisp when Amabel Withers started on yet another of those gloomy anecdotes about local characters who have been drowned or eaten by sharks or caught by an octopus.'

'I expect it's the heat,' said Valerie with a sigh. 'We haven't had any rain for days. A really good shower, and we shall all return to normal—tempers included. *Don't do that, Coppy!* You'll stain your arms!'

Copper, who had leant far out over the window-ledge, drew back sharply. 'Don't do what? Heavens above!—what on earth is it?'

'Sorry,' apologized Valerie. 'I should have warned you. It's some red stuff they stain all the outside woodwork with. We've even got it all over our house on Ross. I believe it's earth-oil, or something of the sort. It's an appalling nuisance because it comes off on everything.'

'It does indeed!' commented Copper acidly, scrubbing her vividly coloured elbows with an inadequate handkerchief.

'No one warned me either,' said Valerie with a grin, 'and I well remember an awful occasion when . . . Good grief! *Look over there! Hi!—Hamish!'* She leant out of the window and yelled down to Captain Rattigan, the earnest and ginger-headed officer in command of the military detachment on Ross who was standing on the drive below: '*Hamish!*—there's a hell of a storm coming up! You sailing people had better get going pretty quickly if you don't want to get caught in it. *Hurry!'*

Copper turned and saw, far to the south-east, a low band of tawny-coloured darkness that lay along the horizon. It had a hard black edge to it, as straight as though it had been drawn with a ruler, and above it an ugly, ochrous stain was spreading upwards into the evening sky.

'But it's *miles* away,' she protested. 'It could miss us altogether. Or fizzle out before it gets here.'

'Perhaps,' said Valerie shortly: 'But I don't like the look of it at all. Come on, we'd better go down.' She turned and ran for the garden, where a discussion was already in progress as to who should sail home and who go by car.

George Beamish and Amabel Withers, Ted Norton of the police and Surgeon-Lieutenant Dan Harcourt of H.M.S. *Sapphire* having elected to return by road, Hamish was busy collecting substitute yachtsmen, and Copper arrived in excellent time to see Mrs Stock take playful possession of Nick Tarrent's arm and demand to be taken back with him in Dan Harcourt's place: 'And don't try and put me off, Nick!' she announced gaily, smiling up into his eyes and wagging a roguish and admonitory finger. 'I'm not a bit afraid of storms and I just *adore* sailing! And you needn't pretend that you are taking anyone else, because Dan has only this minute decided to drive back. Haven't you, Dan?'

'*Dear Ruby!*' murmured Charles gently.

Hamish's voice made itself plaintively audible above the general babel: 'Then that's fixed, is it? Stock, and I are taking one boat, Ronnie and Rosamund and Ferrers another, and Tarrent and Ruby and Shilto will take the third. All right?'

'Cautious chap, Nick,' commented Charles: 'Bang goes Ruby's tête-à-tête!'

Copper laughed and unaccountably felt her heart grow several degrees lighter. She would not have admitted even to herself quite how apprehensive she was becoming of Mrs Stock's determined and mature attractions. The eight yachtsmen packed themselves into the lorry and departed, while the remainder of the party set about collecting rugs and picnic-baskets in a leisurely manner. They would

take less time to return by road than those who were
sailing back across the bay, and since the majority of
them intended to catch the six-thirty ferry from Aberdeen to Ross they could allow themselves another
half hour on Harriet.

The conversation turned naturally to Home—for
this was Christmas Eve and the acute nostalgia of
the Exile for familiar scenes and the years that have
been and will return no more, seized achingly on
the little group under the frangipani trees. Memories
of other Christmases. Of holly and mistletoe, mince
pies and carol singers. Even Copper was conscious
of a brief pang of homesickness, and for a fleeting
moment Nick, Valerie and Charles, the green islands
and the enchanted sea grew dim and unreal, and
she was a child again, climbing on to a nursery chair
to hang gay, glass balls on a Christmas tree . . .

She shook herself as though to be rid of the memory, and having helped to stow the last of the rugs
in the cars, strolled to the far edge of the lawn
where the breeze which had strengthened at the approach of sunset blew her ash-blond hair into a tangled halo about her head. Below and to her left on
the quiet sea off North Bay a tiny white sailing-boat
was moving sluggishly towards Ross. It was too far
out to be one belonging to the Mount Harriet party,
and Copper imagined it must be Valerie's father returning from a peaceful and private afternoon's sailing. She watched it idly for a few moments, and
then as her eyes strayed beyond it, stiffened suddenly to alarmed attention.

They heard her calling from the far side of the
pepper trees, but the breeze took the words away,
blurring them to unintelligible sounds. 'What do
you suppose she wants?' inquired Valerie: 'Charles
darling, do have a good look round and see that we
haven't left anything.'

Copper reappeared suddenly, running across the

lawn, and said breathlessly: 'Come and look at this!' She dragged Valerie at a run to the far side of the garden, the others following more slowly: 'Look!' said Copper, still agitated. They looked in silence; gazing in the direction of her pointing finger to where H.M.S. *Sapphire*, no longer at her moorings, steamed slowly out of the harbour, her bows set to the open sea. 'They've gone!' said Copper blankly.

'No, he hasn't,' said Valerie, correctly translating the thought: 'There hasn't been nearly time for the dinghies to do more than get clear of Hopetown jetty. That is, if they've even started yet, which I doubt—what with Ruby insisting on helping to get the sail up!'

Copper's strained attitude relaxed and she laughed a little unsteadily as Charles said: 'Let's ask Dan,' and turned about to hail Dan Harcourt, who was strolling towards them across the lawn. 'Come and take a last, lingering look at your departing home, Doc. Were you by any chance aware that your mess-mates were proposing to light out and leave you marooned?'

Dan Harcourt glanced along Valerie's pointing finger and his jaw dropped. 'Great Scott! Why—what on earth——?'

'We don't know,' said Copper. 'Don't you know anything about it either?'

'No. There must be something up: someone staging a riot in some insalubrious coastal spot, and the Navy ordered to show the flag for moral effect.'

He grinned suddenly and largely: 'I say, what a bit of luck for me getting left behind! Sickening for all the other poor types having to spend Christmas striking warlike attitudes. I bet they're cursing! Nick will have missed it too: pretty lucky for both of——' The sentence broke off in a little shiver that made his teeth chatter.

Copper swung round sharply and he laughed and

said: 'Sorry. Goose walked over my grave. Hadn't we better get going if we're going to catch the ferry?'

They piled into the three cars and left Mount Harriet behind them. And at no point during the drive down the steep hill road did one of them think to look back to where, behind them, that ominous belt of tawny darkness grew and broadened with uncanny swiftness, blotting out the brightness of the quiet evening sky.

Barely had the last car passed through the gates and rounded the first bend of the jungle road when the new-found silence of the deserted house was again disturbed. This time by the bell in the small telephone box in the corner of the verandah by the dining-room door. The phone rang shrilly, its urgent metallic cry echoing eerily through the silent house.

It rang for perhaps five minutes, and then ceased. And silence flowed back and closed over Mount Harriet like a quiet cloud.

=== 6 ===

'It's getting very dark,' said Copper. 'Are we going to miss the ferry?'

Valerie leant forward and peered at the dashboard clock. 'No, we're all right. We've got nearly half an hour yet and it shouldn't take us more than twenty minutes from here.'

'*Um*,' said Copper dubiously. 'I've never yet been on a picnic with you and Charles when we haven't missed the ferry.'

Charles said: '*Pessimist!*' but applied his foot with more force to the accelerator and took the next bend at fifty.

'Why is everything such a queer yellow colour?' persisted Copper restlessly. 'You ought to switch on the headlights, Charles. You'll run off the road in a minute—it squiggles so.'

'Look, who's driving this car?' demanded Charles. 'You or me?'

Copper apologized hastily and leant out to look back at the sky between the double wall of trees behind them. They heard her catch her breath in a harsh gasp, and Dan Harcourt, who was returning with them in place of John Shilto, leant out in turn and whistled expressively. 'Great Caesar's Ghost——! Here, step on it, Charles, or inside another five minutes we're going to be overhauled by the father and mother of a storm!'

Above and ahead of them the sky was still clear and serene, but behind them it had turned to a leaden pall of darkness against which the tangled mass of the jungle and the tall tops of coconut palms stood black and motionless, and not a leaf stirred. Even the ferns and orchids and the long, delicate festoons of creeper that swung down from every overhanging branch hung so still that they appeared to be rigid, and the rattling swiftness of the ancient car seemed the only sound in all the breathless, waiting islands.

Charles tilted the driving-mirror so as to give himself a view of the lowering sky behind him, and said: 'Crippen! We're going to be lucky if we beat this! Hold on to your hats, and we'll see if we can knock sixty out of this galloping bedstead.'

He switched on the headlights as they bucketed out of a side-turning and swung left with a screech of tortured tyres into a long, straight stretch of road lined with shadowy coconut palms. But the storm was overhauling them with relentless swiftness, and by now more than half the sky was darkened by it and the far hills had been blotted out. 'Hurry, Charles!' implored Valerie.

'It's no good telling me to hurry,' retorted Charles with something of a snap: 'Address your admonitions to this blasted mousetrap!—she's bursting her stays as it is, and even if we could by some miracle kick another five miles an hour out of her, she'd fall to pieces in the process!'

'This *would* happen on Christmas Eve!' mourned Valerie. 'Charles, do you think the others will hold the ferry for us? We were the last to leave and we've got the worst car, so the Dobbies and George and Amabel and Co. are bound to have arrived by now.'

Charles said: 'You forget they've got to decant

Hurridge and Ted Norton first. We'll probably be at the jetty as soon as they are. *Listen!* . . . What's that?'

For some minutes past they had been vaguely aware of a curious humming sound that was barely audible above the noise of the car. But now, suddenly, it deepened until it sounded like the croon of wind through telegraph wires, and grew steadily in volume until the whole island seemed to vibrate to it as the fabric of a church will tremble to the low tones of an organ.

Charles shouted: 'Hold everything—here she comes!' And even as he spoke, the storm was upon them.

It hit the breathless immobility of the evening with the impact of a sixteen-inch shell. Shattering the brooding stillness into a thousand tortured fragments as the wind leapt upon the island; shaking it, savaging it, tearing it as though it were a terrier with a rat: bending the tall trunks of the coconut palms as though they had been saplings, and lashing them to and fro in a wild confusion.

Trails of jungle creeper, ripped from their airy moorings, leaves, twigs and orchids, fragments of branches and startled insects whirled across the windscreen of the car and tangled themselves about the radiator as the car rocked and bucketed onwards, keeping to the crown of the road with difficulty. Valerie could see Charles's lips forming wicked words on discovering that the windscreen-wiper was out of order, and she groped for some cotton waste and leant out, the wind whipping her hair across her eyes. The car lurched to a standstill as Charles applied the brake and dragged her back into her seat with a relentless hand. '—! —!' yelled Charles; his words completely unintelligible against the roar of the wind. He snatched the cotton waste from her and performed the operation himself.

Valerie was aware of Copper shouting something in her ear as the car bounded forward again: *'Nick!'* shouted Copper, white-faced with terror: *'The boats! They'll be out in this!'*

Dan Harcourt, who had caught a word or two above the fiendish flapping and rattling of the aged car and the whining howl of the wind, yelled back reassuringly that they'd be all right and had probably got in about a quarter of an hour ago, and . . .

Valerie turned sharply to look at him. In the reflected glow of the headlights his face betrayed nothing but confidence, but having sailed more than once with him during the past week she knew that Dan must be very well aware of the time it would take to sail from Hopetown to Ross with a fair wind. And there had been no breath of wind for half an hour before the storm . . . They can't possibly be more than half-way by now, she thought with panic: and shrank back against her seat as the first swollen drops of rain splashed heavily against the windscreen.

Copper had never imagined such rain. It came down like a river in full spate. A heavy, opaque curtain of water that descended on them out of the inky sky with the terrifying suggestion of a tidal wave, blotting out the road before them so that they appeared to be driving into a shifting, liquid wall. The aged car leaked profusely from a dozen points, and by the time they reached the outskirts of Aberdeen bazaar its four passengers presented the damp and bedraggled appearance of survivors from a shipwreck.

There was a brief lull in the storm as they arrived at the jetty where they found four occupants of the other two carloads, the Reverend Dobbie and his wife, and Amabel and her George, grouped in an unhappy huddle in the iron-roofed shelter on the quay. The other two members of the party, Ted Norton and Deputy-Commissioner Hurridge, being resident on Aberdeen were mercifully exempt from braving the stormy strip of harbour water in an attempt to return to Ross, and though Amabel also lived on Aberdeen, she had been invited to several Christmas parties on Ross and would be putting up for a couple of nights with the Purvises.

As the Ford drew up under cover of the shed, a bearded Sikh in a dripping mackintosh cape came forward and presented a damp envelope to Charles, who ran his eye down the single sheet of paper and said: 'It's from Amabel's father. Mr Withers says we'd better not attempt to cross over to Ross unless there is a lull. He says he phoned to Harriet to try and stop the others sailing, but as it took ages to get through, he missed us, and that we'd better park ourselves on him and Mr Hurridge for the night.'

'Oh *no*! Charles,' protested Valerie. 'We're giving a party tonight. We *must* get back! The worst is over—it's not blowing nearly so hard now. Do let's go, *please*!'

'We'll put it to the vote,' decided Charles, climbing reluctantly out of the driving-seat and joining the group in the shed: 'Who's for going, and who's for staying?'

After a few moments of animated discussion it was unanimously decided to risk the crossing and dispense with Mr Hurridge's hospitality. 'Come on then,' urged Charles, 'let's make a dash for it. We can't get much wetter than we are already!' And plunging out of the shelter of the shed they fled along the open jetty to where the ferry heaved and shrieked at her moorings.

It needed the combined threats, orders and pleadings of the eight would-be passengers to induce the native crew to attempt the trip, for the wind still howled through the narrow straits between Aberdeen and Ross, and the driven rain, lashing downwards at an acute angle, ricocheted off the heaving waters in a sheet of steel. But since the fury of the rain had temporarily beaten the sea into comparative submission, they cast off hastily: the clumsy craft backing reluctantly away from the jetty and rolling like an elderly and drunken duck.

Copper never forgot the twenty minutes that followed. A dozen times it seemed that they must be swamped or driven back on the jagged teeth of the rocks off the jail point as the labouring ferry heeled over to the wind. '*Hell!*' said Charles after the first five minutes. 'We never ought to have done this. I'd no earthly right to let you come.'

'I expect we'll be swept out to sea,' pronounced Amabel gloomily. 'It just goes to show, doesn't it?'

'Don't be absurd!' snapped Valerie. But it was a disturbing thought, and more than one of the passengers conjured up an unpleasantly vivid mental picture of the ferry being swept through the harbour mouth and out into the angry, desolate leagues of ocean beyond Ross; though neither George nor Copper were among their number—George being occupied with the welfare of his Amabel, and Copper with visions of Nick Tarrent being drowned in the bay, dashed upon the rocks of North Point, or possibly eaten by sharks.

Amabel, struck by a melancholy association of ideas, did not improve matters by suddenly embarking at the top of her voice on a gruesome story of several private soldiers who, long ago, while trying to row from Aberdeen to Ross upon a stormy night were swept out to sea and finally thrown upon the beach of Havelock, a tiny island many miles down the coast. Their boat being smashed upon the rocks and starvation looming imminent, one of their number had attempted the desperate swim between Havelock and Ross to fetch help. But the distance between the two islands being anything from fifteen to twenty miles of shark-infested sea, it is not surprising that he was never seen again; or that having scoured the coasts, the rescue party that eventually landed upon Havelock should find the survivors dead of thirst and starvation, with the details of their tragedy scratched upon a sun-dried scrap of paper.

'—and there's a tablet in the Ross church to the one who tried to get help. You can see it next time you go there,' added Amabel. 'I expect the sharks got him. Or perhaps barracudas; they're worse than sharks. A dreadful thing to happen, I always think.'

Her fellow-passengers eyed her with distaste, and it was obvious from their bleak expressions that including the padre and with the exception of George, they could all of them have thought up several equally dreadful things that they would have liked to happen, immediately, to Miss Withers. Presently Valerie began to turn a delicate and unbecoming shade of green, and Copper shut her eyes and began to think more kindly of drowning. The Reverend Dobbie embarked on a mental recitation of the 'Prayer for Those at Sea', and Charles said: 'By God, we've made it!' as the ferry crashed inexpertly against the pontoon off Ross jetty . . .

Five minutes later, soaked and shaken, they were safe ashore and being packed into the three big Government House rickshaws, known on the island as 'buggies'—a survival of the days when they were drawn by ponies—that had been waiting under the shelter of the sheds by the jetty, Valerie and Copper to return to Government House, Mrs Purvis and Amabel, with George trotting alongside, to the Purvises', the Dobbies to the Vicarage, and Charles and Dan, on foot, to Charles's quarters in the Mess.

But half an hour later there was still no news of the boats, the telephone wires were down and the ferry, having broken its moorings, had made the perilous trip to Chatham and succeeded in reaching anchorage there.

Sir Lionel Masson, who had returned, wet and disinclined for conversation, some few minutes after the arrival of his daughter, had had a hot bath and changed, and on hearing that the telephone had ceased functioning, had donned a mackintosh and gone out into the streaming darkness to get what information he could, while his daughter and her friend, dry and newly clothed though still somewhat damp as to hair, made a gloomy pretence of decorating the dinner table with crackers and artificial holly.

'I can't think why we're doing this,' said Valerie, looping a tinsel ribbon half-heartedly between the tall silver candlesticks. 'I don't imagine that more than three people will turn up, as the forest-launch is sure to land the sailing crowd on Chatham when it's rounded them up, and they'll never get the ferry or anything else across here tonight.'

Copper turned away without answering, and for perhaps the tenth time in as many minutes crossed to the windows and attempted to peer through their rain-streaked surface into the wet darkness beyond. The big clock in the lower hall struck eight as she flattened her nose against a pane, and presently she cupped her hands about her eyes to shut out the light from the room, for she thought she had caught the faint flicker of a rickshaw lamp gleaming through the wild darkness below the house where the drive wound up through an avenue of tossing flame trees. The gleam showed again, more distinctly this time, and a rickshaw drew out from the shelter of the trees.

Valerie dumped a heap of gaudily coloured crackers on to the dining-table and said: '"*Sister Anne, Sister Anne, do you see anyone coming?*"'

'Yes . . . I think it must be your father coming

back. There's a rickshaw coming up the drive. Let's go down.'

They ran across the ballroom which formed the upper hall of the house, and down the stairs to the front door, arriving anxious and breathless as a rickshaw drew up under the wide, covered porch and Sir Lionel descended from it, shaking the wet off his coat. 'They've got back,' he stated briefly in answer to Valerie's urgent query. But there was that in his face which gave her a sudden stab of renewed anxiety. Something horrid has happened, she thought. Aloud she said: 'Come upstairs and tell us about it while I mix you a drink, Dad. And do take off that sopping coat. You'll catch an appalling cold.' She preceded him upstairs to the big glassed-in verandah that was furnished as a lounge, and mixed him a stiff brandy and soda as he sank tiredly into an easy chair.

He sat silent for several minutes, watching the bubbles rise through the amber liquid to burst at the glass's rim, until at last Copper said, sharply anxious: 'What's happened? Are they all safe?' and Sir Lionel appeared to pull himself together. He drank off half the contents of the tumbler before replying and then spoke heavily.

'They were in the water for well over half an hour and the forest-launch had the devil of a time finding them. Apparently all three dinghies were swamped in the first five minutes, but fortunately they were all within yards of each other when it happened— which was just as well, for if they'd been some distance apart, the launch might have been hours rounding them up. They were picked up just this side of North Bay and were landed here. Some of them will be along in a moment. I came on ahead to tell you.'

He paused for a moment, his eyes once again following the streaming line of bubbles in his glass, and suddenly he looked very old and tired. At last: 'They didn't find them all,' he said. 'Ferrers Shilto was missing.'

Valerie drew in her breath sharply. 'You mean he was drowned?'

'Not necessarily. He may have been swept away from the others and caught in a current, and managed to get ashore on North Bay. Or even somewhere on the Aberdeen side.'

Valerie said: 'But you don't think it's likely. And—and anyway, there are sharks,' she added with a shudder.

'*Don't!*' besought Copper. 'What about the others, Sir Lionel?'

The Commissioner turned to her with relief: 'Oh, they're all right—except for Mrs Stock, who seems to be suffering from shock more than exposure. She was rather hysterical, I'm afraid. I have arranged for John Shilto and Tarrent and that young doctor off the ship—what is his name? Oh yes, Harcourt—to sleep here tonight. I hope we have enough bedding. Of course the whole affair is disgraceful. There was a stupid bungle at the wireless station. We should have had a storm warning this morning, and instead of that it was only received about four-thirty. But luckily ships in this harbour have to keep up a reasonable head of steam: otherwise that cruiser would never have got clear in time. As it was, she cut it rather fine.'

'Why did she have to go out?' demanded Copper. 'I thought ships tried to get *in* to harbours in a storm?'

'Not this one. There is not enough deep water. And far too many rocks. Besides, this is only the beginning of the storm. There's a lot more to come, and if the *Sapphire* had stayed here she would have been driven on the rocks like the old *Enterprise*. Her

only chance was to make for the open sea and——'
He broke off as voices sounded from the lower hall,
and putting down his unfinished drink rose and
walked over to the banisters.

Mr Stock, oozing water like a leaking sponge, was
coming up the stairs, rain squelching from his
soaked shoes on to the polished treads and leaving
little gleaming puddles at his every step. He checked
his ascent on seeing the Commissioner, and stood
looking upwards from the well of the stairs, one
hand clutching the banisters and the light from the
hall below him blackly silhouetting his weedy figure.

'Well, Stock?' inquired the Commissioner.

Mr Stock shuffled his feet and cleared his throat
nervously. As ever there was about him a faint, ser-
vile suggestion of cringing, as in a habitually ill-
treated mongrel dog, but in the present instance it
appeared more apparent than usual.

'Well, what is it?' The Commissioner's voice was
unexpectedly tinged with nervous exasperation:
'Have they found him?'

'Yes—er—no. You mean Ferrers Shilto? No. I only
came to inquire if you would be so good as to give
my wife a bed for the night. You see—er—our roof
has gone.'

'Your *what*?'

Mr Stock let go of the banister, swayed dangerously, and clutched at it again to steady himself:
'Our roof. The storm—the storm has blown away a
large portion of it, and part of the house is quite—
er—quite uninhabitable. So I thought that if you
would very kindly allow Ruby—my wife—to sleep
here tonight . . . I—she suffers severely from insomnia you know, and she says that her fear of the rest
of the roof falling would aggravate it. So I
thought . . .' His voice trailed away and his teeth
chattered with cold and fatigue.

Valerie said: 'Why, of *course* we can! Can't we, Dad? And of course you must sleep here too, Leonard. You two can share the big spare room and Nick and Dan can double up in the other one, and we'll make up a bed for Mr Shilto in the turret room.'

Mr Stock muttered profuse thanks, refused a drink, and stumbled out into the night leaving behind him a snail-like trail of dampness. 'Poor little man,' said Copper. 'He looks simply green. It must be a particularly nasty jar after capsizing in a storm and being in the water for hours, to arrive home and find no roof on your house.'

'Not to mention a wife in the last stages of hysteria!' said Valerie. 'If there is one thing dear Ruby really revels in it's a spot of drama, and I bet she'll extract the last ounce of it from the present situation or die in the attempt. Poor Leonard! Come and help me get the rooms ready, Coppy.'

=== 7 ===

Government House was a large, old, two-storeyed and rather gloomy building, full of bats and curious echoes. At sundown the bats swooped through the tall, dim rooms, and once the lights were lit a host of little semi-transparent lizards would appear out of holes and crannies in the high ceilings, to pursue with shrill chirruping cries the moths and night-flying insects that were attracted in by the lamps.

The ground floor was entirely taken up by offices and a guard room, and a wide, shallow-stepped staircase led from the entrance hall to the living rooms above. The upper storey of the house centred about the ballroom; a huge, dim room with a floor of polished boards, into which the staircase emerged, and from which almost every other room in the house led off. A wide, glassed-in verandah ran the length of the house and along part of one end, cutting off most of the light from the drawing-room which was, for this reason, seldom used except by night, and behind the ballroom, separated from it by a couple of pillars and a small section of wall that formed a sketchy passageway, were five bedrooms; one of which, the turret room, was normally used as a morning-room, but was now being pressed into service again as a bedroom for Mr Shilto.

Valerie collected an armful of sheets and pillow-
cases from the linen cupboard and set about preparing for the unexpected influx of guests. 'I expect the
mattresses are all damp and that everyone will get
pneumonia,' she said lightly, 'but there isn't time to
air them. Come on, Coppy; it's no use trying to
dodge those bats. They'll never hit you, anyway!'

'That's what you think! But then you're used to
them, and I'm not. You know, Val, there really is
something very odd about this house. It's quite
cheerful in the daylight, but have you ever noticed
how—how *unfriendly* it gets the moment the sun
goes down? And at night it's sometimes positively
hostile. Or am I being over-imaginative?'

Valerie straightened up from tucking in a blanket
and said slowly, 'No. Even I have noticed it sometimes, and I wouldn't call myself particularly imag-
inative. Perhaps it's because most of the walls are
hollow. Those funny things like portholes, half-way
up some of them, are something to do with ventila-
tion I believe. But it means that bats and rats and
lizards, and goodness only knows what else, can get
between them and run about inside and make odd
noises. And then draughts blow through them and
make even odder ones. Not to mention several families of wild cats who live in the roof and creep about
overhead at night!'

'Perhaps it's that,' said Copper doubtfully. 'That,
and the fact that most of the rooms have no doors,
but only those funny little swinging shutters across
the middle instead. They may stop people seeing
into a large part of the room, but you can't lock
them. And even if you could, anything and anyone
could get in underneath them just as easily as the
bats fly in over the top of them.'

'Oh well, nothing is ever likely to come in,' said
Valerie comfortably. 'Although I must say it would
be nice to be able to shut a door on oneself at night.

But then I'm used to it by now, and this "no doors" system does help to keep the place cool. It lets every scrap of breeze there is blow right through the house. And you mustn't worry about this being an unfriendly sort of house at night, Coppy, because it's much too well guarded.'

That last was certainly true, for the house had a guard from the British Detachment on duty day and night, as well as a permanent guard of Indian Police. Every bathroom in the house had a small outside staircase leading to the ground for the use of servants and sweepers, and at night one of the police guard slept at the foot of each staircase, while as an additional precaution, electric lights burned from dusk to dawn in the garden; one at each corner of the house. But Copper did not feel capable of explaining that the sense of unease that the house gave her was in no way connected with anything that might make its way in from outside, but rather with an almost tangible unfriendliness that the big rooms held in themselves.

They had barely finished making the beds when Mrs Stock arrived, muffled in a dripping mackintosh and supported by the anxious Leonard. Valerie led the way into the spare bedroom, and Mrs Stock, waving aside Copper's proffered arm, tottered across the room and collapsed in a damp heap upon one of the newly made beds. 'Leave me alone!' she commanded fretfully. 'I don't want *anything*. I only want to go to bed. And don't *fuss* me, Leonard! I shall be quite all right if I'm left alone!'

A belated remnant of social poise returned to her, and she turned to Valerie: 'So good of you to have me, dear. I don't know *what* I should have done. The house is in *ruins*, and Leonard has done nothing . . . and after that terrible, *terrible* experience . . . ! I shall never be the same again. Never! No—I'd rather have dinner in bed. *Please go!*' This last was nearer an order than a request, and Copper and Valerie, murmuring helpful suggestions about sending in hot soup and brandy, backed hastily out of the room.

'That's odd,' commented Valerie, surprised. 'I imagined that we were in for the dramatic story of her sufferings, told in minute detail. Oh well, I expect we shall get it tomorrow.'

'There's Nick,' cried Copper suddenly, hearing a voice in the lower hall. She ran across the ballroom and leant over the banisters, listening.

The stairhead posts in the upper hall had been carved by some long-dead Burmese convict, once an artist at the bloodstained court of Thebaw, into the form of gigantic slant-eyed faces with wide, grinning mouths, like the masks of Burmese devil-dancers, one of which, at the top of the stairs, Valerie had christened 'Hindenburg'. Copper had slipped one arm about it as she peered below, and Nick Tarrent, standing in the lower hall, glanced up and for a brief second suffered a savage shock of fear, for it seemed to him as he looked upward into Copper's white, anxious face that someone stood beside her. Someone whose dark, malignant features peered out of the shadows over her shoulder and grinned in evil anticipation.

The impression was so vivid that he had opened his mouth to cry a warning when he realized that the lurking terror was nothing more than a carved block of Burmese teak. But the momentary stab of fear had shown in his face, and Copper's voice held an added edge of alarm: 'Nick!—are you all right?'

Nick's relief made him laugh. 'Yes, of course. A bit damp, but still in possession of life and limb. Charles took us along to his quarters to have a bath and a change. Luckily he and I are about the same size. Dan shoved himself comfortably into a suit of

George's, but you should see old Shilto!—every button and seam working overtime.'

'Where's Charles?' inquired Valerie, joining Copper by the banisters.

'Just arriving. In fact, here's the rearguard now. George and I got off to a flying start.'

Charles, Dan Harcourt, John Shilto and Hamish Rattigan, followed shortly afterwards by the Purvises and Amabel, came in from the wet, wild night, and mounting the stairs, joined Valerie and Copper in the verandah where drinks and salted nuts had been set out. 'The Dobbies aren't coming,' announced Charles. 'Mrs Dobbie is still feeling seasick. They sent their apologies.'

The verandah looked cheerful enough with its gay, chintz-covered chairs and sofas. But outside the rain lashed savagely against the big glass windows that closed it in, while sudden vicious gusts of wind rattled at the hinges and wailed about the house; moaning, whispering, tapping to be let in; screaming like a host of banshees or sighing like a small, lost, lonely ghost . . .

Valerie stopped mixing short drinks and put down the cocktail-shaker with a thump: 'This is too miserable for words,' she said. 'Charles, help me move these things into the drawing-room. The further away we are from the wind and the windows, the cosier we'll be. All those black, wet panes of glass give me the shivers.'

Charles and John Shilto carried the table of drinks between them, and the party moved gratefully into the more cheerful atmosphere of the drawing-room where the sound of rain and wind was less obtrusive. But Copper laid a hand on Nick's sleeve and stopped him as he was about to follow them: 'Nick . . . what happened? We were terribly worried about you.'

'We?' inquired Nick with the ghost of a grin.

'I,' corrected Copper gravely. 'We were only half-way home when the storm hit us, and I was convinced you'd be drowned.'

'Your conviction was shared,' said Nick lightly. 'To tell you the truth, Coppy, I thought we were done for, and I still can't make out how we all managed to get away with it.'

'Not all,' said Copper with a shiver.

'You mean Ferrers? Oh, he'll be all right. Probably been picked up by now, if he hasn't swum ashore.'

His tone was light enough, but he avoided Copper's eyes and she flushed resentfully: 'Don't talk to me as if I was in the kindergarten, Nick! You know he hasn't got a chance, don't you?'

Nick shrugged his shoulders. 'Well—yes. I'm afraid he's done for all right, poor devil. God, what a jolly Christmas Eve!'

'Tell me what happened to you,' commanded Copper, perching on the arm of a verandah chair and clasping her hands about her knees.

Nick hesitated for a moment and jerked his shoulders uncomfortably as if to shrug off an unpleasant memory. Then, 'It was the queerest thing I've ever experienced,' he said. 'We heard it coming. It made a noise like an express train in a tunnel, rushing towards us; very faint at first, but getting nearer and quicker and louder. And then it hit us as though it were something solid made of reinforced concrete. We hadn't time to think and barely time to get the sail down. It caught us broadside on and just flattened us out. One minute we were pegging along in a flat calm, and the next second we were in the water with all hell let loose round us . . .

'We tried to count heads, and as far as I know everyone was O.K. Then the rain arrived, and after that you couldn't see your hand in front of your face. The boats kept bumping into each other, bottom-side up, and the sky was pitch black and the rain ricocheted off the water in a boiling fury. There wasn't anything to do but just hang on like grim death. I don't know where everyone else had got to, but I managed to get Ruby astride the keel of my boat, and I think someone else was hanging on to the other end, though I've no idea who it was. And there we stuck for what seemed like an hour or so, until the forest-launch bumped into us and nearly slaughtered the lot of us.'

'But hadn't you all drifted apart by then?' inquired Copper.

'Oddly enough, no. I'd an idea that we'd be picked up at opposite sides of the bay, but I gather we weren't more than twenty feet apart when the launch found us. Though even then Hamish's boat took a bit of finding; we must have passed her a dozen times without spotting her. It was only when we'd got everyone on board that we realized Ferrers was missing.'

'But didn't anyone see him go?'

Nick gave a short, mirthless laugh. 'No. And it's not surprising, with three boats all barging about in the smother and everyone concentrating on sticking like a limpet to the nearest bit of woodwork. Ronnie Purvis says he thought he was on the end of my boat, but the chap on the launch says he thinks he only pulled in Ruby and myself and that there wasn't a third person with us. So you can see how easy it would have been to lose sight of Ferrers.'

Copper shivered, and said: 'He probably got caught under the boat when it turned over, and never came up at all.'

Nick shook his head. 'He came up all right, because he was one of the first people I remember seeing when I came to the surface. He was hanging on to the next boat, and I remember noticing, in the silly way that one does notice unimportant trifles in moments of stress, that he was wearing a clumsy great garnet ring about the size of a sixpence. His boat bumped into ours just before the rain came, and he was holding on to the centre-board with one hand. I thought for a minute that he'd cut himself. And then I saw that it wasn't blood but a red stone.'

'What wasn't blood?' inquired an interested voice from behind them.

Nick turned swiftly and smiled into Valerie's inquiring face: 'Nothing, Val. Just idle chatter.'

Valerie said: 'Then for Pete's sake come and chatter in the drawing-room! The party is being very sticky, and I can't imagine why anyone turned up. I know if I'd spent an hour or so being soaked in the bay I'd have insisted on going straight to bed. Even Rosamund is looking a bit on edge, and everyone else is frankly bad-tempered. So come in and pull your weight. Hullo, here's Dad.'

'I'm sorry to be so late,' said Sir Lionel, entering upon Valerie's words: 'I'm afraid, Val, that none of your other guests will be able to get here. The ferry can't run, and Norton has gone back with the forest-launch, so he won't be here either.'

'That's all right,' said Valerie. 'I realized that no one else would be able to make it. We were really only waiting for you and Dr Vicarjee and Truda and Frank.'

Vicarjee was the Bengali doctor, Miss Truda Gidney the matron and only European nurse in the small hospital on Ross, and Frank Benton the Commissioner's personal assistant.

'In that case,' said Sir Lionel, 'we can go into dinner, because Vicarjee and Benton went out shooting together and are stranded in Aberdeen and can't get back, and Miss Gidney sent a message to say that both hospital ayahs had leave today and are in the same predicament, so she doesn't think she should leave.'

'Poor old Truda,' said Valerie. 'I wouldn't have her conscience for the world. Fancy having to spend a night like this in an empty hospital, without even a patient to keep you company? No one's sick just now, so she might just as well have come. But I can see her point. Well, if no one else is coming, we may as well go into dinner. Come on, Rosamund, you must be starving.'

She took Mrs Purvis's arm and led the way into the dining-room.

8

Dinner that night was not a cheerful meal. There had not been time to order the removal of the superfluous chairs or to rearrange the seating, and the vacant places lent a gloomy air to the long, gaily-decorated table.

Valerie had ruefully bidden her guests to disregard the place cards and to sit where they liked, and the depleted Christmas Eve party huddled together at one end of the table, sitting close to each other as though in need of mutual comfort and support. But in spite of the artificial sprays of holly, the glittering strings of tinsel and the mounds of gaily-coloured crackers that lay piled on the white cloth, a proper Christmas spirit was noticeably lacking, and conversation plodded heavily through a bog of social trivialities with frequent halts in miry patches of silence.

If only, thought Valerie despairingly for at least the fourth time during the meal, Leonard wouldn't break every silence by saying brightly, 'It must be twenty past—an angel's passing!' . . . I wonder who invented that idiotic saying anyway? If he says it again I shall scream! She sighed heavily, and pushed a piece of plum pudding around her plate with a moody fork, while somewhere behind her in the shadowy depths of the ballroom a monotonous little *drip*, *drip*, *drip*, told her that the rain had discovered a weak joint in the armour of the roof tiles, and that the first of a series of small, gleaming pools was in process of forming on the polished wood floors of the living rooms.

The house leaked abominably in wet weather, and Valerie thought resentfully of the array of bowls and pails that would presently litter the floors and lie in wait to entrap the feet of the unwary, and beckoned reluctantly over her shoulder to a servant who padded forward on noiseless feet and having received a low-voiced order vanished in the direction of the pantry. Presently the dull drip of water on wood changed to the small, metallic *plink* of water dripping into an enamelled bowl, and on the far side of the table Copper abandoned her methodical manufacture of bread pellets and lifted her head sharply: 'Listen—the leaks have started. Now I suppose we shall have to go to bed in a swamp. I wonder if Kadera has remembered to move my bed? The last time it rained, a vindictive leak dripped right on to my pillow and I dreamt I was bathing—and woke up to find that I was.'

Valerie laughed and turned to Mr Shilto who was sitting on her right: 'Is your house as bad as this one, Mr Shilto? The last time it rained we had so many leaks that we might just as well have been living under a sieve.'

But her effort at making light conversation fell on stony ground, for Mr Shilto, who had been staring with blank fixity into the darkness beyond the candlelit table, neither turned his head nor shifted his gaze, and Valerie realized suddenly that he had not spoken since the beginning of the meal and did not know she had spoken to him now. I suppose he's bound to be a bit distrait, she thought, curbing an unexpectedly strong feeling of irritation, after all, his cousin has just been drowned, and even though they were on bad terms with each other, sudden death is always pretty shocking.

Not, she had to admit, that there was anything to suggest shock in John Shilto's pale, puffy face. It wore, if anything, a look of gloating excitement, and it flashed into her mind that he had at that moment an odd look of Kioh, her stepfather's Siamese cat, when she was stalking a bird or a lizard. Becoming aware that she was staring at him, fascinated, she spoke hurriedly and at random: 'The last time it rained, there were so many leaks that we ran out of pails and basins and had to start on the cups and saucers. The P.W.D. are always promising to get it put right, but you know how it is with them. They talk a lot, but nothing *ever* happens!'

Mr Shilto did not reply, but the brief spell of embarrassed silence that followed his failure to respond to his hostess's social efforts was broken with unexpected violence by the repetition of her last statement. Rosamund Purvis, subdued, unemotional Rosamund, who had sat throughout the meal in a silence that had been unobtrusive because she was seldom other than silent, spoke in a queer, high-pitched voice that somehow gave the impression that it did not belong to her:

'*But nothing ever happens!*' she said. And suddenly, shockingly, threw back her head and laughed: a shrill, uncomfortable laugh that held no suggestion of mirth, but was purely hysterical.

'*Rosamund!*' Ronnie Purvis's voice cut across the discordant sound but did not check it.

'*Nothing ever happens,*' gasped Mrs Purvis. '*Ha! Ha! Ha!* That's funny! That's very funny. Nothing ever happens!'

She rocked to and fro, her hands clutching the tablecloth in front of her while the tears of her uncomfortable mirth wet her faded cheeks and Dan Harcourt, standing up swiftly, crossed to the sideboard and poured out a glass of water: the others sitting in stunned silence.

'Stop that, Rosamund!' commanded Ronnie Purvis furiously. 'Stop it at once! You're making an exhibition of yourself!' He jumped to his feet and started towards his wife, but Valerie and Copper were before him. Between them they took the still laughing Mrs Purvis by her arms and lifted her almost bodily from her chair. 'We'll leave the men to their drinks,' said Valerie composedly: 'Come on, Rosamund, let's go and have our coffee in the drawing-room.'

Mrs Purvis's mirth subsided as suddenly as it had arisen. She looked round dazedly at the startled circle of faces, and her own pale features flushed painfully: 'I'm sorry,' she said uncertainly. 'I—I thought . . . It seemed funny; nothing happening——'

'So it is,' said Valerie lightly. 'Dad, don't let them stay swapping stories too long. Come on, Amabel.'

But as though the incident had not been sufficiently unpleasant in itself, young Miss Withers took it upon herself at this juncture to add a further touch of discomfort to the evening's festivities. She rose slowly to her feet, her round cheek bulging with some concealed sweetmeat, and let her prominent blue eyes travel about the table. 'There are thirteen of us,' she announced with gloomy relish. 'It's funny we didn't notice before that we'd sat down thirteen.'

A smile of satisfaction illumined her round, pink face, and she added smugly: 'Well anyway, I'm all right. I didn't get up first, so I shan't be the one who'll die.'

With which pleasing reflection she selected a second lump of coconut ice and trailed away in the wake of Valerie, Copper and Mrs Purvis.

*   *   *

Dan Harcourt, entering the drawing-room some twenty minutes later, noticed with interest that during that interval Mrs Purvis had borrowed some rouge and applied it with an amateur hand. Also that the two uneven patches of pink that now decorated her cheeks merely served to emphasize rather than to conceal the shocking pallor of her face and draw attention to the nervous twitching of her colourless mouth. What on earth's the matter with the woman? he wondered uneasily; she looks as though she was working up for a bad nervous breakdown and I only hope to God she doesn't have it here and now!

There appeared to be some justification for this fear, for Mrs Purvis, who had been discussing a forthcoming tennis tournament when the men entered, faltered on seeing them and ceased speaking, leaving a sentence cut short in mid-air. Furthermore, during the next half-hour, while Valerie served coffee and the conversation became general, she sat silent and rigid; occupying herself with a frightened, furtive scrutiny of her fellow-guests that did not pass entirely unobserved, for Copper's interest too was caught and held by that odd, secretive inspection of Rosamund's . . .

Nick was talking about Calcutta where the *Sapphire* had been before her arrival in Port Blair: 'We thought we were going to be there for Christmas week,' he said, 'and there was a certain amount of sourness when we were suddenly slung off here instead. I remember being fairly outspoken on the subject myself. I'd spent a short leave in Calcutta not long before: stayed at the Grand Hotel, which was a welcome change from stewing on the equator in a two-by-four cabin, and I thought I'd repeat the performance for Christmas. But all things considered this is a decided improvement in programme; hurricanes or no hurricanes. Come on, Copper! take an interest in my laborious social chatter will you, or Stock and Hamish will rope us in to play bridge. They've got that predatory Culbertson gleam in their eye and I refuse to be victimized. Try and look absorbed and interested, there's a good girl.'

Copper said in an undertone: 'Nick—look at Mrs Purvis.'

'Why? At the moment I prefer to look at you.'

'No, seriously Nick. There's something very odd about her tonight.'

'Cotton stockings and a touch of *la grippe*, at a guess,' suggested Nick. Copper ignored the flippancy and continued as though he had not spoken: '. . . she's got something on her mind, and if it didn't seem so absurd, I'd say she was frightened of someone in the room but hadn't quite made up her mind which one. She keeps looking at everyone in turn as if she was trying to work something out. It's—it's almost as though she were playing "*Is it you? . . . Is it you? . . . Is it you?*"'

Nick flung a cursory glance at Mrs Purvis and said: 'Come off it, Coppy! She's merely had a bit of a shock—what with being tipped into the harbour and then this Ferrers business. You'd be a bit jumpy yourself if you'd been in her shoes.'

'Watch her,' urged Copper, low-voiced, 'and *then* tell me that she's only "a bit jumpy".'

Nick obediently hitched himself round in his chair and did as he was commanded, and after a moment or two his expression changed from resignation to reluctant interest.

Rosamund Purvis was sitting on the extreme edge of her chair, her thin, clever hands clenched together in her lap and tense rigidity in every line of her nondescript figure. She was sitting so still that her very immobility served to draw attention to her

flickering gaze, for though she did not turn her
head, her hazel eyes, wide as a frightened cat's,
darted warily, continuously, searchingly, from face
to face in an oddly questioning, oddly disturbing
scrutiny. And it was only after watching her for several minutes that Nick noticed something which had
escaped Copper's attention: that Mrs Purvis's disturbing scrutiny did not extend to the entire party,
but only to certain members of it. Those members
who had made up the sailing party.

He was in the process of digesting this curious
fact when Dan Harcourt came up behind them and
Copper turned her head and spoke in an undertone:
'Dan, what's biting Rosamund Purvis? Look at
her . . .'

'I've been doing so,' said Dan, leaning on the back
of Copper's chair and continuing to watch Mrs Purvis with detached, professional interest: 'She looks,'
he said musingly, 'as though she was wondering
who had buried the body.'

'Cheerful couple, aren't you?' observed Nick irritably. 'Copper has just been propounding a similar
enlivening theory. Well, you're a doctor, Pills—why
don't you take some action? Advise the woman to
take a couple of aspirins and shove off home before
she springs another of those Ghoulish-Laughter
scenes on us. I'm not sure I could take it twice in
one evening.'

Copper said seriously, addressing Dan, 'Nick
thinks she's only edgy because of being upset in the
storm. But it doesn't look like ordinary edginess to
me. She looks—*frightened* . . .'

'So frightened,' agreed Dan Harcourt thoughtfully, 'that if anyone came up behind her just now
and touched her on the shoulder, she'd probably go
off like a bomb and scream the roof off.'

The words were barely out of his mouth when the
correctness of that belief was unexpectedly proved.

Kioh, the Siamese cat, her tail twitching gently like a miniature panther, appeared in the doorway behind Mrs Purvis's chair and having glanced about the room with slanting china-blue eyes, leapt lightly on to the arm of the chair, brushing against Mrs Purvis's bare shoulder. A split second later the languor of that apathetic gathering was as effectively shattered as though a bomb had indeed fallen in its midst, and Valerie's ill-fated dinner party came to an abrupt and shattering close.

Mrs Purvis was on her feet, screaming.

She did not even look to see what had touched her, but stood there for perhaps the space of ten seconds, her eyes starting from her head in stark and horrifying terror and her mouth wide open. Then, before any of her startled audience could collect their scattered wits or move towards her, she crumpled at the knees like a rag doll and fell forward on to the polished floor in a dead faint.

=== 9 ===

'**W**hy did I leave my little back room in Blooms-
bur-ree, Where I could live on a pound a
week in lux-ur-ee?' crooned Copper gently, applying
cold cream to her nose some two hours later.

Valerie laughed.

'I'm afraid it does look like being a pretty
mildewed Christmas for you,' she apologized. 'Today couldn't very well have had a stickier finish,
and tomorrow looks like being as bad—if not
worse.'

'Well, at least it hasn't been dull,' said Copper,
reaching for the hairbrush. 'In fact it's been packed
with brisk incident. But I'm glad it's over. A few
more fireworks from Rosamund and I swear I'd
have started screaming myself.'

'Wasn't it hellish?' sighed Valerie. 'Poor Dad! I bet
it put years on him. He was talking stamps with
Hamish when Rosamund exploded, and he rose out
of his chair like a rocketing pheasant and his specta-
cles fell off, and Leonard trod on them.'

She began to giggle, and Copper, catching the in-
fection, said unsteadily: 'You missed the high spot
of the evening. George was clutching a glass of fruit
cup that he'd just collected for Amabel, and when
Rosamund yelled he nearly jumped out of his skin

and the fruit cup went all over Amabel. She was simply soaked, and that new georgette dress of hers immediately shrunk up like a bashful snail—it was on the tight side to begin with, and you know how that stuff shrinks when it's wet! What with a few slices of banana nestling coyly in her hair and a strip of lemon peel hanging round one ear, she looked incredibly abandoned and rakish, and when George tried to pick them off she slapped him. Poor George! I'm afraid his faith in women has received a nasty crack.'

Valerie leant her head against a mosquito pole and gave way to immoderate mirth, and presently, mopping her eyes and striving to recover her composure, observed that it was not a *bit* nice of them to collapse into giggles like that, as it was simply horrid at the time, even though it might seem funny now. 'I thought poor Rosamund was never coming round. However, she seemed all right by the time they removed her. Dan and Charles went along with her to the hospital while Ronnie went down to fetch her night things.'

'The hospital is much the best place for her,' said Copper firmly. 'Besides, it'll give Truda something to fuss over if she really hasn't any patients at the moment. Funny, the way Rosamund refused flatly to go back to her own house. You'd have thought she'd much rather go home instead of insisting on being taken off to sleep in a ward under Truda's eye.'

'Thank goodness she did!' sighed Valerie, 'I was scared stiff she was going to stay here. I simply *had* to ask her, but I was madly grateful when she held out for the hospital. She'd evidently made up her mind to go there or go off her head, and if she'd stayed here I'd have gone off mine! One hysterical female in the house is more than enough, and Rosamund's yells have evidently brought dear Ruby to the verge of a nervous breakdown. I bet the miserable Leonard is in for a hell of a night!'

' *"We don't have much money,"* ' quoted Copper flippantly, ' *"but we do see life!"* What did they do with Amabel, Val? I lost sight of her in the general flurry after she'd taken that crack at George. Surely they haven't let her go back to the Purvis mansion unchaperoned?'

'Good heavens, no! She's gone along to the hospital with Rosamund, which leaves Ronnie abandoned by his entire harem. Rosamund clung to her like a demented limpet and refused to move without her; though whether from a well-founded mistrust of Ronnie, or because she finds something very sedative and soothing about Amabel, I don't know. Anyway they have both trailed off to Truda's tender care.'

'I wish I'd known that Dan had gone up to the hospital with them,' said Copper. 'I'd have told him to bring back some form of sedative for Ruby. Chloroform, for preference!'

'Oh gosh!' gasped Valerie, giving way to a renewed attack of mirth: 'I *did* enjoy that part of the evening's fun and games! I shall never forget all your faces when she came bursting out of her bedroom on top of Rosamund's big scene, and rushed into the drawing-room like Sarah Bernhardt in pink pyjamas.'

'I didn't notice her pyjamas,' confessed Copper. 'Her dressing-gown was what got me. I might have known that she'd have one like a film vamp's, all yards of train and acres of pink satin edged with marabou trimming. The minute I saw it I knew it was only a question of seconds before somebody fell over it, what with everyone dashing about being helpful, and of course it *would* be the wretched George.'

'I wonder which hurt most?' mused Valerie. 'The smack in the eye he got from Amabel, or the crack on the jaw he got from Ruby? They both sounded pretty crisp.'

'Oh, *poor* George,' gasped Copper: 'It's a shame to laugh! But it *was* funny. At least I thought it was funny until she tripped over her own train and collapsed on to Nick, and then I admit my sense of humour wilted a bit.'

'Personally, I was extremely grateful, because if it had been anyone but Nick the confusion would have been ten times worse. I thought he dealt with her in a masterly manner. "The Silent Service" for ever! Charles, for instance, would probably have felt it his duty to prop her on a sofa and fetch brandy or salts or something, but Nick simply slung her up as if she'd been a sack of coals and dumped her back in her bedroom with, as far as I can make out, instructions to stay there and put a sock in it. She was so astonished she stopped squealing at once and didn't move out of her room again. Which you must admit was no ordinary achievement.'

'I suppose so,' agreed Copper doubtfully. She sat silent for a few moments, slowly removing cold cream with a wad of pink tissue and frowning at her reflection in the mirror, and presently observed thoughtfully: 'Dan says he has a hell of a temper. Ruby was gushing about Nick at that Corbyn's picnic, and Dan told her that if she'd ever had the wrong side of Nick's tongue she'd realize that skinning was preferable. It's funny, because I should have thought he was too lazy.' She rose, yawning. 'I suppose we ought to go to bed. I'm dead tired. What's the time, Val?'

'Nearly midnight. In a few minutes it'll be Christmas Day. Somehow it doesn't seem possible, does it?'

'No,' said Copper, pulling out the edge of her

mosquito net and scrambling into bed, 'but I don't see why it shouldn't. It's odd how one always associates Christmas with snow and icicles and holly, when the first Christmas Day belongs to a little hot town in the East with palm trees and camels and flat-roofed houses.'

'Well I must admit I like the Frost-and-Carol idea best,' confessed Valerie. 'And as for Christmas morning without a stocking, it's a mere hollow mockery to me. But this wretched *Maharaja* having let us down with a thump, there won't be any stockings tomorrow: or many presents either.'

She stopped and lifted her head, listening. The clock in the lower hall was striking midnight, and they kept silence until the last chime died away in the darkness.

'Merry Christmas, Val.'

'Merry Christmas, Coppy darling—and good-night.' Valerie slid off the bed and tucked in Copper's mosquito net for her, and switching off the light vanished through the curtained doorway into her own room. A few minutes later her own light winked out and the house settled down under the blanket of the stormy darkness.

The wind still blew in a half gale, and above the steady drumming of the rain Copper could hear the muffled clamour of the sea raging furiously about the tiny island. There was a certain sullen rhythm in that sound which at any other time might have been soothing, but tonight, mingled with the desolate, wolf-pack howl of the wind and the remorseless thunder of the rain, it held something sinister, and the thought that had been kept at bay all the evening rose as a clear picture before Copper's mental eye; held relentlessly before her by the roar of the breakers.

Somewhere out in that cold, malignant sea, Ferrers Shilto's wizened body must be being dragged and battered by wind and tide; swung and tossed between black, hissing hills of water; pounded in a roaring maelstrom of foam upon the jagged coral reefs of forgotten beaches, or swept out in the close clasp of the currents into that lonely, landless sea that stretched away and away to the South Pole——

Copper dropped into an uneasy sleep . . .

She was standing among the coconut trees on the shore of North Bay in a high wind that tore through the palm fronds and drove the steel-grey seas in upon the rocks at her feet. Something glimmered whitely among that welter of foam: something now half-seen, now hidden by the flung spume. It came nearer—larger—clearer . . . and as the wind blew louder, it shook itself clear of the grey sea, and Ferrers Shilto came walking up out of the bay. Water ran from his soaked garments and streamed in wind-blown rivulets from his shock of grey hair, and a band of seaweed that had caught about his skinny throat fluttered in the wind as though he wore a curiously woven scarf. His small, wrinkled face wore an expression of almost ludicrous astonishment, and as he came nearer, Copper saw that he held his left hand against his breast, and that from between the spread fingers protruded the handle of a knife.

There seemed nothing unnatural in the fact that he should walk up out of the sea, even though she knew that he had been drowned; and fear did not touch her until her eyes fell on the knife. But with the sight of that shining handle the blind panic of nightmare swept down upon her, freezing her, so that she could neither move nor scream. Ferrers's wide, incredulous eyes came nearer and nearer, and there was blood upon his hand: a single splash of scarlet. He was so near her that the wet, wind-blown strand of weed about his throat touched her face . . . And Copper awoke, shuddering with terror, to find a cold drip of water from yet another leak in her ceiling trickling down her cheek . . .

The storm seemed to have blown itself out, though not the rain, and she pulled up her mosquito net and switched on the light. Slow, gleaming drops were forming and falling from the ceiling immediately overhead. She looked about her bedroom in shivering exasperation, and having fetched a soap-dish and the tooth-glass from the bathroom, pushed her bed to one side of the latest leak, threw out her wet pillow, and placing the soap-dish and the tooth-glass where they would do most good, climbed back into bed and switched off the light. But this time she could not go to sleep. The horror of her recent dream, coupled with the necessity for action in the matter of leaks, had awakened her too thoroughly, and sleep had receded beyond recall.

The air inside her shuttered room was warm and damp and heavy, and the swish of the fan blades seemed barely to disturb it. And now that the wind had dropped the house was very quiet. It was still raining, but only very lightly, and after the recent clamour of the gale the silence was an almost tangible thing; emphasized rather than broken by the sound of the sea, whose muffled thunder seemed only to provide a background to the hush that had fallen with the falling of the wind. Yet there was no quality of restfulness in the silence, but rather one of suspense and waiting; as though the storm, far from blowing itself out, had merely called a brief halt in which to collect its forces for a renewed attack. Inside the darkened house the stillness was full of little sounds. Tiny, tinkling sounds in a dozen different keys, caused by water dripping into a varied assortment of bowls and basins. A sudden crack of wood as a piece of furniture contracted, the thin keening of mosquitoes, the flitter of a bat's wings in the darkness and the light patter of rain on the roof. And after a time Copper became aware that there was someone else besides herself who could not sleep that night. Someone who came quietly up the staircase and crossed the dark ballroom floor.

She heard the tread of the top step creak and felt the slight vibration of the floorboards as someone went past her door towards the turret room. It'll be one of the house-servants going round to see that everything's all right, she thought.

A moment later the noiseless footsteps returned, and although she still could not hear them, the familiar vibration of the floorboards told her that the night wanderer had passed her door again. It occurred to her that it might be Kioh on the prowl, but she dismissed the idea almost immediately, for though Kioh was addicted to night prowling, the pressure of her velvet paws was not sufficient to betray her passing in this particular manner.

The unknown promenader returned across the ballroom once more: this time from the direction of the drawing-room for Copper heard the creak of the loose board just outside the drawing-room door. And inexplicably, with that sound the house began to fill with fear.

Fear crept in upon it like the noiseless advance of the monsoon mists across the wet forests, until it pervaded every nook and corner of the dark rooms. Fear blinked from behind the wet, glimmering window-panes, whispered in the rustling patter of the rain and dried Copper's mouth as she shrank back against her pillows, staring into the darkness with eyes that were wide with unreasoning panic. She could hear the beating of her own heart like an urgent, frantic drum in her breast. A drum that seemed to prevent her breathing as she strained her ears to catch a nearer sound. There was a second loose board in the passage to the right of her room, and she was waiting to hear it creak . . .

When at last it did so, she pulled herself together with an effort and reached for the switch of the bedside lamp. But with her finger upon it she hesitated; checked by the unpleasant thought that with a light in her room she would be clearly visible to anyone standing in the darkened hall outside.

Her hand dropped and she sat listening; rigidly erect beneath her shrouding mosquito net and struggling desperately with that rising tide of terror. A distant rumble of thunder blended with the sound of the breaking seas, but the silent walker did not return, and suddenly she could bear it no longer. She slid out of bed and groped her way across the room to the curtained doorway that separated her room from Valerie's, moving very warily for fear of making a sound and agonizingly aware of the pitfalls presented by the various objects that had been set to catch the drips. And when in spite of her caution her foot encountered the cold enamel rim of the soap-dish, it was all she could do to keep from crying out.

'For God's sake pull yourself together!' Copper told herself frantically. 'You're behaving like a hysterical schoolgirl, and you ought to be ashamed of yourself!' But reason failed to make a stand against the fear that filled the dark house, numbing her body and whispering to her imagination that if she continued to walk forward in the darkness, her outstretched, groping hands would not touch the friendly, swaying curtains or the solid wall, but a face—a wet face with a band of seaweed bound like a scarf about its skinny throat.

Copper's own throat stiffened with that fear, and she found she had to force herself forward as though her body was a machine which would no longer obey her will. And then she had reached the curtains, and was through them and dragging at Valerie's mosquito net.

Valerie had been asleep. But few people sleep very deeply in the Andamans, and she was awake almost before Copper's fingers touched her shoulder. She sat up and reached for the electric light switch, and a comforting yellow radiance illumined Copper's white face and the hanging folds of mosquito netting. 'What's the matter, Coppy? Been having another nightmare?'

'There's someone walking about the house.' Copper's whisper was unsteady in spite of her efforts to control it, and Valerie turned swiftly to face the door into the ballroom and listened for a moment or two. But except for the light patter of the rain, the swish of fan blades and the little chorus of drips from the leaking roof, the house was silent.

'Nonsense! No one would be trotting about the place at this hour. You know Dad doesn't let the house-servants come upstairs at night and that Iman Din always sleeps down in the hall at the foot of the staircase. Besides, who on earth would be likely to want to perambulate around on a night like this? I expect it was bats. Or Kioh.'

'It *wasn't*,' insisted Copper, shivering uncontrollably. 'There *was* someone in the hall . . . they were walking around in the dark. I felt the floor shake. You know how it does when anyone crosses the ballroom. And those two loose boards—the one outside the drawing-room and the one in the passage— I heard them creak.'

'Probably Ruby wanting a drink or a biscuit.'

'Then why go along the passage or into the drawing-room for it? And why walk up and down? Whoever it was out there has crossed the ballroom at least three times.'

'You've been having another nightmare,' accused Valerie. 'Own up, Coppy!'

Copper flushed guiltily, remembering her unpleasantly vivid dream of Ferrers Shilto's return from the sea. But since she had no intention of admitting to that at the present moment, she ignored the accusation and said stubbornly: 'It wasn't bats and it wasn't Kioh, and I wasn't asleep. Someone has been walking about the house . . . *And what's more*,' she added, her voice dropping again to a whisper, *'they're still there*—look at Kioh!'

The Siamese cat had evidently been curled up asleep in the cushioned seat of Valerie's big armchair, for there was a betraying hollow that marked where her sleek, small body had rested. But something—perhaps Copper's entry—had disturbed her, and now she was standing upon the floor in front of the chair, facing the door that led into the ballroom.

The doors between the bedrooms and the ballroom were of the type that Copper had previously criticized: two swinging shutters, such as one sees in the taprooms of public houses and railway refreshment rooms, that spanned the centre of the door space, and closed with a latch, leaving a few feet of open space above and below. These half-doors were wide enough to stop anyone outside from seeing more than the extreme upper section of the wall and part of the floor of the bedrooms; and conversely to prevent anyone inside seeing into the ballroom, even by daylight. But cats can see in the dark; and Kioh, from the floor, had an uninterrupted view of the room—and of someone, or something, who was moving about there.

Her short, sleek, cream-coloured coat was no longer smooth but roughened where the hairs had lifted along her back, and she had crouched a little; her black tail twitching and her china-blue eyes glaring fixedly at something that Copper and Valerie could not see. They watched her head turn slowly as her gaze followed someone who moved in the darkness beyond the door, and Valerie cleared her throat, which had suddenly become constricted, and raising her voice called out: '*Kaun-hai?* . . . Who's there?' There was no reply, but once again there came the familiar tremor of the floorboards as someone crossed the ballroom.

Kioh's black, pricked ears flattened and she began to growl softly in her throat—a small, oddly unnerving sound. Then step by step, and still growling, she backed away from the door until she had reached the safe harbourage of Valerie's bed.

'That's funny,' said Valerie, unaware that she too was speaking in a whisper, 'she's usually a most truculent animal.' She reached down to stroke the crouching shape, and the cat, whose eyes were still fixed on the doorway, seemed to explode at her touch as though it had been a small charge of dynamite, and whirling about, spitting and snarling, it streaked across the room to vanish behind the wardrobe . . .

'Oh my God!' gasped Copper. 'I believe I've bitten my heart in half—it jumped into my mouth and now it's in pieces. For heaven's sake let's go out and turn up the ballroom lights and see who's there. I can't stand this!'

'All right,' said Valerie shakily. 'But I didn't hear anything. I'm sure it's only bats.'

'Bats my foot!' retorted Copper forcefully. 'You don't have to hear! You can *feel*. If you don't believe me—' Before Valerie could stop her, she had reached over and switched off the light.

'Copper!'

'Ssh. Listen.'

They had not long to wait. There was no sound, but after a few moments they felt again that soft vibration of the floorboards, and presently, following it, there came the faint, unmistakable creak of the loose board by the drawing-room door.

'*Now* do you believe me?'

'Yes. There's someone prowling about the rooms. Turn the light on, Coppy, I'm going to see who it is.' Once again the bedside lamp made a friendly pool of light in the room, and Valerie said: 'We'd better put something on. If it's one of the servants, we can't go skittering about in our nightgowns.'

She found that she was still speaking in a whisper and was unreasonably annoyed by the discovery; but somehow she could not bring herself to speak aloud. She flung Copper a gaily striped wrap of towelling, and slipping her own arms into a silk dressing-gown, tightened its belt about her slim waist with a savage jerk as though it gave her courage, and added, still whispering: 'I expect we'll find it's only Ruby giving her insomnia an airing.'

'Well, Ruby or no Ruby,' said Copper, 'I'm taking a golf club with me. I admit I'd be happier with a poker, but a steel-shafted mashie makes me feel almost as good.'

Valerie reached wordlessly for the niblick and Copper was suddenly seized with inconvenient mirth: 'Oh g-gosh! we must look such f-fools! And I can't think why I'm laughing, because it isn't really a bit f-funny and I'm scared to death!'

'So am I,' admitted Valerie, 'but I shall have hysterics if I sit here any longer. I was all right until Kioh made that hellish noise, but that finished me. Come on, Coppy, and for heaven's sake hold my hand!'

Holding firmly to each other with one hand and

clutching a golf club apiece with the other, they tip-toed over to the doorway. The main electric light switch for the bedroom was just inside the door, and Valerie turned it on, flooding the room with harsh light. Then pushing apart the swinging shutters, they braced themselves and stepped into the darkness.

To reach the switches for the ballroom involved walking a few yards down the passage to the left of the door. But the light streaming from Valerie's bedroom was sufficient to guide them, and a few seconds later a flood of light wiped out the lurking shadows in the ballroom.

There was no one there, and gaining confidence, they crossed the end of the ballroom and turned on the lights in the dining-room where the long, polished table, cleared of its glittering decorations, gleamed like a strip of dark water. 'Nothing here,' said Valerie, speaking aloud for the first time in ten minutes. But even as she spoke something moved swiftly in the shadow behind them, and they whirled round, white-faced.

Nicholas Tarrent, clad in pyjamas and a dressing-gown, stood scowling at them from the edge of the dining-room.

'Oh God, Nick, you gave me such a fright!' gasped Valerie.

'Nothing to what you've given me! What the hell do you two think you're doing, wandering about at this hour of the night? Brushing up your approach shots?'

Valerie and Copper, who had been endeavouring to conceal their possession of a couple of steel-shafted clubs, had the grace to blush. 'As a matter of fact,' confessed Copper, already slightly ashamed of her recent fears, 'we thought we heard someone walking about the house, so we came out to see who it was. We didn't know it was you.'

'*Me?* Why, you wretched golfing maniacs, I've only this moment torn myself from my bed. I heard someone prowling about, and when lights started springing up all over the house I thought I'd better come and investigate in case someone had been taken ill.'

'Do you usually conduct an investigation round a sick bed with a squash racquet?' inquired Copper accusingly.

Nick laughed. 'You've got me there. I'd forgotten I was still clutching the damn thing. As a matter of fact it was the only weapon within reach, and between you and me, I felt happier with something in my fist. You two ruddy little night-birds have been giving me the cold creeps, tiptoeing around in the dark.'

Valerie and Copper exchanged a swift look. 'In the *dark*?' said Copper.

Valerie turned to Nick: 'Had you heard us for long, before the lights went on?'

'Well, hardly *heard* you. But I felt the floor vibrate every time you passed. And there are a couple of loose boards around: I heard them creak once or twice and I was beginning to think that this would bear looking into when the lights went up. So I came out to see what was up.'

'Then there *was* someone out here!' said Valerie. 'It wasn't us, Nick. We heard the boards too. And Kioh saw something in the ballroom. She stood and watched it moving, and it got on our nerves. So we came out to see who it was.'

They had all been talking in undertones to avoid arousing the rest of the house, but now Copper's voice sharpened: 'Well, what are we going to do? We all heard someone moving about, and unless we make certain that there is no one hiding up here, I for one shan't sleep another wink.'

'All right. Have it your own way,' said Nick. 'Come on. Keep your eyes on the ball and don't press.'

Picking their way among the assortment of bowls and basins set to catch the leaks they made their way across the ballroom into the drawing-room, through the wide, glassed-in verandah and back past the dining-room again. They searched the pantry and the larder and along the passage to the turret room, and opened the doors of the nearby bathroom and the small room beside it. They looked behind and under sofas and chairs, bookcases and cupboards, made certain that all the doors and windows that led out of the house, or on to the two balconies that opened off the closed verandah, were locked, and by the time they returned to the ballroom they had searched the top storey of the house as thoroughly as was possible without entering the bedrooms occupied by Valerie's father, the Stocks, or John Shilto.

Sir Lionel's room and the turret room where John Shilto slept were the only two bedrooms in the house possessed of an orthodox door, and as their doors were closed it was unlikely that anyone other than the owners would have passed through them. The bedroom occupied by the Stocks, which lay beyond Valerie's, closed with the usual ineffectual swing shutters, but a faint, rhythmic sound of snoring suggested that at least one of the occupants was sound asleep.

To make their rounds complete, and more for form's sake than anything else, they looked into Nick's room—this with extreme caution to avoid disturbing the peaceful slumbers of Dan Harcourt—and went through the girls' bedrooms before ending up in the ballroom once more. But with the exception of Kioh, whom they flushed from under Valerie's window-seat, still hostile and inclined to spit, they had found nothing and no one. 'Well I hope everyone's satisfied,' said Nick shortly, his finger on the switch of the ballroom lights. 'Unless it was your father, Val, or Shilto or one of the Stocks, it was bats or the wind. Or too much plum pudding! Take your choice.'

'The last, I expect,' admitted Valerie, yawning. 'Plus a touch of Rosamund Purvis's hysterics thrown in. Well, thanks for your support, Nick. I'm sorry we spoilt your beauty sleep. Come on, Coppy—bed, I think.' She switched off the lights and they turned to go back to their own rooms. But they had barely taken more than a couple of paces into the darkness when they heard Copper gasp.

There had been so much stark fear in that small sound that Nick flung out an arm and caught her against him. 'What is it, Copper?' His voice was sharply peremptory.

'Someone brushed past me,' quavered Copper in a dry whisper. 'They almost touched me—Nick, *listen*!'

All three stood still: and heard, in that stillness, clearly and unmistakably, the creak of the loose board by the drawing-room door, and felt the tremor of the floorboards beneath their feet . . .

'This is ridiculous!' said Nick furiously. He thrust Copper away and took a quick stride back to the switches, and once again the ballroom was flooded with light. But there was no one there, and beyond it the drawing-room doors yawned black and empty.

'Iman Din will be in the hall downstairs,' quavered Valerie. 'He's supposed to stay awake, but he always falls asleep and someone may have passed him. Let's go and wake him up.'

They went quickly over to the banisters, and turning on the lights above the staircase, looked down into the well of the hall.

But Iman Din, the old, white-whiskered *chaprassi** who slept at the foot of the hall stairs by night, was not asleep. He was standing by the bottom step of the staircase, looking up at them as they leaned over the carved banister rail above him, and he did not look as though he had been recently awakened from sleep, but rather as though he had been standing there, listening, for some considerable time.

'Well, I'm damned!' said Nick explosively. 'The old coot must have heard us pottering round hunting burglars, and he hasn't even raised a finger to help us or to find out what all the activity was about. Useful sort of guardian for our slumbers. Ask him if anyone has passed him, Val.'

Valerie leant over the banisters and spoke to the old man in Urdu. He answered her in the same tongue, and Copper saw her start and jerk back, frowning.

'What does he say, Val?'

'Nothing; only some nonsense.' Valerie was plainly disturbed and not a little angry.

Nick said: 'The point is, could anyone have come up those stairs tonight without that whiskered Methuselah spotting them?'

The old man shifted his gaze to Nick, and spoke in slow, accented English: 'Who should enter? The Sahib sees that the door is barred'—he gestured with a claw-like hand towards the massive front door with its heavy iron bolts. They caught a glimmer of light from the guard room through the glass panes of the side door, and heard the sentry on duty ground the butt of his rifle on the stone flags outside.

*Office messenger.

'Don't beg the question,' snapped Nick. 'Could anyone have come up these stairs since Harcourt Sahib came home?'

'Assuredly,' said the old man gravely. He turned again to Valerie and spoke swiftly in the vernacular.

Nick began to lose his temper. The hands of the hall clock pointed to a quarter to three; he had had very little sleep and his experience in the storm had not been pleasant. Above all, Copper's panic had awakened something in him that he had as yet not stopped to analyse. 'See here,' said Nick dangerously, 'if I find that you or your pals have been trying any funny stuff in the house tonight, I'll come down and wring your neck. First you say that the door is barred and no one can come in, and then that someone could have come up these stairs. Well, there was someone up here five minutes ago, and you're coming up to help find out just who it was!'

'The Sahib is angry,' said Iman Din gravely. 'He does not understand. But I will show that no *man* passed this way.' He started to mount the shallow stairs, and Valerie gripped Nick's arm: 'No,' she said breathlessly. 'No, let's go back to bed, Nick. We've looked through the rooms once. Go back, Iman Din.'

'Rubbish,' said Nick curtly. 'Come on up. And you two clear off to bed. Iman Din and I will scoop in this sleepwalker.'

Iman Din, continuing his ascent, put his foot upon the top step of the staircase, and, as always, it creaked sharply.

'There!' said Copper. 'That's the first sound I heard. Somebody *did* come up these stairs.'

'Of course there was someone up here! And I believe this old devil knows who it was. What did he say to you, Val?'

'Nothing. Just native rubbish.'

Nick caught her by the shoulder, and swung her round to face him. 'Well, let's hear it. You're being damned irritating, Val, and for two pins I'd smack you. Odd as it may seem I could do with some sleep. But as long as people are going to perambulate up and down the hall the minute the lights are out, I can't see myself getting any. Come on, out with it.'

'Oh, very well,' snapped Valerie. 'If it's any help to you, he says it's a ghost.'

There was a short and pregnant silence. Then: 'Ghost, my Aunt Fanny!' said Nick angrily. 'No ghost could make the floor vibrate like that, or weigh enough to make those boards creak. Don't be a mug, Val!'

Iman Din's wise old eyes travelled from one to another of the three faces before him, and then past them to the doorway of the darkened drawing-room. He let his breath out in a little sigh and said: 'The Sahib says one pressed upon the board which speaks. Look, and I will show——'

He led the way into the ballroom, and stopped before the open doorway. 'Will the Sahib walk through?' Nick complied, frowning. There was no sound, and Copper said: 'Of course it didn't creak that time. He didn't tread on it. He stepped over it.'

'And why so, Miss-sahib?'

'Because of the water, of course——' began Copper; and stopped, catching her breath sharply. For she had suddenly seen what the old man had seen before her . . . There had been a leak in the roof just above the drawing-room door, and a spreading pool of water saturated the floorboards. But when the three of them had searched the house the lights, as now, had been on, and because they could see they had avoided the various bowls that dotted the floor and stepped across the wet patches. But someone

walking in the dark would not have seen that wet
stain, and so would have walked into it instead of
over it. And the board would have creaked under
their feet. Yet it was not this that had driven the
blood from Copper's face. She had, in the same instant, seen something else. Something they could all
see now—

'*Ah!*' said Iman Din. 'Now the Sahib understands.
When a foot is placed upon that board it speaks in
the darkness. But the wood is wet—the Sahib sees
how wet. Yet no mark leads beyond it, though the
floor is polished!'

Copper and Valerie started back from the gleaming stain and stared at the smooth, polished floorboards. Nick did not speak, but he placed his foot
squarely upon that wet space, which creaked beneath his tread, and walked back to join them.

There was no need for words.

Four clear damp footmarks patched the strip of
floor that he had walked across.

'The Sahib sees,' said Iman Din softly. He drew a
sudden, hissing breath between his yellowed teeth,
and flung out a skinny, pointing hand: '*Look there,
Sahib! There—where the storm returns!*'

The three whirled about to stare where his
gnarled forefinger pointed across the darkened
drawing-room to the verandah beyond. And as they
looked a vivid flash of lightning bathed the inky sky
beyond the expanse of window-panes in a livid radiance that silhouetted, for a fraction of a second, the
figure of a man who stood in the angle of the dark
verandah. A small, wizened figure who appeared to
be wearing about his neck a ragged scarf, the ends
of which fluttered out upon the draught.

With a sob of pure terror, Copper flung herself
frantically at Nick, burying her face against his
shoulder. 'What—who is it?' quavered Valerie, grip-

ping his arm. Nick shook himself free and raced across the drawing-room and into the verandah.

It took him a full minute to find the verandah switch, and it was a further two or three minutes before he returned, walking slowly across the drawing-room, his hands deep in the pockets of his dressing-gown and a puzzled frown between his brows.

Valerie and Copper had vanished, but the old *chaprassi* stood where he had left him, silent and motionless.

'You saw it, Iman Din. What—— Who was it?'

'Sahib,' said Iman Din, 'it is One who returns, seeking vengeance.'

'*Christians awake, salute the happy morn!*' car-
olled Charles, entering the breakfast
room. 'Sorry I'm late, sir. Happy Christmas, darling—and here's your present. I know you chose it
yourself, but let's have expressions of rapturous surprise, just for the look of it. Morning, everyone.
Happy Christmas!'

Valerie had invited Charles to have breakfast with
them on Christmas morning, but the storm was responsible for the unusually large assembly in the
dining-room, and Charles alone appeared to be in
good spirits.

John Shilto, looking if possible even more pasty as
to colouring and morose as to expression than usual,
was helping himself to kidneys and bacon and ig-
noring the timid conversational efforts of Leonard
Stock. Mrs Stock, who had recovered sufficiently to
put in an appearance, was seated, freshly rouged
and curled, between Nick and Dan Harcourt, while
Sir Lionel, a man who preferred to eat his breakfast
in a ritual silence occupied by the perusal of three-
weeks-old newspapers, was moodily sipping coffee
and turning at frequent intervals to glance at the
clock as though help might be forthcoming from the
blandly unemotional dial. He had responded without animation to Valerie's kiss and her 'Merry

Christmas, Dad' and made no attempt to return the conventional greeting.

He's probably got the right idea, thought Copper, avoiding Nick's eye and helping herself to grape-nuts. It certainly can't be called 'merry' at the moment!

Copper was suffering a reaction from the night's alarms; though curiously enough it was not the remembrance of the mysterious prowler that was disturbing her. The terrors of the dark hours seemed less alarming and even a little foolish by the cold light of morning, compared with her own frantic clinging to Nick, and Copper flushed angrily at the memory of her fear-stricken abandonment. And more than angrily at the recollection of Nick's treatment of it. He pulled me off him as if I'd been a nasty type of leech, she thought resentfully, and he probably thinks I did it on purpose; like Ruby, clinging round his neck like a ton of chewing-gum last night—and then I do exactly the same thing a few hours later! I expect, decided Copper forlornly, that he's used to it.

Breakfast was an even less pleasant meal than dinner had been the night before, and with the exception of Charles, no one made the slightest effort to improve it. They ate for the most part in silence, and at the conclusion of the meal dispersed without hilarity: to assemble an hour later in the hall, coated, hatted, gloved, in possession of prayer books and (it is to be hoped) armed with collection money.

Packing themselves under the waterproof protection of the waiting buggies they covered the few hundred yards that separated Government House from the little English church on Ross where, owing to the violence of the storm and the fact that the ferry was unable to run, the Reverend Dobbie's Christmas Day congregation had been reduced to a minimum. Mrs Dobbie had done her best to ornament the altar and chancel in a manner she considered suitable to the season, but the sprays of oleander and wilting branches of casuarina had formed a sorry substitute for holly and evergreen, and the church was very dark, for the doors and windows had been tightly shuttered against the stormy day. But no shutters could keep out the draughts, and the candle flames swayed and flickered, streaming out at right angles to their wicks like small, shining flags, while the timeworn carols sounded thin and strange as they rose in unequal competition with the beating of the rain and the howl of the wind.

'*O come, all ye faithful, Joyful and triumphant . . .*' Copper's voice supported Valerie's against the tuneless but determined baritone of Hamish Rattigan, who occupied the pew immediately behind them, and it occurred to her, with no sense of regret, that a year ago she had sung that same carol in one of London's loveliest churches. There had been hundreds of candles like drifts of golden stars, holly and Christmas roses, a glittering Christmas tree and a world-famous choir: high, pure, boys' voices, with the deeper tones of the men like tolling bells. And in her heart an echoing waste of loneliness and vague, unformulated longings.

And now once more it was Christmas Day, and the four walls of the little dim church with its wheezy harmonium and meagre congregation contained the whole of Copper's heart's desire, while outside the walls, in spite of rain and wind, hurricane and recent death, lay all Romance—a hundred coral-reefed islands scattered over a jade and sapphire sea. Life, Beauty and Adventure: and Nicholas Tarrent, that as yet unknown quantity . . . who had probably got at least a dozen wives in every port, did one but know! thought Copper, taking herself firmly in hand. At which point in her meditations she discovered that the carol having been concluded, the congregation, with the exception of herself, were again seated, and from his place on the opposite side of the aisle the subject of her reverie was endeavouring to draw her attention to the fact.

Copper sat down hurriedly and for the next fifteen minutes endeavoured to fix her attention on the Reverend Dobbie's almost inaudible address.

The afternoon continued as wet and wild as the morning, but towards four o'clock the storm showed signs of having blown itself out at last. The wind had dropped again and the rain died away into a light drizzle, and by the time that the house party, whose numbers had been augmented by the addition of several extra guests, collected in the verandah for tea and Christmas cake, the clouds had lifted and Mount Harriet stood out blackly against a sullen grey sky.

'Let's go for a walk around the island,' suggested Valerie. 'It really does look as though the worst is over, and I'd like to see how much damage has been done.'

'A considerable amount, I fear,' said the Chief Commissioner, joining the group in the verandah and helping himself to an egg sandwich: 'In fact, I'm afraid that you will all have to make up your minds to being marooned on Ross for several days. The hurricane has smashed the jetties and the pier into matchwood, and until something can be done about that no boat can reach us. What is still more annoying is the fact that the telephone wires have gone, and I am told that until this sea goes down there is no chance of repairing them. So for the time being we are completely cut off.'

'But what about our milk and butter, and things like that?' demanded Valerie, dismayed.

'We must make the best of it, my dear. There should be plenty of tinned milk in the house, and we can do without butter and fresh meat for a few days. At least we are in our own homes, instead of being stranded on the wrong side of the bay like Dr Vicarjee and Frank Burton, who, I am afraid, will have to resign themselves to staying in Aberdeen for some days to come.'

'But what about the dance at the Club and——Oh, damn! damn, *damn!*'

'Cheer up, Val,' comforted Charles. 'That's life, that was. Don't let's spend the rest of the day in gloom. Action is indicated. Remember that this is Christmas Day, and as the padre has already pointed out, the motto for the moment is *"Peace on Earth, and Goodwill towards Men"*—which means me. You girls go and shove a mac on and come for a walk. It will do your tempers good.'

The wind might have dropped, but it had by no means disappeared. It was still blowing in steadily from the south-east—driving the grey seas on to the rocks and the sea-wall of Ross as though with each crashing onslaught it must engulf the tiny island—as Nick, Copper, Valerie and Charles walked arm-in-arm down the steep roadway from the Residency to the jetty and the Club.

Behind them, with her escort, came Mrs Stock, who appeared to have recovered both her looks and her spirits. She showed little sign of the collapse that had followed her ordeal of the previous day, and had temporarily transferred her attention from Nick to Dan Harcourt, to whose arm she now clung, uttering little feminine shrieks and cries as the wind dragged at her skirts and fluttered the ends of the gay silk scarf that she had tied becomingly about her carefully waved head. Leonard Stock had not accompanied the party, but Hamish, her faithful adorer, had possession of her left arm, while George and Ronnie, the latter unusually taciturn, completed her entourage. The rear of the procession was brought up by Amabel and John Shilto, neither of whom appeared to be enjoying the other's society.

Amabel's nose was suspiciously pink and her eyes noticeably swollen, and her thoughts ran in continuous and gloomy circles: Why did I have to slap George like that? Not that he didn't deserve it. He did. But it was all Mrs Purvis's fault, behaving like a stupid—a stupid—Amabel's vocabulary failed to produce a sufficiently withering adjective with which to qualify the extreme stupidity of Rosamund Purvis whose regrettable display of lung power had blasted Amabel's young life. I wish I were dead, thought Amabel bleakly, then perhaps George would be sorry!

The storm had left a trail of ruin across the little island. Trunks of fallen palm trees, rent from their inadequate moorings or snapped off like broken broomsticks, lay across the paths and tilted drunkenly down the slopes. Leaves, twigs and flowers, stripped from trees and creepers, carpeted the ground and festooned the broken telephone and electric light wires. Coconuts lay smashed upon the roadways, and even now an occasional nut would fall with a thud, bespattering the earth with milky fluid or bouncing unbroken on to the rocks, to be snatched away by the mountainous seas that still crashed upon the broken fragments of Ross jetty, deluging the causeway in clouds of spray and tossing an untidy litter of wreckage over the Club lawn.

The small summer-house that overhung one end of the turtle tank was now roofless, and the water in the tank was higher than Valerie had ever seen it before as she leant over the edge, peering into its murky depths. A huge dim shape flickered for a moment in the heaving darkness of the shadowed water below her and a horny head emerged for a brief second, regarded her with an austere eye, and withdrew abruptly. Valerie laughed and said: 'If this sea keeps up it may break down the wall, and then you'll all escape. Good luck, chums! Charles, what about walking round Barrack Point to watch the waves? They're gorgeous after a storm.'

The wind met them as they rounded the point, and they paused, entranced, to watch the terrible masses of the steel-grey seas driving down upon the island to crash on to the jagged rocks below the sea-wall in a maelstrom of foam. 'Do let's go down to the beach,' begged Copper. 'It'll look much more exciting from there.'

'There isn't any beach we can go down to,' pointed out Nick. 'And if you think I'm going to let you climb down on to those rocks, you can think again. You'd be dragged off them and swept out to sea inside five minutes. Use some sense!'

'I don't mean here,' said Copper. 'I meant farther along, where the sea-wall stops. Even at high tide there is still a strip of sand there that isn't covered. Look—I'll show you.'

The small curving beach below the house was protected by two natural breakwaters of rock, and they had little difficulty in scrambling down the steep slope between the palm trees and reaching the narrow strip of sand. And as Copper had predicted, the towering waves that swept down upon the island appeared doubly awe-inspiring when seen from the level of the shore. Like dark hills of water that mounted higher and higher as they neared the shore, their crests and flanks streaked with livid bars of foam, to curl over at last and crash down into acres of boiling surf.

'Imagine being wrecked in a sea like that,' shuddered Copper. 'You wouldn't stand a chance. There can't be a lifeboat in the world that could get through it. I'm not surprised that the *Sapphire* ran for her life!'

'Wonder where the old girl's got to?' murmured

Dan Harcourt disrespectfully, screwing up his eyes against the stinging salt-laden wind and peering out to sea: 'I don't suppose she's far off. Except that there isn't a harbour worth mentioning around here, so she may have made for the coast. Anyway, I'll bet the boys are all feeling pea-green and peculiar.'

'What would have happened if they hadn't left Port Blair?' inquired Copper, interested.

'The same thing that happened to the old *Enterprise*,' said Ronnie Purvis: '*Smasho!*'

'Why? What happened to it?'

'Oh, don't you know?' Amabel, who could be counted upon to know the details of any disaster, brightened up a trifle and added her voice to the conversation: 'They had come here on a visit, like the *Sapphire*; only of course it was years and years ago—1891, I think—and a storm got up before they could leave harbour and they got driven on to the rocks off South Point. Ever so many of them were drowned, and there's a tablet to them in the church. Didn't you notice it?'

'No,' said Copper shortly. 'I'm thankful to say I did not!'

But Amabel was not to be deflected from the recital of disaster: 'Well, it's there; and the new *Enterprise* presented the ring of bells in the church steeple in memory of them. At low tide you can still see the boilers of the old *Enterprise* on the rocks off South Point, all covered with barnacles. We sail round them sometimes when we go fishing. I suppose the tide carried the rest of the ship out to sea when it broke up, but these were too heavy. Fancy all those people drowning so close to the shore. It just goes to show, doesn't it?'

'Show what?' inquired Copper irritably. Amabel's story had spoilt her enjoyment in the sight of the thundering seas, and what had seemed so splendid a spectacle a few minutes ago, now appeared sin-

ister and cruel and strangely menacing. All those
people, going to their deaths so close to that same
shore, in that same cold, savage sea . . .

'The natives say,' continued Amabel, determined
to extract the last ounce of gruesomeness from her
story, 'that when there's a storm the noise the tide
makes coming over those boilers is the voices of the
drowned men among the rocks calling for help, and
that on stormy nights you can see their faces coming
up through the water like . . .' She was interrupted
by a sudden gasping cry from Mrs Stock, and broke
off, staring: 'What's the matter?'

Mrs Stock, still retaining her grip upon Dan and
Hamish, was peering intently at the waves, her
head a little thrust forward. She flushed at the inquiry, and laughed a little uncertainly. 'It's funny,'
she said, 'but for a minute I thought I saw a face
looking at me from out of a wave, just before it
broke. I suppose that story about the drowned men
of the *Enterprise* is making me see things. But it
looked so real that it gave me quite a nasty shock. It
was just out there——' She released Hamish's arm
to point with a vermilion-tipped finger: 'In the second line of waves. I expect it was one of those seal
things. A dugong.'

'A dugong?' exclaimed Copper, thrilled. 'You
mean one of those creatures that people used to
think were mermaids? Where! . . . Where!'

They all turned with her to stare into the grey,
crashing seas, their eyes confused by blown spray
and distracted by bobbing wreckage. '*There!*' said
Valerie suddenly. 'I believe I saw something over to
the right. No, it isn't—it's only half a coconut!'

'No, it's not,' said Copper. 'It's—it's—— *What is
it, Nick?*'

The cold ridge of water that was towering to its
fall raced in upon the shore, and from beneath its
curling crest, pale and glimmering against the dark

wall of water and whiter than the boiling foam, there peered a face——

Mrs Stock screamed at the top of her voice as the wave, crashing in spray, surged up the beach and flung its burden at their feet. Ferrers Shilto had returned.

'Don't look, dear!' said Nick sharply. He caught Copper by the shoulder and swung her around forcibly. But Copper had seen, as they had all seen . . .

He lay on his back where the tide had flung him, his feet in the creaming froth of foam and flotsam, his eyes wide open and his face, unmarked by the jagged coral rocks, wearing an expression of almost ludicrous astonishment. His left hand lay across his chest and something glinted redly: a single splash of scarlet.

'There's blood on it!' sobbed Copper. She wrenched herself from Nick's hold and faced the thing that lay on the beach. But the foam of the next wave dragged at its feet, disturbing the limp figure so that its hand fell away from its breast and lay palm down on the sand. And there was no blood. Only the red blotch of the big garnet that winked and glowed from the clumsy bronze ring on Ferrers Shilto's finger.

Nick said: 'Get these women away, George. Purvis, you'd better get up to the hospital and collect a stretcher. Go on, Copper darling. You and Val see to those two women. George will go with you.' Copper turned obediently, and taking the shivering Amabel by the arm, dragged her away up the steep grassy slope above the beach, followed by George and Valerie almost carrying the now completely hysterical Ruby between them.

The noise of their departure died away among the palm trunks, and on the beach Nick, Charles and Hamish lifted the limp, wizened body. There was a small pinkish stain where the head had lain, but as

Dan Harcourt stooped above it the lash of another wave obliterated it, and he straightened, frowning, and followed to where they laid the dead man above the reach of the waves.

John Shilto had made no move to help them, and now he stood motionless beside the bedraggled object that had been his cousin, staring down at it with a curiously unpleasant expression on his pasty features. I believe the bastard's actually *gloating!* thought Nick disgustedly. And turning away, he took out a cigarette and lit it, shielding the match flame from the wind with his cupped hands, and leant back against a palm tree to wait for Ronnie Purvis and the stretcher.

Charles and Hamish followed his example, but Dan Harcourt remained beside the body, staring down at it with an intent expression that suggested, strongly, a terrier at a rat hole. Presently he went down upon his knees and examined the widened pupils of the staring sightless eyes, and then, carefully and minutely, the fingers of both lax hands. The big garnet winked redly as it turned, and he let the cold hand fall and came to his feet again, brushing the sand off his knees.

Charles said: 'It's odd that he hasn't been smashed up at all: you'd have thought all those rocks and reefs would have battered him to bits.'

'Tide,' said John Shilto curtly, speaking for the first time. 'It must have pulled him out of the harbour mouth clear of the rocks. And, as you see, when it turned it landed him back at the one place where there is a clear strip of sand. The current pulls in strongly towards this beach and most of the big wreckage gets flung up here.'

'Oh yes?' said Hamish without interest, and looked anxiously at his watch. They had left the house just before five but now it was well past six o'clock, and aided by the thick blanket of the storm-clouds the swift tropic darkness was closing in on them: 'I wish Ronnie would get a move on,' he said uneasily. 'It'll be dark before he gets back.'

'It's all right,' said Charles, 'here he is now—with young Dutt and a couple of troops, plus stretcher. They must have run most of the way.'

'Truda is behaving like a lunatic,' panted Ronnie Purvis, sliding down the bank on to the narrow strip of beach: 'She says that she won't have the body in the hospital because she's there by herself—except for my wife, who for some goddam reason won't leave, and backs her up. If we insist, we'll have them both in hysterics. What the hell are we going to do? It'll be dark inside fifteen minutes and we can't bury him until tomorrow. We've got to park him somewhere for the night.'

'What about the church?' suggested Hamish, prompted by some hazy notion of lying-in-state. Ronnie Purvis gave a short laugh. 'Can you see Mrs Padre standing for it? Or half the old women in the place, for that matter! No. We've got to get him under cover somewhere. But I'm damned if I know where.'

'If I might make suggestion,' said Dr Vicarjee's young assistant in his soft, imperfect English, 'there is Guest House. It is empty and very seldom used. For many months now no one is using.'

'That's the ticket!' said Mr Purvis with relief. 'Well done, Dutt. Only outside visitors are ever put up in that moth-eaten dump, and they won't ever hear that it's been used as a morgue. If we planted him anywhere else you'd find people refusing to live in the house afterwards. Right, then. Take him along to the Guest House, will you.'

Hamish said: 'I'll go along too, just to see it's O.K. I suppose you'll have to make some sort of examination, Dutt, now that Vicarjee is marooned on the mainland?'

Dan Harcourt took a swift step forward as though he would have spoken, but he evidently changed his mind, for he checked and turned away without speaking, and Charles said: 'See you later then, Hamish; I gather we are both attending a Christmas party up at the house. We've certainly had a jolly day for it! Come on, Nick.'

They turned together and made off in the gathering darkness towards the house whose already lighted windows gleamed through the trees above them, and John Shilto, with one last, long stare at the sheeted figure being lifted on to the stretcher, turned on his heel and followed them.

= 11 =

If the Christmas Eve party had been a failure, the dinner party on Christmas night could definitely be classed, in the hostess's phraseology, as a total frost.

Mrs Stock had taken to her bed, but there had been no question of cancelling the party, for with the house full of guests the table was bound to be fairly crowded. And as Valerie said, one or two more were not likely to add or detract from the general gloom, so if she had to give a dinner party at all she might as well have Charles there to hold her hand under the table and help her through it.

Whether Charles fulfilled the first of these conditions was a matter only known to himself and Valerie, and as he happened to be left-handed the matter was in doubt. But in spite of his best efforts at cheerfulness and his fiancée's valiant support, the conversation at dinner was barely more than spasmodic. Copper looked white and on edge, while Nick was for once strangely taciturn.

Nick had problems of his own to contend with. The sight of Copper's distress had not only disturbed him but made him inexplicably angry: a combination of emotions that caused him considerable irritation, since he was not yet sure of his own feelings towards her. She appealed to him in a way that no woman had ever done before—and a good many women had held a temporary appeal for Nick Tarrent. But Copper was something different. There were times when he would have liked to snatch her up in his arms and kiss her so that she could not breathe, and others when he would have liked to pick her up and throw her into the sea—though whether from a sense of irritation with her or himself, or a desire to be free from her disturbing hold on his heart, he did not know. Nor was he at all sure that he wished to find out . . .

Seated on Nick's left, John Shilto was eating oysters in a manner which caused the majority of his fellow-guests to wish that he would extend his habitual silence to his consumption of food, and beyond him sat Dan Harcourt, absent-mindedly manufacturing bread pills and gazing thoughtfully into space. Valerie, looking drained and tired, was keeping up a desultory conversation with Leonard Stock and Ronnie Purvis, while beyond them Amabel and George sat side by side in a state of congealed gloom and unconcealed misery.

Silly idiots! thought Copper bleakly: they've only got to say two words and they'd be sobbing on each other's necks inside half a minute. I wonder why it's so difficult to say 'I'm sorry?' . . . I wonder why you can't ever be really sensible about the people you care for most? I wonder why I should have dreamt that Ferrers had been stabbed?—everything else was the same, but there wasn't a knife . . .

Her thoughts, back again in that frightening groove, sheered away from it violently, and she turned feverishly to the silent Hamish. 'I had no idea that there were oysters in these waters, Hamish. Do you ever find pearls in them, or are the pearl kind different?'

'Eh?' said Captain Rattigan, waking abruptly from his sombre meditations. The demon of jealousy was gnawing painfully at Hamish's vitals, for although his goddess could do no wrong in his infatuated eyes, Ruby's attentions to Surgeon-Lieutenant Harcourt that afternoon had been more than marked. And almost more than Hamish felt himself able to bear. He had not heard Copper's question and she repeated it.

'Oh—er—yes,' said Hamish, 'I don't think so.'

Charles, nobly following this lead, said: 'I believe there are a lot of oysters around, but the local fishermen are too lazy to go out and dive for them. They prefer hanging over the jetty with a piece of string and a hook and hoping for the best.'

'Last year, one of them went to sleep and fell in,' said Amabel, offering her contribution to the conversational gaiety: 'And he was drowned. Like Ferrers.'

There was a brief silence, during which her fellow-guests regarded young Miss Withers with varying degrees of emotion, and then Sir Lionel said absently, reaching for the salt: 'That reminds me, I had a letter from Ferrers only a day or two ago asking me if . . . the red pepper, please, thank you . . . but I never had time to answer it, and now the poor fellow is dead. Very sad.'

'Yes, indeed,' agreed Leonard Stock unhappily. 'I cannot really feel responsible, but Ruby says——'

'*Responsible?*' The Chief Commissioner looked startled. 'Responsible for what?'

'Well . . . er . . . You see, Ruby thinks—that is . . . Well, what I mean is, I suppose it *was* partly our fault; in a way. If only we hadn't happened to stop off at Ferrers's bungalow yesterday this would never have occurred. It was most unfortunate. But it was really *not* my fault. Mrs Dobbie wanted to ask him about bringing some bedding, and I don't see how I could have . . . But Ruby says——'

Sir Lionel said impatiently: 'I cannot see what you are worrying about, Stock. Or why you or your wife should feel in any way responsible for something that was only an unfortunate accident. It might have happened to anyone.'

'That's exactly what I said. "But, my dear," I said, "it might even have been *you*! Or any of us." But Ruby seems to think . . .'

'That it's all your fault,' finished Valerie shortly. Mr Stock flushed and said incoherently: 'Yes—no. No! I'm sure she . . . I didn't mean . . . You mustn't think——' He gestured agitatedly with his oyster fork.

Copper murmured something that sounded suspiciously like 'apologetic sand-crab' and Valerie threw her a repressive look and said hurriedly: 'What was Ferrers writing to you about, Dad?'

'What's that?'

'The letter. You said that Ferrers had written to you.'

'Did I? Oh yes. Well I do not think we want to go on talking about poor Ferrers this evening. It cannot be pleasant for Mr Shilto.'

John Shilto grinned at him sardonically from across the table, and said: 'I beg that you won't let my feelings concern you, Sir Lionel. Naturally my cousin's death was a great shock to me, but we were hardly on such friendly terms as to make it a mortal blow. And as for this letter, since it is probably the last that Ferrers ever wrote, I am of course—'

But Copper did not allow him to finish, for she too did not wish to speak of Ferrers Shilto; or to be reminded of that pallid face with the astonished eyes. And seized with a sudden and uncontrollable horror of the subject, she said violently: 'Sir Lionel is right. We don't want to talk about him. Surely we can talk about something else?—anything else!'

'Attagirl, Coppy!' approved Charles, seconding the motion. 'What shall we try instead? Let's all decide whom we dislike most and then talk about them. There's nothing like a bit of mutual loathing to draw people together. *"Peace on Earth, Goodwill towards Men!"* What about George? We can probably all find something lousy to say about George. Wake up, George! You are about to be thrown to the lions.'

Copper laughed and had the grace to look ashamed of herself, but the dinner party, finding Charles's guide to conversation a useful one, settled happily down to reviling Europe's least-liked public character, and Ferrers Shilto was temporarily forgotten. But only temporarily . . . The girls had barely left the table to return to the far verandah for coffee when a soft-footed servant announced that Dr Dutt was below and wished to speak to the Commissioner.

'Send him up,' said Sir Lionel, busy with the port; and two minutes later the slim figure of Dr Vicarjee's young assistant entered the dining-room. There were raindrops on his coat and his shoes left damp patches upon the floorboards. 'What is it, Dutt?' inquired Sir Lionel. 'You look pretty wet. Have some hot coffee?'

'Thanking you, but no, sir. I am come only to ask leave for burial of corpse. I have myself held inspection and signed certificate of death, in regretted absence of Dr Vicarjee. Climate here is most humid and corpse should be interred tomorrow morning at latest, with your order.'

Dan Harcourt stirred suddenly in his chair and leant forward across the table. 'Isn't it usual, sir,' he inquired of the Chief Commissioner, 'for two doctors to sign a death certificate?'

Dr Dutt interrupted, bristling slightly: 'That has already been done. Oah yess—I know all procedures. Matron, Miss Gidney, who is lady doctor, has also signed, so all is in order.'

'Yes, yes. Of course, that is quite sufficient.' Sir Lionel did not like being bothered by what he considered unnecessary red tape. 'He had better be buried as early as possible tomorrow morning. I will see that the padre is notified. By the way, Shilto, your cousin was not an R.C. by any chance? No . . . I thought not. Then I will notify Mr Dobbie. I will write the order now.'

He rose to leave the table, and Dan Harcourt pushed back his chair and stood up. 'Forgive me butting in, sir, but—er—could I, as a matter of interest, have a look at the body? I'm a doctor myself and I might be able to help Dr Dutt with his examination.'

'Already the examination has been performed,' said Dr Dutt stiffly, indignation quivering in every line of his slim figure.

'But——'

Sir Lionel turned irritably upon this pushing young man. A surgeon-lieutenant, was he? Well, possibly that meant some kind of a doctor on a ship, but not on shore. 'It seems to me to be quite unnecessary, Mr Harcourt,' he said coldly. 'Come, Dutt.'

Dan flushed and stepped back: Sir Lionel was right. It was no business of his and he had invited that snub. All the same . . . He watched Sir Lionel and young Dutt leave the room, and having finished his drink, went off to play card games in the drawing-room. But the party spirit was lamentably lacking that Christmas night, and it was barely ten-thirty when Valerie stacked the cards and voted for bed. 'It's been such a mildewed day that the sooner we finish it the better,' she said. 'Charles darling, will you and Hamish see that Amabel gets safely up to the hospital? I suppose she *is* still parking there with Rosamund?'

'What about making George see her home?' suggested Charles. 'Then they'll be able to stage a reconciliation on the way, which will ease the present situation a lot. After all, they couldn't very well do the entire trip in stodgy silence. Or could they?'

'Could they not!' sighed Valerie. 'They managed to sit out an entire meal side by side without uttering a twitter. Besides, you know what a fat-head Amabel is. She'd never bring herself to speak a kind word; not with several buggy-men two feet off her and a police orderly trotting along behind.'

Charles said: 'No, I suppose not. I'd forgotten it was raining. I had pictured them wandering hospital-wards, hand in hand, and forgiving each other nobly by the reservoir. However, I do not propose to get soaked to the skin because George has had a tiff with his girlfriend. He can darn well take her back himself, reconciliation or no reconciliation. I'm for bed. Come on round behind this useful screen where Leonard can't see us, and kiss me goodnight. I have had a trying day and I need a spot of cherishing.'

Ten minutes later the last of the guests had departed, and those left behind in Government House had turned out the lights and gone to bed. Christmas Day was over; although Christmas night had still an hour to run . . .

The hall clock struck eleven, and silence flowed in upon the darkened rooms. Outside, a cold sea-mist drifted in from the south to creep across the garden and engulf the quiet house, muffling the guard-lights and blotting out the tall trees, and at the edge of the verandah roof, above the sentry's box, the rain collected in a little pool which presently overflowed in a thin, steady trickle on to the flags below.

'Gawd! what an 'ole!' sighed the sentry bleakly. 'A Merry Christmas—I *don't* think!'

Dan Harcourt had retired to the bedroom he shared with Nick, but he did not undress.

He stood by the window, his hands deep in his pockets, and looked out into the thickening mist beyond the strip of lawn below him, whistling softly between his teeth and frowning into the night.

Nick, who appeared to be in a singularly unpleasant mood, donned a pair of cerulean pyjamas—previously the property of Mr Charles Corbet-Carr—and having morosely requested him to stop that depressing noise and get to bed, climbed in under his own mosquito net and lay down with his back to the light. But Dan made no move to comply with either of these suggestions. His thoughts were fully occupied, and it is doubtful if he was even aware that Nick had spoken, for he continued his tuneless whistling and it was at least fifteen minutes later that he broke off to say abruptly: 'Look here, Nick, I'm in a bit of a quandary and I'd like your advice.'

Receiving no answer he turned from the window and came over to Nick's bed. But Nick had fallen asleep.

For a moment or two Dan debated the wisdom of waking him up, but it seemed an unkindness to do so, and abandoning the idea he switched off the lights and returned to his own bed: but not to sleep. Instead, he lit a cigarette, and getting in under the mosquito net lay down fully clothed and stared up into the darkness where the electric fan blades swished softly in the warm, damp air. It was a pity about Nick. He would have liked to talk the thing over with him. But Nick was obviously dead tired and would probably, if awakened, be more blasphemous than helpful . . .

Dan shifted uneasily on the sheets. What was he to do? Was it any business of his to interfere? After all, but for an accident he himself would not have been marooned on Ross. And but for a freak of the tides Ferrers Shilto's body would have been battered to pieces upon the jagged coral reefs, or else carried miles out to sea and far down the coasts before being thrown ashore. In either case, all that was left would, if found, have been buried hurriedly and without question, and taking that into consideration, was it any business of his, Dan Harcourt's, to meddle with the affair? There was an old and wise adage to the effect that it is always safer to let sleeping dogs lie.

But if it was murder . . . ?

If it was murder there was also another saying, one that was probably equally true in practice, to the effect that a man who kills and gets away with it will live to kill again: and again . . .

And if it isn't murder, thought Dan, it's something so damn peculiar that I shall need a personal demonstration before I believe in it. No, that little man never died by drowning. I've seen men who've died that way, and I'll swear he didn't. But no one is going to believe that unless I can prove it. As for that young snip of an assistant, Dutt, he wouldn't know the difference between a corpse and a case of concussion! I'll bet he never even conducted the sketchiest of examinations—he'd consider it a waste of time. On the strength of the fact that a man is reported to have fallen into the sea on Tuesday and his body gets washed ashore on Wednesday, he would cheerfully have signed a dozen documents certifying death by drowning without so much as taking a second look. While as for that woman up at the hospital who wouldn't even let 'em dump the body there, I'll bet she signed without laying eyes on it!

Dan turned restlessly in the hot darkness while his cigarette burned out between his fingers. They were burying Ferrers Shilto in the morning—early in the morning, Sir Lionel had said. Therefore if he intended to do anything about it he must do so now, since it would be useless to voice suspicions once Ferrers's body was six feet underground. He dropped the burned-out stub of his cigarette on to the floor and lit a fresh one; the yellow flare of the match illuminating for a brief moment his brown, boyish face and the frown between his narrowed eyes. It flickered out in the darkness and he lay back and reviewed the situation once more . . .

Nick had said that the boats had been about halfway home when the storm struck them, which meant that they had foundered in the widest part of the bay and in deep water. There were no rocks within a considerable distance of them, and Nick had seen Ferrers clinging to one of the upturned boats some minutes after they had capsized. That did away with any theory that he might have been hit on the head and killed in the process of capsizing by the mast or the boat itself. Or that he had met his death among the rocks. No one, again quoting Nick, could have managed to swim to the shore in that sea, let alone a frail middle-aged man of negligible physique, such as the late Ferrers Shilto.

Then how——?

There's nothing for it, thought Dan resignedly, but to go down and see for myself. If I don't, I shall worry about it to the end of my days. And if ever I hear that anyone else from these islands has been drowned or otherwise reported accidentally dead, I shall wonder if it really was an accident—and feel like a murderer myself.

He slid off his bed and tossed his cigarette out of the window where it described a thin glowing arc and disappeared into the mist, and having groped about for an overcoat, remembered with irritation that his own was on board the *Sapphire* and by this time probably in the Nicobars, and that he had neglected to borrow one. It would mean getting wet, but resigning himself to the inevitable he turned up the collar of his dinner-jacket—one of George's—

and having collected a torch from the dressing-table, paused to remove his shoes. There was no point in awakening the entire household!

The clock in the hall struck the quarter to midnight as he tiptoed across the silent ballroom and descended the stairs to the hall where old Iman Din lay stretched upon his thin mattress, his turban on the floor beside him and a cloth draped across his face, sound asleep. It is to be feared that Iman Din, although a Muslim and therefore, theoretically, a teetotaller, had also been celebrating Christmas, and had fallen from grace to the extent of imbibing toddy in the Ross bazaar. As a result, his slumbers were particularly sound and his rhythmic snores did not cease when Dan Harcourt stepped over his recumbent body, and replacing his own shoes drew the bolts of the front door.

But with his hand upon the door-latch, Dan stopped and turned back, for hanging on the hall hatstand was a mackintosh cape with a hood of the type worn by the guards and orderlies in wet weather. 'Just what the doctor ordered!' thought Dan; and carefully removing it from its peg he fastened it about his own shoulders, pulled the hood over his head, and thus protected against the rain opened the front door and stepped out into the wet night.

The sentry, yawning in his box, challenged him as he passed, and Dan stopped and came across to him: 'I'm just going out for a breather. Too damned stuffy in the house and I can't sleep. I hope it's all right?'

'Certainly, sir.' The sentry's wooden countenance relaxed into a grin and became human: 'Wish I could join yer, sir! Fair feeds me up, standin' about 'ere ——Christmas night an' all!'

Dan laughed, and pulled out a half-empty packet of Goldflake. 'Tough luck. Have a cigarette.'

'Not allowed to smoke on duty, sir,' said the sentry wistfully, averting his eyes from the betraying stub that glowed two feet away among the wet flowerpots where he had thrown it upon hearing approaching footsteps.

'Keep 'em until you get off,' advised Dan. He pressed the packet into the sentry's grateful hand.

'Thank you, sir. Much obliged. Good-night, sir.'

'Good-night.' Dan turned away, and with no warning premonition of danger to send him back to the safety of his room, walked down the steep pathway and disappeared into the cold embrace of the mists.

The Guest House on Ross was a large, two-storeyed building of dismal aspect, standing just below the grounds of the Chief Commissioner's house at the top of the steep road that led up from the pier and the jetty. It had at that date remained empty for some considerable time, and was only used when auditors and such-like governmental wildfowl descended upon the Islands. The *chowkidar**, as is the custom of such people, was sound asleep with his blanket pulled well over his head, there was no sign of a police guard, and there appeared to be no one to dispute Dan's entrance.

The outer doors were locked, but it did not take him long to find a window whose latch he could force, nor, having once entered the house, to discover which room was doing duty as a temporary morgue.

They had laid the body of Ferrers Shilto on a trestle table in what must have been the living-room, wrapped in a tarpaulin sheet from which slow drops of brine oozed to fall on to the uncarpeted boards beneath and stray away in thin trickles, so that in

*Nightwatchman.

that dim, empty room the dark blot of the makeshift catafalque had the appearance of a spider crouched in the centre of a web. Dust lay in a thick layer underfoot except where the feet of Dutt and the stretcher-bearers had disturbed it, and in that wide space of shadows the beam of Dan's pocket torch made a lonely pool of light, before whose wan glow the darkness retreated a few reluctant paces.

Outside the house the rain trickled from the eaves and gutters of the roof, and wisps of sea-fog pressed against the black, winking window-panes like white faces peering in from the night. But inside the air was dank and heavy, and there was no sound to break the silence save the monotonous *drip, drip, drip* of sea-water from the still shape under the tarpaulin.

A bat that had been roosting on the gaunt frame of the electric fan swooped down with a rustle of leathery wings and fluttered about Dan's head, and he struck up at it involuntarily with his torch. As he did so, the torch slipped from his grasp, and striking the floor, went out, leaving him in a darkness that was so complete as to seem solid.

After a few minutes of blasphemous but ineffectual groping he remembered he had a box of matches in his pocket, and struck one. The hiss and splutter of its lighting sounded astonishingly loud in the silent room, and by its small flame he saw his torch lying near the open door. But as he reached it the match burnt out, and in the brief moment of dark before his fingers closed upon the cold metal, he thought that he heard something, or someone, move in the blackness beyond the doorway.

Pressing the switch of the torch he found to his intense relief that the bulb had not been broken, for once more a yellow beam of light beat back the shadows, and he flashed it about the room and through the doorways. But there was no one there, and except for himself and the dead man the house appeared to be empty. Nevertheless, he found to his disgust that his hands were shaking and that his breathing had quickened as though he had been running.

Of all the damned nonsense! thought Dan savagely: I'm getting as bad as that screaming woman Ruby Whatsername. Astonishing how an empty house at night can give one the jitters! Psychological, I suppose—— He steadied himself with an effort and walked up to the rickety trestle table and its quiet occupant. And it was only then that he saw that the coverings of tarpaulin had been roughly stitched about the body. Evidently they intended to bury it like this if no coffin could be produced in time. Dan fumbled in his pocket, and producing a small penknife, ripped out the coarse stitches and drew back the impromptu shroud.

The stiff folds of tarpaulin fell back with a curious crackling sound and Ferrers Shilto's white face, still wearing that look of incredulous astonishment, gazed up at him, wide-eyed. And suddenly all nervousness left Dan Harcourt and he was once again a doctor, cool and impersonal, and this thing on the table before him was merely part of a doctor's job. He slipped off the heavy mackintosh cape he wore, and turning back the cuffs of his dinner-jacket, bent over the table and began his examination. It did not take him long.

It was perhaps five minutes later that he straightened up with a long-drawn sigh and pulled down his cuffs again. He had seen everything that he had wanted to see, and knew everything that he had wanted to know.

He heard no sound, nor did he see the shadow that moved in the shadows behind him. But suddenly and inexplicably he was aware of danger. Some sixth sense, stronger than reason, rang an imperative alarm bell in his brain, calling on him to turn.

A board creaked behind him and he spun round . . .

An hour later the sentry outside Government House saw a caped and hooded figure walk rapidly up the path towards the house. It nodded a brief greeting to him as it passed, but did not speak, and the sentry, mellowed by illicit cigarettes, followed the dim figure with a grateful gaze.

'I 'ope 'e's enjoyed 'is little stroll,' mused Private Alfred Reginald Weekes: "*Er-iaw-ooh!* Gawd! I couldn't 'arf do with a bit of shut-eye!'

He heard the front door close softly, and then the sounds of bolts being gently pressed home.

Inside the house the clock struck half past one.

= 12 =

'Val, come here a minute. What do you make of this?'

Valerie, on her way to breakfast, paused beside Copper who was thoughtfully examining the intricate carving of the stairhead.

'What is it? Oh, a moth. No, it isn't; it's only a bit of that pink feather stuff off Ruby's dressing-gown.'

'I know,' said Copper. 'But what is it doing here? She never came past here last night. That is, not unless she was prowling around after we'd all gone to bed.'

'What would she want to prowl here for?' asked Valerie reasonably, 'she's got everything she wants in her own rooms.' She reached out, and removing the small scrap of pink swansdown stood for a moment turning it between her fingers and frowning. 'Perhaps she was only taking her insomnia for an airing. Unless, of course, she was——' Valerie broke off abruptly, and turning away said: 'Come on, Coppy, or the eggs will be stone cold. Good-morning, Nick.'

' 'Morning, Val. Hullo, Coppy. Have either of you seen Dan?'

'Not yet,' said Valerie, preceding him into the dining-room. 'Why?'

'He wasn't in his bed when I woke up, and he

appears to have neglected his ablutions this morning.'

'You'd probably been snoring and he was only too glad to get out,' suggested Copper lightly. 'Good-morning, everyone.' She seated herself at the table and poured out a cup of coffee: 'I expect you'll find he's gone for a walk to get up an appetite for breakfast.'

'What—in this weather? Not bloody likely! The fog's so thick you could cut slices out of it with a spoon. And being of a charitable and Christian disposition, I will ignore your first and offensive suggestion.'

Valerie said: 'I'll get one of the servants to hunt him up and tell him that breakfast's ready.' She called a *khidmatgar** and gave a brief order in the vernacular.

'How's your wife this morning, Mr Stock?' inquired Copper. 'I hope she had a good night?'

'What's that?' Leonard Stock, who had been surreptitiously endeavouring to read the back of the Reuters news-sheet that was engaging the Chief Commissioner's attention, jumped guiltily and dropped his pince-nez into his coffee.

'I said that I hoped that your wife had slept well,' said Copper distinctly.

'Oh yes. Oh yes, quite well, thank you,' replied Mr Stock, fishing around in his coffee cup with a teaspoon. 'We both passed an excellent night, all things considered.'

'I only asked,' said Copper mendaciously, 'because Valerie thought that she heard sounds from your room last night, and wondered if your wife had wanted anything.'

Mr Stock looked slightly taken aback: 'From our room? I'm sure she must have been mistaken. Ruby

*Waiter.

would certainly have called out to me if she had
wanted anything in the night.'

'*Called out* to you?' inquired Copper, puzzled.

Leonard Stock flushed pinkly, and abandoning his
ineffectual fishing operations with his teaspoon, re-
trieved his dripping pince-nez with his fingers and
gave a little nervous laugh.

'You see—Ruby prefers a room to herself. She
says that I—er—that I occasionally—er—snore.
And as she is a very light sleeper and suffers terribly
from insomnia, I have had to remove my bed into
the dressing-room, which has a proper door, so that
she can shut it—the door between the rooms I
mean—and not be disturbed. I'm afraid that I myself am a somewhat sound sleeper, but I am sure I
would have heard her if she'd got up in the night,
because in order to get to the bathroom she would
have had to pass through my——' He stopped
abruptly, and crimsoned as violently as though he
had been guilty of unspeakable vulgarity, but Copper's attention had evidently wandered. She was engaged in spreading marmalade on her toast and
thinking deeply . . .

The guest rooms occupied by the Stocks were next
to Valerie's, the tiny verandah outside being shared
by both rooms, and beyond the bedroom was a large
dressing-room which corresponded, on a smaller
scale, with the turret room at the opposite end of
the house—now occupied by John Shilto. The
bathroom led off from this, and as a heavy teak door
separated the dressing-room from the bedroom, it
was unlikely that Leonard Stock would have heard
any but a fairly loud movement from his wife's room
once the door was closed between them. Which
meant that it would have been perfectly simple for
Ruby to slip out of her room into the ballroom without her husband being any the wiser, and if it was
true that he snored, she had only to listen for that

sound to make sure that he was asleep before moving.

A dark and quite unfounded suspicion of John Shilto slid into Copper's mind; to be instantly rejected. She harboured no illusions as to Mrs Stock's standard of morality, having been regaled with too much local scandal by the Island gossips, who had been only too delighted with the opportunity of unloading their choicest titbits on to the newcomer. But John Shilto was not a type likely to appeal to any woman; even one of Mrs Stock's man-collecting proclivities!

Copper glanced across to where he sat silent and morose eating scrambled eggs at the far side of the table. There were heavy dark pouches under his eyes that she did not remember having noticed before, and he looked unshaven and ill and as though he had passed a sleepless night. He's rather like something that's grown up in a cellar, thought Copper; and decided that whatever Ruby Stock had in mind last night, it could not have been John Shilto!

Another and far more unpleasant thought struck her, and she turned sharply to look at Nick; and was as instantly ashamed of herself. I *am* a toad! thought Copper in sudden contrition, ashamed of her own suspicions: I must have a low, mean, horrid sort of mind. But what *was* Ruby doing, creeping about the house last night? Leonard is right. If she'd wanted anything reasonable she'd have woken up the entire house rather than move a finger to get it herself! And she was barefoot too—she must have been. Those silly feather slippers of hers would have made an awful racket, clicking across the ballroom; and if . . .

Copper twisted a little sideways in her chair and surreptitiously studied Nick's attractive profile with anxious eyes. Of course it's nonsense! she thought ruefully. I suppose it's only because I'm jealous of that woman that I think of these things. I *am* jealous of her: I suppose I'd be jealous of anyone who looked at him like that. Even Val . . . Even *Amabel* —— Oh dear!

She sighed a small unhappy sigh. After all, what—apart from the fact that she was in love with him—did she know about Nick Tarrent? Less than nothing! And anyway, he and John Shilto were not the only other men in the house: there still remained Sir Lionel and Dan Harcourt. Sir Lionel naturally did not count. But how about Dan? Ruby had certainly been very charming to Dan on the previous day, and he had not shown himself unwilling to be charmed. What was it that Nick had just said about him? Something about his having got up early and gone for a walk? It seemed an odd thing to do on such a morning, for although the rain had stopped, the fog had thickened until it pressed about the house and the island like a muffling pall of grey cotton-wool.

Copper helped herself to more toast as a red-uniformed *chaprassi* advanced noiselessly to Valerie's side and spoke in an undertone.

'What's that?' Valerie's voice was sharp.

The man shrugged his shoulders, and sketched a gesture with his brown hands.

'But it's absurd!' Valerie turned to her stepfather: 'He says that they've looked everywhere, but they can't find Dan Harcourt. The orderlies say no one has left the house this morning, and the servants say he isn't anywhere inside it. Dad, hadn't we better send someone out to look for him? He must have gone out by one of the servants' staircases without being seen, and got lost in this mist.'

Nick pushed back his chair and rose to his feet. 'In that case, we'd better go and round him up at once. With a fog like this he might well walk off the edge of a breakwater. Anyone coming with me?'

'I'll come,' said Valerie.

'Nonsense!' snapped Sir Lionel irritably. 'I imagine that young man is perfectly capable of looking after himself, and I object to any of you careering round the island in this fog. I expect he went off to the Mess and is having his breakfast down there.'

Valerie stared at her stepfather in some surprise. It was unlike him to be irritable with her, and she noticed suddenly that he was looking old and rather ill, and suffered a pang of conscience; realizing that she had been too wrapped up in Charles of late to pay much attention to his well-being. 'What's the matter, Dad?' she inquired. 'You're looking a bit off colour this morning.'

'There is nothing whatever the matter with me,' said Sir Lionel coldly. 'I merely stated—I will repeat it if you wish—that I would rather you did not go wandering round the island in this weather.' He gathered up the typewritten news-sheets, and disregarding Valerie's hurt and astonished face, left the dining-room.

'He's quite right,' consoled Copper swiftly. 'There's no sense in all of us breaking our necks hunting up Dan. I'll bet he's with Charles. Let's ring up the Mess.'

They excused themselves and left the table, but Copper, looking back from the edge of the ballroom, surprised a curious look upon Mr Shilto's unalluring countenance. He had turned in his chair and was looking towards the windows, and for a moment she thought that he was laughing. It was gone in a moment, but the impression remained that the fat, bulky shoulders in the ill-fitting linen coat had been jerking and quivering with suppressed mirth.

Nick, who had gone to his room for a coat, returned across the ballroom, frowning blackly.

'Look here,' said Nick abruptly, 'I've just found something damned odd: I don't know why I didn't notice it before, but Dan's own clothes are in the bedroom, so he must still be wearing that borrowed dinner-jacket. And his bed has been slept on but not in. I'm going down to make inquiries.'

He turned on his heel, and taking the staircase three steps at a time, flung out of the front door and vanished into the mist. To return five minutes later, with the scowl still on his face——

'I can't understand what Dan's up to. I've been talking to the sentry and the police orderlies, and they still stick to it that no one left the house this morning. Not that that means much! In this fog I expect he could easily slide out by one of the back staircases without being spotted. But what does sound a bit odd is that one of the sentries swears that he left the house about twelve o'clock last night—said he couldn't sleep or something and was going to take a stroll around—and didn't come back until about an hour and a half later . . .

'That old fool in the hall was sound asleep of course and never heard him either time, but the sentry says he remembers that Dan shut the door behind him "very quiet like" when he came back, so I don't suppose he wanted to advertise his return. Anyway, one thing they all swear to is that he didn't go out a second time, and that bearer of yours— blast him—says he didn't notice whether the Sahib was in his bed or not when he brought the morning tea, because the mosquito nets were down. I'm told that a police guard sleeps at the foot of every outside staircase all night, so Dan couldn't very well have gone out again until daylight without falling over someone. What the *blazes* do you suppose he's up to?'

'Val's just phoning Charles to find if he's down at the Mess,' said Copper: 'the Ross wire has been fixed, thank heaven.'

As she spoke, Valerie came out of the verandah

where she had been telephoning, looking both worried and annoyed: 'No,' she said shortly in reply to Nick's query, 'he's not there. *Or* up at the hospital—or down at the Club either. Of course there's still the barracks and Ronnie Purvis. I couldn't get hold of Ronnie. His man said he was out, and didn't appear to know if anyone else had been to the house or not. Oh dear! as if there wasn't enough fuss and unpleasantness without Dan playing the fool!'

'Dan's no fool,' said Nick curtly, 'and if he isn't here it's because he's got a very good reason for being elsewhere! Either that or the silly ass has fallen over something in this bloody fog. Well, there's only one thing to do and that's round up a search-party: I'm off to co-opt Charles and Hamish and anyone else I can get hold of.'

He swung round and bumped into the Chief Commissioner who had been making for the staircase followed by Leonard Stock and Mr Shilto. '*Blast*—I beg your pardon, sir. I——' He stopped suddenly, checked by the sight of their formal attire.

'Valerie, my dear,' said Sir Lionel, 'we are just off to attend poor Ferrers's funeral. I thought that we should excuse you from coming as it is such a wretched day.'

'Oh,' said Valerie blankly, 'I'd forgotten. No, I don't think Copper and I will go, if you don't mind, Mr Shilto?'

'I? But of course not, Miss Valerie. I know that your sympathy will be with us, and that is as valuable a tribute as your presence.' John Shilto grinned maliciously and passed on down the staircase in the wake of Sir Lionel. But they did not reach the hall.

There was a sudden commotion outside the front door, and a dishevelled, unrecognizable figure thrust past the guard and flung itself up the stairs to stop, panting for breath and clinging to the banisters, before the Chief Commissioner.

It was young Dr Dutt, who had apparently run up the steep path to the house, for his gasping words were unintelligible and he appeared to be labouring under the stress of some violent emotion.

The Chief Commissioner, becoming indignantly aware of the curious faces of the orderlies and servants in the hall below, grasped the young man firmly by the arm and propelled him forcibly up the stairs and into the drawing-room. 'Now,' said Sir Lionel, thrusting him into the nearest armchair, 'take your time, and try to get your breath. Stock, will you please fetch a glass of water?'

Leonard vanished obediently, and the young doctor, acting upon the Chief Commissioner's advice, abandoned his attempts at speech, and concentrated upon regaining his breath.

There was something startling about his appearance as well as his sudden arrival. The slim, dapper, self-satisfied figure of the previous night had disappeared, and in its place sat a frantic-eyed youth with disordered hair and clothing. His shoes and trousers were splashed with the mud of the wet roads, and looking at him Copper experienced a premonition of disaster so violent that for a moment it turned her giddy and sick.

It must have shown in her face, for Nick's hand shot out and caught her wrist. He held it for perhaps the space of four seconds, and then dropped it with a little encouraging shake; and perhaps it was that more than anything within herself that held her steady during the moments that followed. For Dr Dutt had recovered his breath.

He gulped down a few mouthfuls of water and stood up, holding tightly to the back of his chair, and though his voice was still breathless and jerky and his English had become more dislocated than ever, his story, which he insisted in relating in strict sequence, was only too clear . . .

He had, he told them, been able to raise a makeshift coffin for the corpse of Ferrers Shilto, and with four men to carry it had repaired to the Guest House some twenty minutes ago for the purpose of coffining the body. But when they removed it from the trestle table on which it rested, they had discovered to their annoyance that owing to the bulkiness of the tarpaulin which had been sewn about it, the coffin lid could not be made to close. There had been nothing for it but to remove the tarpaulin, and after sending out for a knife to rip out the twine with which it was stitched, they presently uncovered the body . . .

Dr Dutt paused to swallow convulsively and renew his grip upon the chair back, his starting eyes once more visualizing the full horror of that moment.

'Well, go on,' snapped Sir Lionel tartly. 'What was the trouble? Don't tell me he wasn't dead after all!'

Dr Dutt licked his dry lips and his eyes turned slowly to Sir Lionel's, and from there to each face in that silent circle.

'I am warn before I open,' he said, his voice barely more than a harsh whisper: 'My hand—it is wet. And when I look upon it, it is blood. But do I warn? No! I think I am cutting myself on knife. Then the cover is remove, and—and there is not Mr Shilto, but the gentleman who speak to me last night and say, "I also am doctor." And—and he is dead!'

'*God!*' said Nick in a queer whisper. '*Dan—!*'

He swung round and ran from the room, and they heard his feet on the stairs, and then the crash of the front door as it slammed shut behind him.

═══ 13 ═══

'Dan!' said Valerie in a small, choking voice. 'Oh, it isn't true! I don't believe it. It can't *possibly* be true.'

Dr Dutt turned to her almost gratefully: 'That is what I speak to myself. I say: "It is not true. Here is much witchcraft!" But the other fellows they are seeing too. They are very poor, ignorant men, but they say: "Here is not Shilto Sahib, but the young Sahib from the large ship. It is evil magic!" and they are fearful and they run away. Then I myself run here with great speed to tell of this terrible calamity.'

Sir Lionel, who had not moved or spoken, let his breath out in a long sigh and said in a curiously halting voice: 'You are certain of this? That it is Surgeon-Lieutenant Harcourt?'

'How can I mistake? Twice I have seen him!'

'And—and you are sure that he is—dead?'

'Most certainly. He is dead as door-nail. There is no doubt.'

'But *how*?' inquired Leonard Stock shrilly, his stunned face a curious greenish white. He took a stumbling step forward and clutched at the young assistant's arm, shaking it violently: 'It's absurd, man! You must be mistaken! A man can't die and

then go off and sew himself up in sacking afterwards. It doesn't make *sense*!'

'Don't be absurd, Stock!' snapped Sir Lionel. 'Is it
likely he'd sew himself up? Pull yourself together!'

'Then—then you think it is—*murder*?' gasped Mr
Stock in a half-whisper, his eyes flaring with a sud
den stark terror.

'*Murder*? What the devil are you talking about?
Why should it be murder? I imagine that the young
fool went down to take a look at the body last night
and probably stumbled or met with some accident in
the dark, and broke his neck. You know what our
local people are like. Always terrified to report any
accident for fear that they will be held responsible
for it. It's more than likely that a native guard or that
fool of a *chowkidar* found him, and realizing that he
was dead, got into a panic and hit on the idea of
sewing him into Ferrers's piece of canvas in the
hope that he'd be buried without anyone being the
wiser.'

John Shilto gave vent to a sudden bark of laughter: a shocking and unexpected sound. 'It's a good
theory,' he said, 'but it won't wash. Why hide one
body at the expense of landing yourself with the
other?'

'I'm afraid I don't follow you,' said Sir Lionel
stiffly.

Dr Dutt said: 'But Mr Shilto he is right, yes! Two
bodies are not present. There is only Mister Harcourt.'

'*What's that?*' Sir Lionel swung round to face John
Shilto. 'You say that Ferrers's body has been removed?'

'Oh, no I didn't,' contradicted Mr Shilto blandly.
'I merely arrived at the obvious, and apparently correct conclusion, that it has been removed. Harcourt
was a slim man, but in spite of that he was a good

deal larger than my late-lamented cousin, and although the thickness of a tarpaulin shroud might have accounted for the rather larger appearance of the corpse, it could never for a moment have been expected to disguise two corpses as one. And if, as I imagine, the substitution of the bodies was intended to conceal the fact of Harcourt's death, it stands to reason that the previous occupant of the tarpaulin must first have been removed.'

'Do you mean to tell me,' demanded Leonard Stock, his voice shrill and quivering with shock, 'that except for the accident of the coffin lid being unable to close, young Harcourt would have been buried as your cousin and nobody would ever have known?'

'You follow me like a shadow,' grinned John Shilto derisively. 'I mean just that.'

The Chief Commissioner turned on him angrily: 'This is no joking matter, Shilto! We are wasting valuable time. I suggest we go down to the Guest House immediately. And the sooner we get the police on to this, the better.'

Mr Shilto gave another bark of mirthless laughter: 'The police? A fat lot of good they're going to be to us while they're all stranded over on Aberdeen! We haven't a single police official here on Ross; and until this sea goes down, and the jetty is repaired, they have as much hope of reaching us as if we were surrounded by a hundred miles of open sea. What's more, with the telephone line to Aberdeen gone, and this fog, we have no possible means of communicating with them.'

Sir Lionel looked at him with a curiously narrowed gaze. 'Yes, of course,' he said slowly. 'I had forgotten that. I suppose, to a murderer, it would be a useful circumstance.' He turned to Dr Dutt: 'You have not told us yet how Surgeon-Lieutenant Harcourt met his death.'

Dr Dutt's lower jaw dropped noticeably, and he shuffled his feet uncomfortably: 'I—I regret, sir, to have made no note as yet. The man is dead, so I do not pause for examination but come hastily to inform yourself.'

'Then in that case, the sooner we get down to the Guest House and find out, the better!'

The Chief Commissioner turned abruptly to the door, and followed by Mr Shilto, Leonard Stock and Dr Dutt, passed down the hall stairs and out into the fog.

As the sound of their footsteps died away, Copper said in a muffled voice: 'I think . . . I think I'm going to be sick.' Her face and voice fully confirmed this statement, and Valerie, jerking herself out of her own horror-stricken immobility, grabbed her by the arm and rushed her out of the room.

'Feeling better now?' she inquired some ten minutes later.

'Yes,' gasped Copper, rising rather shakily from the bed where she had flung herself after putting her recent threat into execution. 'I can't think why I should behave like this. Idiotic of me. I do apologize.' She walked unsteadily over to the windows, and subsiding on to the broad window-seat unlatched them and flung them wide, letting in a cool drift of mist-laden air.

Valerie left the room, and returned a few minutes later carrying two small glasses: 'Brandy,' she announced. 'I think we'd better try it. It may pull us together.'

Copper accepted a glass and drank the contents with a wry face: '*Ugh*—beastly stuff; it always reminds me of being extremely seasick on the Dover–Calais boat. However, I do feel slightly better. How about you?'

'Oh, I'm all right, but—— Oh, Coppy, isn't it

ghastly! Poor Dan . . . and only last night he was alive, and ——'

'Don't!' said Copper violently. 'If we start thinking of it like that we shall go to pieces and start behaving like Ruby and Rosamund. Don't let's go over it all again: I can't bear it! Let's talk about something else instead. No, of course we can't really do that. But couldn't we try and see if there isn't something we could do about it? Then we could at least think of it as a sort of cold-blooded problem, like a crossword puzzle or a cypher.'

Valerie said: 'We can try, anyway. I'm all for doing something. Let's—let's be really female and start by ordering ourselves a cup of tea.' She rang the bell and gave a brief order to the house-boy who answered it, and as the door closed behind him Copper said abruptly: 'Val, I've got an idea. No one has told Ruby yet, have they? About Dan, I mean?'

'I don't think so. No, of course they haven't. They all went straight from the drawing-room to the Guest House. Why?'

'I thought it might be a good idea if we went along and broke the news, just . . . just to see how she takes it.'

Valerie looked puzzled. 'What are you getting at? She'll only have hysterics again. You know what she's like. And frankly, I don't think I could bear another of her scenes just now. She was doing her alluring best with Dan yesterday, and the minute she hears this she'll be able to convince herself that he adored her, and dramatize herself accordingly.'

'I wonder?' said Copper thoughtfully. 'Val, I've been thinking. She must have been creeping about the house last night. Have you any ideas as to what she was up to?'

'Yes,' said Valerie promptly, 'I think she was probably after——' She stopped abruptly, and flushed.

'—Nick,' finished Copper.

'Well, yes,' admitted Valerie uncomfortably. 'Bitchy of me of course, and I've no evidence. But then she *is* a bit of a man-chaser as well as being very attractive in an opulent Serpent-of-the-Nile sort of way, and frankly, I couldn't see any reason for her to be prowling about the house at night, and without her slippers—you've no idea the fuss she makes about possible scorpions—unless she'd staged an assignation with someone. Sorry!'

'Don't apologize,' said Copper sadly: 'I'm a cat myself where Nick is concerned—a hell-cat, I suppose! I thought the same thing until I remembered that he wasn't the only man in the house.'

'You mean it might have been Dan?'

Copper nodded. 'But that's not what I'm getting at. Listen, Val, suppose we were both wrong and it wasn't anything like that? Suppose she knows something? Heaven knows what and I've no idea why she should know anything. But you must admit it's a little odd that she should be prowling about last night of all nights. She could have heard something!'

'Perhaps,' admitted Valerie after some thought. 'Anyway, it's worth trying even if we *do* have to cope with another bout of hysterics! If there really was any connection between her night prowlings and Dan's, she may give herself away when she hears that he's dead.'

'That's why I'd like to be there to see how she takes the news,' said Copper. 'And if we wait until Leonard gets back he'll get in with it first. So what about it?'

'Right! Come on—let's go now.'

They found Mrs Stock sitting up in bed, attired in the same pink satin garment whose abundant supply of marabou-trimming had betrayed her wanderings on the previous night. She was engaged in applying scarlet lacquer to her finger-nails, and though she appeared placid enough, Copper wondered if her unusual high colour did not owe more to rouge than to the natural bloom of which she was so inordinately proud. If there were dark circles below her eyes they had been carefully disguised with cream and powder, and she certainly did not give the impression of having passed a wakeful night.

She greeted the two girls languidly and then, with more energy, inquired fretfully why she had not been informed earlier that Ferrers Shilto's funeral was to take place that morning? 'Of course, I might have known that Leonard wouldn't tell me. He never tells me *anything*! But I do think, Valerie dear, that you at least might have let me know. Shaken as I feel after that shocking occurrence yesterday, it was my duty to attend—if only out of respect for poor Ferrers.'

'You needn't worry,' said Valerie, 'it's been postponed.'

'What's that?' Mrs Stock sat up quickly, scenting mysteries. 'You don't say so! . . . Oh—' she sank back against the pillows: 'the weather, I suppose. But I expect the fog will clear by lunchtime and they'll have it in the afternoon. I wonder, Valerie dear, if you would send down to my house for my hat-box? I shall need a black hat. The *ciré* straw, perhaps—'

Valerie interrupted firmly. 'I'm afraid the funeral won't be this afternoon either, Ruby. You see, when they went to put Ferrers's body in the coffin, they found that it had disappeared.'

'*Disappeared!* But what—?'

'There was a body there all right. But it wasn't Ferrers's body. It—it was Dan Harcourt's, and he was dead. Someone killed him last night and put him there instead.'

If they had wanted a reaction from Mrs Stock, they got it. But it was an entirely different reaction from the one they had expected, for Ruby neither screamed nor indulged in the emotional hysterics with which she had greeted the appearance of Ferrers's corpse on the previous day. She merely stared at Valerie in appalled silence, while every vestige of colour drained slowly out of her face until it was no longer a face but a grey clay mask, crudely patched with staring blotches of vivid pink rouge and gashed with scarlet lipstick.

She tried to speak, but though for a moment or two her lips moved soundlessly, no words came, and then quite suddenly she toppled sideways in a dead faint. 'Now we've done it!' gasped Valerie. 'For heaven's sake come and help, Coppy. Fetch some water, or brandy, or something!'

'Shove her head over the side of the bed,' suggested Copper anxiously. 'It'll bring the blood back to it.'

This treatment, though crude, proved remarkably effective, and a few moments later Mrs Stock was lying back among her pillows, white and shaken, but once more in full possession of her faculties. In very full possession, it appeared, for she neither wept nor dramatized. She accepted an offer of brandy, and having gulped down a few fiery mouthfuls, lay still for a while; staring fixedly ahead of her as though she were remembering something—and making it fit . . .

She seemed to have forgotten that Valerie and Copper were in the room, but at last her enormous eyes turned to them and her lips twisted into the semblance of a smile. 'You really should be more careful, Valerie dear,' she said huskily. 'My nerves are not strong, and bad news always affects me more than it does other people. Such shocking news, too! If you don't mind, I think I should like to be quite quiet for a little; to give myself a chance to recover. You won't mind?'

'No,' said Valerie awkwardly. 'No, of course not. I'm so sorry. Are you sure you wouldn't like one of us to stay with you? I don't like leaving you like this.'

'I assure you I am perfectly all right,' snapped Mrs Stock with a sudden return of vigour: 'All I need is a little peace and quiet.'

Valerie and Copper, murmuring apologies, backed out thankfully and fled back across the ballroom to the safety of a verandah sofa.

'Well, what do we make of that?' inquired Valerie dropping down among the sofa cushions. 'Have we got anywhere or haven't we? I was scared stiff for a moment: I thought we'd given her a heart attack. Do you really think she knows anything about Dan?'

'No. At least, it's obvious that she didn't know a thing about him being dead. She may be a good actress, but I'm quite sure she isn't as good as all that. It gave her a ghastly shock.'

'It certainly seemed to,' admitted Valerie doubtfully. 'But you're wrong about one thing. I've seen her act in amateur shows, and believe me, she is darned good.'

Copper looked thoughtful: 'You mean the whole thing may have been an act?'

'No—not really. I don't believe even Sarah Bernhardt could have made herself turn that horrid colour. She got a terrific shock all right. But there may have been several reasons for it besides the obvious one. If you ask me, I think that something happened last night that she didn't quite know what to make of, but that the minute she heard our story, it—it made sense.'

'I see,' said Copper slowly. 'And her faint needn't have been a real one, but only to give her time to think and to pull herself together?'

'Well, you saw how quickly she came out of it! And how she flung us out of her room as soon as she could. Believe me, that alone is more than peculiar, because if there is one thing that Ruby enjoys more than another it's an audience, and this sort of thing should have been meat and drink to her. The fact that she didn't want to say or hear anything more about it is reasonably good proof, to anyone who knows her, that she either suspects something or thinks she knows something.'

Copper stared reflectively out into the fog beyond the wet window-panes and bit at the tip of one finger and presently she said: 'You know, there's something we've both rather taken for granted. We've both decided that Dan was murdered. But there may be something in your father's theory about someone finding his body and getting scared stiff of being accused of killing him. After all, who on earth would want to kill Dan?—and why?'

'Perhaps we'll know now,' said Valerie, turning her head to listen: 'Isn't that someone coming up the drive at last?' They heard the front door bang and steps ascending the stairs, and then Charles and Nick came into view and joined them in the verandah just as a *khidmatgar* appeared bearing a laden tea-tray.

'I forgot that we'd ordered tea,' said Valerie. 'Would you two like some, or would you prefer something stronger?'

'I could do with a stiff brandy and soda myself,' said Charles. 'Same for you, Nick?'

Nick, who was looking white and grim, answered with a brief affirmative. He lit himself a cigarette from the box on the writing-table, and Copper, watching him, saw that his hands were shaking. Perhaps he was aware of it himself, for he flicked the match into the ash-tray and thrust his hands into his pockets.

Valerie poured out tea, and a minute or two later a house-servant appeared with brandy and soda.

'I needed that,' said Nick, putting down a half-empty glass. He dropped into an armchair and stared bleakly ahead of him into the dim ballroom beyond the dark, carved head of 'Hindenburg', and Valerie said tensely: 'Tell us what happened.'

Nick finished the contents of his glass before replying, and then said curtly: 'He was murdered, of course.'

He heard Copper draw in her breath in a little hard gasp, and turned towards her, his voice suddenly gentle: 'It's all right, Coppy. He can't have known a thing about it. He was hit on the side of the head, and as far as we can tell, it must have killed him instantly.'

Nick did not think it necessary to add that the killer had also taken other precautions to ensure that his victim should suffer no resurrection this side of the grave. He did not like to think of what had been done to Dan.

Charles said savagely: 'Curse this bloody storm! If only the sea would go down we might be able to do something. But as there isn't a decent doctor, or a single police official in the place, it looks very much as if the bastard who killed him is going to get away with it.'

'Why should you think that?' inquired Copper sharply.

'My dear girl, it's obvious! Dr Vicarjee would have been able to give us a lot of valuable information—as, for instance, how long Dan has been dead. But since poor Dutt is in such a flat spin that it's no good going by anything he says, we haven't much idea when it happened. Then there are fingerprints and footmarks and—oh, probably a whole cartload of clues lying about that would mean something to the police. But by the time anyone from the mainland can land on this damned island the case will be stale. Wind, weather, damp and decay will have successfully wiped out or disguised a dozen possible clues, and the murderer will have had lots of time to think things over and, if he *has* made any mistakes, to see that they are rectified. No, I imagine it's the first few hours that must count most in a murder case, and the hell of it is that there's no one here who can do anything!'

'There are four of us,' said Copper shortly.

'And a hell of a lot of good . . .' Charles broke off and scowled thoughtfully into space for several minutes, and then said slowly: 'At least it would give us something better to do than sitting around twiddling our thumbs and cursing.'

Nick walked over to the window, and staring out into the wall of fog that blotted out the world about them but could not silence the thunder of the sullen sea that kept them prisoners, said bitterly: 'Listen to that! It may not go down for days. So if we've got to wait until it does, and until the jetty is mended, we may just as well fill in the time by playing detectives. If the police were here we should merely be a bloody nuisance to them. But as they aren't, I don't suppose we can do much harm. Or good either, if it comes to that! But it will at least be an improvement on trying to make bright conversation or kicking the furniture. And I only hope,' he added viciously, 'that if we ever manage to get our hands on the bloody-minded bastard who murdered Dan, that the police will keep off Ross for long enough to make him look upon hanging as a merciful release!'

'I'll drink to that,' said Charles and tossed off the contents of his tumbler: '*Omne tulit punctum qui miscuit utile dulci—He has carried every vote who has combined the useful with the pleasing.* And as that is about the only Latin tag I remember, it's just as well it's appropriate. We are with you, Inspector Tarrent. Where do we start?'

'With the sentry, I think. He appears to be the last

person, with the exception of the murderer, to see
Dan alive.'

'Right. And after that I suggest we take another
and closer look at the Guest House and the grounds.
I don't imagine anyone else has done that yet. Val,
you'd better see if you can get anything more out of
the servants, and Copper can make herself useful by
wandering round the house with a magnifying
glass. You never know, there might possibly be a
stray clue lying around.'

'I shouldn't recognize one if I saw it,' said Copper
bleakly. 'But at least it will help pass the time. Come
on, Val. See you two later.'

She put down her untasted cup, shivered, and
walked away down the long, dim verandah.

=== 14 ===

A search of the house failed to produce anything resembling a clue, and after a fruitless half-hour Valerie suggested that they try making notes instead, and arming herself with a writing-block, pencils and a notebook, retired with Copper to a quiet corner of the verandah.

'If we both write down every single thing that's happened during the last two or three days, we may spot something that will give us a lead. It always seems to work in books.'

'Only when there is a private detective with a brain like a buzzsaw to spot the clue,' observed Copper sceptically. 'Where are you going to start? The picnic on Mount Harriet, or the day the *Sapphire* arrived?'

'Neither,' said Valerie. 'I've had a better idea. We'll put down the name of anyone who could possibly have had anything to do with it, and then write under each name anything we can remember of what they have said or done in the past few days and nights. What about that?'

'It sounds a pretty hopeless task,' said Copper doubtfully, 'but I suppose we'd better start somewhere. Are we going to cancel out the idea of it having been done by one of the natives? Because if not, it means making a list of everyone on the island. And that isn't possible.'

Valerie chewed the end of her pencil, and after an interval of frowning thought, said: 'I think we can safely wash out the native population. You see, I've lived here long enough to know something of these people and I'm positive, in my own mind, that unless it was the work of a lunatic no islander would have killed a man with whom he had no quarrel. But when Dan was off the ship he was with us, so we know that he can't have had any trouble with the natives, and no lunatic would ever have substituted Dan's body for Ferrers's—or even *thought* of it!'

'That still leaves the British troops,' said Copper, 'and there are a good many of them.'

'Yes, I'd thought of that. We shall have to get Charles and George and Hamish to question them. But there are only about half a dozen of them here on Ross, because all the rest of them were picnicking out at Corbyn's Cove on Christmas Eve and are stuck in Aberdeen by the storm. And in any case, except for the sentry, none of them would have been out of barracks at that time of night, so I think we can fairly safely wash them out too.'

'But that only leaves *us*!' said Copper, appalled. 'Our party, I mean. Val, it can't *possibly* be one of us. It's too fantastic.'

'Fantastic or not, we may as well try and simplify matters by seeing if we can prove that it *wasn't* one of us. That ought to narrow the field a bit, if nothing else.'

'Oh, all right. Here goes, then. Let's start with Ruby. We've got a lot that we can write under her name.'

'RUBY STOCK,' said Valerie, writing it down in block capitals. 'I'd better give her a couple of pages. John Shilto next. I can't think up anything against him at the moment except that he gives me the shivers. Who else?'

'It's no good working on those lines,' said Copper impatiently. 'We must put everyone down, regardless of whether we've anything against them or not. For all we know, almost anyone may be capable of murder if the provocation is sufficient. And I don't suppose the storm helped!'

'What do you mean by that?'

'Only that we were all a bit on edge before it broke. Don't you remember saying yourself that you felt like an overwound watch-spring? Suppose there was someone else who felt like that, and who reached the breaking-point that you described so graphically? Came sort of morally unstuck——?'

'You mean, went mad?' demanded Valerie.

'Not exactly; except that anyone who killed Dan *must* have been mad. I'm not quite sure what I do mean.'

'Oh, all right, let it go. I suggest we put down all the names in alphabetical order, starting with Amabel.'

Despite the horrors of the morning, the vision of Amabel in the role of a murderess reduced the amateur detectives to hysterical mirth. 'It's awful of us to laugh,' said Copper, dabbing her eyes with the corner of the window curtain, 'but that's done me more good than six brandies-and-sodas. Odd what a stimulant a good girlish giggle can be. Where were we? We've put down Ruby and John Shilto and Amabel. Then there's Ronnie Purvis and Rosamund—something against both of them by the way!—and Leonard Stock, George Beamish, Hamish Rattigan and Dr Dutt.'

Copper reached for the list, and after a moment's deliberation wrote down five more names: Sir Lionel's, Valerie's, Charles's, Nick Tarrent's, and finally, her own.

'Two more,' said Valerie, looking over her shoulder. 'In spite of my recent strictures on locals and troops, I feel that we should add the sentry and Iman Din.'

Copper flung down her pencil. 'Look, if we are going to include people like that we may as well give up at once! It's hopeless. At this rate we may as well suspect the padre.'

'That's an idea,' said Valerie calmly. She picked up the pencil and wrote MRS DOBBIE, MR DOBBIE, TRUDA GIDNEY, and had the pencil removed from her hand by Copper, who added a neat cross underneath the last name.

'What's that for?' demanded Valerie.

'X. "The Unknown Quantity". That's to allow for its having been done by one of the locals for some senseless reason that we would know nothing about.'

Valerie put her hand to her head. 'I shall go mad! Let's drop the whole idea, and try working out Einstein's theory of relativity instead.'

'Cheer up,' comforted Copper. 'I admit it looks pretty hopeless, but that's only because we haven't got anything to go on yet.'

'You're telling me! Let's open a few more windows. I feel that a bit of cold air might clear the brain.'

She flung open the window next to her and leant out across the wet sill, breathing in the thick, mist-laden air. The rain had stopped and the wind had fallen, but the surge of the tide about the grey island still rose like the clamour of an angry mob.

'I wonder why the sea hasn't gone down? It must be the swell from a big storm further south. Sometimes a storm that has missed us by hundreds of miles will send colossal breakers rolling in with hardly a breath of . . . Copper! Quick—come here!'

Copper dropped notebook and pencil and leant out beside her.

'Look!' Valerie pointed to her left where, by leaning out of the window, they could see the corner of the house where Leonard Stock's dressing-room on the first floor jutted out into the mist.

There was a shadowy figure standing against one of the pillars of the ground-floor verandah among the pots of palms and ferns that were massed at the verandah edge: a not unusual sight, since guards, orderlies, *chaprassis* and servants were in more or less constant circulation on ordinary days, though they were less in evidence in wet weather. But it was the attitude of the figure that had attracted Valerie's attention, for it stood pressed against the pillar as though hiding from someone or something beyond the turn of the house. And even as they watched, a police orderly came into view and it dodged round to the far side of the pillar; to reappear after a cautious interval when the man had passed.

A breath of wind thinned the mist for a brief moment, and Valerie caught her breath: '*Ruby!* Come on, Coppy!'

Copper needed no second invitation, and a minute or so later both girls were creeping down the small wooden staircase outside Copper's bathroom and had reached the garden, where they stopped, momentarily at a loss, for Mrs Stock—if the skulking figure among the palm pots had been Mrs Stock—had vanished. '*Damn!*' whispered Valerie. 'What do we—— No, there she is! By the orchid trees . . .' The dim figure showed for a brief second beyond the canna beds, making for the shelter of a group of trees upon whose rough bark Valerie had been attempting to grow orchids: 'We'll have to make a dash for it. Thank God for this fog . . . we may be able to get clear of the house without being spotted by one of the guards.'

Footsteps crunched the gravel as she spoke, and the two girls shrank back under the scanty cover of the stairway. But the orderly passed without seeing them, and a moment later they were across the lawn and safely swallowed up by the mist, and though they had lost sight of the quarry, her trail was plain upon the wet grass: 'Lucky she wears such high heels,' said Copper in a whisper.

The small betraying pits in the soaked ground led them across the back of the tennis courts to where the ground fell away steeply on to the road that encircled the island, and below it, to the rocks and the sea. Nothing grew on the slopes below the garden save a few scattered coconut palms, and the sea-mist was not thick enough to blot out a hurrying figure that showed dimly ahead of them: 'It's Ruby all right,' confirmed Valerie. 'What on earth is she up to? Do you suppose she's making for the hospital by the beach road?'

'What about catching up with her and trying a bit of third degree?' suggested Copper, who favoured direct action. But Valerie shook her head regretfully. 'What's the good? She'd have some story or other: probably that she was taking a walk to calm her nerves. No, we must just stick to her heels and see if we can find out what she's up to.'

Despite the mist, this was not as easy as it sounded, for Mrs Stock was continually stopping to look behind her, and with only the inadequate shelter of a few palm trunks upon the steep slopes, the watchers had a bad time of it. She was obviously making for the narrow roadway that curls round Ross, but when she reached it she did not, as they had confidently expected, turn along it, but crossed it and plunged downwards to the beach. 'Val, you don't think that she—that she did it herself?' gasped

Copper, white-faced. 'She couldn't be going to do something stupid?'

'You mean commit suicide? Not Ruby!' said Valerie scornfully. 'But all the same she's up to something pretty queer. Come on, now's our chance.' She broke into a run, and together they fled down the slope and across the road to where a group of palm trees leant out from its edge, overlooking ground that fell away almost sheer to the rocks and the angry sea.

Once off the road, their quarry had become hidden from anyone above it by the steepness of the slope, but from the shelter of the palm trunks they could see her again, almost directly below them. She was making for the huge, piled rocks that formed a natural breakwater at one end of the little beach upon which the sea had given up Ferrers Shilto the previous evening. And since there was no cover below the road, and she could now no longer move out of their range of vision—unless of course Copper's dark suspicion proved correct!—they flattened themselves against the smooth wet boles of the palm trees by the road's edge and watched her slither down the last few feet of grass and clamber on to the rocks.

The tide was out, and only a breath of wind blew in from the south, stirring but not dispersing the ghostly veils of mist. But the piled rocks were wet and glistening with spray from the huge, smooth-backed rollers that swung in from the misty sea, and Copper shivered as she watched. There seemed to her more menace in the endless, towering advance of that gigantic swell, than in all the shrieking savagery of the gale-hounded seas on the previous evening, but it did not appear to disconcert the shadowy figure on the rocks below.

Mrs Stock, stumbling and slipping on the wet, treacherous surfaces, was making her way to where

the sea engulfed them, and Valerie said suddenly:
'I—I think we'd better shout.' She opened her
mouth to do so, but Copper's fingers clenched about
her arm and checked her, for below them Ruby had
stopped——

She stood upon a flat-topped rock, silhouetted
dimly against the grey seas and the flung spray, and
appeared to fumble at her breast. Then of a sudden
they saw her arm come up and back, and then
quickly forward as she flung some unseen object far
out into the boiling waters beyond the rocks.

A moment later she had turned, and was retracing
her steps.

'This is where we move, I think,' muttered Valerie, and they turned together and fled back up the
steep path to the shelter of the trees beyond the tennis-courts, where they waited, panting, until some
minutes later Mrs Stock hurried past them to pause
behind the orchid trees, and seizing a favourable opportunity, slip across the gap between the trees and
the house and vanish up the back staircase that led
to the tiny landing off which both her bathroom and
Valerie's opened.

The amateur detectives, following her example,
reached their own rooms, damp and breathless but
unobserved, some five minutes later. In which they
were luckier than they knew, for while they had
been making lists of suspects and shadowing Mrs
Stock, the entire population of Ross had been
roused to hunt for the missing body of Ferrers
Shilto, and search-parties had been scouring the island. This at Nick's suggestion; though the majority
of the searchers were convinced that it was a waste
of time.

'Sheer idiocy!' had been John Shilto's verdict.
'Surely it's obvious that whoever wanted to get rid
of the body would simply have dumped it into the
sea? It's probably miles down the coast by now!'

'I disagree,' snapped Nick. 'The sea handed it back once. And quite apart from that, there's something else that you haven't taken into consideration. At what point in this island, with a sea like this running, could a body have been dumped into deep water? The answer is: *None!*'

Here he had been unexpectedly backed up by Leonard Stock. 'You see, sir,' Mr Stock explained apologetically to the Chief Commissioner, 'the jetty has been completely destroyed, and so has the pier.'

'No, I am afraid I don't see,' said the Chief Commissioner shortly. 'Perhaps you would be good enough to explain.'

'Look here,' cut in Nick brusquely, 'you saw the sort of sea that was running last night—and for that matter is still running? Well, add to that the fact that the tide is now out, which means that it turned about seven this morning. Q.E.D., it must have been coming in about the time the killer would have been trying to get rid of the body, since it stands to reason he wouldn't wait until daylight. Well, what's going to happen to anything that you chuck into that sort of sea from anywhere on this damned island? It's going to get thrown back at you inside five seconds! And if you want to prove the truth of that, all you've got to do is to take a walk round Ross and see for yourself . . .

'Had the pier or the jetty been standing, there might have been a chance of weighting the body and pushing it off from the furthest point of either in the hope—not very reliable even then—of the current swinging it clear of the island. But as Stock has just pointed out, there is now no jetty. Therefore the body is still somewhere on this island, and I've a strong hunch that when we find it we'll also find the answer to one or two rather pressing questions!'

'The most pressing being why anyone should

have taken the trouble to switch the corpses,' said Charles thoughtfully. 'If you have to dispose of one body by chucking it into the sea, why not chuck in the chap you have just murdered, instead of going in for all this elaborate substitution business?'

'I imagine a small matter of weight was the main reason,' said Nick: 'Dan can't have been more than four or five inches taller than the original corpse, but he was considerably heftier. Whoever killed him would trust to luck that Dutt and his helpers, lifting that bundle of tarpaulin from the table, would not notice that fact. But the extra two or three stone of dead weight would have made a hell of a lot of difference to anyone hauling the body single-handed down to the shore. And there's another thing——

'Once Dan was safely buried as Ferrers, if Ferrers's body had ever happened to turn up again, it would almost certainly be unrecognizable and would be written off as the corpse of some unknown chap off a passing ship. Whereas if Dan's body had turned up, however much damage the fishes had done it might still have been obvious to an expert that far from having been accidentally drowned, he had been deliberately and nastily murdered! I can clearly see why the bodies were exchanged. And I am also prepared to bet that the original corpse is still somewhere on this island!'

The Chief Commissioner had been forced to admit the common sense of these statements, and fifteen minutes later the hunt had been organized and was in full cry.

Copper and Valerie, returning from shadowing Mrs Stock, had missed running into a section of the search-party by a narrow margin.

=== 15 ===

The two girls had lunched alone, for the Commissioner had sent word that he, Nick, Stock and John Shilto would be having something to eat at the Mess.

Mrs Stock had had a tray sent in to her room, and shortly after half past one Sir Lionel had returned to the house, where he had held an informal inquiry into the morning's proceedings. Copper and Valerie had not been required to attend, and they had sat in uneasy silence in the verandah above, listening anxiously to the murmur of voices while the slow minutes crawled past and the fog pressed against the window-panes and crept into the quiet house.

At long last the office door had opened, and they heard Leonard Stock's voice in the hall below, anxious and protesting: 'I feel sure there must be some mistake. Perhaps when Dr Vicarjee is back his verdict will be—will be different . . .'

'There is *no* difference, I am telling you!'—Dutt's voice, shrill and indignant——'All the facts they are plain. As plain as pike-staffs! It is murder! Miss Gidney, she is agreeing too. You will ask her, please. If it is as you say, that the man he is drowned, then there will be water in his lungs. But there is not water. None. It is murder!'

Valerie got up suddenly and ran to call down over

the banisters: 'Leonard—what *is* all this? Who are you all talking about? What's happened?'

'Oh . . . er . . . ah——' The question appeared to have taken Mr Stock by surprise. 'I did not realize that you were there. Perhaps I should not have said—that is——' Dr Dutt's agitated voice cut hurriedly across Leonard's stammered incoherencies: 'You will excuse, please. I go now. There is much work.' The front door banged behind him, and after a moment or two there was a sound of reluctant footsteps ascending the staircase, and Leonard Stock came into view.

He smiled nervously at Copper, and having directed a hunted look at Valerie, observed hopefully that it was still very foggy and that he had never known such unseasonable weather: 'Almost chilly, is it not? In all my years in the Islands, and I think I can safely say that I am the oldest inhabitant . . . well, hardly *inhabitant*, I suppose; after all, there must be people here who . . . what I mean is I really do not think that I can recall such freakish weather . . . there is no other word for it. I——'

Here Valerie, who had no intention of being sidetracked on to a discussion of the weather, cut through Mr Stock's nervous spate of words as unceremoniously as Dr Dutt had done: 'Who were you talking about just now, Leonard? Who wasn't drowned?'

'Well . . . er . . . um . . . Ferrers,' said Leonard unhappily, and cleared his throat with a small embarrassed cough.

'*Ferrers!*' Valerie's white face seemed to turn whiter. 'But that's nonsense! Of course he was drowned. Why we all saw him, and—*Leonard!* . . . Have they found him?'

'Er—yes. I'm afraid so. I mean—— Well, Dutt and Miss Gidney have performed some sort of an—er—an autopsy, and Dutt has advanced the theory that

Ferrers too—was er—was in fact—er—um——'
Leonard's thin bony hands sketched a fluttering
futile gesture and Copper caught her breath and
said huskily: 'Murdered!'

Leonard turned towards her with an expression of
relief: 'Yes. Yes, that is what it amounts to. But Dutt
must have made a mistake. He is—um—not a very
efficient young man as—er—yet. Perhaps when he
has had more experience . . . But I feel sure that
once the sea has gone down and the jetty has been
repaired and—and Dr Vicarjee has been able to return, we shall find that it is all a—um—a mare's
nest. It has to be. Anything else is unthinkable.
After all, who would want to murder Ferrers?'

'John!' said Copper before she could stop herself.
And was instantly appalled at what she had said.

Leonard Stock appeared equally horrified. His
nervous, over-bright eyes widened in dismay and he
threw a quick, frightened glance over his shoulder
in the direction of the staircase and the hall below.
'*Ssh*! He might hear you! No, no *really*, Miss Randal,
you should not—what I mean is——' Leonard became entangled once more in a maze of half-
sentences, and Copper said ruefully: 'I'm sorry. It
was a beastly thing to say and I didn't really mean
it. But I couldn't help remembering that scene at the
Mount Harriet picnic.'

'Oh, I know; I quite see. And you will have heard,
of course, that they did not get on at all well—the
Shiltos, I mean. But *fratricide*! Or—or what amounts
to it. Oh no! . . . unthinkable. You may be quite
sure, as I am, that poor Dutt has made a mistake.
When Dr Vicarjee returns we shall discover that Ferrers was drowned after all, and then everything will
be all right.'

'All *right*?' repeated Valerie, looking at him with a
mixture of amazement and contempt. 'How can it be
all right when Dan—— Oh, it's all awful and horri-

ble and unbelievable! It doesn't seem *possible* that any of it can really have happened.'

'Yes, yes,' agreed Mr Stock earnestly. 'Terrible. Quite terrible! I do feel for you. Such a very unpleasant shock. I shall not enjoy having to break it to poor Ruby. I have not yet dared—er—I mean, I did not like—— Well, the truth is that poor Ruby is particularly sensitive to—er—shock. Her nerves, you know. But I suppose she will have to know sometime. There is no point in putting it off. And yet I must own——'

Valerie said quickly: 'You don't have to worry, Leonard. She knows. I told her myself.'

Some of the nervous tension seemed to leave Leonard's meagre body and he relaxed visibly. 'Oh. Then I need not—um . . . I do hope she was not too upset?'

'I'm afraid she was, rather.'

'Oh. Oh dear. Then I suppose I had better go and see how she is. She will have been expecting me, but I really could not get away before. There were so many things . . . and then your father . . .' His voice trailed away and stopped, and Valerie said encouragingly: 'No, of course you couldn't get away. Ruby will realize that. It's been a horrible day for everybody.'

Leonard smiled wanly, and bracing his thin shoulders, turned and went away across the dim expanse of the ballroom, his shoes squeaking dolefully on the polished boards, and presently they heard him tapping nervously on his wife's door. It opened and closed again, and Valerie said: 'Poor Leonard! I'm afraid he's in for a bad half-hour. And what'll you bet that before dear Ruby is through with him she'll have managed to make out that it's all his fault and that he is personally responsible for the whole thing, and Leonard, poor toadstool, will be apologizing for it. I can't think how he stands it.'

But Copper was not interested in Leonard Stock's matrimonial troubles, and she had not been thinking of him. Only of what he had said. She spoke in a half-whisper, as though she were addressing herself rather than Valerie: '*Murder!*—— He said that Ferrers was murdered too. Then that was why! Dan must have known . . .' She shivered suddenly and violently; and once again a door banged in the hall below and there was a sound of footsteps on the stairs. But this time it was Charles and Nick: Charles for once grave and unsmiling, and Nick looking drawn and grim and exhausted.

Charles said briefly, cutting short Valerie's anxious questions: 'We can't talk here. We'd better all go down to the Mess.' And turning abruptly on his heel he led the way back to the hall and out into the clammy embrace of a fog that seemed to grow thicker by the minute.

Mist filled the long, tree-shaded drive with a dense shifting greyness that smelt as dank as a sea cave uncovered by a spring tide, and when at last the Mess loomed out of it as a dark, dimly seen shape and Charles pushed open the front door, the fog came in with them and eddied about the silent hall.

Charles's quarters, which lay on the far side of the ante-room, consisted of a small bathroom and a large, white-washed and somewhat untidy bed-sitting room decorated with several photographs of Valerie, some depressing school and regimental groups and a clutter of golf clubs and fishing-tackle. 'Hardly the Ritz,' said Charles, ushering in his guests, 'but at least it's reasonably private. And there are quite a few things that have come up for discussion.' He closed the door behind him, and Nick sat down and said tiredly and without preamble: 'We found Ferrers's body, and Dutt says that he was murdered.'

'I know,' said Valerie with a shudder. 'Leonard told us. But he seems to think that Dutt must have made a mistake.'

Nick shook his head. 'Not a chance, I'm afraid. We've been checking back over that half hour in the bay in some detail, and one thing is quite clear: Ferrers Shilto survived the overturning of the boats. I can swear to that myself, because I caught sight of him clinging to the keel of one that bumped into ours, and there was nothing much the matter with him then. But sometime just after that—or it may have been any time during the half hour that we were all in the drink—someone smashed in the back of his head.'

Copper gave a swiftly suppressed exclamation, and Nick turned his head sharply towards her. 'What is it, Coppy?'

'Nothing,' said Copper hastily. 'I only wondered—I mean, how could anyone tell it was murder—a blow on the back of the head? It sounds as if it could easily have happened by accident.'

'This particular blow,' said Nick grimly, 'was given with the end of a tiller. The tillers on those boats are the kind that have a metal-bound slot at one end that fits over the top of the rudder, and the wound on the back of Ferrers's head was made by someone holding the handle of a tiller and hitting him damned hard with the slotted end. There's no mistake about that; the imprint is quite clear. It wasn't spotted before because his hair hid the mark and the blood had been washed off by the sea.'

'But I still don't see why it couldn't——' began Copper.

'Listen, sweetheart,' interrupted Charles briskly, 'the end of the tiller that killed Ferrers is usually attached to the rudder. Therefore it could only have come in contact with his skull once it had come unshipped. If it had been floating round loose and a wave had knocked it against his head, the very most it could have done would have been to leave a bit of a bruise. Instead of which it hit him with enough force to smash in his skull, and also produced a hell of a bruise—and a lot of swelling, which apart from anything else, appears to prove that it was done before and not after death. Now perhaps we can go on? . . . Good! Nick, I think we'd better have a bit of recapping from you. Just to get the record straight.'

'All right.' Nick leant back in his chair and frowned at the ceiling as though arranging his thoughts, and presently he said slowly: 'On Christmas Day—that is, yesterday—we went for a walk round the island at about five o'clock, and very unfortunately for the murderer, Ferrers's body turned up. Even more unfortunately for him, it had escaped being mutilated by fish or reefs, and Dan, who was a doctor, was on the spot. We don't know enough to do more than guess at this bit, but it's pretty obvious that something made Dan suspect that Ferrers had not died by drowning . . . And if I hadn't been a triple-distilled idiot,' added Nick with sudden bitterness, 'I'd have realized that he suspected it from his subsequent behaviour.'

'That applies to all of us,' said Copper quickly.

Nick threw her the ghost of a grin and stubbed out his half-smoked cigarette, grinding it down in the ash-tray with a viciousness that betrayed the state of his nerves. He lit another, and said: 'Dan apparently saw enough on the beach yesterday evening to make him suspect that this wasn't a plain case of drowning, and I can only suppose that he didn't say anything then and there because it wasn't his job to cut in on the local medico. But of course it's quite obvious that that young ass of an assistant is as much use as a sick headache, and could barely be trusted to tell the difference between scarlet fever and heat rash. I gather he barely looked at Ferrers's body other than to see it shoved into the Guest House and sewn up in canvas. And I suppose one can hardly blame him. After all, in justice to young Dutt, it seemed a perfectly clear case to all of us!— except to Dan, who as far as we can make out must have slipped down to the Guest House late last night to take another look at the corpse. And here we stop guessing for a bit and come to the sentry's evidence. Charles can tell you about that. The sentry was one of his chaps and he did most of the talking.'

Charles leant an elbow on the shelf above the fire-place and took up the tale: 'Weekes, the chap on sentry duty, says that Dan came out of the house just before midnight last night. It was raining a bit and he was wearing one of the orderlies' mackintosh capes: they found a smear of blood on it . . .' Charles's voice was suddenly uncertain, and he jerked his shoulders uncomfortably and hurried on: 'The sentry challenged him, and Dan said he couldn't sleep and was going to take a stroll, gave the chap a packet of cigarettes, and pushed off. That sounds all right as far as it goes, but here comes the rub: Weekes swears blind that Dan returned about an hour and a half later, nodded to him, popped into the house and bolted the door behind him. He says he heard the hall clock strike half past one immediately afterwards. Now if he is right, how did Dan get out again, and why?'

'Obvious,' said Copper briefly. 'It wasn't Dan.'

'Don't talk tripe, Coppy. The sentry swears——'

'I don't care *what* the sentry swears! It's so obvious, it simply *screams* at you! You said Dan was wearing one of the orderlies' capes. Well, they have a big hood that goes right over your head and——'

Nick said: 'Charles, you and I should see a brain specialist. Of course that's it! Dan goes down to the Guest House to take a look at the body, and while he's there he's caught at it and murdered. We know that he was killed there, for there were stains on the floor that had been wiped up; but not quite well enough. The murderer substitutes Dan's body for Ferrers's, takes Ferrers's body off and hides it, and having cleared away all traces of his dirty work puts on the mackintosh cape, and with the hood pulled well over his head, walks calmly back to the house.'

Charles said: 'I ought to have a nurse. Of course. It is, as my grandmother's cook used to say, "As plain as the nose on me face".'

'And,' pointed out Copper, 'I notice that the sentry didn't say that Dan actually spoke to him when he came back.'

'That's right,' said Charles. 'He didn't speak. And I don't know if it has struck anyone else, but it seems to me to point to two things. The first being that whoever returned to the house inside that mackintosh was not only the murderer, but someone who must have watched Dan leave and listened to his conversation with the sentry. Otherwise how did he know that he could return to the house without being challenged?'

'But—' Valerie's voice shook—'but that would mean that the murderer was someone in the house!' In spite of her recent suspicions concerning Mrs Stock, the idea that a double murderer might actually be a member of the household was incredibly and horribly shocking. 'Not necessarily,' said Nick. 'It would have been obvious to anyone that to get to the Guest House Dan must have passed the sentry. Therefore it was a fair gamble that the sentry would pass him in again without comment.'

'But Nick—if it wasn't someone from the house, why should they come back again?'

'Alibi,' said Nick shortly. 'Muddy the trail. And a very sound idea too, because if Dan had failed to come back, it's quite on the cards that the sentry would have become uneasy and reported the fact sometime last night. There would probably have been a search within an hour or two of the murder, and then heaven knows what might not have come to light. So Dan *has* to return, because with luck Ferrers will have been buried before any serious attention is given to the fact that he is missing.'

Valerie said unhappily: 'I do hope to goodness you're right. It would be too awful if it had to be someone in the house. But . . .'

'Of course I'm right. That's the hell of it. It widens the field too much. If we could only be certain that the man who impersonated Dan did *not* get out of the house again, we'd be able to narrow down our list of suspects considerably. As it is, the only solid fact that we seem to have got out of all this is that Dan died sometime between midnight and one o'clock. And I'm not sure that that's much help.'

'Yes, it is,' said Charles. 'Because it adds a bit of support to your theory that the chap who came home at one-thirty got out again.'

'How do you make that out?'

'Well, it's really all a matter of timing, isn't it? Dan leaves the house about midnight, chats to the sentry, and shoves off to the Guest House—say at five minutes to twelve. Allow a good few minutes for getting down there, and more for finding a way in— and by the way we found a ground-floor window with a broken catch so presumably he got in by that. We can't tell whether he had time to take a look at Ferrers, or if he was murdered before he had the chance. But I imagine he couldn't have been killed much before twelve-thirty: which gives the murderer just about an hour in which to kill Dan, swop his body with Ferrers's, sew it up again in the tarpaulin, hide Ferrers's body, clear up the blood on the floor and get back to the house again. Can't be done!'

'Why not?' inquired Copper. 'If he worked quickly, surely it's perfectly possible?'

'Possible. But damned unlikely! Nick didn't tell you where we found Ferrers's body. I'm afraid this is going to put you off the soup at the next Guildhall banquet you are invited to attend, but as a matter of fact it was found very cunningly stowed away in the turtle tank.'

'*Ugh!*' said Valerie, shuddering. 'What a place to hide it in. Of course it would float and anyone looking in would have seen it.'

'You're wrong there,' said Charles. 'It was, in fact, very neatly done. And if it hadn't been for the—er—unusual behaviour of the turtles, it might not have been spotted for days. You know that summer-house thing that is built out over the top of half the tank?'

'Of course.'

'Well, the body had been carried round the outer wall of the tank on the seaward side of the summer-house, and lowered into the darkest corner of the tank behind the pillar that supports the floor. It was hanging there by a rope that had been tied under its arms and then fastened to the crossbeams. An ingenious job which must have taken quite a bit of doing in the dark.'

'For goodness sake, why there?' asked Copper breathlessly. 'Of all silly places!'

'Not so silly,' said Nick dryly. 'It would have been a damned good hiding-place if it hadn't been for the turtles, because since it's right on the bay, the minute the sea went down all the killer had to do was to get there after dark, haul up the body, tie a weight to it and push it off the end of the Club breakwater at the turn of the tide. As for Dan, who would not have been seriously missed or searched for until after the funeral, he would be presumed to have taken a toss in the mist and fallen into the sea.'

'Then what we've really got to find out,' said Copper slowly, 'is not who killed Dan, but who killed Ferrers. And then we've got the answer to both.'

'That's about it. The reason for Dan's murder is obvious: he was killed because he discovered, or suspected, that Ferrers had been murdered. What we need now is a motive for the killing of Ferrers.'

'Mount Harriet!' said three voices simultaneously.

'You mean that conversation we overheard at the picnic? Yes: I think that's fairly obvious. So I suggest our first suspect goes down as Mr John Shilto.'

Valerie said: 'Listen, Nick—I don't know about you, but I shall soon be getting hopelessly muddled. This morning Coppy and I decided that we must have some method in our madness, so we made a list of possible suspects so that we could enter up everything "for" or "against" each person. Let's stick to it.'

'Good scheme,' approved Charles. 'Produce your suspects.' Copper handed over the list that they had compiled earlier in the day, and Nick and Charles read it with some amusement. 'Can't you see Amabel spreading death and destruction with a tiller?' grinned Charles.

'The same thought gave us the one laugh of a mildewed morning,' admitted Valerie. 'But Copper said there was no use making a list of suspects unless we put down everyone and then started eliminating by proof to narrow it down.'

Nick said: 'Copper is right. When it comes to murder you can't start by saying, "I'm sure so-and-so can't have done it, he's got such a stupid face," or "Of course she didn't do it! she's got such an angelic disposition." You've got to suspect everyone.'

'We have,' admitted Copper frankly. 'You'll find your own name on the list.'

Nick gave a short and rather bitter laugh. 'Well, why not? You don't really know much about me, do you?'

'No,' said Copper in an oddly uncertain voice: 'That's why I put your name down.'

Nick swung round to face her, his eyes suddenly narrow and angry, but she would not meet his gaze, and after a moment he turned his attention to the notebook in his hand. 'Fortunately,' he stated curtly, 'in spite of Copper's theories we can cut this list down by half. Pencil please, Charles.'

'Why?' inquired Copper indignantly as Charles reached for a pencil from his writing-desk and tossed it across.

'Because, my dear girl,' said Nick acidly, 'we have already decided that although there were two murders, there is only one murderer. Therefore, as Ferrers was killed during the time that the sailing party spent in the water on Christmas Eve, it stands to reason that only a member of that party could have done it. Which brings the suspects down by half. We can now eliminate you, Valerie, Charles and the Commissioner as a start. Amabel and George are out of it too, and the padre and Mrs Dobbie and the sentry. Also "X". The "unknown quantity" I presume, Copper?'

'Yes,' said Copper defensively: 'I thought it might have been one of the natives. But there were none on the boats, of course.'

'That still leaves us with a pretty large list of suspects,' said Valerie despondently.

Charles said: 'Only five. That's a lot better than fifteen!'

'Five?' Valerie rose from the bed and went to lean over Nick's shoulder: 'You mean seven!'

'Look, darling,' began Charles patiently, 'we've already agreed that the man who masqueraded as Dan last night was the murderer, and if so——'

'What makes you so sure it was a man?' cut in Valerie quickly.

'My dear Val!'

'She's quite right,' said Copper. 'We can't be sure. It could just as easily have been a woman. Those capes come down well below the knee, and they're so bulky that you couldn't be certain of the size—or the height!—of anybody wearing one, because the peaked hood would give an impression of height. And anyway I'll bet the sentry barely looked at the person who passed. He would have been so sure it was Dan that his eye would have been blind to details.'

Nick said: 'They're right, of course, Charles. We can't rule out the possibility of its having been a woman.'

'Have it your own way,' said Charles. 'Keep 'em on the list. But as it's half past four and I need refreshment, I propose to call a short interval. Or do I mean "adjourn the court"? Val darling, phone your father that you and Copper will be out to tea: then we can carry on these bloodcurdling discussions after we have fortified the inner man.'

He tucked her hand under his arm and they went out to organize tea and telephone Government House.

═══ 16 ═══

There was a brief interval of curiously strained silence after they had left the room, and then Nick said pleasantly: 'So you think my name should be included among the suspects, do you, Copper? May I ask why?'

'Certainly you may,' replied Copper lightly. 'Always providing you don't expect an answer.'

A spark leapt to life in Nick's grey eyes for a swift unreadable moment, and then he laughed and lay back in his chair. 'Take it that I'd merely appreciate one, then. Do I get it?'

Copper considered him for a long moment. His dark hair was unusually smooth and the eyes that held hers were once again narrowed and lazy. But she saw too, and with a tremor of disquiet, that in spite of his indolent posture and the suggestion of a smile that curved his mouth, there was something about him—some tenseness of line—that suggested wariness.

'I've already told you why,' said Copper defensively. 'Until we can eliminate by proof, we must include everyone.'

Nick said very softly: 'But that isn't what you meant in my case, is it, Copper?'

'No,' said Copper after a moment, in an oddly

brittle voice: 'No. You were right when you said we didn't know anything about you. We don't.'

'And therefore I am probably capable of murder?' suggested Nick ironically. 'Very instructive!'

Copper stiffened and her eyes were suddenly both reckless and angry. 'Do you want me to go on?' she inquired crisply.

'Of course. I'm all for hearing your candid opinion of me.'

'It's not a question,' said Copper coldly, 'of my opinion of you, candid or otherwise. I thought we had already decided—I think you were the one to point it out?—that the murderer of Ferrers Shilto and Dan must be one of seven people. And as you are one of those seven I had supposed, from your question, that you'd like a disinterested opinion on the possibility of suspicion resting on you. Apparently you don't.'

'I accept the correction,' said Nick gravely. 'I shall be more than grateful for a—disinterested opinion.'

Copper got up abruptly, and moving to the window stood looking out into the mist with her back to him and her fingers playing restlessly with the window-latch. The slow seconds ticked away to the tune of the fog-dew dripping from the roof-edge outside, and at last, and without turning, she said in a deliberately cool and conversational voice: 'You were the only one who knew Dan Harcourt before he came to the Islands, and for all we know there may have been some quarrel between you that we know nothing about. They—the police—will think of that. You may have had a dozen reasons for hating Dan.'

'Thanks,' said Nick, without sarcasm. 'You are right. It's just as well to get a "disinterested" opinion' (once again he stressed the word slightly) 'on how people are likely to regard one when it's a case of looking for a murderer. Go on.'

Copper said haltingly: 'I know it sounds rude and—and beastly, but I thought you'd better see—'

'Oh, don't apologize!' interrupted Nick. 'It's very interesting. What about Ferrers? Where does he fit into my murderous schemes?' Copper turned abruptly to face him. The knuckles of her clenched hands showed white and her voice had a defiant edge to it: 'I have no idea—'

'You surprise me!' murmured Nick.

'—why you should murder a man whom you had only met that day. But then it is always possible that you had met him before. Say about a month ago?'

'Meaning what?' inquired Nick softly.

'Meaning . . . just that!'

Copper turned away again and stared blindly out at the drifting mist. Her anger had vanished as suddenly as it had come, but something else had taken its place: an indefinable and disquieting tension. And when at last she spoke, it was without turning her head, and in a voice so low as to be barely audible: 'Ferrers Shilto,' said Copper, 'used to go to Calcutta on business once a year, travelling on the *Maharaja*. I know when he was last there, because he was on board with me when I arrived here. And I know that he had stayed at the Grand Hotel because I saw the labels on his luggage; you couldn't miss them. I know, too, that during the time he was there the *Sapphire* was on a visit to Calcutta, and you told me yourself that you had stayed—' Her voice failed her and she turned stiffly to face him.

Nick was sitting quite still. A faint curl of smoke drifted from the cigarette between his fingers, but there was no other movement in the quiet room, and Copper saw with a tightening of the heart that a

queer little change had come over his face. It was so
slight as to be barely perceptible—yet it was there.
He had made no motion of surprise or denial, but
the lines of his mouth had become fixed and his
grey eyes coldly angry, and presently he said:
'Thank you for defining my position so clearly. Perhaps you'd like to know that your surmise is correct.
I did meet Ferrers Shilto in Calcutta.'

He made no attempt to qualify that terse statement, and Copper drew her breath in a small, hard
gasp, and feeling her knees suddenly go weak, sat
down abruptly on the end of Charles's bed.

Nick came to his feet in one swift unexpected
movement, and crossing the space between them in
two strides, caught her by the shoulders and jerked
her to her feet. She made an instinctive movement
to wrench herself away, but the grip of his hard fingers on her shoulders held her rigid, and she abandoned the attempt to free herself as useless and
undignified.

Releasing his hold on one shoulder he caught her
chin in his free hand, and jerking her head up to
meet his gaze, laughed down at her small startled
face and wide apprehensive eyes. 'I should never
have given you credit for such a vivid and unpleasant imagination, darling. Seriously, do you think
that I may have done it?' His voice sharpened suddenly: '*Answer me, Copper!*'

'It isn't a question of what I think,' said Copper
stiffly. 'I have only pointed out that you *could* have
done it.'

The fingers about her chin tightened convulsively,
but he said coolly enough: 'You haven't answered
my question.'

Copper's lips closed in a stubborn line and she
stared at him in silence, suddenly as angry as he
was. A minute ticked by. Sixty seconds that seemed

as long as an hour—or a day. Then, 'That's all I wanted to know,' said Nick dryly. 'So you think I might even be a murderer, do you, Copper? Well, has it occurred to you yet that if I were capable of committing two murders, I might be equally capable of committing a third? After all, you appear to be the only one who has spotted any connection between myself and Ferrers Shilto.'

The warm strong fingers about her chin relaxed their grip and slid downwards to close gently about her throat, but Copper did not move. She stood as though frozen between anger and fear. A fear that held no considerations for her own safety, but was nonetheless real for that.

It was, of course, absurd to think of Nick in connection with murder, and it would be a mis-statement to say that she had dismissed the idea. It being impossible to dismiss an idea that has never for a moment been entertained. But it had occurred to her that the authorities might well consider Nick as a possible suspect, and her imagination, stimulated by anxiety for him, had instantly presented her with several uncomfortable lines of thought: including an unfortunate recollection of his late sojourn in Calcutta. She had blurted out the results of her anxious meditations from a vague feeling that she must warn him that he might be regarded with suspicion, and she had expected him to laugh at her. But he had not laughed. He had merely been angry. Couldn't he *see* . . . ?

The fingers about her throat tightened steadily, and suddenly Copper became aware of the blood drumming in her ears. She opened her mouth to cry out, but found that she could make no sound. And in the next instant Nick bent his head and kissed her parted lips, long and deliberately.

A moment later the door was flung open behind

them and Charles's voice said: 'What on earth are you two waiting for? A gong? Come along and have some tea. Val's made enough toast for sixty.'

Nick's hand dropped to his side, and Copper stepped back—both hands to her throat and her heart beating jerkily.

Nick swung round with a laugh: 'As usual, Charles, you arrive in the nick of time—no pun intended. I was about to commit my third murder.'·

'Don't let me stop you,' said Charles.

'Copper here,' explained Nick lightly, 'has just been proving, with a wealth of damnatory detail, that I could easily be the local murderer. What are you going to do about it, Charles?'

'Nothing!' said Charles firmly. 'I'm sorry, Coppy: you're probably dead right, but as he is a good deal larger than I am, I shall prudently ignore it and . . .' He stepped back hurriedly as Copper brushed past him into the ante-room, her chin high and her cheeks scarlet.

'Hullo!' said Charles, recovering his balance and disentangling his feet from among a collection of carelessly placed fishing-tackle. 'The lady seems annoyed. Have I put a foot into it somewhere?'

'Both, I imagine,' said Nick with unexpected bitterness. 'And practically everywhere. Copper's dead serious about this question of my having committed the local crimes. She almost convinced *me*!' He laughed shortly, and Charles echoed the laugh; and then remembering Copper's face as she had passed him, stopped laughing and frowned. 'Do you mean to say,' he demanded incredulously, 'that you think Copper thinks——? Of all the unmitigated drivel! Why, the girl thinks you're—— *Ahem!*'

Charles pulled up abruptly on the brink of betraying certain strictly private confidences imparted to him by Valerie, and Nick said curiously: 'Thinks I'm what?'

'Oh, er—I forget. But if you ask me, she's merely been trying to take the mickey out of you. You oughtn't to buy it. Come and have some tea: Val's collected enough to feed a school treat.'

They ate toast and Christmas cake in the ante-room of the Mess, and afterwards, when the cups and plates had been cleared away, Valerie wrote steadily in the notebook and was presently able to announce that she had put down a rough outline of the happenings of the last two days, and that it was time they got back to work. 'Where were we?' inquired Charles.

'Narrowing down the suspects. And now I suggest that we give each of the seven members of the sailing party a page apiece and put down any evidence we can think of, for or against, under each name. Here they are: JOHN SHILTO, RONNIE PURVIS, LEONARD STOCK, HAMISH RATTIGAN, ROSAMUND PURVIS, RUBY STOCK and NICHOLAS TARRENT. And I should think we could cross off at least three of those straight away, wouldn't you?'

Nick said curtly: 'No, don't cut any of them. Who was the first on the list? John Shilto, wasn't it? Well, what have we got against him?'

'Easy!' said three voices.

'All right. One at a time. Come on, Copper. You'd make the best counsel for the prosecution.'

'I've already prosecuted one case this afternoon,' said Copper coldly. 'Charles can take this one.'

'Right,' said Charles, nothing loth. He lifted his tea cup: 'Here's to logic; never sell her short! To begin with, John doesn't—I mean didn't—hit it off with Ferrers. Everyone in the Islands knows that. However, coming down to more concrete evidence, we all overheard a couple of pretty crisp scenes between them on the day of the Harriet picnic, so I think that can go down on his charge-sheet as a start.'

'That's all very well,' said Valerie, scribbling hard, 'but was it enough of a scene to make John want to murder Ferrers?'

'Judging from what I know of John Shilto, easily! But whether it was enough to make him actually *do* the deed is another matter.'

'Yes, it would help a lot if we knew what was behind that row at Mount Harriet.'

Copper said: 'I think I've got an idea.'

'Another one?' murmured Nick, lifting an eyebrow.

'Yes!' snapped Copper dangerously. 'Another one. Any objection?'

'None at all. I was merely expressing admiration.'

Valerie glanced up sharply from the notebook on her lap and looked inquiringly from Copper's face to Nick's. Her brows drew together in a puzzled frown and she said quickly: 'What's your idea, Coppy?'

Copper jerked her gaze angrily away from Nick's mocking eyes, and collecting her thoughts with an effort, said: 'You remember how anxious Mr Shilto was that we shouldn't stop at his cousin's bungalow for water, and how furious he was when he heard that the Dobbies had taken Ferrers on to the picnic?'

'Do we not!' said Charles. 'Said he wasn't going on with us if Ferrers was going to be there, and after making a fatuous fuss about it, suddenly changed his mind and came with us after all.'

'That's just it,' said Copper. 'It was too sudden. And I don't believe for one minute that any change of heart or Christmas spirit was responsible for it. I believe he must have seen something or heard something that made him change his mind about coming.'

'Such as what?' said Valerie.

'I don't know. But he might have seen that the plantation was doing very much better than he had ever imagined it could, and realized that his cousin was on the verge of making it pay at last.'

'And decided to stage a big reconciliation scene and buy it back before Ferrers realized that it was on the upgrade? Yes, I suppose there's something in that. Did he go into the house, Charles?'

Charles considered the point and shook his head. 'I don't think so. He strolled around a bit at the back, but as I thought he wasn't coming with us, I left him to it. And anyway the place smelt like a sewer, so I didn't linger.'

'Oh well, it's a sound idea, Copper. Has anyone else got any more theories on the subject of Public Suspect Number One?'

'I have,' said Valerie. 'You can call it feminine intuition if you like, because I've got no proof. But I'm prepared to bet my entire allowance for the next two years, against Amabel's bridge winnings, that John was delighted about Ferrers's death. He's been going about in a sort of nasty gloating trance ever since.'

'And I'll endorse that,' said Copper.

Charles sighed. 'Righto,' he said. 'Enter two dollops of feminine intuition on the debit side. Anything more? . . . No? All right, account closed for the moment. Nick will please sum up.'

Nick lay back in his chair and stared meditatively at the ceiling again, and presently he said: 'Will this do? Points against John Shilto. One: he had a long-standing quarrel with his cousin, which culminates in a hell of a row a few hours before the murder.

Two: he could easily have murdered Ferrers during the storm. (Against that one, so could any of the other six suspects.) Then, if he *was* the murderer, he would instantly have spotted Dan's unhealthy interest in the corpse, and a guilty conscience would have given him the clue to it——

'His room was at the end of the passage, next to the one Dan and I were in, and he might have heard Dan leave. Or again, he might have been waiting in the ballroom for fear he should do so. In which case, of course, he would have watched Dan go out and wouldn't need to be told where he was going. He collects a weapon, follows him to the Guest House and kills him . . .

'The problem then is how to get rid of the body, and the answer is right under his nose—together with a ball of twine and an outsize cobbler's needle! He sews Dan into the tarpaulin, carries Ferrers down to the Club breakwater where he discovers that it's no good trying to chuck him into the sea again, and hits on the idea of dumping him in the turtle tank. Having done that, all he has to do is to throw the weapon into the sea, put on Dan's mackintosh cape and get back to the house. That's all, I think.'

Copper said: 'Can I add something, please? It—it was only an idea of mine, but when Dan was discovered to be missing and we were all getting a little worried about it, I thought that Mr Shilto seemed to be amused.'

'In that case,' said Nick, 'we'd better add another Maltese Cross, indicating adverse feminine intuition, to the charge-sheet. Anybody got anything else to add? No? Well I have. Write it down, Val. When it was suggested that a search be made for Ferrers's body, Shilto was against it, tooth and nail. Said it was a complete waste of time, and sundry other things, and when I insisted, barged out of the room in a hell of a temper, spitting with wrath. Altogether a pretty peculiar demonstration; and with the discovery of Ferrers's body and the added discovery that he had been murdered, it begins to look even more peculiar. Well, that's about all I think. Who's next on the list?'

Valerie flicked over a page of the notebook: 'Romeo Purvis. Anyone got anything to say about Ronnie? . . . No?'

'What? Not even a Maltese Cross?' gibed Nick. 'Lucky devil!'

'I've got something,' said Valerie, 'and Copper can vouch for it that it isn't just something I've thought up recently, but something I noticed at the time. When Rosamund made that silly scene on Christmas Eve, Ronnie was scared out of his wits. It's not much, but I'm prepared to swear to it. I told Copper about it at the time.'

'Yes,' endorsed Copper, 'and you were dead right, because when she yelled the place down later that evening, Ronnie was scared again. And not for her sake, either.'

'Oh God!' sighed Charles. '*More* feminine intuition!'

Valerie threw a sofa cushion at him and said: 'One more crack like that from you, my own, and I'll throw my engagement ring after it!'

'Is that a promise?' inquired Charles eagerly.

'No. It's an awful warning. So close down, Charles darling, unless you want a two carat diamond in your eye. To return to Suspect Number Two—anything else? No? Very well, Ronald Purvis—no evidence. Go on, Charles, make a case out of that.'

Charles sat up indignantly: 'Good Lord, why me? Give me an easier one for heaven's sake. Oh well——' He subsided gloomily, and cleared his throat: 'In the prisoner's favour: no reason for killing Ferrers Shilto.'

'No *known* reason,' corrected Valerie. 'For all we know he may have had half a dozen.'

'So might Amabel!' retorted Charles with some asperity. 'Are you conducting this prosecution or am I? Then leave me the floor, my love. Where was I? Oh yes. Against the prisoner: as a member of the sailing party he had the opportunity of killing Ferrers Shilto. For the prisoner: so, apparently, had six other people.'

He brooded for a moment or two, and then added: 'From that point on, if Ronnie is our murderer, all that Nick said about John Shilto can equally well apply to him. He spots Dan's interest in the corpse and hangs about outside the house to make sure that he doesn't make a move towards further investigation. Sees Dan come out, hears him speak to the sentry, follows him down to the Guest House, kills him, disposes of the bodies and returns to the house disguised as Dan in order to delay the search for him until the supposed Ferrers is well and truly underground. After which he slides out of the house by a back door and trots off home. And that appears to be all. M'Lud, the case rests!'

He threw himself back in his chair and closed his eyes with ostentation.

Valerie said: 'That's all very well, darling, but you haven't suggested any reason why he should have killed Ferrers in the first place.'

'Don't be silly, sweetheart! He can't possibly have had any reason for doing such a thing. *Ergo*, he did not kill Ferrers. I was merely endeavouring to show that *had* he done anything so fantastic, he could also have killed Dan. Who's next?'

'Leonard Stock,' said Valerie, turning a page. 'Anyone got anything to say about Leonard? No? All right: you take over, Coppy.'

Copper said: 'In the absence of any concrete evidence, I plump for Leonard Stock as the murderer. First, because he's the most unlikely person, and as anyone who has ever read a murder story knows, it's always the most unlikely person who turns out to have done the deed—and fifty thousand authors can't be wrong.'

'I suppose,' drawled Nick, 'that, acting on that assumption, you would unhesitatingly have nominated Amabel if she had been in the running for the Suspect Stakes?'

'Then you suppose wrong!' snapped Copper. 'I should have known Amabel couldn't possibly have done it even if I'd found her standing over the corpse with a bludgeon in one hand and blood all over her! I should merely be convinced that she'd just turned up, at the wrong moment as usual, and picked up the weapon out of mere cow-like curiosity. But I do *not* know that Leonard couldn't have done it. It seems to me that he stands as good a chance as anyone of being the murderer. Because——' She hesitated for a moment, as though doubtful as to how her next observation would be received, and then continued in a tone of some diffidence: 'Have any of you ever noticed that Ronnie Purvis wears a cornelian signet ring on his left hand?'

It was obvious that her question had not only taken her hearers by surprise, but that its connection with the subject under discussion completely eluded them. Valerie's forehead wrinkled in a puzzled frown, and she said: 'Yes, but I don't see . . .'

'I think I do,' said Nick abruptly. 'She means that someone might have seen a hand and thought——'

He broke off without finishing the sentence, and Copper turned to look at him for a moment. It gave her a queer stab of uneasiness to find that Nick should instantly know what she implied by what she had not said. She looked away again swiftly, and turned to Valerie: 'I—I was thinking of Ferrers,' she said uncertainly. 'He wore a garnet ring on his left hand, and in the rain it might have been mistaken for Ronnie's. They were both red, you see.'

'But I still don't—'

Nick said: 'Shut up, Val!'

'Supposing——' Copper was choosing her words with some difficulty, 'supposing that during the storm somebody wearing a red ring had caught at the same boat that Leonard was holding on to? I know Nick said that the rain and spray had reduced visibility to a matter of inches, but Leonard might have seen a hand where he couldn't see a face. He could have thought that the hand belonged to Ronnie, and taken a crack at the owner.'

Charles sat up with some violence: 'But damn it, Coppy, why the hell should Stock want to murder——' He stopped, and then said more slowly: 'You mean—Ruby? I get you. *Hmm!*' He fidgeted restlessly with his cigarette-case for a moment and said at last: 'Yes, I suppose there might be something in it. But supposing you're right about that? I'm not saying that Stock hadn't damned good reason for wanting to do in Ronnie Purvis, but why only Ronnie? God knows I don't want to cast nasturtiums at dear Ruby, but what is Ronnie among so many?'

'Perhaps the proverbial last straw? You must admit it was a pretty blatant straw.'

'Oh, I'll admit that,' said Charles impatiently. 'More like a haystack, if you ask me. But unless rumour lies more than ordinarily blackly, there have been a good many haystacks of that kind in poor old Leonard's matrimonial meadow. Also—forgive me for pointing it out—hadn't one of the members of our jury rather—er—usurped the limelight of late?'

'You mean Nick,' supplied Copper before anyone else could speak. 'Of course. But that might be an added reason in favour of killing Ronnie, because it would provide an alibi. You see,' she added with a touch of malice, 'Leonard would know perfectly well that the minute the *Sapphire* left, Ronnie would move back into favour again.'

Charles shifted uncomfortably: 'Well, as a matter of fact, Coppy, my charmer, I meant you. Ronnie has rather turned from his old allegiance since your arrival on the scene.'

Copper intercepted Nick's amused glance, and flushed hotly, and Nick said: 'Nice to know that as a professional homebreaker I'm in such good company.'

'Charles is quite right,' interrupted Valerie hastily, frowning at Nick. 'I can't see why, if Leonard was feeling murderous on Ruby's account, he should have reached the breaking-point at a time when the Ronnie affair, from both his and Ruby's angle, had taken a bit of a back seat.'

Copper said: 'Because he may never have had an opportunity before. I mean a chance of doing Ronnie in without getting hanged for it. And then the storm may have provided the chance he had been looking for.'

'Oh well, I suppose we'd better put it down as a remotely possible motive,' sighed Valerie. 'LEONARD STOCK. Opportunity: same as everyone else. Motive: Ruby. Bumped off Ferrers in mistake for Ronnie. Rest of the case same as the other two. On the debit side: Copper says he's done it because he's the most unlikely person, and because he thought he was writing off Ronnie because of Ruby. Anyone got anything for the credit column?'

Nick said: 'Yes. You can put me down for the defence. Copper's theory may or may not hold water, but here's something that holds gallons. Has it occurred to anyone that Leonard Stock stands about two foot two in his bedsocks and is about the weediest little specimen, with the possible exception of the late Ferrers Shilto, in the entire Islands? I'm well aware that even the most miserable misfit can wang a man over the head with a marlinspike or a hammer or what-have-you. But it would take a considerable quantity of sheer solid guts and muscle to drag a dead body single-handed from the Guest House to the turtle tank. And it must have taken wrists of iron to carry it round the narrow wall of the tank and hang it from that crossbeam under the floor of the summer-house.

'Fourthly, fifthly and sixthly, the entire performance plainly called for quick thinking, cool-headedness and a packet of nerve. And though I hate to cast cold water on Copper's fresh young enthusiasms, even if Stock possesses the necessary mental qualifications, he quite obviously hasn't the physical ones. So I think we can safely count him out as not being of the stuff that murderers are made of.'

'And of course you'd know about that,' said Copper sweetly.

'Look here, you two!' snapped Valerie in sudden exasperation, 'if you feel you must scratch at each other, you can do it later. Just try and remember that this is serious!'

Nick laughed. 'See what your acidity has let us in for, Copper darling? A public reprimand, no less! That's the stuff, Val. *"Order in court!"* Well, what's the verdict on Leonard? Guilty or not guilty?'

Valerie said: 'I'm not going to put anyone down as either guilty or innocent without positive proof.'

'Oh, all right,' sighed Nick. 'Charles, be a Boy Scout and pour a stiffish whisky into the nearest glass and merely disturb it slightly with soda . . . My blessings on you. Here's to crime!' He drank deeply. 'Next prisoner, please.'

'Hamish,' said Valerie. 'Come on, Charles.'

'Oh, no you don't!' said Charles. 'I've done my stuff on Ronnie. This is your headache, young Portia.'

Valerie shook her head determinedly. 'Sorry. I'm saving myself for Ruby—we've got several lines on her that you haven't heard about yet.'

'Oh, my God!' moaned Charles. 'You women! You cats! You scratchy little hell-cats!'

'I like that!' said Valerie indignantly. 'Here have you and Nick been pointing out half a dozen damning details in connection with John Shilto, Ronnie and Leonard, and did I once rise up and accuse you of being catty?'

'If you two,' drawled Nick gently, 'have a bone to pick, I have it on good authority that there is a Frigidaire in the pantry.'

Charles laughed. 'He's got you there, Val. All right. I withdraw. I apologize. I grovel. Anything, in fact, for a quiet life. I will even, in the interests of peace and justice, strive to make out a case against that old Angora rabbit, Mr Rattigan to wit.'

Clutching a whisky and soda in one hand and his brow in the other, Charles collapsed into the depths of his armchair and brooded deeply, but after several minutes he announced himself defeated: 'It's no good. In spite of remorselessly racking the brain, I can't think up a single damn thing against the old cloth-head. Apart from the fact that he is a promi-

nent member of our Ruby's chain-gang, there is no
blot upon his blameless copy-book. And as he
doesn't wear a ruby on his left hand, he couldn't
even have been killed in mistake for—— Oh, that's
the wrong way round isn't it?'

Charles took a deep draught from his glass and
gazed wildly about the room as though seeking in-
spiration from the walls and ceiling. 'Go on,' commanded Valerie remorselessly. 'You must do better
than that. What sort of thing do you think might
madden Hamish to the point of murder?'

'Unpolished buttons,' said Charles promptly. 'The
old egg nearly busts himself with fury if he spots
one of our chaps sporting a button or a belt-buckle
that you can't actually see to shave in. He may look
like a fluffy form of rabbit, but when he does lose
his temper—happily only about once quarterly—he
doesn't skimp it. Frankly speaking, Hell pops and
strong men take cover.'

Valerie frowned, wrinkled the end of her nose,
and entered: 'Debit: Temper' on the charge-sheet.
'It's not much,' she said doubtfully. 'Couldn't you
improve on it a bit? Rack the brain a bit more,
Charles. Did anything happen on the Harriet picnic
that might have made him lose his temper?'

'That's no good,' said Nick impatiently. 'Half a
dozen things might have done that. Ants in the
mince pies for instance. It's got to be something that
would make him lose his hair with Ferrers.'

'I've got it!' said Charles suddenly. 'See Copper's
brilliant theory re: Leonard, and apply same without
loss of time to Hamish. God will, I trust, forgive me
for grossly maligning the poor guffin, but as I have
already had occasion to point out, anything for a
quiet life. Does that let me out?'

Valerie said doubtfully: 'Well I see what you
mean, and if it's the best you can do——'

'Best I can do!' exploded Charles. 'Isn't that just like a woman? Copper produces a half-baked theory to the effect that that little pip-squeak, Leonard, may have wanged Ferrers in mistake for Ronnie, basing this incredible fabrication of a fevered imagination upon the tottering foundation of a brace of Woolworth rings. It is received with all solemnity. But when I suggest that it might apply equally well to Hamish, what happens? Do I receive a share of the applause? Not on your life! I am instantly reviled. I resign. I throw in my half-dozen towels—two bath, two face and two mat. Will someone please hand me the brandy. I intend to get tight.'

'It's all right, darling,' said Valerie soothingly. 'You're perfectly right, of course. It was very clever of you to think of it. You mean that if Ruby had pitched Hamish a yarn about Ronnie pestering her with improper advances, he might try taking a club to Ronnie?'

'That *was* the idea,' admitted Charles with dignity. 'The poor poop is plain cuckoo about her. She's probably the first woman he's ever fallen for, so he's beyond the reach of reason where she's concerned. I believe she could even wheedle him into thinking lightly of the "Glorious Regiment", let alone mere murder!'

'Rubbish!' said Nick shortly. 'Look here, Val—and you too, Charles—it's about time we stopped fabricating unnecessary fairy tales. I admit I don't know much about Rattigan. But you do. Do you honestly mean to tell me that you think that if Ruby Stock had pitched a "persecution" yarn to him, he'd rush off and try and murder Purvis? Not on your life! He'd haul him off by the scruff of his neck and knock him down with all due ceremony behind the squash court!'

Valerie nodded reluctant agreement: 'You're right, of course, Nick. Which effectively disposes of Hamish. Anyone got anything to add before I close the score? No? Right: then that brings us to Ruby.'

=17=

Valerie drew a deep breath: 'Now listen you two—this is really serious. Copper and I have a few solid clues for you to work on.'

She proceeded to describe in detail Copper's discovery of the fragment of swansdown on the stairhead, together with Mrs Stock's reception of the news of Dan's murder and her surreptitious errand to the rocks. 'It was all rather frightening,' she concluded, 'and I'm leaving it to you to decide if you think there could be anything in it, and if so, what. You see—' her voice broke unexpectedly and she shivered. 'You see she—she must have been near the staircase last night. And—and the murderer must have come up those stairs——'

The sentence dwindled into a whisper of pure terror, and in an instant Charles was out of his chair and had caught both her hands in his. 'I know one thing!' said Charles violently, 'and that is that until this thing is solved I'm sleeping at your house, even if I have to take a mattress and camp on the ballroom floor. It's all right, Val! Don't look like that, sweetheart. There's nothing to be scared of at the moment—Army and Navy both in attendance. And now shall we exchange a passionate kiss here, or in the pantry?'

Valerie's taut nerves relaxed and she laughed tremulously. 'I'm sorry. I do apologize. A momentary spasm of panic brought on by suddenly realizing that Copper and I were probably sleeping in the same house with an honest-to-God murderer last night.'

Charles dropped a swift kiss on to his fiancée's head, and seating himself on the arm of her chair remarked: 'After which brief but affecting interlude, let us return to La Stock. You say you found a chunk of her pink trimmings decorating the stairhead? Well, that presumably means that she was out and about sometime during the night—but not necessarily at half past one. And anyway, it stands to reason that she can't be the murderer if she was parading about the place in forty yards of pink satin profusely decorated with feather frillings. It doesn't make sense.'

'Why not?' demanded Valerie. 'She might have heard Dan cross the hall and followed to see where he was going. And if she saw him put on the mackintosh cape and go out, she could have run back, changed into something more suitable, sneaked out by the back and rushed down to the Guest House. And I would also like to remind you that Ruby weighs around nine stone seven, stands about five foot nine inches in her stockings, and swings a pretty good golf club and tennis racket. So far as mere muscle goes, I imagine that she would be more than equal to dealing with Ferrers, dead or alive!'

Charles whistled gently through his teeth and abstractedly wound a lock of Valerie's hair about one finger: 'Perhaps. But all the same, I don't believe it. And that's not merely because I can't help jibbing at the idea of a woman having done the job, for I imagine that when it comes right down to bedrock, most women are more capable of murder than the average man. But for all that I don't believe it was Ruby. And you can put that down on the charge-sheet as a large blot, signifying male intuition as opposed to female.'

Valerie jerked her head away impatiently and said: 'I don't care how many intuitions you've got about her. They don't alter the fact that she was prowling about the house last night sometime between eleven and half past one, because that bit of swansdown on Hindenburg proves it.'

Nick abandoned his indolent pose and sat up abruptly: 'By jove! I wonder if she was the person that the sentry saw in the office?'

'What's that?' Both girls turned on him simultaneously.

'Forgot to tell you,' said Nick. 'The sentry produced another piece of information this afternoon. He said he'd seen the Commissioner mucking about in the office as he passed the window when coming on duty last night. I've forgotten how he came to mention it, but it was rather odd because the Commissioner denies having been near the office after nine o'clock. He cross-questioned the sentry, and the man said that as he walked down the verandah past the office window he saw there was a light on inside, and as there was a gap in the curtains, glanced in as he went past and saw someone standing by the desk . . .

'He assumed that it was the Commissioner working late; which was a fairly usual occurrence. But when we got down to brass tacks it turned out that the light came from a small green-shaded reading-lamp on the desk and that all he actually saw was the silhouette of someone bending over the desk. And when asked to describe what it looked like, he couldn't swear to any detail of the figure: said he'd only given it a casual glance and was so certain that it was the Commissioner that he hadn't bothered to think any more about it.'

Valerie said: 'You mean it might have been Ruby?'

'It's possible. If you think for a minute, one thing is bound to strike you. Why should the sentry have been so positive that the person in the office was your stepfather? He couldn't explain it himself, but it's fairly obvious that whoever it was or wasn't, it was a European, and that one fact, in the snapshot view he had between the curtains by the shaded light of the reading-lamp, impressed itself on his mind without his realizing it. And if a European, then naturally Sir Lionel: one's brain often unconsciously betrays one's eye, and vice versa. But it could just as easily have been a woman wearing a coat.'

'I see,' said Valerie thoughtfully. 'Ruby might have come to the top of the stairs to see if it was possible to get down unseen, and spotted that old Iman Din was out of play and that the coast was clear. If there was anything in the office that she wanted, she'd be certain to go back to her room and swop that dressing-gown affair for a coat. She's got a heavy brown tweed one, cut like a man's overcoat.'

'Then that may be the solution,' said Nick. 'Probably nothing much in it except another "Possible", to add to a growing list of "Possibles" without a single "Probable" to cheer them up.'

Valerie said: 'But what on earth would Ruby want out of the office? If it *was* Ruby?'

'Heaven knows. Your stepfather went through the entire room with a small-tooth comb, but he said there was not only nothing missing, but that nothing had been moved. So I'm afraid the incident isn't much use to us, except as providing a possible solution for Mrs Stock's night wanderings.'

Charles said: 'What about her day wanderings, comrade? That trip of hers to the rocks smells rather strongly of kippers to me. After all, we haven't yet found the weapon that was used to kill Dan. What about that as a solution to her proceedings?'

'You mean she was disposing of the evidence?' put in Valerie. 'It did look rather like that, but— surely the weapon that killed Dan must have been pretty solid?'

Nick said: 'A club, or a coal hammer or something of that description. Yes; I see your point. Even with the mist, and at that range, you would have been able to see it if what she chucked into the sea had been anything hefty.'

'We didn't see anything at all,' said Valerie. 'And what's more, I believe that she carried the thing she threw away stuffed down the front of her frock, and it stands to reason that she couldn't shove a hammer or a kitchen poker down there without it being pretty noticeable if anyone had stopped her.'

Nick uttered a sound between a laugh and a groan and pushed his hands through his hair so that it was ruffled again. 'God forbid that I should ever meddle with a job like this again! What we need is Scotland Yard and the Ten Best Brains of Britain to cope with this bloody jig-saw puzzle. And I—heaven forgive me!—had an idea that if we dug about we might with luck come across something that would give us a lead. But I didn't bargain for half a hundred separate leads. Let's go and tackle that woman about it at once and see what she's got to say.'

'No!' said Valerie firmly. 'That would be fatal. If we try and bounce her into anything she'll only deny it hotly. Copper and I will wait for a suitable opportunity, and try and lure her into having a girlish chat when she is slightly less hysterical.'

'All right. Then let's get on with the three-ring circus. Who's next?'

'Rosamund Purvis. Take over, Nick.'

'Nothing doing. It takes a woman to prosecute a woman. Take her yourself.'

Valerie chewed the end of her pencil for a moment or two, and then wrote once again in the notebook. 'How will this do?' she inquired. 'ROSAMUND PURVIS. Opportunity: same as everyone else. Motive: possibly the same one as Copper suggested for Leonard, and Charles for Hamish—"Mistaken Identity", i.e. she killed Ferrers in mistake for Ronnie. Goodness knows she must have wanted to do it pretty often. He treats her abominably, and——'

'You know,' interrupted Nick wearily, 'that theory of Copper's struck me as pretty far-fetched the first time I heard it—though I will admit that it did seem to be just within the realms of the remotely possible. But with every repetition it appears less and less so. For heaven's sake let's scrap it for the moment and try another.'

'But I can't think of another,' complained Valerie plaintively. 'I must say I'm inclined to agree with you. But if you can think up any reason why Rosamund would want to murder Ferrers, you're a better man than I am Gunga Din and you can darn well take over the prosecution yourself!'

Nick said irritably: 'It's no earthly good asking me to supply reasons. Damn it all, Val, I've only been on this flaming island a little over a week, so it's hardly likely that I'd know much about the character and private lives of the local inhabitants. All I know is that this ring theory is so thin it's transparent!'

Copper turned swiftly to face him: 'Is it?' she said

tersely. 'Then perhaps this may thicken it a bit. Do you remember the afternoon of the Mount Harriet picnic, just after lunch, when we four were in the lorry and someone came up and put a hand on the edge of it?'

'What's that got to do with it?' inquired Charles impatiently: 'Of course we remember. It was Ronnie, and—— No, by God, it wasn't! It was Ferrers!'

Copper threw Nick a brief, triumphant glance and turned to Charles: 'What made you so sure at first that it was Ronnie, Charles?'

Charles considered the question, wrinkling his nose thoughtfully. 'Damned if I know,' he admitted. 'But now that you come to mention it, I did think it was him, and I was surprised when it turned out to be Ferrers. I certainly can't remember noticing any ring, but that could have had something to do with my jumping to the conclusion that Passionate Purvis was in our midst.'

'Of course it had,' said Copper. 'Not many Englishmen wear rings, and the ones that do usually wear plain gold signet rings. But Ronnie wore a ring with a large red stone set in it, and so did Ferrers. And you are so used to seeing Ronnie's ring that your subconscious mind registered *Ronnie* when you saw a man's hand with a red ring on it. And don't tell me I'm wrong, because I know I'm not!'

'Don't worry,' said Charles, 'I lack the necessary nerve to contradict you. And I dare say you're right. In which case I suppose these series of ring-theories must remain on the books for the present; which appears to thicken the general fog to no ordinary extent.'

'I don't see why it should,' said Valerie obstinately.

Charles moaned and closed his eyes: '*O Woman! in our hours of ease!* Listen, my love, think!—ponder!—consider for a brief moment! If we retain this ring business, it would appear that the whole island is swarming with people who were panting to massacre Ronnie, and that the elimination of the late unlamented Ferrers was due to a mere slip of the spanner. It seems to me to add endless vistas of sinister conjecture to a landscape already overstocked with sinister vistas.'

He drank deeply and subsided on to the sofa, and Valerie said: 'Oh well, let's leave it for the moment and get on with the case against Rosamund. For the prosecution: she plays a good game of tennis and is the best swimmer in the Islands, bar none, so she could have coped with the problem of disposing of Ferrers's body without much difficulty. Then there was definitely something extremely queer behind that display of nerves on Christmas Eve. She was scared to death.'

'She was,' agreed Nick. 'And on thinking back on her behaviour that night, I would like to advance a theory of my own that could account for it. It seems to me just possible that she saw Ferrers die.'

'But you——'

'*Ssh!*—don't interrupt. Let us suppose, for the sake of argument, that she was holding on to the same boat as Ferrers, and saw just enough to realize that someone beyond him had deliberately cracked him over the head? If that were so, the chances are that she would have let go her hold in a panic, and swum around in the smother until forced to grab hold of a boat that she probably hoped was not the one she had originally been attached to. After that there'd have been no point in her saying anything. Unless she knew who had done the hitting, which is unlikely. I think it was Copper who remarked that same evening that Mrs Purvis appeared to be playing a peculiar game of *"Is it you?— Is it you?— Is it you?"* with herself. Which could support the theory that she was aware, even then, that Ferrers had not been drowned but murdered. It would also account for her subsequent behaviour.'

'Um,' said Valerie thoughtfully. 'It does seem to fit. That is, if she didn't do the job herself and wasn't wondering who, if anyone, had seen her do it?'

'For the defence,' said Copper, taking over: 'she wasn't on the beach when Ferrers's body turned up, and neither was she at the Christmas Day dinner party. Therefore she couldn't have known of Dan's interest in the corpse.'

Valerie said: 'Against that we have Amabel and Dutt and Ronnie and Truda. All, or any of them, could have told her something. And even if she hadn't heard any details, if she was the murderer she'd be scared to death at hearing that the corpse of her victim had turned up, and be pretty restless until the body was safely buried. She could easily have got out of the hospital that night, and perhaps gone to the Guest House to assure herself that the murder hadn't been discovered, and found Dan there.'

'Hell!' groaned Charles. 'Then that's six of them who could have done it. Oh well, we might as well make a good job of it and prove that they all did it. Who's next for the electric chair?'

'Nick,' said Valerie, and laughed. She appeared to be the only one amused. Charles was watching Nick over the rim of his glass, and Nick was watching Copper. Copper kept her eyes on the tips of her shoes and said nothing, and Valerie, suddenly aware of tension, looked up from her notebook and glanced from one to another of the three still faces.

She opened her mouth, and then closed it again without speaking.

Nick said dryly: 'Well, Copper?'

He saw Copper's fingers clench themselves together in her lap, but apart from that slight movement she might not have been aware that he had spoken.

'Why this magnanimity, sweet? I can take it, we murderers are tough. Produce your evidence, Coppy. Even if Val and Charles don't see eye to eye with you about it, it's as good as that signet-ring stuff any day!'

Charles saw Copper's chin come up with a jerk, and rushed in where angels might justifiably have feared to tread: 'Yes, come on young Sherlock. Spill the sinister beans and put us out of our misery. Then we can tear up all those appalling notes that Val has been preparing for the purpose of spreading confusion and despair, and fall on Nick in a body. I shall direct operations from behind the bookcase, and you and Val can do the actual arresting. After which we can bury him behind the squash court, and go off to dinner secure in the righteous conviction that we have faithfully administered the King's Justice.'

'I haven't anything to say on Nick's behalf,' said Copper in a small cold voice. 'Either for or against. To misquote him, "It takes a thief to—"' she checked a little ostentatiously. '—I mean, it takes a man to prosecute a man. You can take it over, Charles.'

For a brief moment the knuckles of Nick's hands showed white, and then he laughed and relaxed once more in his chair. Valerie gave Copper a puzzled look, and then turned back to Charles: 'Last prisoner, darling. Take over the charge-sheet, and after that you can come up to the house and I'll make you a mint julep and hold your hand on the drawing-room sofa.'

'A clear case of bribery and corruption,' sighed Charles. 'But then I have always been a weak character. Oh, all right. Prisoner at the Bar, did you or did you not, on the afternoon of December the twenty-fourth, either of intent, or under the impression that you were slugging Mr Ronald Purvis, cause the decease of one Ferrers Shilto?'

'Objection!' said Nick. 'I appeal to the court. That's a leading question.'

Valerie said: 'Objection sustained. Get on with it, Charles.'

'All right—all right. Don't rush me! Case for the prosecution: that the said Nicholas Tarrent, being a member of the sailing party, had full and ample opportunity for slugging the said Ferrers Shilto. Moreover he possesses the physical ability, together with the necessary nerve, guts, brains and what-have-you, to carry out the task to a successful conclusion. Added to which is the damning fact that he shared a room with the second victim, and therefore would certainly have been aware of his suspicions regarding the corpse of the said Ferrers Shilto——

'In fact,' said Charles, reverting to plain English, 'for all we know, Dan may have spilt the beans to him and told him that he proposed to have a look at the corpse. In which case he would have had plenty of time to plan the whole thing before leaving the house: murder of Dan, disposal of Ferrers, the entire works. I will even withdraw my previous assertion that the job couldn't have been carried out inside an hour and a half. Given quick thinking, it could probably have been done in that time and with a few minutes to spare.'

Nick said: 'A bit more of this and I shall burst into

tears and confess all. Go on, Charles. You're doing fine.'

'Matter of fact,' confessed the counsel for the prosecution, 'that about cleans me out of ideas. You see there's the small matter of motive. Just between the two of us and strictly in confidence, what *was* your motive?'

'Objection!' murmured Nick.

'Oh yes, of course. Leading question, an' all that. It's no good, Val, you'll have to enter "No Motive" on the prisoner's charge-sheet. And that, thank God, can go in reference to Ronnie as well as Ferrers, for if anyone had mentioned the word "ring" again I should have screamed aloud and burst a blood-vessel. You can put down that, as far as we know, the prisoner Tarrent had no quarrel and very small acquaintance with Mr Ronald Purvis. Was not sentimentally smitten by Mrs Ruby Stock, and had only laid eyes on Mr Ferrers Shilto a couple of hours or so before the murder. Otherwise all things are equal. Can I stop now?'

'You can,' said Nick. 'And I may say that my case in your hands, as compared with Copper's, is as a bucket of whitewash to a truck-load of coal.'

Charles hitched himself round in his chair and regarded Copper with interest. 'You mean she's suppressing evidence, do you? Well, far be it from me to discourage her. In fact if anyone else has any more evidence against anyone, I'd be everlastingly grateful if they would tie a brick to it and drop it in the harbour. I have had just about as much of it as I can stand in one day, and my brain is reeling. It appears to have been conclusively proved that there are not one, but seven murderers or potential murderers loose upon Ross, and I shall therefore retire to bed tonight wearing a bullet-proof vest under my pyjamas and clutching a loaded shot-gun in either hand. Amateur detectives and intending sleep-walkers, please note!'

Valerie laughed, and turning in her chair slid a hand under his arm. 'Thank God our late librarian didn't have a yen for Ethel M. Dell! I don't think I could have borne a stern, square-jawed hero in this situation. Thank you, darling. Your act has been ter-rific, and for about the first time in weeks I've really appreciated it.'

'It was rather good, wasn't it?' agreed Charles complacently. 'What the dramatic critics would have termed a "fine, sustained performance".'

'If you don't watch it,' observed Copper crisply, 'you'll wake up one fine morning and find that you're talking like that naturally.'

'But I am,' said Charles. 'I do! I find it's a thing that grows on one—like boils. But not to worry. A good strong dose of Hemingway will eliminate the germs.'

'Try Anouilh, darling,' advised Valerie. 'And now listen—I'm going to read out everything I've written this afternoon, and after that I suggest we clear out and go for a quick walk round the island before it's dark. But before I start reading we'll have a five-minute silence during which I want everyone to go over as much as they can remember of the last two days, starting with the Mount Harriet picnic. And if they can think of any incident, however tiny, that strikes them as odd or unusual, to produce it for inspection. Ready?'

The minutes ticked themselves away in a deep si-lence.

'Time's up! What are you frowning over, Coppy? Thought of something?'

'Yes,' said Copper doubtfully, 'but—I know you'll think I'm mad, because it's something that I can't catch hold of. I can only remember that something

happened at the picnic that was odd. I can't even
remember anything about it, except that something
that day made me think "That's queer!" But perhaps
I'll remember it later. Anyway, it couldn't have been
very important.'

'Shove down a question mark, Val,' ordered
Charles. 'Here's a red pencil—catch! Copper may
think of it later. And now, if that's all, I suggest we
get on with the reading.'

Valerie returned to her chair, and picking up the
notebook, added a large red question mark to the
record. 'Now,' she said, 'I'm going to read straight
through everything we've written down here, and I
want you to please concentrate, and if anything
strikes you as particularly important to make a note
of it. Here goes——!'

She sat down and began to read in a clear emo-
tionless voice while her audience sat silent and absorbed. Charles moved to switch on the light above
her head, for it was getting too dark to see, and once
during the reading Copper caught her breath in a
small gasp and stiffened in her chair. The movement
was as slight as the sound, but Nick turned his head
sharply, and saw that her face was very white and
her eyes wide and terrified.

'That's all,' concluded Valerie. 'Has anyone got
anything to add to it?'

Two heads were shaken.

'Did anything strike anyone as being of particular
importance?'

Nick glanced sideways at Copper and saw her
fingers tighten convulsively upon the arm of her
chair. But she did not speak; though neither did she
shake her head in denial as he and Charles had
done.

'Then that's all!' said Valerie, shutting the notebook with a bang. 'And now let's rush out and get

some exercise. It's still horribly misty, but a change of air will do us all good.'

She tossed the notebook into a corner of the window-seat, sublimely unaware of how close one twist to its tangled reasoning would have brought them to the truth.

═══ *18* ═══

It was almost dark when they left the Mess to take a brisk walk around Ross, and the tiny island was still close-lapped in a mist which veiled the last of the lingering daylight.

The faint breeze that had arisen earlier in the day had died with the approach of night, and except for the ceaseless thunder of the surf, which from long familiarity had become barely noticeable, an almost uncanny silence brooded over the island. Not a leaf rustled or a twig stirred, and they could hear the fog-dew dripping from the hibiscus hedges and the gold mohur trees.

For a while the four walked in silence, their footsteps in unison though their thoughts were widely divergent.

Charles, his arm tucked through Valerie's, was thinking of what she had said when she had thanked him for 'putting on an act'. She had thought it was only for her sake and Copper's that he had done his best to keep their discussions on as light a level as possible. But it had also been for his own, because he had not dared let himself look too closely at the picture of Valerie—his own Valerie—lying asleep in that darkened house while a murderer fresh from his killing crept in from the mists of the grey island and barred the door behind him. For beyond that thought lay the knowledge that tonight she would once again pass the dark hours in the same house.

Registering a mental vow to act upon his recently expressed intention of spending the night at Government House, Charles tightened his hold on her arm and Valerie returned the pressure fervently: though she herself had not been thinking of the dark present, but of some golden, hoped-for future when she and Charles were married . . .

Nick, walking between her and Copper, his hands in his pockets and his long, loose stride restricted to their shorter steps, was thinking confusedly of the past. Of Calcutta, and of Ferrers Shilto's face against the background of a corridor in the Grand Hotel. He had looked like a frightened, vicious rat—a cornered rat. Who could ever have supposed that they would meet again, and so soon? And how was Copper going to regard the Calcutta incident? Nick had never yet cared what others might think of his actions, but then Copper was not 'others' . . . His mouth twisted wryly and he scowled into the gathering dusk.

Beside him, her blond head bent and her slim shoulders a little hunched as though against an imaginary wind, the subject of his thoughts walked with her eyes fixed upon the wet road. And for once—perhaps for the first time for over a week—she was not thinking exclusively of Nicholas Tarrent.

Copper was re-living an apparently trivial incident that had occurred two days before, and hearing again a single line from the notebook that was lying discarded on the window-seat in the ante-room of the empty Mess. An incident and a statement that contradicted each other. Had *no* one else noticed it?

Would no one else remember it? Would Valerie? She longed desperately to tell Nick; to beg for his advice and reassurance. But Nick had suddenly become a stranger; and he, too, had got something to hide. Perhaps they all had? Even Charles—even Valerie . . . !

Why had Nick been so angry with her for pointing out that he might lie under suspicion of murder? Admittedly, she had wanted to hurt him. She had tormented herself with the knowledge that he must, in the past, have attracted more than his fair share of fluttering feminine adulation, and she resented bitterly the recurring suspicion that she might appear to him as just another infatuated little idiot who took his casual attentions as proof of something more serious, and entirely non-existent.

Nick, she had thought, would probably expect her to believe that although the rest of the island might be under suspicion, he alone could do no wrong in her too openly admiring eyes, and she had therefore decided to show him that he meant no more to her than any other member of that fatal sailing party. But the result of her ill-advised disclosures had been to turn Nick from a friend into a stranger from whom she could not ask for help. And even if she could do so, would she dare risk it? Dan had been a friend of Nick's, and Nick might——Copper's hunted brain returned helplessly to its original groove and started on the same round once more, like a caged mouse on a wheel.

Silent and preoccupied, the four walked down the dim deserted roads past the hospital and the little bazaar whose doors, close-shuttered against the damp sea-mist, still showed friendly chinks of yellow lamplight in the growing darkness. On a clear night they would have seen the sprinkled lights of Aberdeen across the narrow strip of heaving waters that separated Ross from the mainland. But tonight the mist lay thick upon the yeasty seas, and as they looked into that blank, shifting wall they might have been isolated by hundreds of miles of empty ocean.

They passed the sheds that stood behind the jetty, where their footsteps, muffled until now by the wet ground, suddenly rang loud, and came out by the little bandstand that had once, long ago, been a centre of social life in the glittering tropic evenings, though no band had played there for many a long year. Beyond it their feet left the crushed coral of the roadway and encountered the yielding sponginess of rain-soaked grass as they crossed the Club lawn, beyond which the breakers still sent up ghostly fountains of spray.

A small dark building at the edge of the lawn, barely discernible in the dusk, sent a cold shiver down the spine of more than one of the four who passed it, and instinctively they drew closer together: remembering that sometime last night, in the misty rain-spattered darkness, someone had carried Ferrers Shilto's body to that same small building, and that for more than twelve hours afterwards it had hung there in the blackness above the shadowy tank, while the turtles snapped and splashed in the storm-clouded water below and Dan lay dead in the Guest House.

As if by mutual consent they turned simultaneously and walked quickly across the lawn to where a yellow glow from the Club windows gleamed comfortably through the mist. But apart from the barman and a Burmese waiter there was no one there but Ronnie Purvis, whom they found aimlessly flicking over the pages of a nine-weeks-old illustrated London weekly at one end of the deserted ballroom, and who was plainly the worse for drink.

Apparently he had been there for several hours, imbibing steadily, and had long since passed the convivial stage and the subsequent quarrelsome one, and Nick, eyeing him with detached interest, wondered if this was a usual procedure with him or whether he had merely set himself to get drunk as a relief from other and grimmer realities.

Charles, who knew him better, did not even wonder. Ronnie was a frequent victim of what he himself termed 'one over the eight', but he seldom if ever went in for really hard drinking; and then never alone. Mr Purvis was a man who liked company with his whisky, and rather than drink alone would normally have combed the island for a companion. Yet tonight he had been deliberately drowning something in drink. And it was certainly not sorrow. Funk, diagnosed Charles dispassionately: the fellow's scared stiff about something and has been trying the effects of Dutch Courage. Now I wonder what the hell he's so frightened of?

That Mr Purvis was frightened was as patently and disturbingly plain to everyone in the room as the fact that he was drunk. His usually bronzed features (Ronnie subscribed to the popular theory that 'all handsome men are slightly sunburnt') were a curious putty colour, his hands so unsteady that the leaves of the periodical he held shook as though they were in a wind, while his eyes were as wide and glaring as a frightened cat's, and any unexpected sound or movement caused him to start violently.

There was something about his obvious terror that was infectious, for Nick could see its reflection in Valerie's face. He saw, too, that the fear which had been in Copper's eyes ever since Valerie had read through the contents of the notebook had deepened to something still and panic-stricken, and rising abruptly, he crossed the ballroom floor and switched on every light in the big room. An action that at least had the effect of dispelling the lurking shadows, though it failed to add much cheerfulness to the scene.

The Club had been decorated in honour of the Christmas festivities with branches of casuarina intertwined with strings of fairy-lights, but the branches were already wilted and sad-looking, and the flood of light seemed only to intensify the dreariness of the empty, damp-stained dance floor and make it seem larger and blanker and more deserted than before.

Charles ordered a round of drinks which were brought by the slant-eyed, soft-footed Burmese boy, who materialized noiselessly out of the shadows beyond the ballroom. But alcohol did little towards raising anyone's spirits. Ronnie Purvis was beyond making even an effort at conversation, and though Charles and Valerie struggled valiantly, their efforts to dissipate the general gloom were markedly unsuccessful.

Copper was making a pretence at reading an out-of-date copy of the *National Geographic* magazine, but Nick, who was watching her without appearing to do so, saw that although she turned a page at regular intervals her eyes were fixed and her gaze unmoving and he was unpleasantly reminded of Rosamund Purvis, and Dan's voice saying something to the effect that he believed if someone came up behind her and touched her on the shoulder, she'd scream the roof off. The same, decided Nick, might well be said of Copper at that moment: except that Copper wouldn't scream—she wasn't, thank

God, the screaming kind. But she might easily faint . . .

Outside the Club the sullen swell crashed monotonously against the stone and concrete of the seawall, and occasionally a larger wave, more powerful than its fellows, would fling up an arc of spray to rattle against the ballroom windows, causing Ronnie Purvis to start violently with every repetition of the sound.

Charles put down his unfinished drink and rose abruptly: 'Come on, let's get out of here. Leave that beastly lemon drink of yours, Val; you can get another one up at the house. I've had enough of this.'

His companions rose with alacrity, and Ronnie stumbled to his feet, his mouth twitching. 'I—I think I'll come with you,' he said thickly. 'G-gloomy hole this. R-rotten Club. M-mind if I walk up with you as f-far as my bungalow?' He clawed at Charles's arm as though he was afraid of being refused and as if some special terror lay in having to walk, alone, the few hundred yards that stretched between the Club and his front door.

'Of course not,' said Charles impatiently, disengaging his coat-sleeve from Ronnie's clutching fingers: 'Put down that drink and come along.' He turned on his heel, and Mr Purvis, interpreting these instructions according to his own desires, paused to swallow what whisky remained in his glass before running unsteadily after him.

The air outside felt almost cold after the stuffy closeness of the atmosphere inside the Club, and though night had fallen there was still no breath of wind, and the light rain that was sifting down upon the island barely stirred the leaves beneath its silent fingers. It powdered Valerie's dark hair with stars and turned Copper's pale gold head to silver, and made a glimmering haze about the lamps that lined the roads between the dim sentinel columns of the coconut palms.

They dropped Ronnie Purvis at his bungalow, though it was patently obvious that he would have greatly preferred to accompany them to Government House. 'Can't go home alone,' mumbled Ronnie, swaying dangerously and clutching at a lamp-post to steady himself: 'That's what they're waiting for . . . Ge' me alone, so they c'n shoot me. Shtole m'revolver. S'gone. Looked everywhere.'

'*What's that?*' said Charles sharply. 'Did you say your revolver had been stolen?'

'Not shtolen . . . taken; so's I carn s-shoot 'em first!'

'Listen, Ronnie,' said Charles urgently. 'If you've lost your revolver you'd better go and look for it, and if you can't find it, you'd better report it!'

'Not losht. Just gone. No one in the housh . . . all 'lone. Lesh all have a lil' drink'n be merry—f'r t'morrer we die!'

Ronnie's bungalow was in darkness except for a gleam of light from the servants' quarters, and Valerie remembered suddenly that as both Rosamund and Amabel were up at the hospital, he would be alone in the empty house. Bare charity suggested that she should at least offer him dinner that night. But she could not bring herself to do so, because his drunken terror reacted too unpleasantly upon her own taut nerves. Refusing his invitations and cutting short their goodbyes she dragged at Charles's arm, and they turned hurriedly away, leaving Mr Purvis standing in the pool of light from the nearest lamp, swaying on his feet and casting desperate, terrified glances into the darkness beyond.

Valerie said in a low, breathless voice: 'Did you see—I only noticed it when we were standing under the lamp—he isn't wearing his ring.'

'Yes,' said Charles thoughtfully, 'I noticed. It almost begins to look as though there may be something in that theory of Copper's after all, doesn't it?'

'You mean you think that Ferrers *was* killed in mistake for Ronnie?'

'No. But I think that that possibility has suddenly occurred to Ronnie!'

'But why?'

'Why not? It occurred to Copper. Besides, do you ever remember his not wearing that ring before? He even wears it when he's bathing!'

Nobody answered him. They walked on in silence and at the top of the ascent passed the Guest House: its outline barely discernible through the misty darkness and its windows glinting secretively through the screen of wet leaves, reflecting the glow from the nearest lamp like the eyes of animals caught in the headlights of a car.

Copper turned her head away from it as they passed, but she could not turn away the picture that rose before her mind's eye: the picture of Dan Harcourt walking under those wet branches and through that rusty gate to meet his death. And all at once it seemed to her that there was no safety anywhere in all that misty, marooned island: not out in the wet night, nor in the lighted house above them. She found that her heart was hammering in her throat, and fought down a frantic impulse to turn about and run back down the road they had climbed. But there was nowhere to run to. No safety, no security, no haven . . .

They turned through the stone-pillared gates of Government House and walked up the curving drive under the dark, dripping branches of the flame trees, and they were half-way up when a dim figure materialized out of the mist ahead of them. It proved to be Leonard Stock, on his way down to his house to collect a few more of his wife's belongings.

Leonard was nervous and talkative, and like Ronnie Purvis, inclined to throw quick, darting glances behind him. And Valerie, catching herself doing the same thing, wondered if everyone on the island was equally on edge? She supposed that they must be. It would have made little material difference to their situation if they had been able to communicate by telephone or signal with Aberdeen, but somehow the feeling of being completely cut off—marooned and locked in with murder—was a particularly horrible one. Like being shut into a dark room which you knew to be empty, and then, close beside you, hearing someone breathe . . .

Mr Stock was obviously infected with the same feeling; and even more obviously, intensely disliked the task his wife had set him of going down to his empty, darkened house to fetch some probably useless trifle which she could easily have done without. Valerie, who felt sorry for him but thought him a fool to put up with his wife's shenanigans, inquired what everyone had been doing that afternoon? 'I'm afraid I've been neglecting my guests rather badly. How is Ruby? And Mr Shilto?'

'Ruby is still a little exhausted, I fear. She decided to remain in bed. Shilto's been in his room most of the afternoon, and I'm afraid I've hardly seen him. He came down to the office and borrowed a typewriter and some foolscap, so I imagine he's been getting down to some work.'

Valerie said: 'I hope Dad got my message about not coming back for tea? He was busy when I rang up.'

'Yes. We were making a thorough search of the office,' explained Mr Stock. 'You see, I had a theory that something might be missing, because one of the sentries thought he saw a light in the office shortly before midnight last night, and as your father denied being there, I—we, were afraid that perhaps some unauthorized person had come down after the rest of the household were in bed and—and removed something from it.'

'And have they?'

'Oh no, there's nothing missing, except——' Mr Stock stopped abruptly and looked sly and a little malicious.

'Then there *is* something missing! Do tell us!'

Mr Stock made a pretence of wavering, but it was obvious that he had some special titbit of information that he was bursting to impart. 'I—I don't think Sir Lionel——' He hesitated, fingering his lip, and having glanced nervously over his shoulder, lowered his voice and said: 'You won't let it go any further, will you? I don't suppose it matters very much if you four hear of it, but I should never really have allowed you to get it out of me.'

Nick's mouth twitched at this interpretation of Leonard's obvious desire to impart information, but Valerie said impatiently: 'Go on. What was it?'

'*The letter!*' said Mr Stock in a conspiratorial whisper. 'The letter that Ferrers wrote to your father, which he did not have time to answer. It's been stolen. I'm quite sure of it.'

'Why? Did Dad tell you so?'

'Oh dear me, no. He merely asked me if I had seen an envelope addressed in Ferrers's writing, and when I said I had not, he said it was of no importance: no importance whatever. He was very positive about it.'

'Then I don't suppose it was,' said Valerie shortly.

'It must have been, for if it were not, why should he be so anxious to find it? And he *was* anxious. Oh, indeed he was. You see I—er—happened to return unexpectedly to the office and found your father had opened all the drawers once more and was going through the letters again, though we had already gone through them with the *greatest* care only half an hour before. He was talking to himself too— you know how he sometimes does when he is worried—and I distinctly heard him say, *"But it should be here: I know I left it here!"* He was not at all pleased when he saw me: really quite rude. I don't think I have ever been spoken to like . . . But I am positive that there was no letter there in Ferrers's writing. Positive! One cannot mistake it. Besides, he always used that cheap violet-coloured bazaar ink. It is the greatest pity that I did not—er—I mean . . . Um, I—er—I suppose that none of you have seen it? Or—or would you know what it was about?'

'No,' said Valerie curtly.

Leonard flushed and his eyes darted from face to face in an apparently uncomfortable realization of having said far too much. But somewhere behind them there lurked an avid curiosity and an odd glint of panic—or was it malice?

There followed a brief, uncomfortable pause that was broken by Valerie: 'Don't let us keep you,' she said coldly. 'I'm sure you must have a lot to do, and Ruby will be wondering what has happened to you.'

Mr Stock, encountering her freezing glance, lost himself in a maze of half-sentences, and backing away, scuttled off down the dark leafy tunnel of the drive, and Charles, watching him go, said: 'I wonder what it is that he thinks he knows? Did you see his face? He looked like a cat that has scoffed the canary.'

Nick turned to peer into the misty darkness that had swallowed up the slight figure of their late companion, and said thoughtfully: 'I think that the

sooner we take another look at that notebook of
Val's, the better. However, this is neither the time
nor the place to stand around arguing, and I'm getting damnably damp. Let's get indoors.'

They found the big house ablaze with lights, as
though the servants too had caught the prevailing
unease and with the coming of darkness had attempted to hold fear at bay by turning on every
lamp in the place. But light alone had no power to
banish the fear that pervaded it: a fear that whispered in the swish of the bats' wings, the chirruping
of the little gecko lizards and every creak of floorboard or furniture, and lurked in the shadow of
every curtain and behind each half-opened door.

There was no sign of Sir Lionel Masson, John
Shilto or Ruby Stock, and the big house was uncan-
nily quiet. Charles sent down to the Mess for the
discarded notebook, and while they were waiting
for it Valerie ordered drinks to be served in the verandah. She was annoyed to find herself talking in
something approaching a whisper, and even more
annoyed, on raising her voice, to discover that it had
acquired a slight tendency to tremble.

The air in the verandah smelt stale and faintly
musty, and she crossed to the french windows that
led on to the small balcony beyond the drawing-
room and threw them open. The frangipani tree in
the garden below was in bloom, and its pungent
perfume, intensified by night and the light fall of
rain, drifted in from the misty darkness; cloyingly
sweet and unpleasantly reminiscent, thought Valerie, shivering, of the heavy scent of hot-house flowers at an expensive funeral.

She banged the window to again; bringing down a
pattering shower of raindrops from the bridal-
creeper that grew thickly above the balcony and jar-
ring from its foothold one of the little gecko lizards

which had been crawling across the high ceiling in pursuit of a moth. It fell with a small sharp *plop* at Copper's feet, and Nick saw every vestige of colour wiped from her face and her teeth clench hard upon her lower lip to stop herself from screaming.

He stood up swiftly, and reaching her in two quick strides, caught her by the elbows and jerked her to her feet, and before she could speak had propelled her firmly into the drawing-room and pushed her down into an armchair at the far side of the room. Leaning over her, a hand on each of the chair arms so that she could not rise or escape, he said in a low voice: 'What is it, Coppy? What are you frightened of? Tell me, darling.'

Copper's eyes, dark with fear, clung to his as a drowning man to a spar, but she only shook her head dumbly.

'Why won't you tell me? Is it because you're afraid that I may have had something to do with all this?'

Her eyes did not move from his, and he felt her mind stumble and recover itself. She wet her lips with the tip of her tongue and spoke with a manifest effort. 'No,' she said in a dry, halting whisper. 'No. It's—nothing to do with you.'

'Then tell me what's the matter?'

'I—can't,' said Copper, twisting her hands together. 'There—there isn't anything to tell. Really there isn't. I—I'm only feeling a bit on edge . . . like everyone else.' She essayed a stiff little smile that twisted her lips but did not reach her frightened eyes, and the taut lines about Nick's mouth softened suddenly.

'You're a rotten bad liar, Coppy darling, and just at the moment you couldn't deceive a blind baby. Of *course* you're on edge; we all are. I'm not in too good a shape myself. Look——' He held out a hand for inspection, and she saw that it was not quite steady.

Nick replaced it on the arm of her chair and smiled down at her. 'You see? We've all got the jitters, dear—and with reason. We should be supermen if we hadn't. But it takes more than that to explain why you should have them so badly that a silly little incident like that lizard coming adrift could bring you to within an ace of screaming the roof off.'

'I—it didn't,' denied Copper uncertainly. 'You're imagining things.'

'Am I?' He jerked a clean handkerchief from his breast pocket and with a swift, unexpected movement, leant forward and touched it to her lips. She pulled back with a startled gasp and Nick held out the handkerchief. The white linen was marked with a small scarlet stain.

'Think that's imagination?' he inquired gently. 'It's no good stalling, Copper. You're not scared in the way the rest of us are scared. Or even as that chap Purvis is—which in his case I imagine to be equal parts of alcohol, bad conscience and terror of being the next victim. An hour or so ago you were no more on edge than Charles or Valerie or myself. But you spotted something that frightened you when Val read out the contents of that damned notebook, didn't you? *Didn't you, Coppy!* You either thought of something, or remembered something, that frightened you badly. And you've been thinking of it ever since and twisting and turning it over in your head to see if it fits.'

'No!' said Copper breathlessly. *'No!'*

'It's true. And what's more, you're still frightened! You're frightened now. What is it, sweet? Tell me——'

'I . . . I . . . can't,' said Copper with difficulty.

Nick's hands tightened upon the arms of her chair, and his mouth hardened. 'You mean you won't.'

Copper's voice was barely audible: *'I—I daren't!'*

Nick straightened up and put his hands in his pockets. 'I apologize,' he said curtly. 'I should have remembered that I'm a suspect myself.' Copper flung out a beseeching hand, but he stepped back and turned off the light. 'I think this is where we get back to playing detectives,' he said. 'Here's the citizen who went for the notebook.'

Charles and Valerie called from the verandah, and Copper rose unsteadily from her chair and walked past him to join them.

19

'Here's the fatal volume,' said Charles. 'Now let's see if our newest clue fits in anywhere. The disappearing letter. What do you suppose was in it?'

'We can always ask,' said Valerie. 'In fact I'll go and hunt up Dad now and find out.'

'You do that, honey. It may turn out to be just what we need. And believe me, one really solid lead would be like manna in the wilderness at this moment!' Valerie rose, but was forestalled by one of the house-servants who arrived on the verandah with a message from her stepfather.

Sir Lionel, it transpired, had gone down to see Mr Dobbie—presumably about the burial of both Ferrers Shilto and Dan Harcourt—and had accepted an invitation to stay on for supper: he might not be back until late and Valerie was not to stay up for him.

'Well, that's that,' said Charles. 'Never mind, we can always ask him tomorrow. And I don't suppose that it will turn out to be of any interest, anyway.'

Nick said shortly: 'There I don't agree. If Leonard's guess is right, and someone has swiped it, then it means it contained something of more than ordinary interest. And if it really is missing, it's an even bet that we know who's got it. John Shilto!'

'Why?' demanded Valerie. 'I don't see why it *has* to be him?'

'Use your wits, Val! That "next-of-kin" business. We've already decided that John Shilto changed his mind about coming on to the Harriet picnic because of something that he saw or heard while he was at Ferrers's house, and we all heard him offer to buy back the plantation.'

'We also,' added Charles, 'heard Ferrers turn down that offer extremely nastily. So nastily, in fact, that John's chances of inheriting anything in the sweet-by-and-by could have been profitably swapped for a peanut. But as Ferrers died intestate, John presumably inherits anything there is going. Which could turn out to be plenty. For all we know, copra is due for a rise. Or perhaps Ferrers had found a method of draining his plantation, or fertilizing it, that was making the nuts grow like mad. He may have written to your father to say that he was expecting a bumper crop and wanted extra facilities for exporting the stuff. Something on those lines.'

'Y-es,' said Valerie doubtfully. 'But I still don't see why John Shilto would want to steal the letter. After all, since it had already been read he couldn't hush it up, so why else would he want it?'

'Curiosity?' suggested Nick. 'Or possibly a guilty conscience? He may have wanted to check up on what his cousin had been writing to the Commissioner about, so that he'd know how much of the gaff had been blown.'

Charles said impatiently: 'This is all guess-work. I suggest we try something a bit more practical for a change, and I have a proposal to make.' He rubbed his chin and frowned thoughtfully in the direction of the darkened drawing-room, and after a moment stood up, and crossing swiftly and silently to the door that led into it, peered inside. He stood there for several minutes, listening and letting his gaze wander about the room, before returning to his chair.

'What's the matter, darling?' inquired Valerie with an uncertain laugh. 'Making sure that there are no murderers under the sofas?'

Charles did not echo her bantering tone. 'I thought I heard something move in the drawing-room,' he said slowly. 'Probably only bats or a lizard—or Kioh. But it seems to me that we've all been talking too much and too audibly. So if you will kindly cluster round a bit closer, I propose to lower the old voice a bit. Now listen: what I have to propose is this. You girls, by fair means or foul, must lure the Shilto out here and keep him entertained, while Nick and I go through his room with a magnifying glass and a small-tooth comb.'

Valerie shot out a hand and caught at his sleeve. 'Don't be absurd, Charles! What on earth do you expect to find there?'

'Nothing,' admitted Charles frankly. 'But hope, we are told, springs eternal in the human breast, and you never know what might not turn up. With luck, Ferrers's letter!'

There was a brief silence, and then Valerie rose briskly to her feet: 'All right. But while you're doing it, Copper can try her hand at vamping John Shilto and I'll see if I can't get something out of Ruby.'

Charles said: 'That's my little Mata Hari! And look, Copper, for God's sake keep the Shilto in play for at least half an hour. Or twenty minutes will do, but that's the absolute deadline. We'll wait in Nick's room until you've got the man away, and then sneak in. And for all our sakes don't let him come nipping back to relieve nature or anything, or we're sunk.'

'I'll do my best,' said Copper doubtfully, 'but I can't exactly detain him by force, you know.'

'Nonsense! Sit on his head. Or throw a faint—or

take him off to see your etchings. Use your imagination, girl!'

'You two,' put in Valerie firmly, 'will have to do the job as quickly as you possibly can. And if the worst comes to the worst and he does come back while you're still there, you'll both have to hop out by one of the windows.'

'Thanks,' said Nick grimly. 'A mere drop of twenty feet or so—to say nothing of the possibility of landing on the head of some luckless sentry.'

Valerie laughed. 'It's all right, Nick,' she consoled. 'I wasn't suggesting that you should choose suicide as an alternative to capture. There's a ledge about two feet wide that runs round the outside of the turret room and almost joins up with the balcony outside your room. You can easily get back to your own balcony from it. At least, it's easy by day, though it'll probably be a bit messy by night.'

'I dislike the word "messy",' said Nick. 'It suggests a spade-and-bucket case: *"The driver took a little knife and scraped him off the wheel."* Only in our case it would be the path, or possibly a sentry.'

'It's all right, my timorous mariner,' Charles reassured him: 'She doesn't mean that kind of mess. It's your gent's natty suiting that is doomed to suffer mortal injury. They stain all the outside woodwork here with some red muck that "comes off on you something lovely". Which means that if Copper fails to freeze on to old Shilto for the requisite time limit, we shall either have to go home in Val's pyjamas, or remain in hiding until she can get our suits back from the cleaners. However, these are the grim risks that stare every amateur detective nastily in the eye, so let us give them the cut direct. *"Lay on, Macduff!"*—*"Once more into the breach, dear friends, once more!"*—*"Excelsior!"* '

'For Pete's sake stop being so bloody *Boy's Own*!' snapped Nick, exasperated.

It was some fifteen minutes later that Valerie joined Mr Shilto and Copper in the verandah, and a single look was enough to inform Copper that one assignment at least had proved unsuccessful.

Valerie shook her head in answer to an interrogatory eyebrow, and for the next quarter of an hour assisted in plying Mr Shilto with drink and conversation. Which proved to be a trying ordeal in more ways than one, since Mr Shilto, like Ronnie Purvis, had also been bolstering up his spirits with strong drink. Though unlike Mr Purvis, it had had the effect of making him disconcertingly boisterous, for he talked loudly and disjointedly, punctuating his remarks with frequent bursts of foolish laughter. The minutes seemed to crawl like hours, but at long last Charles and Nick reappeared and Mr Shilto finished the remainder of the brandy and removed himself.

'Any luck?' demanded Valerie in a feverish whisper. 'I had none with Ruby. At the first hint of the subject she closed up like a hysterical clam and almost threw me out of the room. What happened to you two? You were away for *hours.* We thought you were *never* coming!'

'It took a bit of time,' said Charles, 'because we made a pretty thorough search. But it was worth it. Look!' He pulled a piece of crumpled paper out of his pocket and handed it over.

Valerie straightened out its creases, and her eyes widened in a face that had become suddenly colourless. For it was an envelope, addressed in cheap violet ink and in a curious spidery handwriting that she had occasionally seen before, to——

Sir Lionel Masson, C.S.I., C.I.E., C.B.E.,
   Government House,
      Ross.

The writing was Ferrers Shilto's, but the envelope was empty.

20

'—And when they were found,' concluded that indefatigable pessimist, Miss Amabel Withers, 'they were all dead.'

'We have all heard that story at least six times, Amabel!' snapped Valerie with unwonted irritation, 'and if you could possibly keep off the more morbid stories in the Islands' repertoire for this one evening, I'm sure we should all be profoundly grateful.'

Amabel's snub nose glowed pinkly—a distressing habit it acquired when its owner was in any way upset—and her somewhat cow-like eyes filled with tears. Valerie was smitten with sudden compunction: 'I'm sorry, Amabel. I'm a pig. Pay no attention to my beastly snappishness. But if we *could* keep off stories of Battle, Murder and Sudden Death just for tonight, it would be a help.'

Once more they were all seated about the long dining-room table, and Amabel had come over from the hospital for dinner. She had reported that Rosamund Purvis, though by now completely recovered from the 'nervous breakdown' brought on by the accident to the sailing party, had decided to remain at the hospital to keep Truda company. 'You see,' explained Amabel with a characteristic lack of tact, 'Truda couldn't come because she thinks that the hospital cook, who is ill, may be going to die, and Rosamund wouldn't come because she said she'd rather be in hospital with six dead cooks than in a house with one live murderer.'

Her observation had been received in virulent silence, and Valerie, gallantly suppressing a strong impulse towards violence, had managed to turn the conversation to the non-arrival of the S.S. *Maharaja*. But with doubtful results.

'I shouldn't wonder,' offered Amabel with a touch of animation, 'if it hadn't been wrecked. I expect a storm like that could easily turn a ship right over.'

Comment being useless: 'Valerie, my dear,' said the Commissioner, 'I think we had better go in to dinner,' and they had finished their drinks hurriedly and trooped into the dining-room; a silent party temporarily united by a common desire to lay violent hands upon Miss Withers.

During the meal Amabel, who had drunk two cocktails of Charles's devising, with fatal results, had excelled herself. Possibly the unusual silence of the remainder of the house-party was partly responsible for this, since few of them felt equal to manufacturing social conversation, and there was not one among them who did not have his or her own disturbed and secret thoughts. Wherefore Amabel droned on unchecked, and but for the subject-matter of her conversation they might all have welcomed her excessive volubility. But struck by a melancholy association of ideas, stories of murder, mystery, and death by drowning tripped off her tongue in unceasing and morbid procession.

Valerie had endured all these with exemplary patience. But a repetition of the story that Amabel had told on the ferry during the storm on Christmas Eve was too much for her, and had finally provoked her to acid comment. Her belated outburst effectively checked the flow of horrors for the remainder of the evening, but failed to dispel the gloom that their recital had cast over Amabel's fellow-diners, who with one consent hurried over the remainder of the meal and left the table before the arrival of the coffee and liqueurs.

Valerie and Copper left Miss Withers and the men to their own devises, and went off to see Mrs Stock, who had changed rooms with her husband and was now sitting up in bed in the small dressing-room, sipping Ovaltine, with the pink feathered wrap dragged carelessly about her shoulders.

She looked tired and hag-ridden and as though she had suddenly aged ten years, and Valerie noticed with a slight sensation of shock that for the first time since she had known her Mrs Stock had no make-up on her face. Without it, her skin showed coarse and colourless and marked with fine lines about the eyes and mouth, and the fact that she was a middle-aged woman was suddenly and startlingly apparent.

Her hair tangled about her head in disordered black wisps which served to accentuate the pallor of her face, and though she greeted the two girls apathetically, Copper saw that her eyes, like Ronnie's and her husband's and Mr Shilto's, were never still, but darted incessant, uneasy glances about the small room. 'I found I couldn't sleep in the larger one,' she said in reply to Valerie's inquiry about her change of room: 'There were so many bats, and one can't keep them out. And anyway, I am never really comfortable at night in a big room. I think a small bedroom is so much more—more cosy, don't you?'

Valerie, remembering Ruby's own house and her conversion of its largest room—originally the living-room—into her bedroom, had some difficulty in concealing her surprise at this statement. 'Er—yes,' she agreed hastily: 'I suppose so. I hadn't really thought much about it. I suppose they build the rooms large for coolness. I do hope you won't find this one stuffy? There's no wind just now. Would you like me to open one of the windows for you?'

'*No!*' said Mrs Stock with unexpected violence, clutching at Valerie's arm as though to restrain her if necessary by force: '*No!*' She subsided suddenly at the sight of the girls' astonished faces, and forced a smile. 'I—I'll open it myself later when I put the lights out. I do so dislike all those beetles and moths and insects flying in.'

Valerie, refraining from the obvious comment that the mosquito net would effectively prevent them from becoming a nuisance, stayed talking for a few more minutes, and then said good-night.

'I wonder,' said Mrs Stock, 'if you'd give Leonard a message from me? Would you mind telling him that as I'm feeling particularly tired, I'm going to try and get to sleep at once, and that as I don't want to be disturbed I have put his washing things on the chest of drawers in the next room. I'm sure that John Shilto won't mind letting him share his bathroom just for tonight.'

'Of course. Are you quite sure there's nothing else we can do for you?'

'No. No, nothing at all, thank you. Good-night. And please close that door as you go out.'

Valerie and Copper withdrew thankfully, shutting the door of the dressing-room behind them, and they were half-way across the big bedroom—now Leonard's—when a sound stopped them, and they looked back at the closed door of the room they had just left. From the other side of it came the unmistakable sound of a key being turned in the lock, followed by the rasp of bolts pressed home into their sockets. Mrs Stock, it appeared, was barricading herself in for the night.

'I wonder what she's up to inside there?' said Valerie thoughtfully. 'I wonder if—' She frowned speculatively at the teak panels of the closed door, and then turned on her heel again: 'Come on, Coppy. Let's go and rescue Amabel before there's another murder. I should hate to see Charles arrested for homicide, however justifiable.'

But when they rejoined the remainder of the party in the drawing-room, Miss Withers was no longer talking. She was sitting huddled up in a corner of the sofa and complained of a headache. Amabel was unused to alcohol, even in its mildest form, and those pre-dinner cocktails were having after-effects. The Commissioner had vanished, and Charles, Nick, and Mr Shilto, grouped about the empty fireplace, were discussing fishing with a noticeable lack of animation, while Leonard Stock, who was occupying a lonely seat by the bookcase, was yawning over a tattered copy of *Country Life*, and struggling to keep his eyes open.

Valerie paused beside him and delivered his wife's message, which was received without comment: evidently Mr Stock was only too used to being inconvenienced by his Ruby.

On a sudden impulse, which she was afterwards unable to account for, she lowered her voice, and with her eyes on the group by the fireplace added the brief information that they had discovered the envelope of the missing letter in John Shilto's room: 'So you see, Leonard, you were right about it having been taken from the office. But I don't expect Father ever thought of it when he said there was nothing missing.'

Looking down, she surprised an expression of what she could only describe as utter shock in Leonard's pale eyes. It was gone again in a moment, but the little man was obviously shaken: '*John Shilto!*' he said in an uncertain whisper. 'It isn't possible! I thought——' He pulled himself up short. 'I mean, what possible reason could he have had for wanting that letter? There must be some mistake. Yes of course that's it, a mistake . . .'

He babbled on for a full minute, but Valerie received the impression that he was talking at random to cover up some deeper sense of shock or surprise than was conveyed by his words, and she was suddenly angry with herself for having spoken. She cut short his low-voiced incoherencies, and excusing herself, crossed to the far side of the room where Copper was idly turning the pages of a photograph album.

'I rather think I've made an ass of myself,' she confided in a rueful undertone. 'I lost my head and told Leonard that we'd found the envelope of that letter in John Shilto's room, and it seemed to shake him to the core. He's quite obviously got a theory of his own about all this, and it doesn't include John Shilto. Or it didn't, up to five minutes ago! You don't think he *really* knows something, do you? Ought we to ask him, because . . .'

'No, *don't!*' interrupted Copper quickly. 'I mean—he—he could only be guessing, and we're all doing that. Don't let's—' She broke off at the approach of Amabel, and said with some relief: 'Hullo, Amabel, come and play mah-jong, or Slam or something.'

'I dode thig I will, thag you. I thig I'b going to ged one of my colds,' confided Amabel in dismal tones. 'They always start with a headache. Id cabe on suddenly with the puddig.'

Valerie, lending a suitably sympathetic ear, suppressed a giggle with difficulty and said: 'Let's leave the men to talk fish, and see if we can find some aspirin for your head. And when you've taken it, Charles can see you home. You'll be much better off in bed if you're sickening for a cold. Coming with us, Copper?' The three girls withdrew unobtrusively and went off in search of restoratives for Amabel.

'Dad's got something much better than aspirin,' said Valerie. 'It's a sort of powder stuff in a capsule, and it acts twice as quickly. I'm not sure I couldn't do with one myself, to steady the nerves a bit! We'll go and hunt through his medicine cupboard.' She pushed open the door into Sir Lionel's bedroom, switched on the light, and followed by Amabel, vanished through a doorway to the right which led into her father's dressing-room. Copper could hear the chink of bottles as they hunted through the medicine cupboard, but instead of following them she paused instead by the open french windows that gave on to a small creeper-covered balcony overlooking the garden.

Below her in the misty darkness one of the guard lights that remained on all night gave out a dim radiance that touched the creepers with faint gold, illuminating a cataract of scented blossoms that foamed across the wooden balustrade and fell in tangled profusion to the ground. And struck by a sudden thought, Copper walked out on to the wet balcony and peered downwards. But by that faint light it was impossible to tell if the thick masses of creeper had been torn or misplaced.

A breath of wind stirred the mists into ghostly eddies about the old house, and she shivered and turned back again to the comfort of the lighted room. Sir Lionel's bedroom was large and bare and furnished only with a handful of necessities: a cupboard, a narrow bed with a small table beside it, a larger writing-table and a single chair. There were no pictures or ornaments, but a recent photograph of Valerie shared a double leather frame on the writing-table with an older and more faded one of a woman who must have been her mother, for the resemblance between the two faces was remarkable. Copper reached out instinctively, and picking up the frame, examined them with interest. And she was replacing it when something slipped from between the photograph and the back of the frame, and fell upon the table. A sheet of paper covered in thin, spidery writing in cheap, violet-coloured ink. Ferrers's letter . . .

Copper stared at it with a feeling as of cold fingers closing about her heart. It was torn in one place, and it had been badly crumpled, but here and there a few words stood out staringly.

. . . should be most grateful if you could give me some idea as to what the law is on such matters. The lagoon is undoubtedly my property, and therefore anything that it contains is presumably mine, but . . . would prefer to have some official ruling as to where I stand before getting in touch with dealers . . . acquired an aqualung in Calcutta, and the results have been surprising . . . As you will realize, I cannot risk . . . legal angle must be assured . . .

Pearls!—— So that was it! Not the plantation—the lagoon. He had stumbled upon a pearl bed, and—— Why, of course! She herself had asked a question about pearl oysters just before Sir Lionel had spoken of the letter from Ferrers. That should have told her! It had been the mention of oysters that had reminded him of Ferrers; not Amabel's reference to a fisherman who had been drowned. And she herself had put an end to the conversation because she had not wanted to be reminded of that sodden, shrivelled little corpse that the sea had flung ashore.

Pearls . . . John Shilto must have known. That smell that Charles had complained of at the back of Ferrers's bungalow: oysters of course. Oysters rotting in the sun . . .

A voice from the adjoining dressing-room said encouragingly: 'That's right. Swallow it whole. Now in a few minutes you'll feel a lot better.' Copper returned to the present with a start, and thrusting the letter hurriedly back into its hiding-place, turned quickly to face Valerie and Amabel as they re-entered the bedroom.

Returning with them to the drawing-room it was a shock to discover that the fishing story with which Charles had been regaling the company when they left was still in progress, for she felt as though they had been away an hour. But a glance at the clock revealed that they had been absent for barely eight minutes.

Leonard Stock had given up the unequal struggle and departed to bed, and Charles evidently took their reappearance as a signal for breaking up the party, for abandoning his salmon in midstream he jumped up and offered his escort to Amabel as the lesser of two evils—the greater being the continued company of Mr John Shilto.

'I dode thig you need bother,' said Amabel flatly. 'I'b going back in a rigshaw, and one of the orderlies will come along, adyway.'

'Then just let's make sure you get off,' urged Charles, a thought tactlessly. 'Hullo, Copper old girl. You look as if you'd seen a ghost. What's up?'

'Nothing,' said Copper stiffly. 'I'm—I'm a little tired.' And then somehow Nick was standing between her and the inquiring glances that Charles's comment had provoked. 'Same here,' he said lightly. 'Bed for everyone, I think.'

The house-party trooped yawning into the hall, and Nick put a cup into Copper's cold hand and closed her nerveless fingers about it, holding them there with a strong warm clasp. 'It's only black coffee,' he said in an undertone, 'but it's hot. Be a good child and get it down. It'll pull you together.'

Copper essayed a shadow of a smile and drank obediently, her teeth chattering against the rim of the cup.

The others were saying their goodbyes at the head of the stairs by the time she had finished, and Nick took the empty cup from her hand and followed her into the hall. John Shilto departed unsteadily for his room and Charles and Valerie went down into the front hall to see Amabel into her rickshaw. But when Copper would have followed them, Nick put a restraining hand on her arm. He leant against the banisters, his shoulder to the carved stairhead and his eyes on the group in the hall below, and spoke without turning his head: 'What's happened, Copper?'

'I found the letter,' said Copper in a strained whisper.

'The devil you have! Where?'

'In Sir Lionel's room. It was hidden behind a photograph in a leather frame. I—I picked the frame up, and the letter fell out.'

Nick continued to lounge against the banister rail and to watch the departure of Amabel with apparent interest, but his voice compensated for his lack of gesture: 'Take a pull on yourself, darling. It's pretty obvious that whoever took it wouldn't want it found on or near him, but at the same time didn't want it destroyed. And the Commissioner's room would be about the best hiding-place in the house, for no one would think of searching for it there—least of all Sir Lionel!—and when it's wanted again whoever put it there has only to wait until Sir Lionel is safe in his office, and sneak in and collect it.'

'I suppose so,' said Copper in a steadier voice. 'I don't really know why finding it should have scared me so much. It's—it's all this secrecy, I suppose. Everyone having something to hide.'

'Even I,' agreed Nick ironically. 'Tough luck, Coppy! I wonder what dark secret young Amabel is concealing behind that guiltless countenance? And if it comes to that, what are you?'

Copper was saved the necessity of answering by the return of Valerie and Charles.

'*Dear* Amabel!' said Charles, mounting the stairs. 'How I love that girl! Her forebears must have driven a flourishing trade in the undertaking business, and I imagine that Burke and Hare figure pretty prominently in the Withers family tree.' He draped himself limply about the stairhead and added: 'You don't think that we could have been on the wrong track over this murderer business, do you? I mean after this evening's performance I wouldn't put it past Amabel to have pulled off the job herself for the sole purpose of adding another snappy anecdote to her collection of Morgue Memories.'

Nick was not amused. He said tersely: 'Has she gone? Good. Then if the coast is clear, let's get back to the drawing-room for a bit. This spot is a damn sight too public and Copper has got something to tell us.'

They returned to the empty drawing-room where Charles helped himself to a generous nightcap and Copper related her discovery of the letter. And its contents.

'*Pearls!*' said Valerie breathlessly. 'Gosh!'

'Gosh is right,' agreed Nick. 'Pearls. Or in other words, dollars and cents and the pound sterling. Some people might even consider them worth murdering for.'

Charles said grimly: 'Some person quite obviously has!' He finished his drink and put down the empty glass with a thump. 'Well, it's a comfort to have something solid to go on at last, after an entire afternoon devoted to floundering around in a sea of woolly conjecture. That ring theory of Copper's about everyone intending to take a crack at Romeo Purvis and copping old Ferrers by mistake, has been sticking in my gullet. As a motive, it appeared to my limited brain pure dishwash. But here at last we have a good, solid motive for any number of murders. Offered a sufficient quantity of gleaming globules as an inducement, I might very well try my hand at a little murdering myself.'

He turned about and indicated Valerie with a wave of his hand: 'Just cast your eye over there. The small whatnot which, if you look closely, you will observe pinned to my loved one's bosom, was reluctantly donated by myself to mark her last birthday, and set me back a matter of forty-five quid. And what does this bauble consist of? Three—count 'em—three undersized lemon pips which the jeweller who stung me with them insisted were pearls of genuine and not Japanese manufacture, mounted in roughly ten bob's worth of gold. Therefore, by a simple process of calculation—and deducting fifteen quid as an absolute maximum for mounting and making—those three miserable blobs of tallow are worth just about ten pounds apiece, and are barely visible at a distance of two yards. It therefore stands to reason that a pint-size mug of passably decent pips would probably net something in the neighbourhood of fifteen to twenty thousand pounds. Am I right?'

'Just about,' concurred Nick. 'So how's that for a motive for murder?'

'It will do to go on with,' said Charles.

'Then—then it *was* John Shilto!' Valerie spoke in a half-whisper. 'But how did he find out?'

Charles gave a short laugh. 'Probably smelt a rat—or rather a load of rotting oysters—when he went up to the bungalow that morning. You can't open a live oyster nearly as easily as a dead one, so it saves time to let 'em die in the sun and then start in looking for pearls. He probably did a snoop round the back premises to see what in the name of Sodom and Gomorrah Ferrers was using to manure his plantation with, and stumbled across the shells. I know he's been to Ceylon, so he may well have seen the pearl fisheries there, and tumbled to the fact that those shells did not merely mean that Ferrers enjoyed eating oysters.'

Nick frowned thoughtfully into the black night beyond the window-panes, and said slowly: 'Yes. I think it looks more and more as though it must be John Shilto. But I don't think we can just scrub the possibility of its having been someone else.'

'I agree. And I'm not.'

'Oh, nonsense, Charles,' said Valerie impatiently. 'Of course it can't be anyone else! Where would anyone else come in? Ronnie, for instance?'

'Same place as everyone else, I imagine! Ronnie could probably do with a bucketful of pearls.'

'Who couldn't?' asked Nick. 'I don't mind telling you that I could do with them myself. And by the way, Copper, you can now add another black mark to my charge-sheet. If I remember rightly it was only the absence of any motive that stumped you: apart from that you could probably have made out an excellent case against me.'

Copper did not answer, but Valerie, seeing her wince, rushed hotly to her defence: 'That isn't in the least amusing, Nick! If Copper ever suggested that there might be a case against you it was quite obviously to warn you that, outside of ourselves, you might be considered by some other people to be

equally suspect with the rest of the sailing party—
and that you should be prepared to face the fact!'

Nick grinned and said without irony: 'Accept my
apologies, Val: there will be no more acidity in court.
But returning to Purvis, I doubt if he's got the nerve
to commit murder. Though if it comes to that, I
don't believe that the Stocks have either! On the
other hand, it seems to me to stand out a mile that
both Ruby and Leonard know something—or think
they know something. A rather dangerous state of
affairs, I should have thought, with a murderer
around. So I think that at this point a talk with dear
Ruby might be profitable, for if that woman really
was peering over the banisters some time during the
night watches, the chances are that she can make a
pretty shrewd guess at the identity of the murderer.'

'*Um*,' said Charles. 'Possibly. On the other hand,
if Ruby thinks that she knows who did it, why the
hell is she keeping her mouth shut?'

Nick shrugged. 'You have me there,' he confessed. 'I could probably dream up half-a-dozen
fairly plausible reasons, given time, but the only
ones that occur to me at the moment seem a bit
flimsy. However you might consider these: sheer
panic; the inability to produce any concrete proof
beyond her own word which, unsupported, might
be insufficient to secure a verdict. Or black terror for
fear that she might be the next victim on the list if
she admitted to any knowledge of the murder.'

Charles produced a sound uncommonly like a
snort. 'B——! I mean, rubbish! Do you mean to say
she couldn't pick a time when she was surrounded
by a mass of citizens, and then blow the gaff? Of
course she could! She's only got to get in a huddle
with a few of the local inhabitants, and then say,
"There is your murderer! Grab him!" '

'But suppose she wasn't believed?' said Copper in

a low voice. 'Supposing it was someone—someone . . .' Her voice trailed off into a whisper as Charles swung round to face her: 'Supposing it was who, Coppy?'

'I—I don't know,' said Copper uncertainly. 'Just—anyone. I mean, supposing she didn't know for certain, but—but only——' Once again her voice failed, and she stopped.

'Only what?'

Copper did not reply, and Nick's eyes narrowed speculatively as he watched her. But Valerie, who did not appear to have noticed her hesitation, said with a sigh: 'I'm afraid all those laborious notes I made this afternoon are going to need rewriting, now that we've got hold of this pearl motive. What about getting our hands on Ferrers's letter? We could do that easily, because the parent is still working like a beaver down in the office, poor pet.'

Nick shook his head. 'I wouldn't, if I were you. You see now that we know where it is, it seems to me a good scheme to leave it severely alone and tell no one, but merely keep an unobtrusive watch on that door and see who goes to fetch it. Presumably whoever put it there has some reason for wanting it back; otherwise he'd have destroyed it.'

'Which is not quite so easy as it sounds,' commented Charles. 'Torn up scraps of paper can be collected and read. See Crime Club. Also traces of burnt paper, in a house where a paper is missing, are apt to wear a suspicious look. However, just between you and me, what about shelving the entire question until tomorrow? My head is reeling with a varied and malignant collection of clues, motives and suspicious acts, and unless I am much mistaken, a collapse into complete lunacy is imminent. Let's talk about the weather instead.'

He drank deeply, and turned to Valerie. 'By the

way, Star-of-my-soul, what alibi did you hand your respected parent to account for my spending the night here? He murmured something to me about the state of the Mess roof, to which, being unprepared, I had no adequate comeback.'

'I *am* sorry,' apologized Valerie guiltily. 'I should have warned you. I knew Dad would say it was all nonsense if I said I'd asked you to stay here because I was afraid there might be a murderer in the house, so I told him that the storm had broken the Mess roof and your room wasn't fit to sleep in.'

Charles exhaled noisily: 'And what,' he inquired, 'do I say when he comes down tomorrow to view the damage? Just that it was all a hearty little joke? Or that I've just that minute mended it with glue and stamp paper?'

Valerie laughed, and reached out to ruffle his hair. 'It's all right, darling, you know he never goes near the Mess if he can help it. And anyway, it achieved its object. You *are* sleeping here.'

'Not yet,' said Charles. 'But I intend to—and that right speedily!' He drained his glass and stood up. 'Bed, I think, is indicated. And lots of it.'

One by one the lights snapped out until, except for one in the lower hall, the big house was in darkness. And twenty minutes later Copper and Valerie, tucked inside their respective mosquito nets and with their beds tonight placed side by side in Valerie's room, heard Sir Lionel's footsteps mount the stairs and cross the ballroom. Valerie called out a good-night, and a moment after his answer they heard his door shut.

'Night, Val.'

'Night, Coppy. Sleep well.' Valerie slid an arm out from under her mosquito net and switched off the little bedside lamp that stood on a table between them, and darkness and quiet swept down upon the room, broken only by the flitter of a bat's wing and the whisper of the fan blades cutting into the warm damp air. But presently she spoke again, her voice an anxious undertone: 'I'm glad Charles is here tonight. But—but I wish he wasn't sleeping in Dan's bed . . .'

Copper did not reply, and supposing her to be asleep, Valerie turned on her side, tucked one arm under her pillow, and went to sleep.

=== 21 ===

Copper was not asleep. And as the dark hours dragged on, sleep receded further and further from her tired brain.

The house was so still. So deathly still that after a time she realized that the rain must have stopped because she could no longer hear the soft drip of water from the gutters at the roof edge. Even the sea had quietened at long last, and the distant roar of the breakers had softened to a lower key; a soft, drowsy note, like the purr of a giant cat. But the isle was still full of noises, and the apparent stillness was, as ever, made up of a hundred small sounds which welded together made up the sum total of silence, and Copper's taut nerves separated each sound from its fellows.

Every unexplained creak or patter, every whisper of a bat's wing or tap of a night-flying beetle against a window-pane—even the familiar sound of the hall clock striking the slow passing of the hours—made her pulses leap with terror; and when a nightjar cried harshly in the garden her heart seemed to jump into her throat and she found herself clutching at her bedclothes with frantic fingers to keep herself from screaming.

She tried not to think of Dan and Ferrers—and death. Or of any of the horrible happenings of the last three days and the sheer terror of the night between Christmas Eve and Christmas Day. But it proved to be beyond her powers, for her weary mind betrayed her and took her stubbornly back over every hour of those long hours and through every detail of those grim little notes that Valerie had written down in her sprawling, schoolgirl hand. And with every recollection her fear mounted.

They had been mad—mad and stupid and conceited—to imagine for one moment that they could help to unravel this ugly, bloodstained tangle. Their interference and probing could not possibly help . . . but it might well end by placing every one of them in terrible danger, for someone who had already killed twice might, if sufficiently frightened, kill again.

Supposing that unknown killer were to grow suspicious of them? Of their actions, their inquisitive interest, their questions—and begin to fear that between them they might stumble upon the truth? The prospect was too frightening to contemplate. Yet it was impossible not to ask questions. Not to guess—and be afraid.

What was Nick hiding? What was Ronnie afraid of? Why had John Shilto drunk so steadily that evening and talked so disjointedly and wildly? What had frightened Rosamund Purvis and why had Ruby changed her room and locked and bolted herself into it that night? Why hadn't Dan told anyone of his suspicions regarding the death of Ferrers Shilto, and why had the news about the finding of the envelope in John Shilto's room come as such a shock to Leonard Stock?

The questions shifted and jostled through Copper's aching brain like pieces of a jig-saw puzzle, and it seemed to her that they lacked only the addition of one key piece to fall swiftly and easily into place. And suddenly it was borne in on her, with inexplicable conviction, that the clue to the whole murderous tangle lay concealed behind that final question mark in Valerie's notebook. A red question mark that stood for a trivial incident at the Mount Harriet picnic that had struck her as odd. If only she could recall what it was, the pieces of the puzzle would fit together and the answer to all their questions would be found in the completed picture.

But she could not remember. Try as she would it eluded the grasp of her tired brain, and she turned back wearily to the long procession of information and conjecture that lay between the covers of the notebook, pressing her palms against her aching forehead as she added up the sum of whys and whats and whens. But the only answer that presented itself was too frightening to be faced, and she shied away from it as though it were something tangible that must be avoided at all costs.

Her hunted mind turned desperately to Nick. But with no sense of relief, since Nick, like everyone else, was hiding something: and that in itself was as terrifying to her as the actual fact of Dan's murder, for the core of her terror lay not in any fear that Nick might be implicated in the crimes, but in the fear that he might possess some vital piece of information that was of danger to the murderer, and for the suppression of which he must be silenced. As Dan had been silenced . . .

Copper sat up in bed, clasping her hands about her knees and staring into the darkness. Tomorrow she must warn Nick—she must warn them all—that in meddling with this affair they were playing not so much with fire as with high explosive. She felt a little sick at the remembrance that it was she herself who was mainly responsible for their activities, since it was she who had suggested that they try and help track down Dan's murderer. But Dan was dead. Nothing that they could do would alter that fact or bring him to life again, but their continued meddling could easily lead to another death on the island. To-morrow, before it was too late, she must make the others see this.

Before it was too late . . . ? All at once it was as though a cold finger had reached out of the dark-ness and touched her, stilling the beat of her heart: for suddenly, sickeningly, she remembered Ronnie's missing revolver.

How could she have forgotten it? How could *any* of them have forgotten it? Why hadn't they realized its deadly significance? Ronnie had been so drunk, and they had been impatient of his alcoholic bab-blings and anxious to get away. And then Valerie had startled them with the remark that he was no longer wearing his ring, and a few moments later they had met Leonard Stock, whose news about the missing letter had sidetracked them on to Ferrers. Sidetracked them when all the time here, surely, was proof that a third murder was not only con-templated, but already planned.

Copper gripped her hands together and tried to think what she must do.

In the morning, as soon as it was light, she would wake Charles and Nick, and after that there must be no rest for anyone on the island until that revolver was found. Thank God the heavy sea swell seemed to be running itself out at last, and perhaps tomor-row they would be able to establish communication with the mainland. The arrival of Dr Vicarjee and Benton, the P.A., of Ted Norton and his police, and of Mr Hurridge, the Deputy Commissioner, would lighten the tension on Ross to a considerable extent.

Copper sighed wearily and laid her aching head against her knees, and as she did so something touched her arm very softly, and once again her heart seemed to stop beating. The next moment she realized that it was only her mosquito net which had billowed inwards, stirred by a draught from the open windows. A breeze had at last arisen to disturb the stillness of the mist-laden air, and outside in the garden it rustled the leaves of the mango trees, set the dry stems of the bamboo clusters clicking together, and passed in a cooling breath through the darkened rooms.

The hall clock struck two, and in the stillness that succeeded its metallic chime, Copper thought she heard a floorboard creak somewhere in the silent house. And instantly she was terrifyingly alert: waiting, with every nerve taut, for the faint vibration that would betray the passing of anyone . . . of anything . . . through the ballroom. But she could not have told whether it came or not, for as she waited another puff of breeze, stronger than the last, billowed her mosquito net again and shook the iron rods that supported it. When it had passed, though she continued to strain her ears for any further sound from the ballroom, none came, and after a few minutes she lay back on her pillows and tried to relax.

A faint measure of ease returned to her, probably due more to nervous exhaustion than to anything else, and a blessed drowsiness began to steal over her, drugging her brain. Tomorrow, thought Copper sleepily. Tomorrow I must tell Nick . . . the revolver . . . it isn't safe . . . Tomorrow . . .

It was then that she heard the shot.

The crashing reverberations of that violent sound shattered the silence into a hundred savage echoes that seemed to fill the house and give no indication of direction. It was followed by a frozen moment of utter stillness; and then the house was full of noises.

Copper was half out of bed, struggling frantically to free herself from the clinging folds of mosquito netting, when the light snapped on and Valerie was standing beside her, clutching at her, her face blanched and even her voice drained of blood: *'What was it?'*

'Ronnie's revolver!' sobbed Copper in a harsh, choking whisper. And free of the mosquito net she snatched up her dressing-gown, and without pausing to put it on or to consider what danger she might be running into, tore herself free of Valerie's clinging fingers and ran out into the passage.

There was a blaze of light in Nick's room, and as she reached the doorway someone running out collided violently with her flying figure.

'Nick!' said Copper in a breathless sob, *'oh, Nick!'* The next instant she was lifted off her feet and held so closely that she could hardly breathe. Her own arms were tight about his neck, and she was sobbing in hard, dry gasps.

'Are you all right?' Nick's voice was harsh with fear, and he held Copper as though he would never let her go.

'I thought you'd been killed,' she sobbed. 'I thought he'd killed you!'

Nick kissed her hard and savagely, holding her close. Lights were flashing on in room after room and the house seemed full of people in pyjamas and dressing-gowns, and noisy with fear-filled voices. Charles, whom the shot had barely awakened, came blundering out into the passage and crashed into them. 'Left, I think,' he said breathlessly, and Nick thrust Copper away from him, and the two men raced along the passage towards the turret room, Valerie and Copper at their heels.

The turret room was in darkness, and for a blasphemous minute Charles groped for the electric light switch and called John Shilto by name. Then

there was a click, and the lights flashed up, and
Charles said: 'Damned if he isn't asleep—or drunk!'
for they could see the bed with its close-tucked mosquito netting, and through its shrouding whiteness,
the dark bulk of the body that lay on it.

But John Shilto was not drunk. He was not even
asleep.

Something was dripping from the bed on to the
smooth uncarpeted floor, and each slow drop fell
with a monotonous little splash into the small, grinning pool that had already formed beside the bed
and was spreading sluggishly along the joins of the
floorboards.

Nick tore out the mosquito net with a savage
hand, and after one swift look, dropped it and spun
round: 'Get out of here, Copper,' he ordered curtly.
'You too, Val! You can't do anything. He's dead.'

Neither girl moved. It seemed as though they had
lost the power to do so. Then, suddenly, the Commissioner was in the room, and Leonard Stock, his
feet thrust hastily into tennis shoes and wearing a
vividly patterned dressing-gown that looked as
though it must belong to his wife.

Orderlies, *chaprassis* and one of the sentries were
thronging the entrance to the turret room, and of all
the household only Ruby Stock appeared to be con-
spicuous by her absence.

The Commissioner pushed past Valerie and strode
to the bed. 'What is it?' he demanded. 'What happened? *Good God!*' His voice cracked harshly as he
swept the mosquito net aside.

There was a sudden frozen silence in the crowded
room, broken only by the slow splash of falling
blood, and for a moment it seemed as though the
house itself were holding its breath from horror.

John Shilto was very dead. Where his head had
been there was now only something blotched and
shapeless and dripping. One lax hand lay outside

the sheet, its fingers loosely clasped about the barrel of a heavy service revolver, a bullet from which had so recently and violently awakened the house. There was a faint reek of cordite in the air, and pinned neatly to one corner of the pillow was a folded sheet of foolscap. '*Suicide*, by God!' breathed the Commissioner. He stretched out a hand towards the revolver and Nick said sharply: 'Don't touch it— fingerprints!'

But he was too late. Sir Lionel's fingers had already closed about it, and he swung round and glared at Nick: 'Don't talk such damned nonsense! Who else's fingerprints should there be on it, other than his own?'

'At a guess, Purvis's,' said Charles.

'*Purvis!* Then how the devil——? Here, Stock, you'd better take charge of it for the moment.'

Leonard Stock stepped back hurriedly, treading on the toes of an inquisitive house-servant who, taken unawares, yelped sharply.

'I——? Oh, er—of course. Certainly.' He accepted the weapon reluctantly, as though afraid that it might explode in his hand, and held it as far away from him as possible, eyeing it unhappily, while Sir Lionel, having ordered servants and orderlies from the room, turned back to the bed. 'And now—' began the Commissioner. But he was not allowed to finish, for Charles cut unceremoniously across his sentence: 'Val darling, you and Copper clear out, will you? At once, please.'

'No,' said Copper in a taut voice. 'I'm not going until I know why he did it. If—if he did it. Why hasn't someone read that paper?'

Sir Lionel swung round with a muffled exclamation and ripped the folded paper from its fastening. It proved to consist of a single closely typed sheet of foolscap with the final signature in a bold sprawling hand. He glanced swiftly through it, and then, very deliberately, read it aloud:

I, John Chalmers Shilto, being of sound health and in my right mind, have decided to put an end to my life. The circumstances which have brought about this decision are as follows:

The estrangement between my cousin, the late Ferrers Shilto, and myself is common property, but few have realized how bitter it has been. I do not propose to weary others with an account of our private dispute. It is enough for them to know that the bitterness of years culminated, on Christmas Eve, in a difference of opinion, on a private matter, which convinced me that the Islands were not large enough to accommodate both my cousin Ferrers and myself. I therefore decided upon his removal.

Fate played into my hands, and during the storm on the evening of the same day, my cousin and I shared for a few moments a hold upon the same upturned boat. At the moment at which we overturned I had grasped at, and still retained, the tiller of my boat. It made an excellent weapon. I struck my cousin on the back of the head and I believe that he must have died immediately. A few moments later another boat bumped into mine, and I left mine and clung to it. The visibility was so poor throughout that I do not believe anyone noticed the exchange, for it was next to impossible to see who was one's neighbour, and I should not have recognized my own cousin except for a ring he wore upon the hand with which he had grasped the keel beside me. No one noticed his absence, and it was not discovered until we were taken aboard the forest-launch nearly half an hour later, when it was naturally assumed that he had been drowned.

However, an unlucky freak of the tides returned his body, undamaged, to Ross; and by an even more unlucky accident, Surgeon-Lieutenant Harcourt was pres-

ent on that occasion. He saw what Dutt missed, and unfortunately for himself went down to the Guest House on the night of December 25th in order to verify his suspicions.

But since he had already displayed them too clearly I was prepared for some such action on his part. I managed to get clear of the house without being seen, and followed him to the Guest House, where I killed him.

I sincerely regretted having to perform this act, but I had no choice in the matter. It was a case of my life or his, and I preferred, not unnaturally I think, that it should be his. But once again I was unlucky, for the lack of a few inches in the size of the coffin destroyed what I flatter myself was a well-thought-out plan of action.

Since then I have had to realize that the chances of discovery are increasing hourly, and that to diminish them, I should have to kill again. I may say that I enjoyed killing Ferrers, but the elimination of young Harcourt was distasteful to me, and any further killing— perhaps, of necessity, even women—would not only be distasteful, but would also add to the risk of discovery. Life under these conditions would not be worth living, and so I have decided to cut the Gordian knot of a situation that has grown too complicated for me. My regards and apologies.

John Chalmers Shilto

There was a brief silence after Sir Lionel had finished reading, and the page of foolscap crackled harshly as he refolded it. He said heavily: 'I think we had better send for a doctor. Dutt will have to do.'

Charles took Valerie's arm and propelled her towards the door. 'You and Copper had better go back to bed, darling.'

Valerie said beseechingly: 'We can't, Charles— you know we can't!'

'All right then, go and sit in the verandah. I'll come along as soon as I can. Here, Leonard'—he grabbed Mr Stock by one gaily-coloured sleeve—'be a good scout and take these two kids off to the verandah. And just see that they don't start having hysterics. It's all right, Val, Leonard will keep you company and I'll be along in a few minutes.'

He hustled the two girls out of the room, and Mr Stock followed with grateful alacrity.

22

'I don't believe it!' said Copper, breaking a long silence.

The three of them were sitting in that part of the verandah that lay beyond the drawing-room, for as though by mutual consent they had come as far as possible from the thing that lay in the turret room.

Ten minutes had passed since Charles had ordered them from the room, and for ten minutes they had not spoken. True, Mr Stock had made an abortive attempt at conversation, but the blank and unresponsive stares of his two charges had caused him to drop the idea and he had taken instead to tapping a nervous little tattoo on the arm of his chair.

Valerie turned her blank gaze from the dark window-panes and asked listlessly: 'What don't you believe?'

'I don't believe he killed himself.'

'What's that?' Valerie sat up with a jerk, staring at her, and then relaxed again. 'Oh, don't be ridiculous, Coppy,' she said wearily. 'It's quite obvious that no one else could have done it. Besides, what about that letter?'

'That's just what I mean. Would you have thought that he'd write like that? I mean, express himself in that way?'

Valerie shrugged her shoulders. 'It was a bit pedantic, but then I imagine that writing one's Last Will and Testament, so to speak, would be inclined to make one go a bit legal and pompous. What do you think, Leonard?'

Mr Stock, who was looking grey and strained, started slightly on being addressed, and thought for a moment. 'Yes, I think perhaps you are right,' he admitted cautiously. 'And then, too, anyone contemplating suicide cannot really be considered normal; although they are probably quite sane. So it is not to be expected that they would write a normal letter. I imagine that the majority of suicide notes are either hysterical or dramatized, and the slightly pedantic phrasing of poor Shilto's letter was probably the latter.'

'*Poor* Shilto!' said Valerie violently. 'A low-down, cold-blooded cowardly murderer! He at least had the excuse of a quarrel with Ferrers, but he killed Dan just to save his own beastly skin. Poor *Dan*——!' Her voice broke.

Mr Stock shuffled his feet uncomfortably and murmured something about '*De mortuis*', and Copper said: 'Personally, I'd consider the saving of one's own skin a much better reason for committing murder than a mere difference of opinion. And that's another reason why I don't believe he did it. We overheard part of that second quarrel, and however much they spat at each other it didn't seem—— Oh, I don't know!' She sighed impatiently and turned to stare out into the darkness.

'What's that?' inquired Mr Stock eagerly. 'You actually heard the Shiltos quarrelling on another occasion?'

'Yes,' said Copper, and repeated, verbatim, what she could remember of the dispute, while Valerie peered apprehensively into the shadows of the darkened drawing-room beyond them and Leonard Stock looked interested and malicious and, finally, disappointed. When she had finished he shook his head and said: 'No, I agree it does not seem enough by itself to have driven Shilto to committing murder. It is a great pity, of course, that you didn't hear more. But you must not forget the years of enmity behind it. Taking that into account, I think his act is understandable—though hardly forgivable.'

Copper turned to stare at him in frank contempt. The bathos of the phrase 'hardly forgivable' applied to an act of deliberate and cold-blooded murder struck her as little short of ludicrous, and even managed to bring a wry smile to Valerie's weary mouth.

The three of them were sitting in a solitary pool of light thrown from a heavy bronze standard-lamp; for although most of the lights in the rest of the house were burning, the drawing-room and the verandah had been in darkness save for the standard-lamp. But the small pool of light in which they sat seemed to form a charmed circle in the dark verandah, holding them safe from the shadows of the rooms beyond and the grim, quiet figure that lay hideously illumined in the turret room at the far side of the house.

Copper shifted her gaze from Leonard's restless fingers to the comforting immobility of the huge bronze dragons, fashioned by some long-dead Burmese craftsman, that writhed in frozen fury about the massive base of the curiously wrought standard that had once held high an incense burner in some forgotten temple, and was now relegated to the lowly task of bearing a couple of electric bulbs. And as her eyes followed the curves and twists of the metal, her mind traced again the tortuous curves and twists of recent events.

She had forgotten her earlier terror and her resolve not to meddle further in this murderous business, for John Shilto's letter should have completed a pattern; but it had not done so. There was still something missing. The key piece of the jig-saw puzzle——

She lifted her head and spoke abruptly: 'I don't understand why he didn't give the reason for that quarrel with Ferrers. If he'd decided to kill himself, surely there was no reason why he shouldn't speak of it? He didn't strike me in the least as a man who would mind washing dirty linen in public. Especially if it was Ferrers's dirty linen.'

Valerie said impatiently: 'Are you still harping on the idea that it wasn't suicide? Because if that's one of your reasons for thinking it wasn't, it's a poor one. I can't see why he should have made his statement longer than it was. If he'd started out to put down all the whys and wherefores and ins and outs of his quarrel with Ferrers, he'd probably never have had time to shoot himself before he was caught.'

'Yes, I realize that,' said Copper, stirring restlessly. 'But all the same I can't help feeling that there's a catch somewhere. He—well, he didn't seem to me the type of man who'd ever kill himself. Anyway, not until he was actually cornered.'

She pressed her hands to her aching temples, thinking again of the thing that had haunted her ever since Valerie had read through the contents of the notebook: a picture and a statement that contradicted each other. Nick had said that only seven people could lie under suspicion of killing Ferrers Shilto, because only seven were out in the bay with him when he was murdered. But Copper, looking down on the bay from Mount Harriet barely twenty minutes after Ferrers and those seven had left, had seen a sail. A tiny, white triangle against the expanse of opalescent water below her, that could not have belonged to any of the three boats that had left from Crown Point jetty . . .

Leonard Stock cleared his throat apologetically. 'If I may make a suggestion,' he said hesitantly, 'are you not making rather a mistake in—er—perspective?'

'I don't think I know what you mean?'

'Well—er—even supposing that it was unlikely that a man of Shilto's temperament would shoot himself, surely, in this case, it is even more unlikely that anyone else did? I imagine you were asleep when the shot was actually fired, and therefore ——'

'I wasn't,' interrupted Copper. 'I was awake.'

'Oh. Then that will probably help to prove my point. May I ask what you did when you heard it?'

'Jumped out of bed,' said Copper.

'And ran out *immediately*?'—there was a slight emphasis on the last word.

'Well, almost immediately. You see I forgot about the mosquito net, and I got myself tangled up in it.'

'Then how long was it, would you say, between the firing of the shot and the time it took you to reach the door of your room?'

Copper considered for a moment. 'Not much more than a minute, I imagine. I didn't even stop to put on my dressing-gown. I just grabbed it up and streaked for the door.'

'Did you meet anyone in the passage?'

'Only Nick—and Charles.'

'No, I mean coming away from the turret room.'

'No,' said Copper slowly, 'I didn't. But it was dark except for the light from our room and Nick's.'

Valerie said: 'It's no use, Copper. I can see what Leonard's getting at, even if you can't. And he's quite right. There simply would not have been time for anyone else to fire that shot and get clear of the room before we all came rushing in. No one would have dared risk it, because the chances of someone being awake and running out in time to cut off their retreat would have been too great.

'And if you're going to suggest that it might have been someone who got in from outside, _don't_! Once the shot was fired, sentries and guards would have been dashing around the house, and the risk of trying to pop out of a window would have been terrific. And quite apart from that, it would need another Douglas Fairbanks to take a jump of about twenty feet on to a gravel path and then get up and dodge a gang of sentries!'

Copper looked unconvinced, and Leonard Stock cleared his throat again and said diffidently: 'You see, it's the time factor. To fire the shot and then pin a paper to the pillow, tuck in the mosquito net again and get out of the room and down the passage, and be out of sight before anyone arrived, would not, I think, have been possible.'

'No,' said Valerie positively. 'Of course not. So shut up, Coppy.'

Copper did not answer, and Valerie saw that she had shrunk back into the far corner of the sofa, and that her slim figure was all at once curiously rigid, while her eyes were staring into the shadows beyond them as though she had seen something move in the darkened drawing-room.

'What is it, Coppy?' asked Valerie sharply. 'What are you——Oh, it's only Kioh.'

The lithe form of the Siamese cat advanced into the pool of light, purring amiably, and rubbed against Copper's ankles, and Copper bent forward to stroke the dark head with a hand that was noticeably shaking. Valerie saw her pass her tongue over her lips as though they were dry, and presently she straightened up a little stiffly and said in a voice that in spite of her struggle to control it was more than a little unsteady: 'I—I saw her move, and—and it gave me a fright. I'm afraid I must be going to pieces. Nerves or something, I suppose.' She looked across at Mr Stock and essayed a stiff little smile: 'Cats are creepy things, aren't they? Would you be very kind and move the lamp to the other side of your chair so that it throws some light into the drawing-room?'

'I'll switch on the ones in the drawing-room if you like,' offered Mr Stock, rising hopefully.

'*No!* No, don't go in there! It—it feels cosier sitting in just this little patch. The house seems so huge and empty when all the lights are on—'

'Now, now, we mustn't let ourselves get nervy, you know!' said Mr Stock with an attempt at roguishness. 'There, is that better?' He placed the lamp so that its light penetrated into part of the darkened drawing-room and thinned the close-packed shadows.

'Thank you,' said Copper shakily. 'You're very kind.'

A pulse was hammering in her throat and her eyes were wide and frozen as she stared into the shadows beyond the reach of the lamp. But behind their fixed gaze her mind was working frantically. She knew now who had murdered Ferrers and killed Dan Harcourt. And who, a short half-hour ago, had shot John Shilto.

The question mark in Valerie's notebook was no longer a query but the key piece to the jig-saw puzzle; and with it, as she had known it would, the other pieces had fallen into place. But there was still another and more difficult problem to face. How could she prove it? What could she do? For the moment, at least, she could do nothing. She must wait until Nick came, and tell him everything. Nick would know what to do . . .

And then, suddenly and horribly, her heart seemed to leave her breast and jump chokingly to her throat. For Valerie was speaking: 'Good heavens, Leonard! You've got blood on your hands! You must have touched him! *Ugh,* how beastly!'

Leonard Stock looked down quickly at the palms of his hands, and his eyes widened as he looked. For the lamp-light that fell on them showed them smeared and blotched with red. But it was not blood . . .

Copper was on her feet and had flung out a frantic hand in a desperate attempt to check Valerie's next words, but she was too late: 'No, it's not blood. It's only that stain off the woodwork of the balcony. Why, Leonard, you're covered with it! Where on earth have you—'

Then she stopped, and in the frozen moment that followed there sprang into her dilated eyes, fully fledged, the implication that hung on those words. Valerie stood up slowly, staring at him, her mouth dry and her hands shaking.

'*You!*' she said in a whisper. '*It was you!*'

Leonard Stock let out a long breath like a sigh and rose to his feet, stretching himself. And it was as though a harmless, dried-up twig had suddenly uncoiled and shown itself to be not a fragment of dead wood, but a live and poisonous snake.

'Yes,' he said very softly—almost complacently, and as though he were speaking a thought aloud rather than answering a question. 'Yes. It was I.'

'*It isn't true!*' said Valerie in a choked whisper. 'It can't be true. You're only making fun of us, aren't you?'

'No,' sighed Leonard Stock. 'I would deny it if it

were not for the fact that I made a slip just now. My very first slip—and a bad one. It was extremely careless of me, but I hoped that it would pass unnoticed. However, I'm afraid Miss Randal is sharper than one gave her credit for being. A pity.'

He chuckled. It was a remarkably unpleasant sound.

'Yes,' said Copper steadily. 'I did see it. It was a great pity.' Her eyes did not leave his face, but her ears were straining for the sound of voices that would tell her that Nick and Charles were coming.

'For *you*, I fear,' said Mr Stock with another cold little chuckle. 'Much as I regret the necessity, I can clearly see that I shall now have to add two more— er—perhaps I had better say *"eliminations"* to my list.'

Valerie's fingers closed over Copper's arm: 'Scream, Coppy!' she said breathlessly.

'No!' said Copper sharply: and Valerie's own scream died unuttered. She had forgotten that Leonard still held Ronnie Purvis's revolver. 'Very wise of you,' grinned Mr Stock.

The lamp-light glinted wickedly along the barrel of the weapon he held in his hand, and the realization of their complete helplessness swept over Copper in a sickening wave. Beyond the stretch of the dark verandah there was a continuous coming and going of hurrying figures between the hall and the turret room. But none of them had entered the verandah. And since neither she nor Valerie could call out, for all the help they could give they might as well have been a mile away. Would Nick and Charles *never* come?

Crowding close on the heels of that thought came the blinding fear that when they did so, the cornered little maniac before her might be goaded into killing from sheer terror. Copper had no knowledge of firearms, but she possessed a hazy idea that a service revolver contained several bullets—was it six? Only one had been used for the murder of John Shilto, which meant that five remained. One for herself, one for Valerie. Still three left. Charles . . . *Nick!*

Cold panic took possession of her brain: to be ousted by colder logic. Her taut muscles suddenly relaxed and she said quite steadily: 'May I sit down? If I don't, I think I shall fall, and that might make rather a noise.'

Mr Stock grinned. 'Of course. Very sensible of you. You too, my dear.' He gestured with the gun barrel at Valerie, who obeyed him; moving as stiffly as though she were a jointed doll, her dilated eyes still fixed upon the weapon in his hand. 'Closer together, please. Thank you.'

Copper saw his eyes leave them for a brief instant and flicker towards the ballroom from where they could hear the sound of voices as a *chaprassi* called down instructions to someone in the hall below. Then his gaze came back again to the two girls, and slid from them to the windows behind them.

'It's no good,' said Copper quietly and very distinctly. 'You know quite well you can't kill us. You daren't fire that revolver because of the noise. And if you tried hitting either of us over the head, the other one would scream the place down and you'd have lost your last chance of escape.'

Leonard Stock nodded in grave agreement. 'You're an intelligent young woman. Yes, I had just reached the same conclusion myself. *Hmm.*' He shifted his weight from one foot to the other with a little rocking movement and squinted down at the weapon in his hand, and after a moment or two he said: 'I'll tell you what I propose to do instead . . .

'I propose, presently, to walk out of this house. And if I should hear any cries or sounds of pursuit I shall shoot the first person I see after that; and probably the next four as well, as this admirable weapon still contains five bullets. Therefore, unless either of you prefers to have the blood of several innocent persons on your head, you will watch me go without screaming or calling for help, and you will also refrain from raising an alarm for at least half an hour afterwards. Have I made myself quite clear?'

Valerie and Copper nodded wordlessly.

'In that case,' said Mr Stock, 'I will wait until Dutt's arrival, which will ensure the removal of most of the household from the hall to the turret room and give me a clear field. It will also allow me a few more moments in your company, so if those two somewhat thoughtless swains of yours should join us, I am sure you would not be so foolish as to arouse their suspicions. May I add that I am an excellent shot?'

He returned the weapon to the pocket of his dressing-gown, and to Copper's bewilderment, reseated himself and lit a cigarette.

'Valerie, my dear,' he said smoothly. 'I am very much afraid that I shall have to trouble you. I do not really think I should leave the house in these garments, so perhaps you would be so good as to go to my room and fetch me the pair of stout walking shoes you will find there? Also the flannel trousers and the tweed coat, both of which are hanging over the back of a chair, and my shirt, hat and raincoat . . .

'You will please do this without being seen. A simple matter if you keep in the shadow and select a time when someone is not actually passing through the ballroom. I will ask you to be as quick as possible, and warn you, in case you have forgotten, that if I get suspicious at the length of time you are away, or if you return in company with anyone else, the consequences will be most unpleasant for your young friend here.'

'I won't go!' said Valerie in a dry whisper.

'Go on, Val,' said Copper evenly. 'It's all right. He won't shoot unless he is cornered, and if you do as he asks you'll at least lessen the chances of his shooting Charles or Nick.'

'Your friend has grasped the situation admirably,' approved Leonard Stock. 'I advise you to do the same.'

Valerie stood up uncertainly. 'All right,' she said shakily. 'I'll do it.' She turned away and, fear lending wings to her feet, ran through the doorway into the drawing-room and vanished into the shadows.

Copper sat tensed and waiting, and with every second that dragged by she saw Leonard Stock's face become more strained and his eyes more wary. Watching him, she wondered how she had ever thought his face was characterless or weak, for in the yellow lamp-light it looked neither. And all at once she knew why. That curious flickering light that seemed to burn behind the pale eyes was suddenly revealed for what it was: a consuming desire for revenge. And with that knowledge cold panic clutched once more at her hammering heart. Weak he had been, possibly characterless. But now he was neither, for hatred had given him both strength and character.

She wondered how long the spark of revolt had been smouldering in his heart. And what had suddenly caused it to flare up and consume him? . . . Had it been the storm? What long years of disappointment and lost opportunity, of snubs from social and official superiors and incessant nagging and bullying by an overbearing wife, lay behind the sudden metamorphosis of a small, diffident man into the merciless and cold-blooded little killer who had already murdered three men, and was perfectly capable of putting a shot through her head should Valerie fail to keep to the letter of his instructions?

His sudden pedantic turn of speech. Was that too a sign of hate? What he himself had described as 'dramatization'? He was acting—even the nonchalance of his present pose was acted—but his pale eyes remained tense and watchful, and as the moments ticked by and Valerie did not return, Copper saw his hand move stealthily towards his pocket, and in spite of the close atmosphere of the verandah she was suddenly ice cold . . . What did it feel like—being shot? A cold bead of sweat ran down her forehead and smeared her cheek: and then Valerie was back again, light-footed and breathing in quick gasps, her arms laden with clothing.

'*Ah!*' said Leonard Stock on a short sigh. 'I was beginning to think that you had been stupid. Sit down beside your friend, please.'

He slipped out of the dressing-gown and began to clothe himself; drawing on the garments over his pyjamas, swiftly but without undue haste. And as he dressed he talked in a low, precise voice that made his words seem like so many drops of ice water.

'Yes,' he said, 'it is strange how in spite of exercising the greatest caution one can yet make such unpardonable slips. Throughout this affair I have made no mistake which might have been avoided. I think I put the case clearly in that typescript that I pinned to poor Shilto's pillow. The discovery of Harcourt's body, owing to the unexpected production of a coffin that proved to be a few inches too small, was a quite unavoidable accident. But the plan for the elimination of John Shilto appeared to contain no flaws. I thought it all out very carefully from every angle and down to the last detail, though the broad outline was of course childishly simple . . .

'I had only to walk from my room to his, and after pinning the letter to his pillow (he was fortunately drunk enough to be sleeping soundly) shoot him, allow myself a margin of roughly fifteen to twenty seconds to complete the scene, and then step out of the window. This admirably patterned dressing-gown of my wife's served as an excellent camouflage to anyone looking up from below, but the mist proved even more valuable.

'The moment those two young men in the next room had run out into the passage nothing was more simple than to enter their room from the balcony, and walking through it, pick my time and join those who were crowding into the turret room. But I forgot that damnable stain, and I followed it up by the almost worse slip of forgetting about the mosquito net. I congratulate you on spotting that, my dear. You did, didn't you?'

'Yes,' said Copper steadily. 'Valerie and Charles and I were the only other people in the room when Nick pulled out the mosquito net to look at Mr Shilto. No one else could have known that it wasn't like that when we found him. Unless it wasn't suicide, but murder. And then only the murderer could have known.'

'Ah, yes. It was regrettably careless of me. A bad slip.'

'There was another one,' said Copper conversationally, her voice unstrained but her eyes intent. 'Not exactly a slip, but a useful clue.'

'You surprise me,' murmured Mr Stock, stooping to lace his shoes—the revolver beside his foot and within easy reach of his swiftly moving fingers. 'I had imagined that outside those two glaring examples I was blameless.'

Copper said: 'On the day of the Mount Harriet picnic I saw you carry a packing-case full of bottles from the car to the far side of the lawn, single-handed; and I remember being surprised. Then later, when we decided that you couldn't be the murderer because you hadn't the strength, I had forgotten about it and could only remember that something had happened that afternoon that had struck me as a little peculiar. I couldn't even connect it with anyone in particular. But when you made the slip about the mosquito net, and I realized that you must have been in John Shilto's room before we were, I thought: "It's impossible, because whoever shot him must have killed the other two, and he isn't strong enough." And then quite suddenly I remembered the box of bottles, and so I asked you to move the lamp, to make sure. It takes two of the servants to lift that lamp, yet you lifted it easily.'

Mr Stock straightened up and laughed his little bloodless laugh: 'Clever!' he approved. 'Very clever of you. Yes, I once wanted to be a gymnastic instructor at a private school; before I came out to India. But Ruby thought athletics of that description were undignified, and so I gave it up. But I used to practise in secret. I've never missed doing a few press-ups every morning.'

His thin lips stretched to show his teeth, and the sheer concentrated malignancy of that smile chilled Copper's blood and made her shrink back involuntarily. But Leonard Stock was not thinking of her . . . '*Ruby!*' he said softly, and his lean fingers tightened convulsively about the weapon he held. '*Dear* Ruby! I'd put a shot through her head before I go, except that she'll hate this worse than death! I think she suspects even now. For the first time in her life she's frightened—and of me!'

It was plain that he was no longer addressing

Copper, but speaking his thoughts aloud: 'Seventeen years I've put up with her. Seventeen years from my life——! And for a good many of them I've been planning how I'd kill her. It's been my one recreation—planning the details of her murder. But this was better. Who would have supposed that that little rat Ferrers would stumble on a pearl bed? If we hadn't stopped at his bungalow that day I might never have found out. It must have been in that tidal lagoon behind the house. He'd left the shells to rot in the sun—the fool!'

Once again, and too late, Copper remembered something. A look she had seen on Leonard's face when the Shilto cousins had met at Mount Harriet. Yes, he had known even then; and had realized in that moment that John Shilto also knew . . . !

But he was still speaking, and now his voice held a note of injury and bewilderment: 'I didn't mean to kill him. It wasn't my fault. It was the storm. I'd felt queer all day—keyed up and on edge—and when it broke, something seemed to snap. He was beside me, and suddenly it came to me that if I killed him I could get the pearls. Freedom and money. Freedom from these damned Islands—freedom from Ruby! With the pearls, I could walk out—disappear . . .

'So I killed him. Harcourt was a mistake—his mistake, not mine. And as it seemed that John Shilto had also found out about the pearls, I realized that he would have to go too. Besides, it was useful to have those two murders pinned on someone else. And then for the whole thing to fall to pieces over a smear of red wood-stain and a slip of the tongue!'

Leonard Stock jerked back his head and laughed: so suddenly and so shrilly that involuntarily Copper started to her feet. In a flash the barrel of the revolver was levelled at her breast, held in a perfectly steady hand. 'No tricks, my dear,' urged Leonard Stock.

He reached behind him, and picking up his rain-coat struggled into it; changing the revolver from his right hand to his left and back again in the process. There were voices from the direction of the hall, and he said: 'Ah, that will be Dutt arriving. Yes, he is going to the turret room, so I shall be able to leave without attracting undue attention. May I remind you both not to go rushing to your friends with this story until I have had ample time to get clear of the island? Say half an hour?'

'Are you mad?' interrupted Valerie breathless: 'You're marooned on this island like the rest of us!'

'Oh, dear me, no.' Leonard Stock laughed with genuine amusement. 'You forget that I always keep my own boat in the old swimming-bath. And after the discovery of Harcourt's body I took the precaution of provisioning her—just in case of accidents. This is no weather to be setting out in a sailing boat, I will admit. But she has a good engine, and luckily the sea appears to have fallen considerably, so I shouldn't do too badly. Half an hour should see me well off the premises. So remember, no immediate hue and cry if you wish to avoid further bloodshed.'

He wagged the heavy revolver at them with a grim joviality, and grinned maliciously. 'Well—*au revoir*, my dears. I trust we shall not meet again, but one can never——'

He stopped suddenly. There were voices in the ballroom, but this time it was Charles. Charles and Nick.

Copper swayed sickeningly and caught at the arm of the sofa to steady herself. She saw Leonard Stock slip the heavy revolver into the pocket of his rain-coat, but his hand still kept a grip on it and she knew that his unshaking finger was still upon the trigger.

He did not again remind them that at least one life, if not all their lives, depended upon their behaviour during the next few moments. Perhaps he knew that they needed no reminder. He began to speak in his usual rather diffident voice, and they saw, with a fresh stab of fear, that his face had once more become weak and characterless and rather foolish, as though he had drawn a mask over that other face whose owner had murdered three men.

Valerie gave a hysterical laugh and said: 'And I once said that story about Jekyll and Hyde was far-fetched! One lives and learns.'

'What's that about Jekyll and Hyde?' inquired Charles. And then he and Nick were standing beside them: real and solid and alive in an unreal world.

Nick looked sharply from Copper to Valerie and said: 'You two look pretty done up. A stiff brandy all round would about suit the case I think.'

'Suits me all right,' said Charles. 'God! What a night! Hello, Leonard, old man, what are you all togged up for? If you're thinking of fetching Dutt, you're too late. He arrived a few minutes ago and they're all poring over the body again. So we beat it.'

'Er—as a matter of fact,' fluttered Mr Stock, 'Ruby is a bit upset, and she says she cannot go to sleep again without some tablets which she sometimes has to take, which are unfortunately down at our house. I said that I would slip down and fetch them—it won't take me a moment.'

'Jeepers, these wives!' said Charles. 'Who wouldn't be a bachelor?'

Copper attempted a laugh. 'That's a nice thing to say in front of your future wife, Charles. Are we going to get those drinks or aren't we?'

'Of course. Come on.' They moved off down the verandah, Leonard Stock walking a little behind them, and paused at the top of the stairs. 'I think I should appreciate that drink more when I come back,' said Mr Stock.

'We'll save you one,' promised Charles. 'Don't go breaking your neck in the dark.'

'I shall do my best to avoid it,' said Mr Stock primly. 'Good-night.'

He began to descend the stairs slowly and rather stiffly. And as he did so, Sir Lionel Masson came quickly across the ballroom: 'Hullo, Stock—where are you off to?' He did not wait for an answer, but hurried on in a preoccupied voice: 'By the way, that revolver of Purvis's—I'd better take charge of it.' He held out a hand, and Mr Stock stopped upon the staircase and made his fourth and final mistake.

Had he said 'I put it in your room,' or any similar lie, the events of that night might have had a very different ending. But some instinct of obedience betrayed him, and mechanically he had begun to draw the revolver from his pocket. A split second later he had recognized the error. But by then it was too late, for the Commissioner had seen it.

'Thanks,' he said. 'I'll see Purvis about it in the morning. It's quite disgraceful that he should not have kept it locked up.'

Mr Stock did not move, and Nick took a step forward as though to take the gun. But as he did so Copper moved quickly and stood between him and the figure on the staircase below, her cold fingers clinging to his. She could see rage, uncertainty and cunning contending together in the eyes of the shrivelled little killer in the raincoat, from whose features the mask had once more slipped to show the face of murder. Then the Commissioner had brushed past her, and descending the few steps that lay between them, held out his hand.

With a curious little sigh, Mr Stock drew out the revolver. He looked once more into the faces above him, and was silent for a long moment. Then suddenly and unexpectedly he laughed, a loud, shrill peal of laughter; his lips drawn back from his teeth in a curiously animal grimace. And startled by the sudden shrillness of that sound, Kioh, who had followed at the Commissioner's heels, spat indignantly, and bounding forward, streaked between his feet and down the stairs . . .

It was all over in a moment, before anyone could move or cry out.

Leonard Stock, taken unawares, stepped backwards and missed his footing. Instinctively, his hands came up and his finger must have tightened upon the trigger, for as he fell there was a blinding flash and a crashing detonation, and his body tumbled backwards down the shallow steps and came to rest at the turn of the staircase, where it quivered once, and then lay still.

The bullet had entered under his chin and come out at the back of his head, and he was dead long before they reached him.

23

It was a glorious day. The pearly sheen of morning had melted before the shimmering sunlight of mid-day, and beyond the curving sands of North Corbyn's the sea was an expanse of smooth, translucent turquoise that stretched away, island-dotted, to the far horizon, where it met and merged into the blue of a cloudless sky.

Valerie and Copper, accompanied by Nick and Charles, had boarded the little fishing-launch *Jarawa*, and complete with bathing-suits and picnic-baskets had anchored off North Corbyn's to spend a day of alternate sun- and sea-bathing.

The Commissioner had been deeply thankful to see them leave. He hoped that they would be able to put out of their minds, if only for that day, the horror and confusion of the night on which John Shilto and Leonard Stock had died; though he doubted if he himself would be able to do so. It had taken some little time to get a coherent account of the events preceding Leonard's death from his overwrought stepdaughter and her friend, and at first he had not believed them. In fact it was not until dawn had broken that an inspection of the sailing boat in the disused swimming-bath, and a long and harrowing interview with Stock's wife, had finally convinced him that a murderer had indeed paid for his crimes by becoming his own executioner.

Two crowded and grimly unpleasant days, full of endless inquiry and discussion, had followed. The bodies of Ferrers, Dan, John Shilto and Leonard Stock had been buried, and though the mists still clung thick about the tiny island, the sea had fallen and communication with the mainland had at last been restored.

Sir Lionel had made an abortive attempt to keep Valerie and Copper in bed, but they had rebelled against staying there and had wandered about the house and the fog-shrouded island looking worn and hollow-eyed; flatly refusing to discuss any aspect of the recent murders and starting violently at every unexpected sound. But on the third day the sun had risen into a cloudless sky, the mists had melted with the dawn, and the harassed Commissioner had instructed his stepdaughter and her friends to remove themselves off the island and to stay off it for as long as possible.

'And if I so much as see a *flicker* of you before dinner,' said Sir Lionel, 'I shall give the whole lot of you seven days' hard labour. So now you know! You can have the *Jarawa* for the day and go out fishing or picnicking or bathing. And now get out and leave me to my labours.' He kissed Valerie, and hustled them firmly out of the house.

The Islands, new-washed by storm and mist and drenched in sunlight, appeared greener and lovelier than ever before, and there were lime trees in blossom in the jungle behind North Corbyn's. Huge, gaudily painted butterflies lilted to and fro on the windless air, the sands of the long white beach were wet and firm underfoot, and the sea that had recently raged so wildly was now as flat as a looking-glass, its water crystal-clear and patched with lavender and lilac where the reefs of coral patterned the sea-floor.

The *Jarawa* had anchored as close to the beach as possible, and its four passengers had waded ashore with the baskets and bathing-towels on their heads to spend the morning swimming and sun-bathing. Afterwards they had eaten a picnic lunch under a tree that spread its branches far over the sands, before settling down to a prolonged and peaceful siesta: from which Copper had been the first to wake, aroused in the late afternoon by the crying of a gull overhead.

Propping herself on one elbow she had looked out across the beach at the tranquil sea, and found it hard to believe that barely a week ago it had risen up in a shrieking frenzy to lash out at the Islands, smashing and tearing. For by now the waves and the wind had already swept away most of the traces of their recent rage, and save for a few prostrate coconut palms and the unusually large number of shells that strewed the sand, there was little visible evidence of those wild days and nights. 'Except on Ross,' thought Copper soberly. There were four new graves on that little island to mark forever the passing of the great storm.

For the first time since that terrifying night when John Shilto had died and Leonard Stock had become his own executioner, she found herself able to think of it all calmly and with a certain amount of detachment; and after a while, with curiosity. And apparently Valerie too had been awakened by the gull, and her thoughts must have been moving on the same lines, for she turned on her elbow and her voice broke the drowsy afternoon silence: 'Charles—'

'Mm?'

'Charles, how did everything happen? I mean

about Leonard, and the Shiltos and everything. Did you ever find out?'

'Ask me some other time,' murmured Charles into the hat that he had tilted well over his nose.

'I don't want to know another time. I want to know now. I haven't wanted to know before, because I felt that if anyone so much as *mentioned* the grisly subject to me, I'd go off the deep end. But getting away from Ross, and all this heavenly sun and peacefulness, has been like a tonic, and I suddenly feel sane again—and full of curiosity.'

'I, on the contrary,' said Charles, 'am full of food and drink, and I require repose and not conversation as an aid to digestion.'

Valerie consulted her wrist-watch: 'You've had more than two hours, and you've got the digestion of an ostrich. So wake up and tell us all about everything or I shall point you out to a few hermit crabs.'

Charles groaned and turned his back on her: 'Ask Nick. He knows much more about it than I do.'

'Nick is included of course. We want lots of information from both of you: don't we, Coppy?'

Copper nodded. 'I didn't feel I wanted to know before,' she admitted, 'but I do now. I suppose it's because this place is such heaven that battle, murder and sudden death seem unreal and not so very important by contrast. Sort of "turnip-lanternish", if you know what I mean. Whereas back on Ross, even on a day like this, it all still seems far too real and frightening, and the turnip-lantern isn't merely two inches of candle and a hollowed-out pumpkin, but a real and rather horrible ghost.'

Nick tilted his hat back from his eyes and grinned at her. 'And you think that hearing all about the whys and wherefores would help to lay the ghost. Is that it?'

'No,' said Copper after a brief pause. 'I don't think anything but lots of time, or perhaps lots of happiness, will lay this particular ghost for any of us. But knowing something about the whys and wherefores will make it less frightening.'

Nick sat up and brushed the sand out of his hair, and propping his back against a conveniently curving tree root, lit a cigarette and said: 'Fair enough. Wake up, Charles, a voice cries, "*sleep no more!*" In this case, two voices. So let conciliation be your policy.'

'*Hell!*' moaned Charles, propping himself on a reluctant elbow and reaching for the beer. 'All right. Which bit of the recent unpleasantness do you two harridans require me to elucidate?'

'We don't want a "bit",' said Valerie. 'We want chapter and verse, right from the very beginning.'

Charles imbibed half a glass of beer and ruminated, and presently he said: 'Remember that sort of lagoon that was part of the "plantation" which John Shilto palmed off on to Ferrers? Well, it turns out to be simply crawling with pearl oysters.'

'Do you mean to say that all these years it's been right under——'

'Look,' said Charles, 'if you propose to interrupt this enthralling narrative with girlish cries, I shall return to my slumbers. You confuse me. Where was I? Oh yes. Well somehow or other, we shall never be certain how, Ferrers discovered the fact that though half his plantation was worth about fourpence ha'penny, the other half was probably worth, at a conservative estimate, about a million sterling.'

'*Gosh!*' said Valerie, awed. 'I didn't think there was that much money in the world!'

Charles grinned. 'It is a pretty good slice, isn't it? A pity we didn't do a bit of paddling there ourselves. Imagine old Ferrers's fury on realizing that he'd spent fifteen or sixteen years in a state of extreme poverty and simmering rage, while all the time a film star's salary was sitting in his backyard, only needing a bathing-suit and a bucket to be collected. I'll bet that thought did something towards tingeing his cup of joy with cascara!

'Well, to continue with the saga, the little man popped over to Ross, borrowed the *Encyclopaedia Britannica* off the padre, and read up everything he could find under the expression "Pearls". He then took to spending half his time in a bathing-suit in the lagoon, and evidently hauled up a goodish few shells, which he spread around in the sun behind his house until the flesh rotted and he could open them and dig in the debris—which accounts for the appalling stink that was hanging about the place. He must have collected more than a hundred fair-sized pearls this way, but he realized that he was only touching the fringe of the matter. To get at the real boodle he needed a diver. Or better still, a diving-suit. So one day he packed his toothbrush, pocketed his pint of pearls, and made tracks for Calcutta.'

'Of course!' said Copper. 'What a fool I am! I wondered, when Val first told me about him, how he'd managed to put up at the Grand if he was so poverty-stricken. I suppose he sold the pearls?'

'That is the supposition, my sweet. Anyway, he managed to bring back a complete diver's suiting with him, and he couldn't have swapped *that* for a sandwich! He got going with it, and business boomed. He hauled up bucketloads of shell and the plantation began to smell like a sewer. And here the first fly mixed itself up in the ointment. Someone, it was quite obvious, was shortly going to ask questions about this extraneous perfumery. And when they did, where exactly did he stand in the eyes of the law? Had he complete and legal right to the produce of his pond, or would the Board of Agriculture and Fisheries, or some similar collection of bewhiskered bandits, sneak up on him and collar two thirds of the loot? It was certainly a problem, and after a bit of brooding he wrote off to the Commissioner and popped the question—disguising the reason for this request with some merry tale about an argument with a friend in Calcutta.'

Valerie laughed. 'I shouldn't have given the little man credit for so much imagination,' she commented.

'Oh, he had a certain amount of brain under that thatch,' said Charles. 'And this brings us to Christmas Eve: "*Noel! Noel!*"'

'On Christmas Eve we stop at Ferrers's bungalow to get water, and John Shilto smells a rat—or, let us be accurate, about a ton of rotting oysters. I smelt it too, and it meant nothing more than nasty stink to C. Corbet-Carr. But John Shilto had been to Ceylon, and the odds are that he's smelt that smell before. This bit is only guess-work of course, but I imagine he snooped around and stumbled on the truth. Not the complete truth, but only half of it—probably due to the fact that Ferrers had a passion for oysters, and as his servants were a slovenly crew, there were certain to be a goodish few shells permanently cluttering up his backyards. But "pearl" shell is a bit different. And John Shilto spots that difference all right!

'Placing two and two together and adding them up to a total of six, he erroneously decides that Ferrers *hasn't* spotted it; and legging it down the path after us, pitches that yarn about the soothing effects of Christmas and how he yearns to clasp his cousin by the hand—which is not surprising, considering that to all intents and purposes the hand contains a fistful of pearls! But alas for day-dreams, Ferrers not only knows the difference between edible and pearl oysters, but he is sitting on both his hands and has every intention of continuing to do so.'

Valerie said: 'Yes, that bit seems all right. But it

wasn't John who killed Ferrers. It was Leonard. How on earth did Leonard get on to it?'

'Cast your mind back, my angel,' urged Charles. 'Remember when we stopped at Ferrers's bungalow his boy told us that the Stocks had been in and had taken him on with them? The Stocks had the Dobbies on board, and Ferrers was coming to Ross to spend a couple of nights with them. Behold the peculiar workings of Fate! Mrs Dobbie wishes to shove in some inquiry about bedding—is he bringing his own or isn't he?—and it is a hot day and Ruby wants a lemon squash. So they all troop up to the bungalow where, according to Ruby, they find Ferrers in high spirits . . .

'They suggest that he comes on to the picnic with them and goes back with them to Ross afterwards. The idea is well received, and while he's packing a toothbrush, Leonard, who was always a bit of a snooper, takes a stroll round the back of the house to see if Ferrers is using a school of stranded whales to manure his plantation—which is what it smells like. Here he stumbles across a quantity of pearl shells, but they only appear to indicate that Ferrers likes oysters. And it is not until he pokes his nose into the shed behind the house that his brain begins to buzz a bit. You see, there was a diving-suit in that shed.'

'How do you know all this?' demanded Valerie.

'Ferrers's Burmese house-boy saw him rubber-necking around. And here Ruby takes up the tale. She says that Leonard came back looking rather excited, and as Ferrers was still absent and they were tired of waiting, they popped into his room to assist with the packing. Apparently they walked in without knocking and caught the master of the house on his hands and knees, with the matting rolled back from a corner of the floor——

'Leonard's arch inquiry as to whether he was

looking for something produced a quite unaccountable explosion of wrath, and for a brief space high words buzzed briskly to and fro. Then Ruby appears to have suggested acidly that from the fuss he was making anyone would suppose he had something to hide, which pungent truth seems to have brought him to his senses, and he apologized all round and mumbled something about having seen a scorpion. He put back the matting and something rolled out of it. Ruby says she saw her husband put his foot on it, and when Ferrers's back was turned, pick it up and put it in his pocket. She meant to ask him about it afterwards but forgot. However we now know that it was a pearl, and that Leonard, who was no fool, was also putting two and two together, and unlike John Shilto, totting them up to the correct total.'

Valerie shifted restlessly: 'Do you mean to say,' she demanded, 'that Ferrers went off to Harriet leaving a lot of pearls lying around the house?'

'They weren't lying around. They were very neatly stowed away under a loose floorboard. And he wasn't looking for a pearl that he'd dropped. He can't have known that he'd dropped one. He was merely stowing away the swag, and the one Leonard picked up was just sheer bad luck as far as Ferrers was concerned.'

'And for that matter,' interrupted Copper, 'as far as Dan and John Shilto and Leonard himself were concerned.'

'Well, yes. If you care to look at it that way,' admitted Charles. 'Now let's think. What comes after that? Oh yes. Quarrel between the cousins Shilto and departure of sailing party.' He turned to Nick, who was meditatively blowing smoke rings at the chips of blue sky that gleamed through the network of green leaves overhead, and said: 'As a member of the sailing party, Mr Tarrent will now take over. *En avant, mon brave*—the floor is yours.'

Nick blew another smoke ring and said: 'You already know what happened when the storm hit us, and since we now have an accurate account of the murder, typed by Stock himself for the purpose of shoving the blame off on Shilto, we know how he spotted that his next-door neighbour was Ferrers—which proves that there was some sense in Copper's ring theory after all! The idea of knocking Ferrers on the head probably jumped into his mind then and there.

'He had been steering his boat and was still clutching the tiller, which had come adrift when they turned turtle. He wanged Ferrers over the back of the head with it, causing an impacted fracture which laid him out in one. Ferrers vanished abruptly, and Leonard decided that murder was child's play. But he hadn't seen that there was somebody on the other side of Ferrers—Rosamund Purvis!

'It's not surprising that he didn't spot her, for her head was a good deal nearer the water than Leonard's because she was holding on to the rudder, and she herself saw very little; what with smashing rain and splashed-up sea, and that howling wind. *But she saw enough to realize that someone had been deliberately murdered within two feet of her!*'

'Of course!' said Valerie suddenly. 'We ought to have realized from the way she behaved that something more than ordinarily nasty had happened. She was much too sensible and stolid a person to have reached that pitch of hysteria over a sailing spill and the fact that one of the party, whom she disliked, had been drowned.'

Nick flicked the stub of his cigarette at an inquisitive hermit crab, and leant back with his hands behind his head: 'I agree. But we can now understand why the poor woman was so worked up. You see, she knew that Ferrers hadn't been drowned.

She knew he'd been murdered for she had actually seen it done: he'd been killed within a foot of her. But she had no idea who had done it! She says that she let go of that boat as though it was red hot, and after a few minutes crashed into what she hoped was another one. After that of course it was no use saying anything, as having once let go of the original boat, she had no means of finding out who else had been on it.'

'But what about Ronnie?' asked Valerie. 'Why was he so scared? Don't tell me *he* saw it done too!'

'No. He didn't see it done, but he got hold of the weapon.'

'The tiller? But I thought Leonard threw it away?'

'He did, but being wood it floated, and some time later it biffed into Ronnie, who grabbed it. The sea was getting rougher by this time and he was afraid of being washed off his boat, so he stuck the tiller through his braces with some hazy idea that it might help to keep him afloat if he lost his hold.

'It was still there when the forest-launch picked him up, and he says he hauled it out and dropped it on the floor of the cabin, and it wasn't until about half an hour later, when they'd given up the hunt for Ferrers and were heading home, that something about it caught his eye. There was a band of metal about the business end of that tiller, and something had got wedged between it and the wood. The sea had washed off all traces of blood, but it hadn't been able to dislodge that bit of flesh and a tuft of grey hair.'

'*Ugh!*' shuddered Valerie. 'How beastly!'

'Yes, it gave Ronnie a bit of a jar too. He picked the thing up to take a closer look at it and discovered that there not only *was* a ragged scrap of flesh and grey hairs wedged between the wood and the metal, but it was quite out of the question that it could have got there by accident. By that I mean the tiller could easily have biffed into someone while floating around loose, but unless it had been applied with a considerable amount of beef behind it, that scrap of flesh could not possibly have got wedged so far down the crack . . .

'Even then, the idea of deliberate murder didn't enter his head. He says he was too shaken up to think straight, and his immediate feeling being one of disgust, he heaved the tiller overboard. But after a bit, when his brain began to function, he started putting two and two together. With the result that at the dinner party that night there were actually three people present who knew that a murder had been committed: the one who had done it, and the two who knew that it *had* been done, and how, but had no idea who had pulled it off.'

'Hence Rosamund's acute attack of St Vitus's Dance,' put in Charles. 'Not a particularly comfortable feeling, having to sit around in a party one member of which you know to be a murderer, but without the least idea which one it is. I don't wonder she was a bit jumpy. Or Ronnie either! If I'd been in their shoes I should have locked myself in my own room and refused to move without a strong police guard. I rather imagine—though of course Ronnie denies it hotly—that his dear wife's firework-display made him suspect that she'd done in Ferrers herself.'

Valerie said: 'And I suppose Rosamund will also deny that she ever thought Ronnie did? Of course it's obvious she did from the way she insisted on going off to the hospital and wouldn't stay with us or go back with him. At least she could be certain that Truda hadn't done it!'

A brief silence followed on Valerie's last words, for they were thinking, all four of them, of the same thing. The dark hours that followed Rosamund's departure.

'How do you explain that?' asked Valerie at length. It was not necessary to ask what she was referring to.

'There isn't any explanation,' said Nick slowly. 'Unless you're prepared to accept Iman Din's.'

'You mean,' said Valerie with a shiver, 'that—that it *was* Ferrers who came back that night?'

'God knows,' said Nick. 'I'm not prepared to swear to it one way or another. It may only have been an optical illusion due to the lightning, and the noises may have been made by cats or bats or rats. On the other hand, after a brief stay in these islands I'm prepared to believe almost anything. And then of course there is always that time-worn remark of the late William Shakespeare's: *"There are more things in heaven and earth, Horatio, Than are dreamt of in your philosophy"*—and that goes for Copper's nightmares too! So let's leave it at that, shall we?'

'Yes, *do*,' said Charles cordially. 'And here I too propose to leave you and take one last, long, lingering splash into the sea before giving my attention to tea. Anyone coming with me? Right! I'll race you for the last marron glacé!'

The four rose simultaneously and raced down the beach into the water.

'I,' said Copper, shaking salt water out of her eyes, 'am going to get tea ready while you finish the story. Go on, Charles.'

Charles ceased rubbing his head with Valerie's towel, and looked indignant. 'Good Lord, Coppy, you don't want to hear any more, do you? I thought I had successfully glutted your appetite for meticulous detail.'

'Don't be silly, Charles! Of course you've got to finish it. Go on.' Copper vanished round the back of the tree where they had built a little fire of driftwood, while Charles took up the tale once more.

'We now come,' said Charles resignedly, 'to Christmas Day and the reappearance of Ferrers. Which you must admit was a shocking bit of bad luck for Leonard—Ferrers being washed up on that particular beach. Practically anywhere else, and he'd have arrived so badly bashed up by rocks that neither Dan nor anyone else would have spotted anything odd about him. But as it was, there were probably several things that made Dan brood a bit. What was it Vicarjee said, Nick?'

'Oh, just that a drowned man usually goes a sort of bluish colour, and as I remember, Ferrers was anything but blue. And that there should have been froth round his mouth and nose—or anyway inside his mouth, and something peculiar about "washerwoman's hands" that I didn't quite follow. Anyway, there were evidently enough signs missing to make Dan wonder if the man really had been drowned. He can't have spotted the crack on the back of the head, because he never turned the body over; and it wasn't easy to spot unless you were looking for it, for twenty-four hours in the water had washed it clean, and that mop of hair covered it up fairly thoroughly. But I suppose the more he thought about it, the more certain he became that there was something fishy about the whole thing, and—well you know the rest. He pushed off to see for himself . . .

'Here Leonard Stock reappears on the scene, and we are back again at guess-work. But this is what seems to have happened. Leonard must have got a nasty jar when Ferrers's body was reported to be present and correct, but a much nastier one when Val's father mentioned during dinner that night that he'd had a letter from Ferrers—possibly on the subject of pearls. As far as we can make out he must have slipped out that night and gone down to the office to hunt for it, but failed to find it. For the simple reason that John Shilto had got there first. In fact he was probably on his way back from the office when he saw Dan cross the ballroom, and realized what he was up to.

'After that he presumably slid back to his room, pulled a pair of pants on over his pyjamas, shoved on a raincoat, and left by the back staircase that leads out of his bathroom. He must have calmly stepped over the Indian guard, who, it now appears, was asleep for the greater part of the night with his mackintosh over his head.'

'What *I* don't understand,' said Copper, appearing abruptly from behind the tree with her eyes watering from the effects of wood smoke, 'is why Ruby didn't hear him; considering that he had to go through her room to get to the ballroom and the office.'

'Because, my sweet,' said Charles, 'Ruby's reported insomnia is pure baloney. She apparently sleeps like the proverbial log, and the insomnia racket was merely another method of annoying Leonard and making a fuss over herself. In other words, it was a complete myth and Leonard knew it, though he found it convenient to play up to her sometimes. You remember how he told us the next day how badly Ruby had slept? Well, as it happened, though he wasn't aware of it, he was right for once.

'Ruby wasn't sleeping so well that night, and she *did* hear Leonard go out. *And* come back again! It puzzled her considerably. So much, in fact, that she didn't immediately rise up and inquire what the heck he meant by it, but after a bit of brooding got out of bed and went into his room to institute inquiries. He wasn't there, and what's more, the back door from his bathroom was open.

'Being Ruby, she seems to have jumped to the conclusion that he was carrying on with some woman, and she put on her dressing-gown and went out into the ballroom to investigate. I cannot suppose that she ever *really* expected to find either of you two holding her husband's hand in the verandah, but anyway she evidently had a good snoop round, and after leaving a chunk of feathers as a souvenir on Hindenburg, got back to her room and found there was still no Leonard.

'It was just about then that she began to get nervous. There was something a bit sinister in this silent popping to and fro, and she wondered if Leonard was beginning to suffer from softening of the brain? She says that she must have stayed awake for nearly an hour, waiting for him, and it was during that time that it occurred to her to go through his pockets and see if they didn't contain some betraying note suggestive of a rendezvous. She found something all right! Knotted into a corner of his handkerchief was a pearl.

'It was evidently a pretty good line in pearls, and to Ruby, "money talks". She seems to have had quite a chat with it that night, and the upshot was that she lay doggo and didn't see her husband again until after you two had broken the news about Dan.'

Valerie looked bewildered: 'But—but why did she behave so oddly when she heard about it? Copper and I thought that she must either have done it herself or seen it done. She very nearly had a fit!'

'Use your brain, my small angel. Put yourself in her place. She has been wondering what on earth her husband could have been up to on the previous night, and suddenly she hears that at just about the time that he was out and about, a murder was committed. I don't wonder she had a fit. If I'd been in her shoes, I'd have had a dozen. She obviously jumped to the instant—and perfectly correct—conclusion that her husband had done it——

'You know, I feel we all owe Ruby an apology if we've ever spoken slightingly of her brain. She's got brains all right—the cunning kind. Having flung you two out, she ties a wet towel round her head and thinks things over. Why was Dan killed? What was he doing in the Guest House? Why has Ferrers's body disappeared? The answers that we missed, she got in one. And the pearl gave her the clue to the murderer of Ferrers. Oh, she's clever all right, is our Ruby!'

Valerie said: 'Then it was the pearl that she threw away? Why?'

'Because she lost her nerve. She had no idea how many people knew about those pearls, or how long it would be before everyone knew and the motive for the murder begin to look obvious. She wasn't taking any risk of being mixed up in it herself, so she took that pearl and heaved it into the sea. And it must have broken her heart to do it. About a hundred and fifty quid in the ash can!'

'But what about John Shilto?' asked Copper. 'Why did he go about grinning to himself in that revolting manner? And why did he borrow that typewriter?'

'Taking your questions in order,' said Charles, 'he had good reason to be pleased with himself. He discovers that Ferrers is on to a fortune in pearls, and when he tries to get in on it, is told to go and boil his head. A few hours later Ferrers is dead and he, John, is the next of kin. As to your second question, Shilto senior, just to make assurance doubly sure, borrows a typewriter for the praiseworthy purpose of forging a will, purporting to be Ferrers's, leaving all his worldly goods to cousin John in the hope that he will forgive and forget. It was an extremely touching document, and in spite of the solemnity of the occasion we all laughed like a row of buckets when we read it. It was found in his coat pocket, and I imagine the main reason for his pinching that letter from the office was because he needed a signature to forge from.'

'What did we pack the tea in?' demanded Copper, reappearing for the second time: 'How did the letter get into Sir Lionel's room?'

'In that thing like an aluminium soap-dish,' said Valerie. 'Yes, how did it get there, Charles?'

'I expect one of the *khidmatgars* shoved it in with a spoon——Oh, you mean the letter? Well, your father too evidently had his suspicions about John Shilto. He'd lent him his bathing-wrap to wear as a dressing-gown—that striped towelling one.'

Valerie said: 'Charles, what *are* you babbling about? What on earth has a bathing-wrap got to do with all this?'

'Only that there was a thread of striped towelling caught on the broken edge of the office desk that morning. That's why, when he found the letter was missing, your father didn't say anything for fear of putting Shilto on his guard. But he watched his opportunity and sneaked into the turret room later that day where, sure enough, he unearthed the letter. He left the envelope where he found it, and took the letter away to go through it later and try to discover why it had been pinched; hoping Shilto wouldn't spot that it had been removed. Result—we find the envelope in Shilto's room, and Copper finds the letter in your father's. Dense fog of confusion all round.

'As for John, if his fate hadn't already been decided upon before, it was definitely sealed when you told Leonard that the letter—you didn't say "envelope only"—had been discovered in John's room. Leonard didn't know exactly what Ferrers had written in that letter, but he guessed that it would be enough to put John Shilto on to the right track as regards the pearl bed, and shortly afterwards he pushed off to his house. Presumably in order to compose and type that "confession" and to plan out any odd details.

'He'd already pinched Ronnie's revolver; I suppose the discovery of Dan's body made him realize that he might at any moment have to pin the murders on someone else, and what better way of doing it than a third murder, dressed up to look like suicide? He went down to his own house at about a quarter to ten, taking an orderly with him for the look of the thing, and was away more than two hours, for it was roughly about midnight when he got back. And then of course Ruby played right into his hands.

'She was certain that he was the murderer, and she was scared to death. Here was a man whom she'd bullied and brow-beaten for years, and now he had killed two men in cold blood. She was in mortal terror for her own life, and she changed her room so that she could lock herself in for the night. But even then she daren't sleep, and although she heard the shot and the general uproar afterwards, she didn't stir from her room until morning.

'Well, that's about all that's new. The rest is pretty well what Leonard told you himself. Shilto had drunk too much and was out like a light, so it was money for jam. All that Leonard had to do was just stroll in about two a.m., switch on the small bedside light, pull out the mosquito net, pin that "confession" to the pillow, and, wearing a glove of Ruby's on his right hand, put the muzzle of the revolver to Shilto's head and pull the trigger . . .

'The moment the shot was fired he put the thing in Shilto's hand and closed his fingers round it, tucked in the mosquito net, snapped off the light and stepped out of the window. The whole thing can't have taken more than ten or fifteen seconds, and he knew he could count on a margin of at least half a minute after the firing of the shot. He'd even chosen his costume with care. That jazz-patterned thing of Ruby's was a perfect camouflage against the criss-cross patterns of the woodwork and the tree shadows on the wall. But he forgot about the mosquito net, and worst of all he forgot about that red stuff on the outside woodwork. Anything else you want to know?'

'Yes,' said Valerie promptly: 'What about Ronnie? Why was he in such a hopeless panic that last evening?'

Charles chuckled. 'Ah, that was Amabel! You see, two murders on two successive days had been too much for Ronnie's nervous system. He hadn't an inkling as to why they had been done, and then Amabel-the-Ever-Bright, by some curious fluke, produced the same theory that had already occurred to Copper.

'She made some fatuous remark about his ring while Ronnie was up at the hospital that afternoon, and then, remembering that Ferrers had also worn one, offered the suggestion that perhaps red rings were bad luck, and he might be killed too. A typically Amabelish remark, which might have passed over his head if she hadn't followed it up by adding that perhaps the murderer had mixed him up with Ferrers?

'At the time, Ronnie apparently laughed it off, because it sounded so ludicrously far-fetched that only Amabel's unfaltering determination to take the worst possible view of everything could have thought it up. But after a bit he began to wonder if perhaps there mightn't be something in it? He couldn't imagine why anyone—even John—should bother to kill Ferrers, and the thought that perhaps someone had meant to take a crack at him instead gave him no ordinary jar. And when on top of this he discovered, around five-thirtyish, that his revolver had taken unto itself legs, he went straight off the deep end and drank about half a bottle of whisky, neat. After that, there being no more alcohol in the house, he pushed off to continue the good work at the Club. Which is where we came on the scene.'

'I see,' said Valerie thoughtfully. 'Poor Ronnie! It shows he realizes that he's not all that popular if he could think up several reasons why someone should want to kill him.'

'Do him a lot of good,' said Charles callously. 'Nasty little philanderer! With any luck it will have given him such a heck of a jolt that he'll turn over a whole tree full of new leaves, and blossom into a Perfect Husband. In which case, if I may coin a phrase, "*Good will have come out of Evil*".'

A meditative silence fell upon the group under the big tree, in which they could hear the friendly bubble of a boiling kettle and the snap and crackle of flames. 'Tea!' announced Copper, appearing round the tree trunk with an outsize teapot, her cheeks flushed from the fire.

=== 24 ===

The sun dipped below the rim of the horizon as they packed up the picnic-baskets and strolled back along the shore to the anchored *Jarawa*.

The retreating tide had transformed the wet sands into a curving silver mirror that reflected the colours that flooded the pale sea and pearly sky in waves of wonder. The far islands had lost their look of shimmering transparency and become silhouettes of violet velvet against the opal sea, and a dimness had crept over the flaming green of the jungle-clad hills; softening and blurring it with a blue, grape-like bloom.

Sky and sea turned slowly from shell-pink to primrose and gold, and then to lavender and green. And a full moon rose through the twilight above the quiet glassy floor as the little *Jarawa* throbbed her way home across the darkening sea past dim romantic shores and lonely reefs uncovered by the retreating tide, towards the tiny island of Ross that was already pricked with pin-points of light. Presently in the gathering twilight a single star gleamed palely; to be joined before long by another, and another, until the dim bowl of the sky was sequined with them: their brilliance dimmed by the growing glow of the moon.

Nick, lying prone upon the roof of the launch and

following up a private train of thought, said: 'My ship gets in tomorrow.'

He did not add that it also left on the morrow, and that this was therefore his last evening in the Islands, for they already knew that.

For a moment no one answered him, and then Valerie said: 'Let's not go home. Let's take our supper to Corbyn's Cove. It's such a heavenly moon, and it's going to be a heavenly night.'

Charles gave his unqualified approval, and then observed, more practically, that they would have to return to Ross for food. 'All right,' agreed Valerie. 'We'll collect some from the Club, and ring up from there for a car to meet us at Aberdeen, and phone Dad and tell him we shan't be in to dinner. Then we shan't waste any time.'

'My practical Penelope!' murmured Charles approvingly. 'What an organizer the little woman will make! With her at my side, a Field Marshal's baton is as good as in my pants pocket.'

He relapsed into a contented silence which was broken by Copper's suggestion that they should add George and Amabel to the party. 'Heaven forbid!' said Charles, sitting up in alarm. 'I have no wish to spend the evening refereeing. Romance is what I yearn for; moonlight and tropic shores to delight the eye, and some of the more soupy and sentimental recordings of Bing Crosby to soothe the ear—plus caviare and Guinness to stay the inner man. An evening with Amabel and George in their present humour can only lead to high words and indigestion.'

Copper laughed, but stuck to her point with unexpected stubbornness.

'Oh, let 'em come, Charles,' said Nick lazily. 'Can't you see that Copper's gone all sentimental? She wants to try her fine Italian hand at playing Cupid, or Providence, or something of the sort, and reunite two sundered hearts. Isn't that right, Coppy?'

Copper flushed and frowned. 'You're too acute, Mr Tarrant, but I suppose you're right.'

'Of course I'm right. And I agree with you. Left to themselves, those two fat-heads will spend the remainder of George's term of penal servitude drooping about the island like a couple of bereaved earwigs and avoiding each other's eye. But if we plant them on a nice strip of moonlit beach, and then sneak off and leave them to it, they'll be publishing the banns by the time we get them home. I defy anyone to resist a night like this.'

Copper gave him an odd sideways look, but made no comment, and Charles said: 'Oh, all right. Let us sacrifice ourselves on the Altar of Romance. It can only lead to our being stung for an expensive plated fish-slice and/or toast-rack apiece, but what of it? *"It is a far, far better thing that we do now, than we have ever done before,"*— or words to that effect. Hullo, here we are!' The *Jarawa* bumped alongside the rough-and-ready structure that temporarily replaced the damaged jetty, and the picnickers disembarked.

An hour later, packed into the same aged Ford that had taken them up to Mount Harriet on that fateful Christmas Eve picnic, they were speeding along the moon-drenched road to Corbyn's Cove.

Nick, who was driving, had Copper and Amabel and an assortment of biscuit tins beside him, while Valerie, George and Charles shared the back seat in company with the picnic-basket, a variety of bottles and several travelling rugs. And it was, as Valerie had predicted, a heavenly night.

Moonlight striped the road with lines of white satin between the ebony shadows of the tree trunks, the air was warm and still and heavy with the scent of flowers, and the lovely, curving bay of Corbyn's Cove was a silver arc fringed with tall palms that leaned out across the sands, cutting clear patterns against the moon-washed sky and barring the sands with shadows, 'sable on argent'.

A gramophone provided undemanding music while a picnic supper was eaten on the dry sand in front of the palm-thatched bathing-huts, and though the records that had been borrowed at random from the Club proved to consist solely of dance-music, played by popular bands and sung by crooners, the slurred sweetness of the trite melodies that drifted out across the white beach and the glimmering bay were transmuted by the wizardry of the night into pure magic.

'George, dear,' begged Valerie charmingly, at the conclusion of the meal, 'would you be a darling and see if I brought a torch in the pocket of the car? It doesn't matter if it isn't there.'

George trotted off obediently, and having dispatched Amabel to the water's edge with a pile of dishes to be washed, the remaining four members of the party removed themselves hurriedly from the scene.

'*Phew!*' gasped Valerie, flinging herself down panting and breathless on a bank of sand at the far end of the beach. 'I haven't run like that since the days when for my sins I played right wing in the school hockey team! I wonder what Amabel will do when she finds we've left her to it?'

'You mean,' corrected Charles, 'when she finds that we've left her to George. Well, if she has a spark of intelligence—which I doubt—she will fling herself into his arms and say, "George darling, if you will only forgive me, I'll never touch fruit cup again!" But judging from what I know of the young dim-wit, she'll give her famous imitation of an underdone doughnut instead. And the same, I fear, will apply to George.'

Copper, who had been lying on her back gazing

up at the moon, sat up and brushed the sand out of her hair. 'I will bet you ten rupees,' she said, 'that by the time we get back they will be closely entwined and rapturously forgiving each other. Any takers?'

Charles looked up at the moon and down the long curve of the beach, and finally out at the silver sea and the tiny black shape that was Snake Island. Somewhere behind them a frangipani tree was spilling its sweetness on the warm night air, and the sea murmured drowsily among the rocks of the point. Charles sighed. 'No,' he said. 'No takers. I believe Nick was right, and that to resist a night like this is beyond the power of mortal man—or mortal woman either. It isn't merely romantic, it *is* Romance; and with a capital R. Val, my star, hold my hand. I am inspired.' He breathed deeply and wriggled down on to his spine.

'Copper,' said Nick abruptly, 'do you mind if I return to this murder business for a moment?'

'Not particularly. Why?'

'Something that's been puzzling me. What was it you thought of that scared you so badly when Val was reading through the notes in the Mess?'

Copper did not answer, and after a short interval of oddly embarrassing silence Nick repeated his question. 'It was nothing important,' said Copper in a restrained voice.

'I'll tell you what it was,' said Valerie surprisingly.

'*Val!* But you don't—'

'Yes, I do. She thought Dad might have done it,' said Valerie calmly. 'Didn't you, Coppy?'

'Good God!' said Charles. 'Sir Lionel? *Why*, for Pete's sake?'

'Well I—I remembered the sail. There was someone else sailing in the harbour, and when we got home they told us that Sir Lionel had been out. You see all the time we'd been saying that there could only be seven suspects, because only seven other people were out in the bay when Ferrers was killed. But there were eight; and Sir Lionel was the eighth.'

'I see,' said Nick soberly. 'Poor Coppy! A nasty thought to take to bed with you. Why wouldn't you tell me?'

'I—I suppose I was afraid you'd—do something. And he was Val's father and——Oh, I don't know. I was scared silly. I worked it all out how he could have done it, and I thought perhaps that explained why Ronnie, who obviously knew something, wouldn't tell; because he wouldn't be believed. Then when I found the letter, I nearly went crazy. Val, I do apologize: I must have been crackers!'

'Nonsense, darling. It was very intelligent of you. You notice that the fat-head by my side never spotted the significance of that other sail? I did though, and it gave me a few nasty moments. But then it was different for me, because of course I *knew* he couldn't possibly have done it. Charles, darling, may I use your arm as a pillow?'

'Certainly, my sweet. All that I have is yours—even after that last dirty crack at my expense. Nick, chuck me over a cigarette. Thanks.'

They settled themselves comfortably in a row with their backs to a tide-driven bank of sand, looking out across the shining sea in a silence deep with content, while the soft murmur of the waves and the monotonous trilling of the cicadas among the trees on the hillside behind them sang a song more sweet than that of any night club crooner.

'Does anyone remember,' said Nick, breaking a long and peaceful silence, 'what Copper said this afternoon about only a lot of time, or a lot of happiness, laying the ghost of the late unpleasantness on Ross?'

'Umm,' said three voices, in drowsy affirmative. 'Why?'

'I have been brooding,' said Nick, 'upon the latter half of that remark.'

He relapsed into silence.

'Well?' inquired Valerie curiously.

'Well, what?'

'Well, go on.'

'Oh—only that the second proviso appears to me to be more attractive than the first. I don't think I particularly want to wait until I'm middle-aged before I stop waking up with nightmares and dreaming I'm back among the murderers.'

Valerie laughed softly. 'In that case, why not try the second method?'

Nick twisted round to face her. 'Then I take it that you agree with Copper as to its reliability? I wouldn't like to go in for it, only to find myself still haunted by grim spectres.'

'Speaking for myself,' said Valerie, 'the remedy has my fullest approval. And in partnership with this slumbering object on my right, I propose to put it to the test in the near future. Signed: Valerie Anne Masson.'

'What about you, Charles? Do you endorse this damsel's view?'

'I'll endorse anything tonight,' said Charles. 'You only have to show me the dotted line.'

Nick said: 'Oh well—in that case——' He lay back against the sandbank and clasped his hands behind his head.

'*"He either fears his fate too much, Or his deserts are small"*—' quoted Valerie wickedly.

'What's that? Oh, of course; Jamie Graham. "*That puts it not unto the touch, To win or lose it all.*" I wonder. Copper?'

'Yes?'

'Will you marry me?'

'What!'

Three figures out of the four were no longer

prone, but sitting bolt upright. Nick continued to lie on his back and gaze at the moon.

'*What* did you say?' demanded Copper.

'You 'erd!' said Charles.

'I asked you if you'd marry me,' repeated Nick obligingly.

'Oh!' said Copper.

'Charles,' said Valerie firmly, 'I think this is where you and I fade rapidly away behind a palm tree.'

'Not on your life, my sweet! I am intensely interested. Besides, we men must stick together. How do I know that Nick won't shortly be needing my shoulder to sob on or my services as Best Man? Go on, Coppy; a fair answer to a fair question. We hang upon your words.'

'Don't be absurd!' flashed Valerie, jumping to her feet. 'Nick, you ought to be ashamed of yourself!'

'Don't go,' said Copper surprisingly. 'I think I may need a bit of support too.'

'Of course she does,' approved Charles. 'Sit down, Val, my treasure. Go on, Coppy. I demand on behalf of my client that he shall be put out of his misery. A plain straightforward Yes or No, Miss Randal.'

'I think,' said Copper thoughtfully, 'that there are one or two questions I'd like to ask first.'

'Oh, that's all right,' said Charles, 'the man's stiff with money, if you're wondering if he can keep you in Chocky-Bix. In fact, his yearly income, quite apart from the salary donated to him by a benign Government, is of such proportions as to make my own not-too-miserable pittance look like a trouser button in the collection plate. My advice to you is grab him quickly before he regains his senses, because——'

He subsided abruptly with his mouth full of sand.

'That'll hold him for a bit,' said Valerie serenely 'Go on, Coppy. What is it you want to know?'

Copper turned to look down upon Mr Tarrent's recumbent figure: 'Nick——'

'Darling?'

'Did you mean to ask me that question tonight?'

'No,' said Nick unhesitatingly. 'To be frank, I had every intention of leaving without asking it.'

'I thought so,' nodded Copper. 'Then why didn't you?'

'Because I found that I had no alternative between that and living out a ghost-haunted existence.'

'*Don't!*' said Copper sharply. 'I wasn't being funny. I want the real reason.'

'Neither was I. And that is the real reason. I wasn't referring to Leonard's victims, sweet. The ghost would have been yours, and I should have been persistently haunted by the fact that I'd once seen the Real Thing, and failed to grab it.'

'Love-fifteen to my client,' said Charles, spitting out sand.

'Shut up, Charles!' said Valerie.

Copper said gravely: 'Why were you so angry that afternoon in the Mess?'

Nick did not answer for a few minutes, and in the clear moonlight Copper saw the shadow of a frown etch itself between his eyebrows. Presently he said: 'I wasn't only angry. I was blind furious, if you want to know. You had thought up so many things against me that I believed you really thought I might have done it. And it hit me pretty hard to realize that I ranked so low in your estimation that you could even suspect me of murdering one of my own friends. I was so damned angry I could cheerfully have strangled you!'

Copper said: 'I was only trying to warn you.'

'I know. Though I have my suspicions of that "*only*". I believe you intended it as a slap in the eye as well. Didn't you?'

Copper flushed, but she was too honest to beg the question. 'Yes.'

Nick laughed shortly. 'Well, you succeeded all right. I've seldom had a worse one. Any more questions?'

'Two more. When did you meet Ferrers Shilto before, and why did you keep quiet about it?'

Charles sat up again with some violence. 'Do you mean to tell me,' he demanded, 'that you've been concealing a skeleton in your closet all this time? Good God!—if I'd known you were holding out on us I'd have arrested you without a qualm!'

'I'm sure you would,' said Nick dryly. 'Perhaps that was what I was afraid of. How did you know, Coppy?'

'I told you. I saw the labels on Ferrers's luggage, and you told me yourself where you'd been staying. The times fitted. But it was just a shot in the dark— that you might have met him. And when I saw that it had gone home, and you wouldn't explain, I was frightened.'

'May I ask you something before I answer this? Why do you want to know?'

Copper considered the question for a moment.

'Partly curiosity, I suppose. But mostly because it's the only missing piece of the story. I know everything else except that, and once it's explained, the story is complete.'

'The same,' said Charles, 'goes for me—with the accent heavily on the curiosity. Produce your skeleton.'

Nick pulled out another cigarette and lit it with some deliberation before replying. Then he lay back again, and looking up at the black patterns of the palm fronds against the moonlit sky, spoke in a voice that was entirely without expression—slowly, as though he were choosing his words: 'I met Ferrers Shilto while I was in Calcutta. We were both stopping at the same hotel. I—there was a friend of mine in Calcutta; a woman. She was attractive and popular and—married . . .

'To cut out a lot of unnecessary narrative, she was seen leaving my room at four o'clock one morning by the late unlamented Ferrers. He happened, unfortunately, to be occupying the room opposite mine, and recognized the lady. She and her husband were very well known. Next morning he went round to her house and tried his hand at a little light blackmail. He may have been finding it difficult to get cash down for the pearls—I don't know. Anyway he had no success, for the lady, doubtless remembering the masterly tactics of the late Duke of Wellington under similar circumstances, replied that he could publish and be damned, since it would be a case of her word against his.

'If he'd had the sense to leave it there, he might have got off scot-free. But he came to me and suggested that I might find it advisable to pay up. Disregarding the old school tie, and elderly as he was, I tore him into small shreds and threw the remains into the street. I also told the Manager that he had been attempting to blackmail me, and as he hadn't paid his bill, he was requested not to return. And—that's about all. I had no idea where he came from or where he had gone to, and it gave me no ordinary jolt to find him on the lawn at Mount Harriet. My only consolation is that it must have given him a much worse one!'

Nick stopped speaking, but he did not look at Copper.

'*Um*,' said Charles thoughtfully. 'A bit tricky for you all round.'

'Damnably,' agreed Nick. 'I hope now you appreciate my reasons for suppressing that information.'

'Like hell I do! I wouldn't like it to be widely

known that I'd been recently threatened with a particularly nasty form of blackmail and had soundly
beaten up the blackmailer, who was later discovered
murdered. People might begin putting two and two
together and making the answer thirteen.'

'Exactly,' agreed Nick. 'And after all, except for
Dan I was the only stranger in your midst and, as
Copper kindly pointed out, no one really knew anything about me. In addition to that, there appeared
to be no motive for the thing. "*Cui bono?*" is apt to
be shouted a bit after a murder, and I imagine "*the
victim of blackmail*" is as good an answer as any. So I
kept my mouth shut and hoped for the best; both
for my own sake and——'

He stopped abruptly and frowned.

'You mean Copper,' said Charles, '——it's no good
kicking me, Val, my sweet. We all know what he
means. It's quite obvious to one and all that half the
reason he kept his mouth shut was because he was
afraid Copper would give him the bird on receipt of
said information. Isn't that right, old man?'

Nick remained silent, and after a moment or two
Copper said: 'Were you in love with her?'

He did not reply for so long that Valerie began to
think that he had either not heard the question,
or did not intend answering it. But Nick had both
heard it and realized that it must be answered. Only
he dared not answer it quickly or thoughtlessly.
Instinct warned him that if he said 'No,' he would
lose Copper. Only the truth would serve him now.
But what exactly was the truth? *Had* he been in love
with that electric, red-haired lady? Certainly she had
been very fascinating, and he had been quite willing
to be fascinated. Even more certainly, she had
ended by falling in love with him. But for himself
the attachment had never gone very deep, and despite her obvious wish for something more serious,

had remained no more than a surface affair of froth and sparkle.

Even that fatal four a.m. visit had been no more than a mild indiscretion. They had been to a dance at the Saturday Club, and afterwards had driven to Tollygunge to bathe. Judith had offered to drive him home, and on dropping him at the hotel had invited herself in for a drink. It was late and he had been sleepy. Too sleepy to be sensible, and not sleepy enough to appear ungallant. Judith had stayed for fifteen minutes, during which time he had yawned at least fifteen separate times. She had laughed, and told him that his manners were abominable, kissed him in the middle of the fifteenth yawn, sighed, and left him—to walk straight into Ferrers Shilto who was returning after an equally late night.

But would Copper believe that? Nick had never cared before what anyone believed of him, but now . . . Copper's question was still waiting.

He said slowly: 'I was very fond of her. She was beautiful and intelligent and amusing; and a good companion. Perhaps if you'd asked me that question a week or so ago, I might have said "Yes", because I didn't know then what being in love meant.'

Copper said: 'What does it mean?'

'I'll answer that one,' said Charles firmly. 'Shut up, Nick! I arrived at the same fence a few months ago, and so I knew the answer before you did. He means, Coppy, that even though he had no intention of getting engaged or married, or otherwise entangled, and had firmly intended to dodge it or die in the attempt, he has discovered—probably with disgust—that the light of Reason has been put out and that he has been forced, against every prompting of intelligence, common sense and willpower, to chuck himself and his future at your feet, because he knows that unless you can be persuaded to pick them up, neither the one nor the other will ever be of any value to him again.'

Charles paused for a brief moment, and lifting Valerie's hand, touched it lightly to his cheek and continued more slowly: 'He knows, too, that even if you won't pick them up, the fact that you once touched them will be the only really worth-while thing that ever happened to them.'

Copper said: 'Is that what it means, Nick?'

'Yes,' said Nick. 'It means, too, that even if you turn me down and I never see you again, I shall still go on loving you.'

'The whole thing in a nutshell!' said Charles. 'A masterly summing up, combining sentiment, sincerity and a touch of pathos with a manly independence of spirit. Come on, Caroline Olivia, the court awaits your verdict. Make it snappy!'

Copper sighed and looked up at the moon. 'But Charles darling, I can't rush into this. How do I know that I should like spending half my life in places like Malta and Gibraltar and Jamaica and Java and Plymouth and——'

'Listen!' interrupted Charles firmly. 'Arithmetic, and not Geography, should be the key-note when selecting a suitable mate. My client possesses large quantities of cash, cleanliness and charm, so let us have no more of this waffling. Do you or do you not take this man for better or for worse? My advice is a hurried affirmative before the offer is withdrawn.'

'Do I, Val?' asked Copper.

'I think so, dear,' said Valerie tranquilly.

'The casting vote,' sighed Copper. 'The Ayes have it.'

'Val,' said Nick, 'would you mind removing your property further up the beach? In about ten seconds I propose to kiss this girl with considerable fervour, and I should prefer to do so without helpful instructions from Charles.'

'Darling,' said Charles, 'the man is an ungrateful polyp, and I deeply regret having tendered him my valuable advice during the recent crisis. However, there is an excellent clump of palms on our left, where, under the cover of darkness, I can get engaged to you all over again. Let us withdraw the hem of our garment.'

They drifted away down the moonlit beach.

Mr Hurridge, Deputy Commissioner and confirmed bachelor, had driven out to Corbyn's Cove to smoke an after-dinner cigar and meditate upon the recent dark happenings on Ross.

He would have to write a report. Several reports in fact. It was all very terrible—dreadful! A shocking affair. His deepest sympathy went out to all on Ross who had endured those days and nights of terror: in particular the young people, over whose youthful lives this dark affair would cast an ineradicable shadow. He pictured them sitting in the Commissioner's house, silent and subdued; awed by their recent contact with swift and violent death. Graver, older . . . I wonder, thought Mr Hurridge, if it would be considered indelicate if I were to arrange a picnic—say next week? A little soon after these recent bereavements perhaps, but I feel that they should not be allowed to mope.

He had been somewhat taken aback, on arrival at the Cove, to find the Ford parked among the palm trunks, but had decided that it must be Mrs Stock—come to be alone with her shame and sorrow.

Mr Hurridge could observe no lonely figure walking by the sad seashore, but on approaching the bathing-huts with the intention of seating himself on one of the wooden benches that stood outside, he became aware of voices and paused involuntarily. The conversation was hardly edifying:

'It was all my fault, darling!'

'No it wasn't; it was mine, darling!'

'Oh no, darling! I was horrid!'

'You weren't horrid, darling!'

'Anyway, it was really all that horrid Rosamund's fault—it just goes to show, doesn't it?'

'Then you do forgive me?'

'Oh George!'

'Oh Amabel!'

Mr Hurridge averted his head and hurried past. He was profoundly shocked. It seemed—under the circumstances—little short of indelicate that young Amabel Withers and George Beamish should drive out to Corbyn's Cove with no better object than to indulge in sentimental reconciliations, when after all . . .

He slowed his steps and made for a patch of shadow where a fallen palm trunk, victim of the recent storm, offered an inviting seat.

It was, alas, already occupied.

'We'll be married as soon as I can get home. That'll be about April. Oh Val, darling—only four months!'

'Oh Charles! Oh bliss!'

Mr Hurridge felt like an elderly maiden-lady who has discovered a burglar under the bed.

It was indecent! It was outrageous! Was *Murder*— three murders no less, not to mention one accidental though well-deserved death!—a matter of so little moment that the young people of Ross could thus ebulliently discuss love up and down the Islands?

'Disgusting!' said Mr Hurridge, and coughed with loud disapproval.

He decided to pause for meditation and a quick cigar upon the sandbank at the far end of the beach.

But it was not to be. Mr Hurridge's luck was out and Romance was definitely in.

'There's still one thing I forgot to ask you. Do you love me, Coppy?'

'Oh Nick!'

'Oh *damn!*' said Mr Hurridge.

He wheeled about, tripped over a piece of driftwood, dropped his unlighted cigar upon the sand, stooped to retrieve it and was sharply bitten by a crab, and abandoning it, departed blasphemously down the beach—a misogynist for life.

As Amabel would doubtless have said, 'It just goes to show, doesn't it?'